MW00781322

This is a work of fiction. All characters and events are either a product of the author's imagination or used fictitiously, and any resemblance to real people or events is entirely coincidental.

SERPENT'S TEARS

Cover art by Beth Alvarez

Edited by Savannah Grace Perran

First Edition: May 2020

ISBN-13: 978-1-952145-05-6

SERPENT'S TEARS

BOOK TWO OF THE SNAKESBLOOD SAGA

BETH ALVAREZ

Elenhiise Island

Kardis

Trell

Quaris

Giftless lands

Rilstran

Ilmenhith

Pengast

River Quaris

Lake Ards

Lake Alwhen

River Ilmenie

Charth

Alwhen

The Ruins

River Alwhen

Erdael

River Erdael

Core

River Core

Pell

Andel

Kirban Temple

Underling outpost

Wethertree

Eldani lands

River Eldani

Winfell

N

Eldril

CONTENTS

SETBACKS

ASH STILL SMOLDERED IN THE TEMPLE.

Heaps of ruined furniture and books sat in the courtyard, mages clustered around them to supervise their destruction. Firal tried not to linger, though the gilded lettering on the scorched spines of records still called to her. She struggled to shut out the worry that came with seeing them on the piles waiting to be burned. It seemed a waste, though she knew there was nothing left to salvage from the piles now. The magelings had worked to the point of exhaustion on a daily basis, scouring Kirban Temple for anything that could be saved after fire ravaged the grounds. In the wake of the disaster, destroying the rubble that remained with more fire seemed tasteless, but she knew there was no other choice.

No matter how she reminded herself she'd chosen to move on, the loss of the records still stung. Firal had spent so much of her life chasing her parents' ghosts that moving on without finding them seemed an impossible feat. But the records had been her last hope of finding them; that dream, along with the temple's library, was ash—and she only had herself to blame.

Her friends had been quiet, sheltering her secret, but she saw their furtive glances and caught the way their conversations ended when she drew near.

Fat plumes of dark smoke wafted to the sky as the remnants of the library were disposed of. She swallowed and made herself move on. The infirmary waited, and it was one of few places where she could make a difference.

The temple had suffered, but a few sections were well on the way to recovery. The infirmary had been one of the first areas cleaned, and the box of supplies in her arms had survived in one of the undamaged storerooms.

A handful of workers stood outside the infirmary, marking measurements for a new roof on large sheets of parchment. Canvas had been drawn over the top of the building to form a temporary shelter, and magelings came and went with boxes in tow. Shymin—Firal's classmate and one of her dearest friends—stepped from the open doorway with an empty box dangling from her fingertips, but she offered no more than a smile before hurrying on her way.

Firal bowed her head as she slipped inside. Her companions had every right to be angry with her. It was her own selfishness that had ruined things. Her desperation for answers had pushed her to impatience, drove her to seek aid from their enemies—from Daemon.

After their time traversing the ruins outside the temple, it hurt to think of Daemon as an enemy. Firal couldn't bring herself to think of him as a friend, but he'd been an ally.

Yet a true ally would not have set men upon the temple, or destroyed her home with the very power he'd begged her to teach him. Resentment stuck in her throat and she used it to fuel her determination. She thumped dark glass bottles of tinctures and medicines onto the new shelves erected against the sandstone walls, turning all of them so the new labels were meticulously aligned.

She'd been a fool. Foolish to think her path would be easy and foolish to trust an Underling.

"You seem angry." Vahn swept into the empty space beside her, another box of supplies in his arms. He flashed her a grin and tilted the box to offer its contents for her approval.

Firal finished stocking her own bottles first, then removed one from his box to inspect. "Not angry. Disappointed, perhaps. You've seen the damage. It's such a waste."

He gave a helpless shrug. "There's nothing we can do about it now. The temple has lost a great deal, but it will recover. It recovered after the first fire, too."

The first fire. Firal had heard something about it before, but no one was eager to speak of it. After living through Kirban's destruction, herself, she understood why the mages remained tight-lipped, and she suspected her feelings would be raw for some time. Vahn was different, a soldier from the capital city, stationed at the temple to aid its reconstruction and defense. The fires meant nothing to him. She studied him from the corner of her eye. "What do you know about it? The first time the temple burned?"

"Not a lot," he admitted. "Just what my father told me. He still served as Captain of the Guard when it happened. From my understanding, he feared something like the fire might happen. Well, maybe not fire, exactly, but he always said the temple's lacking defenses would invite problems. But the generals ignored his warnings."

She put her empty box aside and selected another pair of bottles from the one he held. "When did it happen?"

"Not long after the founding. It came after some sort of dispute, but he never said more than that." Vahn's head turned when another mageling entered. His face fell when it wasn't the one he'd hoped for.

Firal couldn't help but smile. "You're looking for Kytenia. She'll be back before long."

His eyes widened and a hint of a flush crept up his neck. "I wasn't looking for—I mean—"

"No?" She tapped the corks of bottles in the box as she

counted them. More than she had space for. She turned back to the shelf and rearranged the bottles she'd already aligned to make more room. "She'd be disappointed."

"You think so?" he replied, a little too fast. The redness stole into his cheeks.

Firal felt a twinge of shame. "Goodness. I didn't think it was that serious." She hadn't meant to tease him that severely. Vahn was a shameless flirt, but it seemed his own sensitivities lurked nearby.

"No, I... I appreciate candor, if you're serious. I enjoyed her company at the solstice ball." He averted his eyes. "I enjoyed it a great deal."

"And yet Ran was the first person you asked after when you arrived at the temple," she said.

He rolled his eyes. "For entirely different reasons, I promise you."

"Oh, no, I understand." She cast a glance over her shoulder and then lowered her voice, mindful not to be overheard. "He's gone to great lengths to hide his position and his father's identity. I imagine he makes an effort to be unknown most places. Though I suppose it will be harder to scrape by unnoticed now that he's in Master white."

Vahn almost dropped the box. "White? Ran? You can't be serious!"

She arched a brow. "You mean to say you haven't seen him? He's been parading around in white robes since we returned from Ilmenhith."

"I thought it was gray! A Master? But he can't even..." A look of consternation drifted over his face and he thrust the box of bottles into her hands. "Hold this. I need to go."

The box was heavier than Firal expected and she squeaked when the weight jerked her downward. "Wait, what do you mean he can't? Can't what?"

"I'm sorry, I've got to go!" He waved a farewell and rushed for the door, narrowly missing a collision with a mageling.

Firal's eyes narrowed. She eased the box to the floor and straightened as she wiped her brow. Would that she was a Master, herself. The rank would have more benefits than just letting her teach. It would give her information, and she was getting tired of all these secrets.

———

SETBACK WAS NOT THE TERM DAEMON WANTED TO APPLY TO THE situation. It was a disaster. The biggest failure he'd ever experienced. It had torched all hopes of progress and left him farther behind than when he'd started. But *setback* was a gentle term, one his men would accept. It implied he had control, that he'd already planned a way forward. If only he had.

Daemon buried his face in his scaly hands and rubbed as if he could scrub away his frustrations. The privacy of his quarters was the only place he dared shed his mask. With the burden that weighed on him now, he was grateful for whatever freedom he could gain.

A half-dozen reports lay spread across his desk. None were good news. He'd read each of them twice and still hadn't decided how to respond. Food was the most pressing concern; he'd have to address that first. Agriculture was difficult in the concentric rings of the ruins and while their raids had supplemented their stores for a time, he'd always known they were not a viable long-term option. On the heels of the temple's destruction, raids were not an option at all.

But food, at least, was a problem he'd already devoted thought to. He'd laid enough groundwork to make a difference. They would simply have to reach north to bolster their supply, take care to avoid places where news of the temple may have spread. If they moved fast enough, the trade routes he hoped to create would be established before word of what his queen had done reached the remote areas of the island.

Lumia was a problem, herself. Daemon pressed his fingers

against his eyes, mindful of his claws. The rune-shaped scar that decorated his hand tingled as if in acknowledgement of the queen. He'd sworn himself to her service, but his tolerance for her temper had worn thin. They were supposed to be working together for the benefit of the ruin-folk, pushing to claim space on the island's surface and eliminate fears of famine. Once he had his power in hand, not even the mages in Kirban could hope to stand against him.

He'd adhered to his half of the plan, struggling to gain control of his wild magic so he could defend them from opposition. She, on the other hand, had shattered his hopes of progress. He shouldn't have been surprised. Lumia's loathing for the temple ran deep, and he had to accept that the teacher he'd found—short lived as their cooperation was—had been a temple mage, herself. All their knowledge had been at his fingertips.

Then the temple burned.

Growling in frustration, Daemon reached for his mask. It was a setback, he decided; nothing more. His plans had failed, but he had no time to sulk over what should have been.

His people were starving.

2

DISMISSAL

Though Ran had worn them for more than a week, the white robes that marked him as a Master mage still startled him every time he looked down. The fabric caught on a stack of books and he brushed it loose. The material snagged on his rough hands as badly as it caught on everything else. He'd gotten hung up on the corners of every object between the tower's ground floor and the top, where the Archmage's office waited. The robes were too long, he decided. He'd grown used to wearing them knee-length, but he suspected his position as a court mage would allow him to wear a tunic instead. It wasn't as if anyone other than mages wore white, after all. The robes swished around his legs as he moved on. The Archmage's door was just ahead. He rapped twice before he let himself in.

"What is it now?" the Archmage snarled at the creak of the hinges. Books and artifacts piled on her desk hid her slight figure from sight.

"Not quite the greeting I expected." The path from door to desk was barely wide enough to walk through. Ran struggled to follow it without overturning anything.

Envesi thrust herself from her chair and glared over the

clutter. "You thought I'd be happy to see you? This mess still isn't cleaned up, hundreds of artifacts were destroyed in the fire, and with Kifel's men underfoot, I'll never get anything done." Small as she was, little more than her snowy hair and icy blue eyes were visible. Though her glower was meant to be intimidating, Ran found it hard not to laugh. But the Archmage's position demanded respect, and he did his best to give it. He'd come for assistance. Mockery would not help.

"I never would have thought you'd be displeased to have an army at your disposal." He glanced down as a book snagged on his robes and tumbled from a stack at his feet. He picked it up and paged through it. It was written in a language he didn't recognize, the lettering sharp and angular. He put it back with a frown. "Alira sent word by messenger pigeon. She will return by morning, with an ambassador from Relythes following to make arrangements. I imagine you're going to need my father's soldiers out of your hair before an ambassador from the Giftless king arrives."

The Archmage grew still, and her pale blue eyes narrowed. "What do you want?"

"In return for what?" He gave her a hard look, matching the ice in her stare. "Surely you don't think I have a way to move all of Father's men before tomorrow?"

Envesi gritted her teeth and pushed books aside. "Kifel's men don't belong here. He knew what might happen, what your mistakes might bring down on us, and yet he did not send an army until after my temple burned."

His mistakes. The accusation made his hackles rise, but Ran refused to take the bait she dangled in front of him. There was a little room in front of her desk, just enough space for one small chair. He pulled it back until it hit a crate and then sat down without permission. One corner of her desk poked out from under the mess. He leaned back and propped a boot heel on it, crossed his ankles, and smirked at the look of disdain on her face. "Very well, then." He clasped his hands together atop his stomach. "If you want them sent back to Ilmenhith, how about this? I see that the soldiers are gone before midday tomorrow, and you take care of a small matter for me in return."

"I don't have time for your games, Lomithrandel," the Archmage snapped as she shifted a pile of books from the top of her desk to a towering stack behind it.

"What a shame, a chess match would have been pleasant. Do you still play?" He paused just long enough to stir her temper again. "Maybe you'll have time for a match after Kifel's army receives their orders. They might be sent north before sunrise, I've heard."

Envesi watched him for a long time before she spoke. "You guarantee they will move before the ambassador arrives?"

"My word should be as good as guarantee." Ran picked dirt from his fingernails, feigning indifference. "Besides, I thought you were the one pulling the strings. The whole purpose of keeping a leashed pet is to have it do tricks."

Her mouth drew tight and one fine white brow arched. "A bold change in your opinion. I ask again: What do you want?"

"Nothing extraordinary," he replied, though his heart pounded. More than once, he'd considered letting go of what had transpired, but irritation still needled beneath his skin. How else was he supposed to protect his interests? Neglecting it would only make things worse. In the Archmage's eyes, his request would mean little. For him, it was peace of mind. "I just ask that you move a mageling to another station."

"I beg your pardon?" The Archmage's face remained stern and unchanged, but her eyes hardened. He wondered if she knew the steely glint gave her away.

"You heard me. Nothing complicated. There is a green mageling here by the name of Firal. I understand she's become something of a troublemaker for the Masters. She has also become aware of my rank and my position within the king's household—knowledge that could make it difficult for me to perform my duties, should it become common around the temple."

Envesi lifted her chin as she cleared her desk and sank into her chair.

He went on. "I want her out of the way. Preferably a southern chapter house, away from the soldiers who have been stationed here. The only tongue looser than a mageling's is a soldier's." He shrugged. "Transfer her to another post, send her as apprentice to another Master, I don't care how you do it. Just send her away. Perhaps she could go east. I'm sure the Masters in Quaris could use a new assistant."

Envesi regarded him thoughtfully. She leaned forward to rest her elbows on her desk. "A simple request. Consider it done."

"Then consider those men moved." Ran stood, righting his robes and brushing dirt from her desk. "If you'll excuse me, I must return to Ilmenhith." He dipped in an insincere bow and turned to leave without regard for the books that toppled in his wake.

He hadn't expected the Archmage to agree so easily, but perhaps he'd underestimated her desperation. Still, he was aware of the cold smile that pulled at the corners of her mouth, the weight of her eyes heavy on him as he departed.

He ignored it. She thought she pulled the strings. Sometimes, she did. But a leashed beast could still force its master to move.

———

A BRISK KNOCK AT THE DOOR STARTLED FIRAL BADLY ENOUGH THAT she clapped a hand to her chest. Her face twisted with displeasure—more at her own jumpiness than the interruption—and she smoothed her green robes. Though wrinkled and dirty, the soot-stained robes were all she had. "Just a moment," she called as she got to her feet.

A number of makeshift rooms had been established in the Archmage's tower, spaces previously used as offices and inhabited by Masters. Though the rooms were cramped, they held proper beds and even washbasins, and the magelings took turns freshening up.

Firal had intended to wash her robes and enjoy the privacy while they dried, but at least she'd had the opportunity to wash her face and hair. Brant knew she'd needed it. The water in the basin was almost as black as the wet ringlets that curled around her pointed ears. She flicked her wet hair over her shoulder and opened the door, pausing when she came face to face with a girl she didn't recognize. She'd expected one of her friends, or perhaps another classmate hoping for a turn to wash.

"Miss Firal?" the girl asked, her eyes skimming Firal's filthy clothes. Perhaps they'd found more storerooms that survived the blaze. The girl's robes were a crisp blue, freshly pressed. The contrast made Firal more conscious of her own sooty training robes.

"Yes," Firal replied, more cordially than she felt. She had been guaranteed two hours to wash and rest. It hadn't yet been one. "Can I help you?"

The girl offered a quick curtsy. "Your presence has been requested in the office above. Master Nondar asked me to retrieve you in his place, as the rain has caused his arthritis to ail him."

"Oh, of course." Firal left the door open behind her. She paused and considered emptying the basin before she dismissed the idea. Her teacher would not want to be kept waiting.

The girl turned without a word and started for the stairs.

The tower was all but empty. Most of the magelings returned to cleaning after they had a chance to bathe. Firal had planned to assist in the restoration of the dormitory after she'd washed, but with fortune, whatever task Nondar had for her wouldn't take long. Kytenia's embroidery basket had been found untouched in their room, according to Shymin, which encouraged all of them to hunt for belongings that might have survived. Firal doubted there would be much, but she hoped to find some of her own possessions intact.

"This way." The girl's words interrupted her thoughts and Firal hurried to close the distance between them.

Firal thought Nondar had been among the first back to his office—she'd seen him rearranging things in the infirmary—but as the leader of the House of Healing, he was found just as often in the meeting rooms at the top of the tower.

"What did Nondar need me for?" Firal's brow furrowed as she glanced up the stairway. Surely Nondar hadn't climbed that many steps if his joints were ailing him.

"Not Master Nondar. He was only told to retrieve you." The girl stepped aside and gestured for Firal to move ahead as they crested the stairs. The path before them was no wider than her shoulders, narrowed by crates stacked from floor to ceiling.

When Firal paused, the girl smiled in reassurance. "You're expected, don't worry. Just go on in, the doors won't be locked."

"Thank you," Firal murmured as she squeezed into the narrow pathway. Behind her, the girl retreated down the stairway they'd just climbed.

Stacks of crates gave way to piles of books and the path widened at the doors. Firal hesitated again, worrying her hands. When the girl had said she was to report to the offices above, she had not expected that meant the Archmage's office.

Swallowing thickly, Firal reached to open one door. It was heavier than she expected; she had to heave back to move it. It issued a squeak of protest as it swung open on polished brass hinges. The room beyond was brighter and she squinted against the sunlight as she stepped inside. Brighter, but no less crowded.

"You took longer than I expected." The voice across the room was unfamiliar and cold.

"I'm sorry?" Firal faltered. She inched forward as the room came into focus. It was whitewashed from floor to ceiling, books and wooden boxes lining the walls beneath the windows. The path ran straight to a large, dark wooden desk. A woman in white sat behind it with her hands clasped together at its edge.

"What I mean is, you are late. Though whether it's your own tardiness or the incompetence of the messenger sent to retrieve you, I don't know." The woman's voice held very little emotion. She gestured toward the small chair before her desk. "Sit down."

Firal's heart fell to her stomach as she realized who sat in front of her. "Yes, Archmage." By the time she reached the desk, her knees quivered. She sank into the chair, feeling flushed and chill at the same time.

"Do you have any idea why you are here?" the Archmage asked.

"No, Archmage." Firal struggled to keep her voice from quavering.

Envesi arched a brow. "Really, now?" She tilted her head, white waves of hair spilling over her shoulder. "What a shame. Ignorance is a poor quality in a mage."

Firal ducked her eyes. "I'm sorry."

"You should be." Steel chilled the Archmage's words. "The rules of this temple were implemented for the safety of not only the magelings, but of the Masters and civilians as well. If you think your misconduct has gone unnoticed, then you are sorely mistaken."

"What?" Firal's amber eyes widened. She hadn't told anyone other than her dearest friends about Daemon. "Misconduct? How could—"

"You are in no position to ask questions," the Archmage snapped. "You sit in my office because of your own actions. By entering the ruins, you have violated one of the most important rules Kirban Temple upholds. Your actions were verified by the Master you study beneath just this morning, and I am appalled such behavior was allowed to go on for so long."

Firal leaned forward in her chair, gripping the edge of her seat with both hands. "But I—"

"No buts!" The Archmage's eyes flashed with fury. "Have

you no shame? For all we know, your actions could have been what led to the razing of the temple and everything we have struggled to build. Due to your repeat offenses, you receive no warnings. You have until nightfall to collect your belongings and remove yourself from the temple. You, mageling Firal, are hereby expelled."

3

SECESSION

TORRENTIAL RAIN CHURNED THE ROAD TO MUD BENEATH THE horses' hooves. The animals walked with their heads down, but they carried on without fuss. Rikka squealed at the crash of thunder and shrank in the saddle. Alira tried not to sigh. She led the procession, though it was far from the sort of entourage she deserved.

Relythes had provided a change of clothing and a good wool cloak for each of them, though the cloaks did little to keep them dry. Had she not been in the presence of magelings, Alira would have made an energy barrier to deflect the rain. As a Master mage, she could use magic for whatever she pleased, a privilege the mageling girls with her hadn't earned. But there were precedents to be set. It wouldn't do to give them ideas.

Adjusting the hood of her cloak, Alira thought again of the ambassador they'd left behind. They had departed from Alwhen at the same time, but when the weather turned foul, the man had backtracked to the city's edge. She had considered stopping with him, but only briefly, knowing the Archmage awaited her return. Alira grumbled to herself at the idea of the ambassador lounging in a dry, comfortable room while she suffered out the storm, but the complaint was more out of jealousy than annoyance.

"I can't recall the last time it rained this hard," Kytenia said, raising her voice over the static din of the storm. Though the three of them rode with their mounts abreast, Alira pretended not to hear.

Rikka heaved a sigh. "I was hoping we'd reach the temple before nightfall. I don't think we'll make it in this weather."

"We're closer than you think." Alira said, squaring her shoulders. The magelings twitched when she spoke, which made her frown. Maybe they hadn't meant for her to hear what they were saying, after all. "Perhaps the two of you should pay closer attention to your geographical studies."

Rikka stared at her for a time before she looked to the sky. "Well, it's not like we'd be any more comfortable in the temple, what with this rain. Though I suppose even the tower floor would be better than trying to sleep in the saddle."

Alira's lip curled with distaste at the reminder. Everyone would be crowded into the tower with nothing to do but wait for the storm to pass. Sharing the tower with the other Masters was bad enough, never mind the magelings and the soldiers. As Master of Fire, she might be granted a private bed, which would make her more fortunate than many. But many Masters would be expected to stay together. If that meant sharing quarters with the Masters of the other Houses of affinity, she would prefer to refresh herself with nearby energies and stay awake the whole night. Despite her position as Master of a major element, she often found herself treated as if she'd just graduated to the white.

No one said anything more, leaving Alira to her sullen thoughts as the three of them rode through the rain.

The storm tapered off after dark. The path grew dimmer and more narrow, the crumbling walls of the ruins looming to one side to show they neared home. The cool glow of mage-lights ahead beckoned, encouraging them to pick up their pace. Alira wasn't the only one to breathe a sigh of relief when they reached the temple gates. Stable hands met them in the courtyard to take their mounts. Kytenia slid from her horse with a groan, though her face twisted when her slippered feet hit the muddy ground. She rubbed her thighs as she stretched her legs. Alira couldn't blame her. The use of her Gift was enough to keep them fresh, but not enough to keep them from being saddle sore.

"Both of you stay here," Alira ordered as she dismounted and left her horse to one of the grooms. "Watch the road for half an hour or so. The ambassador might have decided to follow us after all. We'd hate for him to arrive without anyone at the gate to receive him. If he makes an appearance, take him to the Archmage at once."

Neither mageling protested, though their expressions made it clear they wanted to. But the desires of magelings didn't concern her, and Alira hurried into the tower. She waved a hand over her shoulders and down her front to draw the rain from her robes. Water spilled from the hem and splashed around her feet as she strode through the building.

Crowded into the Archmage's tower, the mages in the lower floors looked bored, irritable, and uncomfortable. There wasn't a single soldier to be seen, Alira noted with a bemused frown. She tried to ignore the magelings she passed, preserving her reputation as cold and aloof as she hurried to the Archmage's office. The office doors stood open and Alira peered inside. Envesi was at the window, rather than her desk. Most of the boxes that had crowded the Archmage's space were gone. A promising sign for cleanup efforts.

Alira lingered beside the doors. "You saw us arrive, Archmage?" She never knew what sort of mood the woman might be in. If the Archmage was in sour sorts, even positive news might be unwelcome.

"I gave up watching when the storm came in. It was merely good timing that I looked out the window as you cleared the gates." Despite the placid tone the Archmage used, Alira had a distinct feeling her words were not truth. "I trust all went well?"

"Yes, Archmage. I assume you received my message about an

17

ambassador to discuss the finer workings of the arrangement?" Alira waited for Envesi's nod before she stepped inside. She closed the doors and went on. "I expect he will arrive tomorrow, perhaps the day after. How convenient that Kifel's men are already gone."

The Archmage ignored the observation. "Then we shall make our announcement tonight." Envesi raised a hand. Gestures were unnecessary for magecraft, though often used to help maintain focus. In the Archmage's case, they were used for grandeur. Threads of light spun around Envesi's fingers and rushed through the window, out into the night sky. They wove themselves together over the temple's grounds, creating thin ribbons that flowed in the current of the wind.

With her other hand, she twirled her fingers, drawing the storm clouds in the sky into a tight whorl. The air currents seethed with energy, protesting her use of power. Alira cringed as the Archmage cast the clouds aside. Weather did not take kindly to manipulation; nature's energies often struck out against the mage who tried to shift them. It was a testament to Envesi's strength that she could bend a storm to her will on her own.

As the clouds parted, a pure, sweet resonance filtered through the air. Alira tensed as she felt it slide across her skin.

"I've Called the Masters," the Archmage stated, as though Alira wouldn't know what the sensation was. The Calling, as it was named, was a strange thing. A prickling sense of energy only tangible to those the caster sought, it filled those summoned with a sense of urgency tied to an impression of the mage who issued the Call. "See that the magelings are assembled in the courtyard."

"Yes, Archmage." Alira bowed her head and inched toward the door. The Calling wasn't used often, reserved for urgent matters and taught to mages only after they had proven themselves responsible. That the Archmage chose to summon *all* the Masters with it made her skin crawl worse than the

Calling itself. Envesi's eyes were all too heavy on her back as she left.

Magelings cast her curious looks as she passed on the order and Alira's hackles rose each time another pair of eyes turned her way. But she was a Master, her eyes marked with ink resembling fire, and the magelings heeded her orders. They filtered out to the courtyard one by one. Alira ran her hands over her upper arms as if to brush away the prickle of the Calling, and nervous weight settled in her stomach. She did not know how the news would be received, but the thought of the impending announcement gave her chills.

———

THE DISAPPEARANCE OF THE RAIN WAS PUZZLING, THOUGH MOST magelings were more interested in the fluttering ribbons of light that played overhead. Kytenia reached to touch them and laughed when the streamers passed through her fingertips without so much as a tingle.

Mages poured into the courtyard to see the lights. Fascinated, Kytenia watched the streamers ripple in the breeze and only tore her eyes away when Rikka nudged her shoulder. Delight lit her face when she spotted Shymin and Marreli hurrying across the flagstones to join them. She swept her sister into a hug as Rikka greeted Marreli in the same way.

"You're home!" Marreli looked ready to cry, her dark eyes glassy and her hair a mess.

"Of course I am, you goose." Rikka tugged the smaller girl's braids and craned her neck to search the growing crowd. "Where's Firal? Isn't she with you?"

Kytenia cringed at the gentle reminder. "We need her right away." She caught Shymin by the shoulders and lowered her voice to keep from being overheard. "We must get a message to the king as soon as possible." She still wasn't sure how it could be done, but none of them had overlooked the king's apparent interest in Firal. If any of them had a chance to gain an audience with Kifelethelas, it would be her.

Shymin's face darkened. "Firal isn't here. And we can't discuss this right now." She cast a meaningful glance toward the Masters joining the crowd.

Kytenia worried her lower lip. "Then we need Ran," she said. If Ran really was a court mage, as Firal had mentioned before Kytenia and Rikka were whisked away to Alwhen, then he made a logical second choice. But as a Master, he served the temple before he served the king, and she wasn't sure where his allegiance rested.

"He's not here, either."

Rikka made a sound of exasperation and threw her hands into the air. "Blight it all, then, who *is* here?"

Kytenia hushed her as the crowd shifted away from the temple's central tower, and silence took the crowd. Masters formed a half-circle around the tower's doors, forcing the mages back, clearing space as the Archmage emerged into the courtyard.

Kytenia's throat tightened. It was only the second time she'd seen the woman. With the way her white hair glowed beneath the ribbons of light, she seemed more a specter than a person. The shifting sea of magelings grew utterly still as the Archmage took them all in, her face as serene and cold as her eyes.

Kytenia shuddered as the Archmage's gaze swept over them, but the woman's eyes did not linger. Beside her, Rikka exhaled in relief. Kytenia felt her own shoulders sag with relief, too. Perhaps the Archmage didn't know who Alira had taken with her, but the knowledge they bore—and what they intended to do with it—meant scrutiny was the last thing Kytenia wanted.

Rikka watched until the Archmage faced the other way, then leaned toward Marreli. "Where has Firal gone?" she asked in a harsh whisper. "Is she off hiding in the ruins again? We can't send this by carrier pigeon, you never know who will read it!"

"We don't know where she is," Marreli replied. "Master

Nondar said she was expelled from the temple this afternoon, just before the king's men were summoned back to Ilmenhith."

Kytenia's jaw dropped. *"Expelled?"*

Shymin pressed a finger to her lips with a scowl as the Archmage spread her arms to the sky.

"Tonight..." the Archmage began, power amplifying her voice and making it boom across the temple's grounds. "Tonight marks a new beginning for Kirban Temple, for all mages here. At moon's zenith, we begin our new legacy. The sun will rise on our new path, our new pursuits, our newfound power and freedom." She paused, skimming the crowd again. "I am sure the absence of the king's men has not gone unnoticed."

A number of magelings shifted at mention of the soldiers. Almost unconsciously, Kytenia leaned into her sister's arm. She'd noticed the men were absent, but she hadn't had time to discover why.

The Archmage went on. "They will not return, because as of tonight, we stand alone. The temple has severed its ties to the old ways, from the influence of a neglectful ruler. Let it be known that, from this moment on, we have seceded from King Kifelethelas's control."

The announcement sent an uproar through the crowd. Kytenia exchanged glances with her friends, all their faces pale in the mage-light.

Rikka linked arms with Kytenia and Shymin and pulled them back as a wave of argument rose in the mages around them. Even the Archmage's gestures and commands couldn't calm the sudden fury that spewed from Masters and first-year magelings alike.

"Come on," Rikka said. "We've got to send word now, while the Masters are distracted. We'll discuss what happened to Firal later."

Kytenia turned back and caught Marreli's hand. The younger girl's face was ghostly white, her eyes wide with fear as the group slipped from the crush of people. Kytenia swallowed. If

21

they hurried, they'd have just enough time to pen a letter before someone noticed they were gone. If luck was on their side, they'd find a way to send it without being seen. And if not, then perhaps Firal was more fortunate than they realized.

———

"You seem troubled, my liege."

Kifel frowned and lifted his quill from the paper before him. "Do I? I was hoping it wouldn't show." He leaned back in his chair as he looked to the doorway. Medreal rarely knocked, though it never seemed an intrusion when she slipped into his office. She had been his nursemaid, once upon a time, which made her seem more like a mother and less like an adviser.

She'd worn the eye markings of a court mage then, a practice she stopped not long after he had risen to the crown. He had always assumed her a mage trained in the old ways—a powerful one—but he'd never asked about her education. Now that he thought of it, she had stopped marking her eyes around the time the temple had been founded. He'd never noticed. He should have.

"You do a fine job of concealing it, my liege. Only the watchful eye of one who knows you could see it." Medreal let the door click shut behind her. She balanced a tea tray on one arm, a rolled and sealed letter in her hand.

Kifel dropped his quill into its inkwell and rubbed his eyes. "Something doesn't feel right, that's all. It's been several days since I received a report from the men I stationed at Kirban Temple. I don't expect anything too eventful, but I do expect regular reports."

"It's natural to be distressed by such things. You worry enough about the temple as it is, what with your son and our kindly Archmage." Medreal made her way across the room as he tidied his desk.

Kifel snorted with a wry smile. Kindly? There were many

words he might use for Envesi, but that wasn't one of them. Regardless of her tasteful phrasing, though, Medreal was right. "Nothing gets past you, does it?"

"I don't mean to make you feel transparent, my liege."

Rain beat against the high arched windows of his office, leaving the interior dismal and dark, befitting his sour mood. Kifel gazed outside almost wistfully as Medreal laid the tray before him. "I also should have received word about the mages I requested for Ilmenhith. We're always in need of more healers. Temar received word they graduated Lomithrandel to Master, though I don't think him ready. I'm not even certain what he can do. He doesn't speak of his abilities. Still, there were several other students I had my eye on."

"Are you worried our people may soon need healing, my liege?" Medreal raised a thin brow. "All has been calm for what, thirty pents? Do you fear injury, or illness?"

He sighed, pressing fingers to his temples. "I don't know."

The old woman pursed her lips and extended the sealed scroll to him. "Well, perhaps this contains something to brighten your day. It does not bear the army's crest, but I believe it's from a temple Master."

Kifel all but snatched the scroll from her hand. "It's too big to have come by pigeon. How did this get here?"

"It was on my table, my liege. I do not know how it came." Medreal bowed her head.

Frowning deeply, he broke the seal and unrolled the smooth paper. The message inside was written in a neat and elegant hand. "I don't recognize this writing," he murmured, but he read on.

FOR THE ATTENTION OF KING KIFELETHELAS ALONE:

One day past, as you read this letter, your men were dismissed from the temple by word that came from Ilmenhith. The order bore your seal.

A messenger from King Relythes of the eastern province will arrive in Kirban today to discuss control of the temple.

    Last night, the Archmage announced secession from your rule.

    Please advise, but address anonymous response to Mageling Rikka.

    N.

KIFEL SAGGED AGAINST HIS CHAIR, THE PAPER CURLING AGAINST HIS tense fingers.

"My liege?" Medreal questioned. Anxious, she tugged the neckline of her dress. When he did not reply, she leaned closer. "My liege, what is it?"

He flung the tray from his desk. Tea spilled across his papers. The teapot shattered on the floor. "This is how she repays me?" He slammed a balled fist against his desk and rose so fast, his chair fell backwards. He backhanded the teacup that had fallen from the tray. It crashed into the window beside his desk.

"Majesty!" Medreal staggered back from the cacophony of shattering glass. "Calm yourself!"

"After everything I've done for her! After everything I've given her! How dare she?" Tea streamed across his desk in steaming rivulets. He planted his hands on the desktop and did not feel the burn. Cold rain blew in through the broken window. The droplets left dark stains on his sleeve. "How *dare* she?" Rage flashed in his emerald eyes. "She's declared herself independent of me! After all I've done to fund her follies, all I've done to raise —" He bit his tongue and stifled the words before they escaped. No. He wouldn't stoop to that. He wouldn't misplace the blame.

Wary, Medreal drew back another step. "The Archmage? She can't stand independently of you, can she? Does she even have the means for it?"

Kifel clenched his teeth and inhaled through his nose. His palms pressed harder against the desktop, the heat of the spilled tea seeping into his fingers. He leaned against the desk with his head down. "Relythes has his fingers in that pie, it seems. After so many years of peace."

"I'm not certain I would call it peace, my liege," Medreal cautioned. "A truce, perhaps, but not peace. There has been no trade and no contact with the eastern half of the island since you brought the skirmishes to an end."

The king shook his head. His shoulders bunched tight and he willed them to relax, but they slumped instead. "She's sent my soldiers away. The men I sent to protect her. How did she convince them to leave? How could she?"

"I can't answer that, my liege. Only she can."

It was an honest response, but the calm way Medreal said it still made him sigh. "Then I must go to the temple immediately." He stepped away from his desk and lifted his hands. His fingers were red and sore. Resigned, he drew the tiny tea towel from the tray and dried his hands, leaving behind bright, angry marks.

Medreal laced her fingers together at her waist, as composed as ever. "How shall I contact you while you are there?"

Giving her a pointed look, he said, "Don't."

Despite the anger that still burned in his chest, Kifel smoothed his hair and righted the gold circlet above his brow. His face showed nothing but cool neutrality by the time he set foot in the hall. He did not wear a crown often and he couldn't say what made him pick it up that morning, though he was glad for its presence as he straightened his sleeves and stepped into the parlor where his court mages waited.

The mages in blue-trimmed white all but leaped to their feet when he appeared at the doorway, abandoning their chessboards and books. Kifel's eyes narrowed. Ilmenhith's mages had enough duties to tend that they shouldn't have been lounging about and playing games. They were fortunate he was in a rush. "A Gate to Kirban Temple. The Archmage's office, now."

The Masters bowed and hurried to take their places around the stone archway they used to anchor Gates. In no time, the air crackled with power. Kifel hadn't often thought of his Giftless lineage, but he cursed it now. Had he been born with a Gift, perhaps it would be easier to keep the mages in hand.

The Gate grew still and the image within it stabilized. He waited for one of the mages to nod before he stepped through. The air in the Archmage's tower was hotter than that in the parlor, and he grimaced when it struck him. He drew a breath, his face stony once more as he strode down the narrow path to the doors of the Archmage's office. He flung open the doors so hard they banged into the wall, spilling a shower of dust from the doorframe.

"Temper, temper," Envesi chided. She lowered her book and brushed snowy white curls away from her face.

"Do not dare chastise me," Kifel said icily.

Her eyebrows lifted. "Of course. You are a king, after all."

As cool and respectful as her words sounded, there was no mistaking that they were meant as a taunt. His eyes sparked with anger. "I am *your* king. And this is a school that I founded, if I must remind you."

"Oh, yes." The Archmage leaned back in her chair, drumming slender fingers against her chin. "I'm afraid I would forget, if you and that boy of yours weren't so determined to remind me. He's so very like you, one might fail to recall he isn't yours."

His breath caught.

She chuckled. "Or perhaps you want them to forget? What a pitiful creature. I don't know why you dote on him so."

"You gave me a child, but you gave me no heir. What else do I have?"

"Ah, yes." Envesi's eyes narrowed at the corners, hinting at a smirk she couldn't contain. "In that case, I suppose you'll be forced to pass your position to your mages when you die."

"I have no intention of dying any time soon," Kifel replied. "Your interest in my demise is unsettling."

She gave him a disdainful look and then shifted her gaze to the tall windows that rimmed her office. "Please. We both know you aren't afraid of me. Besides, I can count those who still know who I truly am on one hand. A single generation, and already

26

the island has forgotten. You doomed me the moment you refused a public wedding. Without an obvious heir to tie us together, what would I gain from your death?"

"And what do you gain from abandoning my rule?" he asked. The surprise on her face gave him a small twinge of satisfaction. He wasn't supposed to know. He straightened and continued. "Your connection to me makes this even more absurd, whether the island knows it or not. Or do you want me to be remembered as the king who let an estranged queen tear his legacy apart?"

She folded her arms over her chest. "Your expectations are unrealistic and your ability to protect the temple is wanting. Spare me the dramatics. You shouldn't take everything as a personal affront. I don't love you, but I don't hate you, either."

"You used to."

"Hate you?"

"Love me." He leveled his gaze with hers, searching her mage-blue eyes. Despite everything, the cold lack of emotion was disappointing.

Envesi regarded him solemnly for a long time before she pushed herself up from her desk. "People change, Kifel."

"No," he said. "Minds do."

She strode to the windows and peered down into the courtyard. "This exchange is over."

"You're right," Kifel agreed, brushing dust from his coat. Not dust; ash. It left a pale streak on his sleeve. "There was never anything to discuss. If you think you have the authority to pull Kirban out from underneath me, you're mistaken. You might think the temple is yours, but it rests on my land, and the mages answer to me. Don't think escaping me is as simple as telling my men to leave. You'll do well to remember your place before this is settled."

He strode out of her office before she could respond, his jaw set. He drew the door closed behind him, and his shoulders sagged as it clicked shut. It wasn't hard to tell she had not been intimidated. Perhaps he'd let her go unchecked for too long. But he'd never thought he needed to fear her—or any of the mages, for that matter. That overconfidence became clear now.

Why had he come without any of his court mages? He was the king, but Envesi held no respect for that. He was powerless in her eyes, un-Gifted, and he'd walked into her office like a fool. Had she wanted, she could have crushed him. Kifel looked at the ash on his sleeve and dusted at it again as he started down the tower's stairs.

It had been decades since the temple's founding. It was foolish to think something might have changed between them, yet he hadn't been able to smother the hope he'd kept kindled. She was not who he remembered; she didn't even look the same. He always remembered her as she'd been the day they met. The memory haunted him, even now. He tried to shake it from his head.

As the only child left to his bloodline, Kifel's right to the throne had been uncontested. But heirs did not choose their futures, and Envesi had been chosen for him. Despite that, he'd hoped they would have the sort of relationship his parents had shared. They had not started their life together in love, but it had ended that way, and they had passed within hours of one another.

He turned to descend another flight of stairs. In the heat of the day, with the magelings out cleaning the burned temple, the tower was all but empty. The library on the lower floors was desolate, nothing but lingering ash to show its books ever existed. He thought again of the smudge on his sleeve. The temple's destruction clung to him, whether it was his fault or not. Clearly, the Archmage felt it was.

Envesi had been an odd choice from the beginning, and so their union had been kept quiet. The daughter of a minor lord on the mainland, she had been selected specifically because of her heritage as a mage. Her power gave her prestige on Elenhiise, where their culture prized magic. Her eyes had already been mage-blue when she came to him, her tresses the blackest he'd ever seen. She had been striking, if not beautiful, and he had foolishly thought nothing mattered aside from appearance and respect. She had both, and if she had truly wanted to marry him, perhaps everything would have been different.

As Kifel reached the ground level, his expression shifted to something as solemn as stone. He'd made many mistakes. He had been headstrong and rash, hadn't valued his bride as he should have. But her bitterness toward him had formed long before they were married. He couldn't blame it all on himself, and he had tried to make her happy. He had given her the temple, after all, in exchange for a child.

The king stepped from the ruined tower and squinted against the sunlight.

"You," he called, singling out a mageling with her arms full of books.

She froze. Something about her russet curls tickled his memory, but he'd seen so many magelings during the solstice that all of them seemed familiar.

"Where can I find a mageling named Rikka?"

The girl bowed and murmured something about retrieval before she dashed away.

Kifel waited at the doors of the tower, his face unchanging. Mages gave him a wide berth and worried glances. He couldn't blame them; Envesi's announcement had already been made, and he knew he did not look pleased.

After a time, the mageling returned with a red-headed girl in tow.

He straightened. "Rikka, I presume?"

The red-headed girl's eyes widened, but she regained her equanimity fast enough. She spread her skirts and offered a deep curtsy. "Yes, Majesty."

"Good," Kifel smiled, though there was no mirth in him. "We have much to discuss."

All Rikka managed was a nod.

4

A PLACE TO BELONG

DAEMON SHIVERED DESPITE THE MORNING'S HUMID WARMTH. Clouds hung in thick sheets over the ruins, glowing soft pink in the sunrise. He rose from his perch atop a ruin wall, his rain-chilled muscles protesting movement. The morning's sentries would be out soon, his soldiers quick to follow.

He dropped to the ground and knuckled his back beneath his cloak. A handful of men had camped with him at the edge of the ruins, though they left the wall-climbing to him. Some eyed him with solemn faces as he rejoined them, as if they sensed his doubts. But they had his armor ready and waiting, so he unfastened his cloak.

Armor was something he didn't really care for; it was cumbersome and sometimes too showy. But he recognized his need for it and tried to cooperate while his soldiers helped him don it. One of the men pressed something into his hand and he turned it over to see what it was. "For good luck," the man said.

It was a simple jade carving of a scorpion, similar to the one he'd left in the village of Charth during his first raid. Daemon wasn't sure where the man had gotten it, but it was a pleasant surprise. If nothing else, it showed his men paid closer attention to what he did than he thought. A good omen for a new leader.

He belted his sword at his side as the rest of the soldiers filed into the camp and the captain of the group joined him. He'd chosen Davan's group because he knew he could work with the man, and strengthening relations with the captain could only serve to aid him. "Is everything ready?"

"Yes, sir." Davan's reply was hoarse and uneasy, but the captain looked more confident than he sounded.

"Good." Daemon adjusted his mask and fastened his cloak around his shoulders again. Then he tied the scorpion amulet at his throat. He drew a claw over the rough jade, reminding himself why he'd liked the symbol in the first place. Venom wasn't a scorpion's only weapon. Often, it was a last resort. "We're moving now. Be ready. We don't know what we'll be facing today."

Silence met his words. Davan moved aside to let him pass, organizing the ranks as Daemon led the way. The cacophony of footsteps behind him shifted into the steady drumming of a marching army.

Three days for the village to decide to meet them as friend or foe had been too much time and yet not enough. Daemon didn't think he'd need the two hundred men he'd brought, but he couldn't be too careful. He'd threatened to wipe them out if they didn't cooperate. It wouldn't do to show up without the means. The line of soldiers behind him threaded through the curving hallways of the ruins like a black snake, the rhythmic sound of their march driving concern from his head. The weight of his armor brought a pleasant warmth back into his limbs, and he took each step with growing vigor.

They spilled from the ruins like flowing water and filed into formation on the side of the grassy hill. Daemon breathed a sigh of relief. No rival army stood between them and the village ahead.

The morning bustle in the village slowed as they approached. Men gathered to stare at the approaching army, while the women and children disappeared from sight. Hidden in case of violence, no doubt, but the village men clustered in the streets were armed only with the garden tools they wielded for the morning's work.

The march slowed as the army formed a wide half-circle to envelop the town's edge. Daemon strode forward from its center with his head held high, one hand resting on the pommel of his sword. "Gentlemen," he offered in greeting as he surveyed the men gathered before him. "It seems a fine day for business. It appears you agree."

"It is a fine day." The response came from a voice he'd heard before, though Daemon couldn't pick Rolan from the crowd until he moved to the front. "Mark us, though, General, we don't want you thinking us cowards for not wanting to fight."

Daemon laughed. "The wiser man is he who avoids conflict, my friend. The stories of my people may tout ruthlessness, but I assure you we are not savages."

"And you'll pay us?" Rolan asked, uneasy. His eyes flicked between Daemon and the captain at his side.

"That was the agreement, was it not?" Daemon swept his cloak back over his shoulder. The village men shifted nervously at the sight of the sword at his hip, but his hand passed the hilt and settled instead on the bulging leather purse tied behind the blade. He pulled the pouch loose and upended it over his palm, spilling a shower of gold into his hand. A whisper of excitement passed through the cluster of men. Excitement and relief.

"Unmarked and unminted, for your own protection, of course." Daemon flexed his hand to let the gold catch the light. "Mined beneath the ruins by the hands of my own men. There are some impurities, but I hope the quantity we're offering rectifies that problem." He poured the handful back into the purse and gave it a shake to settle its contents.

"And it's real?"

"You think I'd bring you fool's gold after all this?" Daemon snorted and held the purse out in one hand. "You're all free to inspect it for yourselves. As I don't know what the current prices for goods are, I trust you will divide it fairly among your people once we have what we came for."

Rolan snatched the purse from Daemon's hand. A handful of men inched closer to inspect its contents. "All right." Satisfied, Rolan closed the purse and gestured for the other villagers to move. "You've got a deal. Give us a few minutes to get things together, and we'll give you everything we can spare."

Daemon signaled to the half-circle of soldiers behind him as the village men retreated to collect their goods. The army parted to allow a handful of soldiers with narrow wagons into the street. Tension dissolved as the village men began to reappear with sacks of grain and bins of vegetables. Several chickens in crates appeared, and farther down the road, a man led a hog on a short rope. Soldiers met the men halfway, and they worked together to load the wagons.

Rolan posted himself at Daemon's side, watching the men at work. "I think this arrangement will benefit us both. We can provide food enough for ourselves, but we've no cobbler and no weaver. Everyone in the cities wants money for goods, they're unwilling to barter. Trade being reestablished with either kingdom would give us back our livelihoods."

"We're from neither kingdom," Daemon said dryly, shifting on his feet. He relaxed his shoulders, mindful that the motion not be mistaken for discomfort.

Rolan turned his head, confused. "You're not? But—"

"Your people call us Underlings," Daemon answered before the man finished the question. "Though if we have our way, everyone will know us by a different name before long."

Surprised, Rolan looked to the wagons. "Underlings," he repeated, the word full of wonder.

Daemon allowed himself a smile behind his mask. "We would prefer to be known as ruin-folk. That's what we call ourselves." When no response came, he left the man to marvel and returned to the job at hand.

He walked between the clusters of village men and his soldiers, but they did not need oversight. His men were efficient, working in teams they'd arranged themselves, loading wagons and moving them to the edge of town to form a neat procession. Calling them wagons might have been generous, Daemon thought as he watched another join the line. The carts were no wider than the span of a man's arms, built with high wheels designed for the uneven ground and narrow hallways of the ruins. Even fully loaded, they weren't heavy enough to require animals to pull them. Fortunate, as their collection of livestock was limited. With time, Daemon hoped that would grow, too. He savored the sounds of men joking and laughing, letting thoughts of the future play in his head as business was settled.

The sun rode high in the afternoon sky by the time Daemon thanked the village men for their aid and his soldiers departed with their new supplies.

For the first time in a while, a tingle of contentment touched Daemon's spirits. He split the men into three companies and directed each down a different path as they moved into the ruins. The hardest part was over. A burden lifted from his shoulders. With the sky clear overhead and his men safely back inside the ruins, the rest of the day promised nothing but smooth sailing.

———

FIRAL BOWED HER HEAD AGAINST HER KNEES. SHE WOULDN'T CRY. She refused.

Why now? Why after everything had settled? She thought of her conversation with Shymin and Marreli and her face flushed with anger. She hadn't dared to remain at the temple long enough to find the girls or tell them what happened. Not that she needed to. Her expulsion would be gossip on every mageling's lips before nightfall.

Even had she sought her friends, she doubted she could think of a kind word to give them. No one else knew of her frequent visits to the ruins; no one else could have betrayed her. Firal clenched her teeth and balled her fists in the dirtied gown she held bundled in her arms. She had nothing else. Without the temple, she had nothing at all.

She had fled through the temple's open gates before the guards on duty could catch her, her face burning with shame under the weight of unfamiliar eyes. Her escape into the ruins provided little comfort, though the low, domed canopy of the familiar sigil-marked tree offered shelter from the rain. Firal waited with her back against the tree and tried to ignore the clouds overhead. Birdsong halted when the storm began, leaving only her occasional hiccuping sobs to fill the silence.

It was well past dark before she decided to venture on, though the storm persisted. She was soaked to skin and a dull ache in her middle reminded her she'd left without food. Her eyes skimmed the tops of the walls and searched openings into passages she didn't take. The entry to the long, straight underground road to Ilmenhith couldn't be that far, though she didn't know where to look. With the cold, pelting rain, she could only hope to find it soon—before she, herself, was found.

Undeterred by the weather, night insects whirred in the grass and jumped around her feet as she walked. It seemed like ages since she'd quarreled with Daemon, but it had only been a handful of days. She glanced over her shoulder at every opportunity, each twist and turn of the corridors making her more nervous. How far could she travel before he found her? Firal tried not to think of it. He hated her, she knew. She hadn't seen his face, but there was no need. There was no reason to think he would hurt her, but a confrontation now was the last thing she wanted. Everything from the way he'd stood to that otherworldly light in his eyes had radiated anger.

Shymin was right; it hadn't been her place to teach him. Firal should have known it would go sour somehow. But it had only come to shouting, and that single warning against setting foot in the ruins again. She hadn't intended to return to the ruins at all, never mind so soon.

Though she hated to, Firal made a mage-light and held it near the ground. The light would make her too easy to spot, but she didn't stumble quite so often when she could see where her feet were going.

By the time she found an opening into the underground, the storm had grown so intense, it was impossible to know whether it was day or night. The passage did not lead into the tunnel she'd hoped for. Instead, it ended at a spiral stairway of black stone Firal was certain led to the catacombs of Lumia's underground palace. That was the last place she wanted to be. But respite from the storm was welcome, and she crept into the cavern's mouth.

Firal's green robes were saturated, a fact unpleasantly emphasized by the cold breeze that whipped into the stairwell, and water plastered her dark hair to her head. She pressed her fingers to the fabric of her robes and caught the flowing energy of the water, twisting her own energies with it. When she moved her hand downward, the water followed, her magic stripping the rain from her clothes.

She repeated the process for her silk gown. The black dye bled onto her hands when she touched it. Dark, marbled stains ruined the red silk panels in the bodice and skirt. She studied the dress with a frown. Her only remaining possession, and it had been rendered as useless as her dreams. Morose, Firal curled against the cold wall and pulled the gown to her shoulders, reducing the once-magnificent garment to a blanket as she succumbed to her exhaustion.

Sleep came fitfully, and not long after sunrise, she began to walk again.

Gray clouds veiled the sky throughout the day and made it

difficult to tell which direction was which. Not that it mattered, with the way the ruins doubled back on themselves. It was unlikely Firal could have done anything to keep going the same direction. A handful of plump blackberries scrounged from leggy bushes took the edge off her hunger, though a single handful was all she found.

Her legs burned with fatigue and her feet grew clumsier the longer she traveled, but she didn't stop until the sound of voices on the other side of a ruin wall caught her by surprise. She didn't think she had gone far enough to reach civilization again, though the sound of men's voices and deep laughter indicated otherwise.

With as much stealth as she could manage, Firal crept forward until she could almost make out words. Smoke rose from the other side of the wall ahead, carrying scents that made her mouth water. Hunger and curiosity proved too much for her. Using gaps in the stone as handholds, she scaled the wall and peered over the top.

On the other side, pale canvas tents filled one of the large, circular rooms she'd come to expect in the ruins. Men milled about the tents, some in worn armor, some in nothing more than breeches. A few sat in clusters around a fire built in the center of the camp, joking and laughing as they filled bowls from the deep iron pot that sat in the coals. The good smells made Firal's stomach gurgle. She grimaced and slid back to the ground.

The men hadn't looked unusual, though they certainly weren't Eldani. They were stocky and bronzed, with thick beards and dark hair. Their complexion was more common among the Giftless men from the east. But humans, this far into the ruins? She shook her head and hurried down the corridor. Just looking had been a mistake. If she made it to Ilmenhith in one piece, she would send word to the king. Beyond that, their presence was none of her concern, and the last thing she wanted was more risk.

Firal rounded the corner and collided with an armored body.

She screamed, but the man caught hold of her and clamped a hand over her mouth to cut it short. Someone shouted, and metal rasped as dozens of men in the camp behind the wall drew steel.

Her captor wrenched her arm behind her back, forcing her to drop the bundle of silk in her arms. "I've got her," he called, turning with her to face the small party of armed men that spilled into the hall. They stopped when they saw her, mingled surprise and suspicion drawn on their faces. A moment later, their leader pushed through the crowd.

Firal's stomach dropped and her knees went weak. She sank to the grass.

Though his face was hidden by the same plain steel mask as ever, the eye slits of Daemon's mask glowed red in obvious anger. He motioned with a clawed hand and his men fell back, though they held their swords ready.

"Is she a temple spy, sir?" Firal's captor asked. He kept firm hold of her, though his hand slipped from her mouth. She considered screaming again, but abandoned the idea. What difference would it make? The men were the only ones who would hear.

Daemon snorted. "Don't be ridiculous. She's tactless and graceless. Spies demand guile, charisma, and good social placement."

The implication that she had none of those made her cheeks burn with shame.

The big hands wrapped around her arms clenched tighter and gave her a hard shake. "What are you doing here, Eldani?"

Her stomach churned beneath the nauseating claws of fear and for a moment, she was grateful she'd found so little to eat. "I'm traveling to Ilmenhith." Tears welled in her eyes and she blinked furiously to clear them. "I have nowhere else to go."

"Well, I'm sure the king will be happy to have you," Daemon replied snidely.

The man who held Firal twisted her arm again, forcing her back to her feet. "What should I do with her, sir?"

"She had her warning. Get rid of her, however you see fit. What you do with her is no concern of mine." Daemon turned back the way he'd come and waved the rest of his men away. Some of them sheathed their weapons and trudged back toward their camp. Others watched her, and the gleam of entertainment in their eyes made her sick.

"I've been expelled." Firal called, and her voice cracked.

Daemon paused mid-stride.

"I've been stripped of my rank. All my possessions burned with the temple." She wiggled to free an arm, but the soldier who held her was too strong. Unable to dash away her tears, Firal grimaced as they rolled freely down her cheeks. "I have no family and no friends outside the temple. I have no other home. If I can get as far as Ilmenhith, perhaps I can..." She trailed off. What could she do? Cast out from the temple, it was unlikely she would find anyone willing to train her further. Aside from magic, she had no skills.

The silence dragged on until even the men behind Daemon shifted with discomfort.

"Begging your pardon, my lord," the man beside her began, "but if you've no preference what we do with her, perhaps I ought to take her to Core."

Daemon glared over his shoulder. "Core?"

"You promised us a mage, my lord. I know you remember." The man licked his lips and cast Firal a thoughtful look before he went on. "It would fulfill your promise, my lord. The people would love it. We can take her to my Minna, sir. She'd be glad to set things right."

Daemon was quiet for so long that Firal wasn't certain he would reply. Even so, a tiny light of hope blossomed in her chest at the idea of having somewhere to go—even if she didn't understand where. She tried to smother it, but the small flame of hope twisted to longing instead.

Eventually, Daemon spoke. "Very well." The words were defeated, resigned. But they were enough.

The soldier let go and Firal almost fell. She teetered sideways and put out both hands to catch herself against the wall. When she looked up, Daemon's eyes were on her, but their threatening glow was gone.

They regarded each other for some time before he tore his gaze away. "Let's go."

The men behind him parted to let him pass. Then, in pairs, they moved after him.

Firal turned at last to look at the soldier who'd caught her. He smiled, and the kindness in his brown eyes startled her.

"Come along, now, miss." He motioned her forward and, obediently, she gathered the dress she'd dropped into her arms and turned to follow the soldiers around the corner.

The camp grew still when she appeared at its entrance. Her pointed ears burned with the weight of the eyes on her.

Daemon stopped by the fire to scoop a bowl of stew from the pot. Firal shuffled toward him, hugging her gown to her chest. "Daemon, I—"

"Don't talk to me," he growled. He pushed past the men clustered around the fire and slipped into a tent, closing its flaps behind him.

She stared after him, uncertain, and blinked when someone held a bowl of stew right in front of her. That soldier again. He smiled, a gentle, fatherly spark in his eyes. He pushed the bowl toward her again and, not knowing what else to do, she took it. He pointed one callused finger toward the large stones that surrounded the fire, and she sat.

"Thank you," she said as she settled. The food's pleasant aroma was enough to make her stomach growl.

"Don't mind the general, miss mage," the man said as he seated himself beside her. "It's best to leave him be when he's in a mood. He'll get over it. Or he'd better, what as he's the only one of us free to take you back to Core."

As if she wanted to travel anywhere with Daemon now. Uneasiness stirred in the pit of her stomach again, but hunger overpowered it. She reached for the wooden spoon in her bowl. "Where is Core?"

He chuckled. "You'll see, miss. Just wait."

5

CORE

Aside from the occasional curious glance, the men paid Firal little mind. Daemon didn't say a word to her during their trip through the winding corridors of the ruins, did not even explain where she was meant to go when the small army divided into smaller groups. She stood at the crossroads where the groups parted until the man who'd caught her in the first place took her arm and directed her toward the stairs, just as Daemon disappeared down them.

He didn't ask for a mage-light, but she created one anyway. She'd seen enough of the underground before, and after so much travel, she did not trust her feet on the uneven stairs.

They passed four landings, each of which branched off into winding pathways of their own. Firal gazed down the meandering tunnels and couldn't help but wonder if one of them led to Ilmenhith. She didn't know where they were going or why she was going along with it, really. All she could think of was having somewhere dry to rest.

Her body ached with fatigue, but the stairway stretched ever farther into the earth. With one hand on the wall to aid her balance, she crept down the steps at as slow of a pace as she could manage while still keeping Daemon in sight. The longer they traveled, the more she wondered if they would ever reach the bottom.

And then, without warning, the stairway ended. A smooth-walled hallway stretched on at length, and at the far end, a dim glow beckoned them onward.

Daemon never looked back, but when they reached the end of the hall, he paused. When Firal reached him and saw what waited ahead, she couldn't help but gasp.

The corridor emptied into a natural cavern, its walls so steep and smooth she might have thought them man-made, save the way they tapered to the ceiling some hundred paces above. The entire cavern bustled and roared with the noises of life. Wide stalls with colorful cloth tops created a market that spread almost from wall to wall, its narrow avenues packed with people.

A shallow river intersected the cavern, splitting it into two distinct halves. Children played along the riverbanks while women washed laundry against the rocks. At the mouth of the river, far to the right, a towering waterwheel turned lazily against the cavern wall.

"Come on." Daemon jerked his head to the left and started into the throng of people. He led her downstream, where matching flights of stairs descended on either side of the river. A deeper pool waited below the wide waterfall, where children splashed in the foam.

Firal's eyes traced the water and then scaled the walls. Doorways, walkways, and windows were chiseled into the stone walls beyond the market, some of them glowing with candlelight. The sense of awe that washed over her made her feel as if she'd shrunk. "I can't believe there's an entire city down here."

Daemon made a sound of displeasure. "Where did you think we lived? In a dirt hole?"

"I just didn't think it would be like this." She hurried to close the distance between them. "There are so many people."

"Our numbers aren't as small as the stories tell," he agreed.

The stairs tapered and then flattened into a narrow path that meandered alongside the river. Some distance ahead, a sheer, black stone wall rose to block the way. Narrow archways in its face allowed a thin stream of people to pass farther into the underground. The crowd parted with warm smiles and bows of deference as Daemon led her that way.

"You certainly are well respected," Firal said.

"I am their general and the right hand of their queen. If nothing else, they would respect the title." He sounded indifferent, though the stiffness of his shrug implied otherwise.

"Are we speaking now?" she asked.

"You're speaking."

And he was angry at her, she concluded. No surprise. She wasn't thrilled, either, but at least she was out of the rain. "That man in the ruins above," she began quietly.

Daemon paused and turned an ear toward her.

She swallowed. "He said you promised them a mage. What did he mean?"

He stood still for a time, not seeming to notice the stream of people who flowed around them like a parting river. Eventually, he resumed walking. The stiffness was still there. "I would have thought you'd take the time to learn at least something about us before returning."

"How was I to do that?" She lifted her chin. "The temple's library burned, remember?"

He grunted. "What you heard is everything you need to know. I promised the Underlings a mage. Though when I promised that, I meant me."

Firal stopped dead in her tracks as they stepped through the archway. Narrow shafts of sunlight spilled in from far overhead, illuminating a wide avenue that ringed what she could only describe as an underground tower, the railless walkway spiraling both upward and down in perfectly spaced tiers. To Firal's right, a graceful stone bridge spanned the river. The water poured off a ledge beneath the bridge without a sound, the noise of the waterfall lost somewhere below. The wide central shaft of the tower plunged so far into the earth that the bottom could not be seen. Suddenly weak in the knees, Firal staggered back against the wall.

Daemon snickered at her terrified expression. "Don't worry. You'll get used to it. Walk beside the wall, you'll be fine."

"Walk? I can't even stand!" she cried as her legs tried to buckle beneath her.

A man with a rough wooden cart passed between them. As if to torment her, Daemon stepped backward, toward the edge. He watched the cart go by, then moved to assist her. Or, she'd thought it was meant to be assistance. There was nothing kind in the way he grasped her arm and hauled her to her feet.

"Keep a hand on the wall," he said. "Even if heights make you dizzy, a hand on the wall will keep you grounded."

Firal clutched his arm with one hand and draped the gown she still carried over her shoulder with the other. When her free hand found the wall, the black stone was glass-smooth beneath her palm.

Daemon led her downward through the tower's counter-clockwise spiral. Hallways branched from the main path at regular intervals. Glass-paned lamps dotted their walls, though few were lit. The foot traffic grew thinner as they traveled, revealing the reason so many halls were dark.

"Where are we going?" Firal shuffled along with both hands on the walls and tried to retreat into each dark hallway they passed. Daemon refused to let her, and she found herself scowling before long. Dark was infinitely preferable to the pit, especially when she could make her own light.

"To your new home," Daemon said. "As Davan said, I promised them a mage."

She sniffed. "And you never thought to ask me whether I wanted to live here before abducting me?"

His head rolled back in the most exaggerated gesture she'd

ever seen. "No one is forcing you to do anything. You were free to go from the moment Davan let go of your arm. You chose to come with us. You walked here and followed me into the underground of your own accord."

Her cheeks heated. He was right; she'd come willingly, had not so much as questioned her own decision. And why not? Why, after everything that had happened, did she immediately feel so comfortable with Daemon and his men? She eyed him, suddenly ill at ease. "Why are you the one bringing me here? Why not the man who suggested it?"

"Because I am the one with the authority to allow you to stay here. Davan is free to offer his home, but there are only two who can allow you into Core. I don't imagine you want to try your luck with the other."

Firal swallowed. She remembered the frigid hate in the Underling queen's eyes too well. "Where will I be staying? With Davan?"

"For now. There are empty rooms all throughout Core, but nothing ready for occupants. Davan's family will be glad to keep you, for the time being. They'll be pleased to meet a mage in person, I'm sure." He paused and turned, his snakelike eyes raking her from head to foot. "You'll have to do."

The insult made her breath catch and a heated response burned on the tip of her tongue, but she swallowed it back and let it burn in her belly instead. Whether or not she liked it, she'd gotten herself into a precarious situation. If Daemon was being truthful and she *was* there of her own free will, then it was an opportunity she couldn't lose. The market beside the underground river presented a valuable chance to gather supplies for the trip to Ilmenhith. She had little to barter with, but if the Underlings truly desired a mage's presence, perhaps that was enough.

Of course, if they kept creeping downward into the belly of the earth, she wasn't certain she could bear to return alongside that dreadful chasm. "How much farther?" she asked.

"The home you'll be staying in is on the third ring down from the waterfall," Daemon said. "If you moved faster than a snail, we'd be there already."

Firal leaned to the side to see past him and groaned when she spotted the waterfall just ahead. They'd not even made a full revolution around the cylindrical pit. Frustrated, she hurried forward and attached herself to his arm. He twitched in surprise and his step faltered.

"If I fall, you're going with me." She set her jaw and held tight, half expecting he would shake her off. Instead, he responded with an almost imperceptible shrug and continued down the spiral.

They drew curious looks from the passers-by as they walked. Firal stared back at them with a frown. "I don't understand why all these people are here," she murmured. "They all look human."

"What is there to understand?" Daemon asked, a hint of amusement in his voice. "They look human because they are human. What did you think Underlings were?"

"I... I don't know," she admitted as she glanced up at him. He'd been the first she'd seen. She'd assumed the rest of their kind would be like him. Foolish, in retrospect. Lumia had been human. Or at least human enough.

He gave her a sidewise look. "And what are the Eldani but humans with longer lifespans?"

"Humans can't use magic," Firal protested.

The light of his eyes flickered behind his mask. "Of course they can. Anyone can use magic, but they have to believe in it, first."

She couldn't resist an eye roll. "Believing in something doesn't make it exist."

"No, but when people stop believing in things, they eventually stop existing." His shoulders rose in another faint shrug. "Myths remain, but nothing else. Stories of things like dragons persist, yet they stopped existing long ago. How long until things like magic and the Eldani join their ranks?"

Firal scoffed. "People would never stop believing in magic."

"Do you believe in fairies?"

A frown tugged at the corners of her mouth. "No."

Daemon gave his head a grim shake. "Well then, I hope you realize you're contributing to their extinction."

The absurdity made her grimace, but she thought better of challenging it. "In any case, I've never seen a human who was Gifted."

"Half-bloods, even humans, can make perfectly adept mages." Daemon turned to lead her into a hallway. There was nothing remarkable about it, nothing to distinguish it from the rest of the halls. Firal scanned the walls in search of markings like he'd shown her before, but saw nothing. How did he know where to go? The curve of the central walkway meant there were no turns to keep track of, no clear markers to show how far they'd gone.

"Half-bloods are uncommon, though," Firal said. "Their numbers are so minuscule they hardly account for anything."

"And yet, if they're so rare, how come you know several? There's even a half-blood Master, is there not?"

"There is, but..." She gave him a sudden suspicious glance. "And what about you? You're Gifted, and you're certainly no half-blood."

"Prying won't get you far. I'm not entirely sure what I am, myself."

Her brows lifted, then knit together in confusion. "You don't know?"

"It's difficult to explain." His shoulders moved; she thought he winced behind his mask. "I'd rather not discuss this now."

Despite the new questions that itched in her mind, Firal didn't press.

They walked for some time before Daemon stopped to rap on a door. The entire corridor was lined with doors that looked the same, though each bore an etching of a different symbol just above the latch. She could not read them, but it was little wonder he could.

The door swung open without a sound and the woman behind it caught Firal off guard. She was small of stature and kind-faced, with rosy cheeks and dark hair. Fine lines skirted the corners of her eyes and mouth, but she didn't look old, merely worn.

"My Lord Daemon," she gasped, giving a deep bow. "And a stranger! Oh, goodness. Please, come in, both of you. I am honored. Please, I've just set water on for tea."

"I believe I owe you an extra set of hands, since I've had your husband with me for the last several trade runs." Daemon gestured for Firal to precede him. When she hesitated, he shoved her through the doorway.

The room beyond was little larger than the temple's dormitory rooms. Two beds filled half the space, crates and boxes stacked cleverly around them. The rest of the room was cramped with a narrow table and chairs, a washstand, and a small couch before a recessed fireplace. Unfazed by the lack of room, Daemon settled on the couch before the hearth.

"Oh, Davan told me he'd be needed for some time before he left. I know his place, as I know mine. We all do what we must." The woman fastened the door's latches as she closed it behind them. "Ah, but where are my manners? Excuse me, my lady. My name is Minna."

"A pleasure to meet you. I'm Firal." She twitched her skirts in her hands and stepped back, uncertain what to do.

"She's a mageling from Kirban," Daemon added.

"A mage!" Minna gasped. "And my lord general, in my house at the same time! Goodness me. Please, sit, my lady mage. Make yourself at home. Lifetree's mercy. What have I done to deserve the honor?" She clicked her tongue as if to scold herself and hurried across the room. A moment later, she placed a tea tray before Daemon, complete with tin cups, a battered kettle, and a jar of something amber-colored.

"Oh, no." Daemon raised his hands in protest. "Not on our account, please."

"Now, my lord, you know right well molasses isn't fit for sweetening tea, and it isn't very often that I have such respectable guests." Minna settled on the floor beside the tray and poured a thin stream of hot tea into each cup. She beamed as she opened the little jar, spooning the half-crystallized honey into their cups while adding none to her own.

"Where did you get honey?" Firal padded to the small couch to sit, though she perched on the end, as far from Daemon as she could manage. In the king's palace, honey wouldn't have seemed out of place, but its price was higher than what even the temple's Masters could afford.

"It was a wedding gift, near a decade past, now. That's the wonder about honey, it is. It'll turn to crystals, but it'll never go bad." Minna stirred their cups before she held them out in offering.

Firal took the warm cup with a grateful smile. "I thought honey had to be imported."

"It does," Daemon grumbled. "Almost all of it comes from the mainland. There are hives in the ruins, but they're hard to find, even for us. Aside from that, there's practically nowhere to get it on Elenhiise." He only took his cup when it was clear Minna wouldn't allow him to turn it down. He muttered a dour thank-you as she settled it in his hands.

"And for all that land out away from our little island, here we are fighting just to stop living in caves." Minna shook her head, though she laughed.

Daemon said nothing, staring down at his tea.

"Oh!" Minna exclaimed. "Begging your pardon, my lord. I completely forgot." She hurried to a box by the fire and fished in it for a time before she produced a thin reed from the kindling.

She rinsed it at the washbasin, shook it dry, and finally presented it to Daemon with an apologetic smile.

"Thank you," he murmured. He dropped the reed into his cup and slid the free end of it beneath his mask. "Regardless, I'm sure the surface will find the island is big enough for all of us."

Firal sampled her own tea and licked her lips. The drink was good, the mellow flavor of the honey better than she'd imagined. She studied Daemon as she took another sip. "Why don't you just take that off? It'd be easier to manage without it, wouldn't it?"

"A mask is a small price to pay for anonymity," Daemon said.

"There won't be a need to hide yourself forever, my lord," Minna said.

Daemon shot her a harsh look, a flicker of red lighting his eyes.

The Underling woman winced. "Forgive me, my lord. It's not my place."

A long, uncomfortable silence passed before he spoke again. "In any case, I have scouts I must speak to, and I'm sure the two of you have much to do. I trust there's a house free that she can take over?"

Minna nodded. "Aye, Lord Daemon. I'll see that she's looked after. Don't be a stranger whenever you're at market. You're more than welcome in my home."

Daemon handed his near-empty cup back to her as he rose. "I'll let you settle, then. Thank you, Minna, for your hospitality. I'll be back to speak with Firal tomorrow afternoon." He stepped around the couch to let himself out without waiting for a response. The door clicked firmly shut behind him.

"He's a kind soul, that one." Minna nodded toward the door. "A good mate, he'd be."

Firal choked on her tea.

"Oh!" Minna lifted her hands and laughed. "Begging your pardon, my lady! I mean nothing by it. It's only that he reminds me of my Davan, when he was younger. All business and responsibility, but a good heart underneath." She grinned and held out a hand to take her cup.

Firal downed the last sip of tea before she handed it back. "Davan is your husband? I met him in the ruins." She chose not to mention the man had caught her trespassing. "I traveled with some soldiers on the way here. Is he away often? If I may ask, that is. I don't mean to intrude on your family."

"It's no intrusion, my lady, rest assured of that." Minna chuckled. "Yes, he is away from us quite often. He's with the army several weeks at a time. The duties all rotate, so it stays fair, but it does get a bit lonely for us women-folk. I'm fortunate, at least, having Tobias."

"Your child?" Firal guessed.

"My son, aye. Out to play with his friends, or I'd have introduced him already. He's a good boy, but he's only eight. Not much company for a grown woman, my lady."

"Just call me Firal, please." She grimaced. "I really don't deserve any such title as lady."

Minna shrugged and carried the dishes to the washbasin. "Very well, then, Miss Firal. But begging your pardon, I'm sure you'll have high honors on your name among our people, being a mage and all."

"Being a mage is far from being noble." Mages were certainly respected, but aside from the highest-ranked Masters, Firal had never heard any of them referred to by title.

"It's not as far off as you think, I promise you that. We've been desperate for a mage with the ways of healing for many years, though many gave up thinking we'd find one. Then again," Minna said, and the caution in her voice made it clear she chose her words with care, "Lord Daemon promised us a mage, and he's the best leader our people have ever had. Not to speak ill of Queen Lumia, of course, but people stopped starving when Daemon became general." She rinsed each cup and put them upside-down on a threadbare towel to dry. "But that's enough of that. Tobias will share my bed while you're staying with us. Tomorrow, we'll see about finding your own house space. For now, you just worry about getting settled, then we'll get supper started."

Firal's face fell.

"What's wrong?" Minna perched on the edge of the hearth like a wary bird, ready to take flight.

"I can't cook."

"You can't?" Minna cried. "What are they teaching you at that temple?"

Firal's ears reddened, but before she could speak, the woman waved a hand.

"Goodness me, I apologize. 'Tis not my place, and I'm certain your training takes a great deal of time." Minna fluttered a hand as if in dismissal. "Don't worry, dear. I'll teach you everything else you need to know."

"Thank you," Firal murmured. Her shoulders sagged with relief as Minna stood again and busied herself with preparing linens from a box beneath the beds.

Yet in the moment of peace that came with Minna's quiet, cheerful humming, a creeping sense of dread pricked at the edge of Firal's senses. A single day after her world had capsized, there had been Daemon, ready to stabilize it again.

She'd been offered shelter, food, a place to belong. But how could she trust the people who had destroyed her home?

6

HOMEMAKING

"I DON'T KNOW HOW ANYONE CAN WALK NEXT TO THIS," FIRAL groaned. She pressed a hand to her uneasy stomach as she stepped into the hallway where Minna and Tobias waited.

"Hurry up, now!" Minna called. She put a hand on the shoulder of the boy beside her to still his grumbling.

Tobias was a pleasant boy, if quiet. He had dark hair and somber brown eyes, cheeks that should have been plumper, and a smile that was missing teeth. The child looked impatient now, but Firal couldn't fault him. She was slow. Their trip into the market had been one thing; the water in the river was shallow, and she had no difficulty walking along its rocky banks. But the chasm in the middle of that spiraling ramp... She shook her head and tried not to shudder.

They hadn't made her carry anything, since she had such difficulty walking next to the railless pit, but Minna and her son both carried baskets filled with goods. It had been strange to see how similar this market was to the ones above-ground, though Firal supposed its location shouldn't make a difference. Markets were all the same.

"You'll get used to it, don't worry." Minna patted her arm sympathetically and started down the hall at a brisk pace. Firal recognized the symbol on Minna's door when they reached it, but they did not stop there. Instead, they continued down the corridor for some distance and shadow swallowed their small group. The daylight that filled the underground tower didn't spill far into the tunnels, and lamps were few and far between. Firal looked back now and then, stealing glimpses of the daylight behind them until they rounded a curve and it disappeared. The hallways sprawled like natural tunnels, and perhaps they were. The ground underfoot was obviously smoothed by hand, but it was possible the tunnels themselves had been shaped by branches of the river in ages past.

They stopped at a door that bore no markings, though there was a place above the latch for a plaque. There was no lock on the door, but it still resisted when Minna pushed it. Rusted hinges groaned and dust stirred in the musty room as the door gave way and let them inside.

"Who lived here?" Firal covered her face to ward off the dust, though it still made her cough.

"Nobody I ever knew. It seems our numbers dwindle every year." Minna waved the dust away and grinned when Tobias sneezed. The boy scampered into the room, his feet kicking up dirt.

"Do they? There were a lot of children in the market," Firal said as she peered inside. There were a few shadowy shapes she guessed were furniture, though it was too dark to be certain. She crouched beside the doorway and ran a hand over the floor in search of a pebble she could use to make a light.

"Yes, but few families can support more than one child. Some years we do well. Others are more difficult. The labyrinth overhead isn't the best for growing food." Minna watched as Firal took a stone in hand and blinked in surprise when it took on a warm glow. The mage-light intensified until it was uncomfortable to look at. Firal squinted and shifted her hand to block most of the light as she held it up and looked inside again.

Roughly squared, the room was similar to the cavern-house

Minna called home, though it was a little smaller. The hearth was nestled in one corner, a cobweb-covered chair beside it. There was a bed frame in the opposite corner, though it held no mattress. A thick coat of dust covered its plank bottom. Aside from the small bedside table, there was nothing else in the room.

"There's not even a blanket," Tobias said, bending over to look beneath the bed.

"We'll find her one, silly," Minna laughed as she put down her baskets and rolled up her sleeves. "Run back up the lane and get the broom for me."

"Yes, Mama." The boy hurried past the two women, his bare feet slapping on the stone as he ran out the door.

Firal couldn't help but sigh. She'd gone straight from cleaning the temple to cleaning here. "Where am I going to get a real bed?" She didn't know how she would pay for it, but she didn't share that worry aloud. How she would get supplies for her planned expedition to Ilmenhith hadn't yet crossed her mind, either.

Minna set her baskets on the hearth. "Well, you'll have to work for it. No one can spare it without something in exchange. We'll find some way to fill up your little house, but for blankets and such, I can help you get started."

Firal lifted the mage-light high into the air and held it still for a moment before she pulled her hand away. The light bobbed in midair, settling into its suspension. Levitation was something she'd never quite mastered. She had set the energy flow into a cycle it could sustain on its own until spent, but she was sure it would fall before long. She never knew how much energy to cycle. "I don't think there's much I can do that would be worth trading for."

Minna raised a brow and glanced toward the light floating in the air above them. "I'm sure there's something."

Tobias returned to the doorway breathless and with a broom in hand. He panted as he presented it to his mother. "Mama, Miss Firal can have my old blanket, if she needs it."

Firal chuckled. "I might borrow it from you, but I don't think I'll keep it."

"Step out, both of you. I need to sweep and you're in the way." Minna shooed them toward the door with the broom. They both skittered into the hallway. The older woman started in the far corner and worked toward the middle, a cloud of dust dimming the light.

Tobias leaned forward to peer at the mage-light through the haze. "Miss Firal, how did you hang the light up there? I don't see no strings or nothin'."

"I just told the air to hold it," Firal said, unsure how to explain. The concept of the ebb and flow of energy was difficult to describe to someone who lacked the Gift.

"Can you teach me to do that?" he asked, his dark eyes alight with excitement.

She hesitated. It had only been a day since her arrival in the underground, but she hadn't sensed any other mages. If anyone else bearing magic had been present, she would have sensed them. The power of others always made a small warmth at the edge of her senses, like an ember. She'd felt nothing. "Not everyone can learn, Tobias."

"Why not?"

"That's enough, now," Minna called. "Miss Firal will have her hands full, being the only mage here in Core. If she finds anyone who can learn, I'm sure she'll be right quick to pick them out."

Tobias looked at her again, anxious. "Can I learn, Miss Firal?"

Firal opened her mouth to reply, but closed it again it when her conversation with Daemon drifted to mind. It seemed ridiculous to think someone who lacked the glimmer of the Gift could learn to wield such power. But until she'd met Daemon, she'd thought only the Eldani were Gifted. If he believed it possible others could bear magic, perhaps there was a reason. "I don't know," she admitted. That, at least, was true. She felt nothing in the boy, but he was young. There was still time for power to manifest in him, though she was reasonably sure nothing would.

"Save your questions for later, Tobias. We've lots to do." Minna swept the dirt out the doorway and paused to clear dust from her throat with a cough. "We'll need water to scrub the hearth. Take the pail and fetch some, if you would?"

"Yes, ma'am." Tobias ducked his head and retrieved the empty bucket. He cast Firal one last wistful look before he ran for the river.

Firal watched him go with a frown. "You really don't need to send him on every errand. I can get some things, if you need me to."

"Nonsense," Minna said. "It's good for the boy to do some running. Goodness knows he doesn't get up to the gardens enough to stretch his legs properly."

Firal perked up. "There's a garden?"

Minna nodded as she wiggled the cuffs of her sleeves up past her elbows. "Up above, there is. Right in the middle of the ruins. It's not much, but everyone does their part, and it gives us fresh produce. Not enough to feed the whole of Core, mind you, but it's nothing to sneeze at, either."

That was a relief. If there was hope for vegetables to grow, there would be somewhere to grow herbs. Gifted in healing as she was, Firal could make do without them, but she preferred to have them on hand. Even before the temple burned, she'd kept a small amount of the most useful herbal remedies in her room. Finding seeds would be the next challenge. Firal crept back into the house and checked the suspension of her mage-light. "I'd like to see it some time."

"There will be plenty of time for gardening." Minna flashed her a grin as she put aside the broom and retrieved a stiff-bristled brush from the baskets on the floor. "Cleaning comes first. You'll earn a few callouses for your pretty hands before the day is done." She pushed the brush into Firal's hands and found another for herself.

It didn't take long for Tobias to return. Eager to show her capability, Firal set to scrubbing the fireplace, though her vigor waned fast. It was a more difficult task than she expected and before long, her hair clung to her forehead and temples, tickled the back of her neck and made her swipe a wrist across her sweaty forehead in irritation.

Minna and the boy both worked hard, scouring away cobwebs and dust, though the dark room looked little cleaner for the effort.

The lack of sunlight made it impossible to tell how long they worked, but by the time Minna deemed the cavern-house clean enough to live in, Firal's muscles screamed in protest at every hint of movement. She grimaced at the weight of the linens Minna piled in her arms, but bit her tongue to keep from fussing. Several trips back and forth from Minna's home filled the little room with mismatched dishes and spare cookware, blankets, and even an old down-filled pillow. Despite Firal's insistence she would repay their value, Minna waved her away with a huff.

"You'll have more than enough work to do, don't be in such a rush. Besides, it's all old. Only taking up space in my house," the Underling woman assured her, though the sparseness of her home's furnishings made it an obvious lie.

Firal thought better than to argue and simply put her new things away. "Well then, don't hesitate to come to me if there's something I can do to help." She turned around in a slow circle and inspected her new home with a wistful eye.

Minna smiled and patted her arm. "Don't fret. I know it's different, but you'll get used to it soon enough. It's not such a bad place to live. We have everything here we need." She caught Tobias by the shoulders and turned him toward the door. "It's been a hard day's work. I think we're all ready for a good night's rest. You know where to find me if you need anything."

"Thank you, Minna. I appreciate everything you've done." Firal touched her fingers to her heart as she escorted the two of them to the hall and saw them off with a small wave. That

Minna's home was not far off was a blessing, and she was grateful, but Minna's home was exactly that—warm and welcoming, a true home. Firal shut the door and sighed at the drab emptiness of the new space she had to call her own.

The cavern-house was even more forlorn with the door closed. She rattled a few plates together and was staring at their mismatched colors when a thud against the door made her jump. It swung open with a creak to reveal Daemon on the other side.

"Oh, of course." Firal crossed her arms over her chest. "Come right in, there's no need to knock."

"I don't want to hear it." Daemon nudged the door open wider with one green-scaled foot. He had satchels slung over both shoulders, a canvas bag in one hand and a beheaded chicken in the other. He thrust the fowl into her hands and dropped the bag onto the table with a thump. One of the satchels slid down his shoulder and he swung it forward to leave it beside the bag.

"What am I supposed to do with this?" Firal glanced at the stump of the bird's neck. Her stomach gave an unpleasant flutter and she looked away. She extended her arm to hold the dead thing as far from her as she could manage.

Daemon slid the second satchel to the table with more care. "You eat it. Unless you brought other food with you that I don't know about?"

She bit her lip and looked toward the old stew pot Minna had hung above her empty hearth.

"Let me guess. You can't cook."

"It's not something one generally needs to learn at the temple," she said, a little more defensively than she intended.

Rolling his eyes behind his mask, Daemon snatched the chicken from her hands and thumped it down on the table. "Helpless girl. And you're welcome, by the way. I'm sure you're glad you won't starve to death."

"I'd have found skills to trade for meals," Firal muttered as she peeked inside one of his bags. It bulged with radishes and carrots, sweet potatoes and turnips. "Where did you get these?"

"Oh, I don't know if you noticed it when we were coming in, but it seems there's a very large market down here." His tone was as light and nonchalant as his words were needling. "It's by the river. As it happens, there are a number of merchants who offer food."

She glowered at him, but he didn't notice. He worked fast, piling feathers on the table. Even those couldn't be wasted, it seemed. Firal watched him for a minute before she abandoned the bag. "Did Minna tell you where to find me?"

Daemon shook his head. "You're the talk of Core. I don't think there's a soul in the city who doesn't know where you live."

"Reassuring." She moved to close the door.

"Don't."

She frowned and peered into the empty hallway. "Why not?"

"It would be extremely inappropriate for a woman to shut herself in her home with a man who is not her husband." He gave her a shadowed look. "There are enough rumors about you flying around as it is. I'd rather not be part of one."

Firal shot him a glare.

"Get a fire started," Daemon ordered. "I've been out in the ruins all day. I wasn't planning on fixing your dinner as well as my own."

She did as he said, though she promised herself it wasn't because he'd told her to. Regardless of his wishes, she had to eat, and the stew pot was all she had. "No one is asking you to cook for me." She emptied the only bucket of fresh water she had into the pot and piled firewood beneath it. A small basket of tinder sat beside the hearth and she frowned at it. There was tinder, but there were no matches.

Hesitantly, she drew her fingers over the surface of the wood. There was no reason not to use her magic, but it was strange to think she'd never seek a Master's permission again. She closed her eyes and flames leaped up to answer her call. The golden light that spilled across the room helped drive away the chill of bare stone. The wood crackled pleasantly and Firal held out her hands to the warmth.

Daemon grew still behind her and she turned toward him. He watched the fire with a distant look in his eyes.

A chill swept through her and for a moment, they sat in silence.

"I didn't do it." His words were soft, yet there was a hint of strength in his voice.

Firal licked her lips. "I know."

He met her gaze and held it. There was an intensity in his stare she hadn't seen before. She shrank back an inch before she caught herself and steeled her resolve.

"That is, I believed as much," she said. "I... hoped as much."

"I was in Ilmenhith when the temple burned." His eyes closed, and the slits in his mask went dark. It was as if a shadow fell over him, a deep, dark remorse that threatened to swallow him out of her room.

"I remember," she replied softly. His grace on the ballroom floor had haunted her dreams.

"When Lumia set her sights on the temple, it was to obtain something the Archmage held. An artifact, one mostly useless to mages. I agreed to go along with it because it was something that could be useful to me, too. Then she did not want me present when she went to retrieve it. If I'd known—if I'd been there—"

"You don't have to explain yourself," Firal said. "It doesn't matter anymore."

"It does matter," he insisted, meeting her eyes again. "It matters that I clear my conscience. If you're going to be here, I need to know there is no bad blood between us."

Her throat tightened. "I appreciate what you've done in bringing me here. You didn't have to, and I... I'm sure you're still angry with me."

From the way he straightened and the light of his eyes

flickered, the admission had caught him off guard. "I'm angry at myself," he said after a time. "The destruction of the temple set me back farther than I could have imagined. I did everything I could. I even warned the Eldani king, but it was too late. I hate the temple. And I hate the mages for what they've done to me. But I didn't want..." He trailed off and squeezed his eyes closed. When he reopened them again, their light was steady. "I made a promise to my people and it must be kept."

"You keep saying that. That you promised them a mage." She rubbed her arms and shifted closer to the fire. "When Minna's husband said it, I feared you meant... well, something else. Revenge. But your people have been nothing but kind to me. I don't understand. I thought our people were enemies."

Daemon's head tilted ever so slightly to the right. She recognized the movement as a frown, even with his mask on. "The ruin-folk have never thought of the Eldani as enemies."

"But we were at war," Firal said.

"The Eldani were at war. The ruin-folk were—you mean to say you don't know any of our history?" His tone shifted up a note, both surprised and incredulous.

She shook her head.

Daemon sighed, finally returning his attention to the half-plucked chicken on the table. "The Eldani were settlers who came to Elenhiise from the north. I'm sure you know that much. They sought wealth through sea trade, starting with the island's inhabitants."

Firal shook her head again. "We were settlers, but the island was uninhabited. There were only the ruins to show anyone had ever been here."

"Elenhiise was not uninhabited," he said, though his tone was that of correction and not argument. "The Giftless were already here, and they were not pleased with the idea of sharing their prosperity. That was what began the war between the eastern and western factions, Giftless men against the Eldani. Not everyone agreed with the war."

"There are always dissenters." She stood and stretched her stiff legs.

"But their punishment isn't usually so harsh. The Eldani brought magic, and with it, healing. There were those among the Giftless who thought it a blessing. When the Giftless king called for a hard stand against the mages, the dissenters were cast out." Daemon stepped to the side and motioned for her to take over.

She cringed, but joined him at the table. She grasped a fistful of feathers and looked to him for instruction.

He continued instead. "They sought asylum with the Eldani. The Eldani refused, and the Giftless would not take them back. They were caught between the two factions, rejected by both and caught at the border between two warring kingdoms. Where do you suppose they went?"

Firal's mouth fell open. "You're saying the Underlings wanted to ally with us?"

"They saw the benefit of magic," Daemon said. "They still do. That was one of the reasons I promised them a mage." His eyes drifted back to the fire and he gazed at it with such longing that it made her heart ache.

She glanced toward the hearth. Tingles of energy still lingered there, betraying her use of magic. "Do you still want to learn?"

"Do you still want to teach?"

She lifted her chin and forced herself to swallow the lump in her throat. "Teaching is what I thought I was meant to do."

He nodded, and the words he whispered gave her chills.

"Show me."

7

DISSENT

"HURRY UP. AT THIS RATE, IT'LL BE NOON BEFORE WE GET UP there."

Firal pressed her back to the wall and forced her eyes open. "Isn't there another path to the top?" She shuffled along the spiral path, her fingers searching the wall behind her for handholds. Though the avenue was easily fifteen feet wide, her heart hammered in her chest as if she stood at the edge.

"No, and if you're going to be working up here every day, you're going to have to get used to it. Come on!" Daemon didn't try to hide his exasperation anymore.

"I can't walk next to that!" she cried. "What if I fall?"

His head tipped to one side and he heaved a sigh. "You're not going to fall. Nobody falls."

Firal slid her leading hand farther along the wall. When she found nothing to cling to, she inched after it. "You're lying."

"I am not lying. Nobody falls. I have never, in the entire time I've lived here, heard of anyone falling. Never." He put a clawed hand to his chest in sincerity.

"You'll have to excuse me if I find that hard to believe." She glowered at him, but the sight of the pit at his back made her sick. She turned away.

"It's perfectly safe." Daemon took a step backwards.

Her pulse soared. "Don't you dare!"

"Don't what?" He took another step. "Stand at the edge?"

Firal tried to look in every other possible direction, but her eyes snapped back to him no matter what she did. "I will not attend your funeral!"

He spread his arms and inched backwards, until he teetered at the very edge of the chasm. His cloak fluttered over the void.

"Daemon!" she shrieked.

His arms dropped back to his sides and he rolled his eyes. "Fine." He strode forward and grabbed her arm. She yelped as he hauled her away from the wall and set a brisk pace for the top of the inverted tower.

Firal supposed that name made sense for the place, though she would have given it a title befitting the dread it put in her belly. *The abyss*, perhaps, or simply *the pit*. The drop beside them hovered in her peripheral vision and she tried to focus on Daemon's back instead. Gradually, his grip on her arm eased, and his hand slipped down until his scaled fingers wrapped around hers.

As eager as Firal had been to see the gardens, both Daemon and Minna had insisted it best that the visit wait for clear weather. Daemon had been at her door nightly for lessons in magic, and she'd received lessons of her own in between. Minna took time each morning to teach her a bit more about cooking and how to manage a household. By the third night, the remnants of the chicken Daemon brought her had become a proper soup, and she'd started a small collection of culinary herbs, beginning with several small vials of seasonings Minna had presented as a gift. Firal hoped she would find more in the garden. If they ever made it to the garden, that was.

"Do you think I'll have to tend the plants every day?" Her voice quavered. It was hard enough to move beside the pit with Daemon holding on to her. She didn't know how she would make it up and down the ramp on her own.

"I'm sure once you see the garden, you'll want to." He kept her close to the wall, though she doubted it was for her comfort. The closer they were to the wall, the faster she walked.

"Because it's beautiful?" she asked. "Or because it needs care that badly?"

Daemon did not reply.

A steady stream of people worked their way down the spiral. Many had dirt on their hands and knees, and some carried baskets of produce. The passersby studied the two of them with everything from curiosity and smiles to narrowed eyes and thoughtful frowns. The latter made Firal uncomfortable, but she was new to Core and could not blame them for having reservations. Between Minna's visits and Daemon's, she'd had no reason to leave her new house, and that meant no time spent with the rest of Core.

Not that she had time to spare. Minna always arrived soon after Firal finished dressing and pinning up her hair. Sometimes she came with Tobias in tow. Those days were Firal's favorites. She grown fond of the boy's ready grins, and of the stories Minna recited for her son.

Both in between and during stories, the Underling woman taught Firal to mend and sew, cook and bake. As mouth-watering scents from cook-pots began to fill the hallways each night, Daemon would arrive with a satchel of some supply she hadn't yet realized she needed.

After the first two nights of lessons, she had stopped being self-conscious about the open door. Spectators were few and far between, but Daemon had cautioned her the first night. The number of gawkers would increase as word spread there was a mage in Core.

"Dragging your feet will only force you to look down there even longer," Daemon said.

Firal squeezed his hand in response, a silent plea that he not let go.

It grew brighter as they walked and eventually, blue sky

showed overhead. She didn't realize how much she'd missed the wind until a gentle breeze stirred her skirts and tossed her dark curls. The fresh air promised freedom, and she hurried to escape the walkway and its awful pit. Firal let go of Daemon's clawed fingers and ran ahead, blinking hard as she emerged into the blinding morning light.

The top ring of the underground tower was level with the garden walkway and rimmed by tall black stones with jagged tops. Four wide arches opened in the black wall, one at each of the cardinal directions. People came and went through three of the openings, though the fourth arch hung over the gap where the walkway emerged from the earth.

Beyond two of the arches, narrow pathways wound through tall grasses until they disappeared behind a line of trees. The third arch gave way to a trail that was edged with stone and more manicured than the others. All along the hard dirt path, people stirred among rows of carefully cultivated plants. Fat purple coneflowers bobbed in the sunlight. Firal paced between them with a sense of awe. She drew her fingers over their petals and turned back to face Daemon. "I thought this was a vegetable garden!"

"There are gardens throughout the ruins for growing food. Some of these require more care, so we keep them here." He shrugged his cloak back over his shoulder and hooked one thumb under the strap of a satchel she hadn't realized he was carrying. "Most of the women know enough about herbs to get by, but none of them are really experts."

"Well they certainly could have fooled me, what with everything they have planted here." Firal scanned each section as she walked. "I see valerian. Comfrey, too. And this is feverfew, isn't it? How did all of this get here?"

Daemon shrugged as followed her, his head bowed against the sun. "The garden was here before I joined them. I think they've been nurturing it for a long time. Look there. Those trees mark the edge of the clearing. The walls begin just beyond them."

She studied the treetops that loomed above the tallest walls she'd ever seen in the ruins. "What is this place?"

"We're right in the heart of the ruins. That's why they named the city Core."

Firal couldn't help but turn her eyes toward the south. This far into the ruins, she knew she wouldn't see anything, but she envisioned the Archmage's tower on the horizon just the same. Not even a week past, she'd been collecting herbs from the ruins of the infirmary and ruminating on how valuable they'd be. It seemed almost too serendipitous that she'd find herself collecting them again. She frowned. "Why are you showing me this?"

"You wanted to see the gardens. You also need something to keep you busy. And besides, I figured you'd want to keep some of these herbs on hand. You're a healer, aren't you?" He cocked his head in a manner that reminded her of a bird.

"I am," she replied cautiously.

Daemon prodded at a coneflower with one claw. "Out of all the elements and affinities, that's the one that I can't seem to work with. I'm no good with healing. My people needed me to be, but I just... I can't."

She raised her brows. "I think that's the most sincere thing you've said to me yet. But I think I understand." Her hand drifted back to the flowers, to the familiar prickly heads and fuzzy-textured stems. They were a comfort, if only because they reminded her of home. "Herbs are useful to any healer. I'll teach you what I can, but it's no substitute for magic."

"I don't need it to be," he said. "I just want to know enough to fill in the gaps. The brunt of the healing work will be on you, especially once word gets out that it's your specialty. You'll have visitors wanting remedies and healing every day. Even if I weren't involved, you'll need to have herbs on hand."

Firal crossed her arms and cocked her hip to the side. "What makes you think I'll be here long enough to have visitors?"

"Won't you?"

She didn't want to admit she hadn't thought about it. Initially, she'd imagined Core as a stepping stone to Ilmenhith. Things had changed as soon as she'd met Minna. She was fond of the woman, fond of Tobias, and in a few short days, Minna had become the mother figure Firal had always lacked. She rubbed her arms and did not reply.

Daemon's eyes flickered. "Or are you trying to get out of our arrangement again?"

"I don't think I'd have visitors every day." She sidestepped the question and turned her attention to the flowers again. She'd already spotted a few to cut and hang to dry.

"You'd be surprised," he said. "These people have needed a proper medic for a long time. You're the best fit for the job. If you take it, you'd surely be well compensated."

"Compensated?" Her brow furrowed.

"Everything is based off barter, remember? You heal someone's injured leg, let them return to work, and they bring you part of the fruits of their labor. That's the way it works down here." He slid the empty satchel from his shoulder, drew a knife from his belt, and offered her both.

"I can just take anything I need?" Firal asked as she accepted them.

"As long as that's all you take. We don't have the means for excess." He looked across the fields, and his eyes darkened. "You go ahead and cut what you wish to dry for your remedies. We'll have no lesson tonight."

"You're leaving me here?" She cast a nervous glance back the way they'd come. "How am I supposed to find my way back down?"

"I'm sure anyone you ask would be happy to help you find your way. Besides, it's best you get comfortable going back and forth on your own, especially if you plan to visit the garden often." Daemon shrugged his worn cloak forward over his shoulders and lifted the hood so that it framed his mask perfectly. "I trust you can find your way around an herb garden on your own?"

"Of course." She forced a smile.

"And you'll be in Core when I get back?" he asked, softer.

Her smile faded. Why did he care? He made it sound as if she were eager to go. Maybe she would be, if she had anywhere else she *could* go. There was still Ilmenhith, she supposed, but that was a gamble. In Core, she had a space of her own, a service she could provide, even a friend.

Two friends, she corrected herself as she met Daemon's eyes. Or, she hoped he was a friend. Not that long ago, she'd still held him as an enemy in her heart. She didn't understand why he hadn't harbored the same resentment.

"You owe me more lessons," he said.

The moment shattered, she rolled her eyes. "Fine. I'll be here when you return, but beyond that, no promises."

Daemon chuckled and held up a finger. "We'll work on that."

She scowled as he disappeared into the tall grasses that ringed the garden's edge.

"No promises," she repeated.

LUMIA STIFFENED AS THE DOOR CREAKED OPEN BEHIND HER AND THE too-familiar rasp of claws against the stone floor filled the silence. Her shoulders bunched and she tried to ignore the sound. Her grip on her ivory-handled comb tightened until her knuckles turned white.

"Didn't feel like sitting on your throne today?" Daemon turned a disinterested eye around her bedchamber. She wasn't sure she still considered him welcome. It had been a long time since he'd set foot there. That he'd entered without knocking smacked of arrogance.

Lumia lifted her chin and stubbornly drew the comb through her golden curls again. She didn't turn to face him, though she spared a glance for his reflection. "Oh, I thought you'd be keeping it warm for me. Goodness knows you've been making enough decisions without direction." Her tone was goading, but Daemon didn't rise to it. He stood unmoving, staring at her from behind that infernal mask, begging her eyes to wander. He so seldom wore it in when they were in private. That he wore it now dug at her like a nettle. She refused to look at him again and stared at her own face in the mirror, instead.

"I've done very little that needed direction since we last spoke." His voice was infuriatingly level. "Direction is why I've come."

"And is that the only reason you've to come to me? To ask direction? Permission?" Her lip curled with disdain. She tossed her hair over her shoulder and turned at last to face him. "Nothing more?"

"You are my queen and I am your general. There should be nothing more than that." His slitted eyes locked with hers, all ice and formality.

He had been cold toward her since the temple burned. She liked his newfound confidence, though she hadn't imagined he would turn it against her. Anger prickled beneath her skin, but the last thing she wanted to do was show she was upset.

She stretched her arms languidly overhead and sighed when she dropped them. The front of her dressing robe fell partway open. She left it. Her wiles had worked on him before, and his response would make a good measure for how far her hold on him had slipped. "A queen ought to have what she wants, when she wants it. What do you want?"

"A queen's job is to see to her people," Daemon said. His words were sharp, and she raised a brow. Seemingly thinking better of his tone, he continued in a more subdued manner. "I'm sure you've heard by now that the temple is leaving Eldani rule.

Relythes will be the new power over the island. I want to speak with him."

Lumia frowned. "What reason do you have to speak with the Giftless king? It's not his throne we're after."

"This is an opportunity we shouldn't pass up."

Her brow furrowed. The eastern half of the island was just as densely populated as the west, but the settlements clung to the coast. Relythes left his borders unprotected and contributed next to nothing to the temple, which meant Underlings and Giftless men rarely crossed paths. Establishing communication after centuries of silence seemed absurd, but Daemon went on before she could object.

"A shift in power could put us at risk, but Relythes would be pleased to have us recognize his new position as chief power over Elenhiise," he said. "And the visit would open new opportunities. Our mines line our pockets with gold and gems that are precious to others and worthless to us. If we take a small sampling of our riches as a gift, he may be open to an alliance. We have money. He has the temple to feed. And if we make ourselves agreeable, he may not mind when we finally move our people out of this hole in the ground."

"And what if our people are happy in this hole in the ground?" Lumia thrust herself from her chair. "What's so wrong with the life we have now?"

"Life?" Daemon scoffed. "What life? We're barely existing. Why would you balk at this? We have a right to reclaim the ruins, but if we're caught between both sides of the island, we'll be crushed. If I wanted to seize land from Kifel's holdings, you'd be at the bit to speed it along."

"It would change everything!" She flung her comb to the floor. "Why not return to Kifel, whimpering with your tail between your legs? To ally with Relythes would be to ally with the mages at this point. Have you forgotten what started all this? Have you forgotten what they've done?"

"How could I?" He flexed his hands at his sides. The soft

rasp of his scales against themselves filled the air. "But my fight with the Eldani is mine alone. I will address it my way, on my own."

"Your way?" Her eyes narrowed. "And does your way involve giving them free passage through my territory and shelter under my roof?"

A flicker of color behind his mask gave him away. His eyelids fluttered, just slightly, before he caught himself. But he did not deny it.

"Did you think I wouldn't hear? That I'm so disconnected from my own people that I wouldn't know what you've done? I know who she is. And that you failed to kill her." Cold fury seethed inside her, knotting her stomach and chilling her skin. She moved forward with the slow, calculating grace of a viper, her expression deceptively calm. Something less familiar burned in her chest, white-hot in her lungs and sharp in her eyes. Jealousy, she realized. Her ears burned with a curious mix of agitation and shame.

"Core needs a healer," he said with an indifferent shrug. "And I need a teacher. Her ties to the temple have been severed. She'll never be welcome among their ranks again. She is the best choice we have, since you cannot do these things."

Though he said it without malice, the suggestion she had failed still stung. It wasn't that she couldn't heal. But there was her pride to think of, and she could not spare the time to see to menial injuries. She was a queen, after all. Her power might have been why the Underlings allowed her to rule, but it was fear that kept them under her thumb.

But his education was something else. He had outstripped her in ability from the moment he'd set foot in the ruins, and she could offer nothing to help him learn. She would never admit she feared his power. Her hold over him was weakened enough already.

"And just what is she teaching you, pet?" Lumia sidled against him and drew her fingertips across his mask. "How much knowledge will she share with you? How much time do you have before she learns what you've done? What we've planned?" Her fingers darted for the ties that held his mask in place. He caught her wrist before she could pull them. His grip tightened until his claws drew blood.

"Why, Lumia," he murmured, tilting his head. "You're the only one who knows. Or were you planning on having a conversation with the little mageling you hate so much?"

Any other time, she'd found it easy to get under his skin. Why was he suddenly so unshakable? She scowled. "Don't pretend there isn't something else you hope to achieve. She can offer you nothing." She twisted her arm in his grip and winced when his claws slit her skin as easily as parchment. "You think she'd accept you as you really are? Look at you! How long can you hide behind masks and magic and disguises? What woman would have a monster like you? What woman but me?"

Daemon shoved her arm away. "You overestimate the value of a boy's plaything."

Her eyes widened and she recoiled as if struck.

He righted his mask and pulled up his hood. "I will leave within a fortnight to speak with King Relythes. I will select my own envoy. You will need to sign a waiver allowing me to fill chests from your coffers, so that I might take the king a fitting gift on your behalf."

Lumia rubbed the bleeding slices that decorated her arm, leaving thin orange streaks across her alabaster skin. "She won't have you. I'm sure of it."

"I'll return for the waiver in a few days, after our next trade meeting with villagers to the north." He gave a stiff bow. "My queen." He turned to excuse himself from her chambers, and she did not try to stop him.

She lifted her hand from the three identical gashes that marred her perfect skin and stared at them in disbelief.

8

DOUBTS

TREN DRUMMED HIS FINGERS AGAINST THE EDGE OF HIS DESK AS HE looked over the maps again. Whether or not he'd been stripped of his rank, not everything had been taken from him. He still had his office, decorated to fit the title of general he'd had before. Weapons hung upon the walls as tools and decorations both, with numerous charts and maps of the island suspended between and behind them. The lavish furniture remained, the dark wood polished to a glassy shine. An opulent patterned rug still lay underfoot, one of many spoils he'd claimed for himself before that whelp of a boy had taken his place.

Stroking his beard, Tren sat down. He still had men in the ranks who were loyal to him, soldiers he could count on for information. He didn't like what they'd brought him today. It wasn't unusual for Daemon to come and go from the ruins, but leaving northward was something he didn't do often. The boy almost always departed southward, skirting temple grounds. From what Tren had gathered from his eyes and ears, Daemon had not ventured near the temple since the Eldani king's soldiers had departed and visitors began to arrive from the east, instead.

So was the boy avoiding the mages? Or was Daemon a part of their envoy now? All of Core was aflame with talk of their general learning magecraft. With the way things between the temple and Ilmenhith teetered on the verge of eruption, that seemed like the last catalyst they'd need for a disaster.

He'd felt from the beginning that using Daemon was a mistake, but who was he to argue with the queen? If the boy were not so volatile it would have seemed a decent strategy, but his temper and mood swings complicated things. With Daemon's grudges against both the royal family and the temple mages, he made an ideal pawn, and he'd still been an impressionable child when Lumia ensnared him. Tren couldn't condone her methods, but the idea was sound enough. By setting Daemon up to seize the western throne, she'd put herself in position to become his queen. A convenient accident could remove him and leave her with all the glory she craved.

Glory meant nothing to Tren. His game had always been power. Losing his title as general had been a minor setback, but it might spare him trouble in the long run. Let Lumia and her pet do the leg work. Once she removed Daemon from the picture on her own, she'd be more vulnerable than she knew.

King. Now there was a title with a powerful ring to it. He ran a hand over the map spread across his desk and smiled at the expanse labeled as the Eldani kingdom. There would be no more cowering in caves. No more desperate struggle to survive. Sometimes he couldn't understand how he'd been born to these pitiful people, with their weak wills and lacking ambitions. But some were born leaders. He wouldn't say much for Lumia, but at least she'd recognized that trait in him. Yes, King Tren, that sounded right. After all, it was only right that his people be ruled by one of their own again.

Tren folded the day's notes and tucked them into his pocket before he slipped out of his office and into the busy hallway. He adjusted the stiff collar of his coat and closed the door behind him. No one would have dared steal from him, but he locked it, nonetheless.

His office wasn't far from the main marketplace of Core. The barracks at the end of the hall gave the avenue a steady stream of traffic. It granted him anonymity, in a way. So many people came and went that no one noticed when he visited his office, nor when his informants joined him.

"Afternoon, sir."

Tren suppressed a frown and turned to face the soldier who had stopped in the hall beside him. Had he arrived a moment sooner, they could have spoken in private. To retreat into the office again would have been noteworthy. He opted to remain in the hall instead, choosing to ignore the carefully respectful greeting the soldier had used.

The men did not seem to know how to address him since Lumia's removal of his rank. That was something Tren would have to remember to speak to her about. They lacked the forces for titles to be anything other than formality, but titles still held power in the minds of men. Surely there was some other title he could adopt. Colonel, perhaps.

"Afternoon," Tren replied, cold and formal. He tried to avoid giving extra attention to those who still acted as his men, tried to treat them no differently than any other soldier. Less likely to arouse suspicion that way. One never knew who was listening. "Is there any news?" It was the same thing he always asked, the wording innocuous and tone nonchalant. The soldier fell in step beside him as he made his way toward the market.

"There's been no activity in the ranks since the mageling's arrival," the soldier replied. Tren was pleased the man's choice of phrasing sounded half complaint, half gossip. "We're all itching to move again, but the general seems distracted."

"By the mageling girl?" Tren brushed dust from his sleeve and raised his chin as they stepped into the bustle of the lantern-lit marketplace. The military cut of his coat yielded nods and curtsies from people who bowed out of his way.

"Of a sort." The soldier paused, and a hint of a frown pulled at his mouth. "By learning her craft, at least. I've no desire to watch their lessons, myself, but I hear they can be quite a spectacle."

Tren slowed. "She teaches him here?"

"Where else? She's got her own place a few levels down." The soldier adjusted his pace to match the hesitance in the former general's step. "He's there a lot, from what I gather. I've heard talk it's not just her magic he may fancy."

Tren grunted. From the way the man beside him nodded, he found the notion disgusting, as well.

When Tren said nothing, the soldier went on in a disinterested tone. "I hear Firal—the mage—is up in the gardens most afternoons. Seems harmless enough, but plenty of folk avoid the place like the plague whenever she's there. Not everyone is as trusting of mages as the general seems to be. They wronged us before. There's no saying what they might do now." Then the man fell back and touched a finger to his brow in a gesture of respect. "See you in the training arena, then?"

"Of course," Tren murmured as his informant vanished into the crowd. He stopped at the archway into the inverted tower at the end of the river. The branching hallways there housed most everyone in Core, Tren included. He'd planned on retiring to his private quarters, but the new knowledge made him reconsider.

Despite living near the temple his entire life, Tren knew little about the mages—beyond their politics, at least. If the mageling girl sought to manipulate Daemon, he wouldn't be surprised. But there were enough hands pulling those strings already. Whether Lumia knew it or not, Tren would be the first to endorse her puppetry. The queen's intentions paved an easy road for his own.

He altered his course, climbing up the spiral path rather than delving farther into the earth.

The afternoon sunlight was harsh after the dusky lantern light of the underground. Tren grimaced as he waited for his eyes to adjust. He spent little time outside of Core. Even when he'd been in charge of raids—before that, too, had been taken from him—they'd gone under the shadow of nightfall. It would certainly take time to grow accustomed to living beneath the sun.

There were few enough people in the herb gardens that it wasn't difficult to see her, though the first glance caught him off guard. Though he wasn't sure what he'd expected from the Eldani girl, she certainly wasn't it. Her black hair was pulled into a bun that was coming undone, her homespun dress the same as any other woman in Core might have worn. She wasn't as fair or fine-featured as he'd always heard Eldani women were supposed to be. Aside from the definite peaks of her ears and the milkier tone of her skin, there was nothing to distinguish her from his own people.

Dirt smudged Firal's face and caked beneath her fingernails. Muddy splotches on her skirt showed she'd spent most of the day on her knees. She banked soil beneath a plant with a trowel and sat back to inspect her work. A swipe across her forehead with the back of one hand left a dusty streak on her pale skin. Tren frowned. Somehow, he hadn't expected to see her working for her keep.

He strode closer and clasped his hands behind his back. "I imagine this sort of work is unusual for you. I suppose mages would be more at home among piles of books."

The mageling twitched as her eyes swept toward him. Her gaze lingered on his uniform, though she was clearly uncertain what to make of it. "I'm no stranger to work," she said after a time. She rose and brushed dirt from her skirts.

"I didn't mean to imply that you were," Tren replied. "You're fending for yourself quite well, from what the city has to say. I figured it was time for me to meet you."

"And you are?" The question wasn't quite sharp, but there was an edge to her voice that he wasn't sure he liked.

"Tren Achos. I'm an officer in Queen Lumia's army." The latter tasted sour as it rolled off his tongue. If colonel was what he was going to call himself, he needed to embrace the title before Lumia could take it away. "And you are the mage Firal, who has the whole city in a buzz?"

Firal made a face. "Would that they speak to me and not of me." She tucked the handle of her trowel into the ties at the waist of her dress and pushed her hair back from her face.

He shrugged. "Well, it's not as if you can blame them. Magecraft is something rather unknown among our people. It's caused a bit of a stir, you teaching our general the ways of a craft so foreign to us."

"I've heard people say your queen is Gifted, as well," she said dryly.

"Not quite in the same way Daemon is." He paced forward to inspect the neat rows of well-tended herbs. "You look at home among the plants. Are herbs useful to you? Or are they just part of the lessons?"

Firal gave the plants an indifferent glance. "Herbs are useful to everyone. Tending them gives me something to do. I've a lot of time and little to fill it with."

"Do your lessons with him take so little time?" Tren arched a dark brow.

Her eyes narrowed. "You seem awfully concerned with Daemon and his abilities."

"Less concerned with him and more concerned with your safety, my lady. I've heard you are a skilled medic. That's something we desperately need. I'd hate for you to get caught up in his schemes. Especially those involving your people." His eyes flicked to her ears.

Firal did not reply right away, but her lips pressed into a thin line. "I'm not a part of any schemes," she said finally, though a wary look flitted through her amber eyes.

"Is that what he's told you?" Tren chuckled and rubbed his beard with his thumb. "You're involved whether you like it or not, my dear. All of us are. He'll use anyone in Core to get to the throne. It's not bad to be along for the ride, as long as you know there's a place for you at the end of it. As long as you're mindful and keep yourself useful to him, I'm sure he'll make room for you in the palace in Ilmenhith."

Firal drew back. He saw the uncertainty in her posture, though her face remained unchanged. Good. Let Daemon try to keep his secrets. Tren was eager to see how well he'd be able to use the girl now.

"My work in the gardens is done for today," Firal said with a stiff nod of farewell. "If you'll excuse me, Sir Achos."

"Colonel Achos. And of course, my lady." Tren bowed as she picked up her skirts and hurried past him. He didn't smile, but a definite sense of satisfaction filled him as he watched her leave.

"IT'S GOOD TO SEE YOU IN THE PALACE AGAIN."

Ran jumped and snapped shut the book in his hand. It slipped out of his grasp and clattered onto the desk. The sight of Medreal in the doorway should have been a relief. Instead, his heartbeat thundered in his ears and throbbed in his fingertips. He swallowed and moved the book back to where it had been, never tearing his eyes from the stewardess. "I thought you would knock."

"I thought the office was empty." Medreal closed the door behind her as she joined him in the king's office. "Don't look at me that way. You know perfectly well I won't bite. Has the temple set you free, then? I imagine it's been busy, putting things back in order."

"Not everyone is needed at this point." He tried to sound casual. It was harder than he expected; his voice caught in his throat and threatened to choke him. Uncomfortable under her gaze, he turned his attention to the papers on Kifel's desk instead, stirring them as if bored. Some must have gotten wet. He squinted at the lettering. The ink was almost illegible. "With everything going on, I figured it was best to just stay out of their way."

The old woman smiled, though her eyes remained as sharp as ever. They cut through him like knives. "Well," she said, "I'm sure there's plenty here that you can do. I'm sure you know more about the rumblings in the temple than we do. Your father will likely have questions for you. He is holding audiences with mages who have declared their loyalty to the crown. They wish to unify the mages stationed outside of Kirban."

"What do the chapter houses think of that?" If he was supposed to be a court mage, he would be required to be involved, but he was careful not to sound too interested, lest she drag him off to be included in those meetings. He was not ready for that.

"Who can say? Not all of them have been contacted. Of course, the temple itself may yet break. There are some Masters within the temple who I cannot imagine agree with the direction the Archmage has chosen."

Ran stepped away from the desk. "Actually, I'd hoped to speak to Father about that. Or find information on it." He waved a hand at the scattered papers. Had they been in the locked boxes or drawers, they would have been off-limits. His father never left important documents where they could be seen. Were it not for Medreal's presence, he might have retrieved the set of keys hidden elsewhere in the office. But he wasn't supposed to know the king's secrets, and while he was certain Medreal was fond of him, it wouldn't spare him her wrath—or his father's—if they learned he knew where the keys were kept.

"What sort of information?" Medreal asked.

"What I'm supposed to do. I assume the court mages are away to aid him with Gates? Or else they defected." The word left an unpleasant taste in his mouth. Though he was no stranger to diplomacy, there were times bluntness worked in his favor. There were appearances to keep up, and as far as his former nursemaid was concerned, he was still an inexperienced child. "It doesn't seem they've left anything for Father, or for me. I had hoped to find some indicator of who should be giving me orders, and who I could trust."

Medreal raised a brow and he shifted in discomfort. Surely she hadn't thought he would join the mages in their rebellion against his father. She paced across the soft carpeting with her hands clasped at her waist. "Given the circumstances, I think the mages are being particularly careful with correspondence. I'm sure if Kifel wanted you to do something, he would send word directly."

Ran fought not to grimace. Where could word be sent? Kifel certainly wouldn't send anything to the temple, where his orders and plans could be intercepted with ease. If he had orders for Ran, they would have been left somewhere in the palace.

Well, not necessarily left for *him*. Court mage or not, Ran was a Master trained in Kirban, and Kifel had more reasons than that to doubt his allegiance. But a message to or from any of the mages would have sufficed. All he needed was an idea of what was going on, what he'd missed, and where he needed to be to avoid the growing strife. A list of loyal contacts in the temple would have been useful, as well. He had no intention of allying with the temple mages, but as a newly-appointed Master, he still had responsibilities and needed direction.

When he did not speak, Medreal turned her gaze to the mess of papers on the desk. She bent at the waist to pick up one that had fallen to the floor. "Will you be returning to the temple soon?"

Ran shifted to face the tall windows and pretended he wasn't interested in the letters and notes his father's adviser shuffled into order. "I've a few errands to attend to in the city before I go anywhere."

"No need to be so cold and formal, boy." She chuckled. "I was your nursemaid once, you remember. There was a time I rocked you to sleep on my bosom."

He moved away when she rounded the desk. "There was a time I was not involved with the temple, as well."

That drew a hearty laugh. "My dear child, you've been involved with the temple from the moment you were born."

His ears grew hot, though whether from anger at the reminder or embarrassment over the correction, he didn't know. Medreal raised a brow and a hint of a smile played at the corners of her mouth. But she did not comment on the faint flush that colored his cheeks. She tapped the thick stack of papers against the desk's edge to align them, checked the dates and headings that were still legible, and tucked them into the carved wooden box Ran had stolen them from in the first place.

He righted his white robes. "See that you tell my father I came to visit, would you?"

"Of course," Medreal replied, only half interested. She studied the last handful of pages with a thoughtful frown.

Ran stalked toward the door, but felt his spine itch under the weight of her dark eyes as they settled on his back. He closed the office behind him and freed himself of her scrutiny.

What he'd spread across his father's desk were reports, but not on correspondence between mages. Reports on the whereabouts of the soldiers he'd dismissed from the temple were something else entirely. He didn't want to stay put long enough for her to ask questions. He could only manage redirection for so long, and he feared he was about to run out of time.

9

FRACTURE

"Do you think they find it suspicious, the way the rains have washed out every crop this year?" Envesi chuckled as she turned away from the window. She left the shutters open and ignored the rain that spilled in to leave wide puddles on her office floor.

Anaide's nose wrinkled, but she said nothing, though she lifted her feet so the growing pool of water would not saturate her shoes. The meeting had been unpleasant enough without wet socks.

The Archmage's office had been the first space cleared. Wagons full of books and relics were well on their way to Alwhen by now. All that remained was the great desk in the center of the room and a handful of chairs in a half-circle before it. Anaide disliked the arrangement. The Masters sat before the Archmage as if they were children to be disciplined, instead of some of the most powerful mages in the temple—if not the world.

Anaide pursed her lips and looked to the sky beyond the window. It was clever, really. The sensations that came with the flow of magic were so common around the temple that none of the younger Masters thought anything out of place. The rivulets of energy the Archmage had cast into the sky were almost imperceptible now, riding on the wind and bending the weather across the island to her will.

"They have no reason to assume it's anything but ill luck." Edagan gave Anaide a sidewise glance. "Outside the Masters of the five Houses, no one knows that weather can be manipulated so easily."

Envesi sniffed as she regarded the four women gathered before her. "Yes, well. I'm sure it will stay that way. Regardless of how smoothly the shift of power goes, we don't want Relythes to be privy to such information, either."

The whole situation still gave Anaide chills, but she kept her thoughts to herself and held her expression carefully neutral as she glanced over the other women. Alira, with her half-bleached hair, made no effort to hide she was eager to move from Eldani lands. Arrogant child; she'd learn better soon enough.

Melora, sour-faced and sharp-eyed as ever, was harder to read. The Master of Wind had little love for the royal family. She'd been passed over as court mage before she rose to lead an affinity, and she still complained about it from time to time. But she also had little love for the Giftless people of the east. Perhaps she could still tilt either way.

Edagan, Master of the House of Earth, was the only one Anaide was sure she would win over. Edagan was level-headed and would hear them out without immediately reporting their intentions to the Archmage.

Unsure of her next move, Alira returned her eyes to the Archmage. The situation was frustrating, to say the least. Nondar had started the effort and Anaide had been the first he'd approached. Futile as the effort seemed, she was all too happy to aid the old half-blood. Gathering the mages loyal to King Kifelethelas would be no small feat, but one of Nondar's magelings had already received some correspondence on the matter. If the messages were to be believed, a number of the chapter houses spread across Elenhiise were ready to stand with the king.

"There have already been reports of hunger in the more remote parts of the island." Alira folded her arms over her chest as she spoke. She'd looked smug enough already, but now Alira wanted to slap her. "Relythes verified that the weather in his region has remained unaltered. We can assimilate the borderlands almost immediately. Relythes is equipped to feed the hungry, so once the food supply in Ilmenhith begins to run low, it will be easy to remove Kifel from power."

"Good." Envesi settled behind her desk and clasped her hands together against its edge. "Send word to Relythes about the impending famine. The sooner he gains favor in the eyes of the western cities, the better. We shall paint him as a hero for their benefit."

Anaide couldn't help her frown. That Envesi spoke so casually of starving her own people made her blood run cold. She shouldn't have been surprised to learn the Archmage had manipulated the weather, yet she cursed herself for not thinking of it sooner. Had she known, she could have tried to unravel it. Melora was better equipped for altering weather, what with her wind affinity, but as Master of the House of Water, the wellbeing of Anaide's students demanded she try.

Unlike Melora, Anaide had once been offered a place as a court mage—and she had turned it down. It had been an honor that King Kifelethelas trusted her so, but her heart was with her students. Now was her opportunity to repay that trust.

"Is everything organized for the Gate to Alwhen?" Melora asked.

Alira spoke before the Archmage could open her mouth. "Nondar has seen to the organization of the magelings. They stand prepared, though most of our belongings and supplies will not reach Alwhen until well after we've settled. I regret it wasn't possible to Gate them, too."

"I understand our new headquarters is to be quite nice." Edagan gazed absently at the water spreading across the floor.

"Not that I'm fond of eastern architecture, but it is a definite improvement over having to rebuild."

Those words put a grim smile on Envesi's face. "Destruction of the temple was not part of my original plan, but it has worked out well enough. I didn't anticipate any trouble from that meager band of ruffians out in the ruins, but now that they've entangled themselves in matters, we shall have a few more pieces to play on the board."

"They do make a very convenient target for the king's ire." Melora's smirk was none too flattering to her withered face. "And a perfect distraction. It couldn't have worked out better if you'd planned it."

"Do we mean to abandon the child to them?" Anaide folded her hands in her lap.

Envesi snorted. "The entire group has no further use. Allowing the emerging war to consume them will solve several problems."

"Very well." Anaide pushed herself from her chair and offered as deep a bow as her aging bones allowed. "With your leave, Archmage, I'll begin preparations for the opening of the Gate."

"Of course." Envesi gave a careless flick of her fingers to grant dismissal.

Anaide did not miss the glance Edagan threw her way as she departed. It was hard to be certain, but Anaide took it as a good omen. Edagan had said little during the course of the meeting, but she was a woman of few words. Having her on their side would mean the divide was equal. Anaide would not hold her breath on turning Melora to their side.

The few magelings who remained in the lower levels of the tower were uninterested in yet another Master in their midst, and so Anaide's descent through the tower was unhindered. That, too, was beneficial. As long as no one cared to watch her, no one would notice how often she approached Nondar.

Anaide gave her head an irritated twitch at thought of the

man. He was a strong mage and a valuable asset to the king, but he was utterly incapable of hiding his opinions. Through his stark silence in previous meetings, he conveyed his disapproval more loudly than he could with words. It was a wonder the Archmage hadn't scheduled any convenient accidents to remove the man from his seat of power. But Nondar's loyalty to the crown was unwavering, even when such loyalty could threaten his life. For that, Anaide had to give him respect.

Nondar had chosen to organize affairs for the move from his old office, and it didn't take long for Anaide to reach the mostly-ruined building. A few magelings crowded his desk, but a single glance from her mage-blue eyes made them scatter. Nondar met her eyes and a barrier sprang up around them to keep their words from prying ears. Sometimes Anaide forgot that not all mages favored flamboyant gestures to guide the energy flows they manipulated.

"The meeting went well, I take it?" Nondar's voice held a sardonic edge.

"I believe Edagan will join us. Her level-headedness is a good counterbalance to Alira's impulsiveness. The Archmage will have a rash council remaining." Anaide drew out a chair and sank into it with a sigh. A rash council that would retain control over the majority of the temple, she reminded herself. "Are we really doing the right thing?"

"We are doing the only thing we can. Whether it's right or wrong is something we have yet to see." He shrugged. "Are you having second thoughts?"

Anaide shook her head. "My family has stood behind the throne since long before the temple was founded. To turn against Kifelethelas now would be to spit on my mother's grave."

"Then is it loyalty to the crown, or to your family that sets you on this path?"

She didn't like the way he looked at her. "Can it not be both?"

The old healer chuckled and bowed his head, though he

swayed a hand in a placating gesture. "We shall see, Anaide. With fortune, we shall see."

A desire to recite her reasons for loyalty rose within her, but Anaide forced herself to return her thoughts to her orders. "The Archmage wishes for us to prepare the Gate."

"Then it shall be prepared," Nondar said, reaching for his cane. "I shall see to the magelings."

"And our plans?"

Nondar stood and shrugged. "They continue, unchanged. It makes no difference whether we are here or in Alwhen. When the time comes, it will come. But the time is not now." He dropped the ward.

Anaide understood and fell silent. There would be no more discussion on the matter until then. Not in the ruins of Kirban, and not in Alwhen. All she could do was wait.

THE AIR SIZZLED WITH SUCH ENERGY THAT KYTENIA'S HAIR STOOD on end. She never liked the sensation of Gates. The opening was the worst—so much raw power manipulated by so many hands. She shuddered and then flinched when her sister laid a hand on her shoulder.

"It'll be okay," Shymin said.

"I know it will be, but that doesn't mean I have to like it while it's happening," Kytenia whispered back. She knew her sister meant well, but the Gate was only half of what unsettled her. She did not want to return to Alwhen.

Mageling robes of every color swirled around them as they moved into ranks. The Masters had tried to sort them at first, but had given up after only a few minutes. Students crowded the courtyard and sorted themselves into groups. Shrill voices called for friends and classmates over the noise of the crowd.

Kytenia's group had formed early. Marreli clung to her arm and watched the crowd with wide eyes. Now and then, Rikka reached out to pat the smaller girl's head and smooth her braids. The group felt incomplete without Firal, but there was no helping that now. Kytenia could only pray her friend had made it to safety.

Streaks of energy sparked from nothing and arced across the sky in crackling bolts. A tremor of fear rolled down Kytenia's spine as the lines of pure magic intersected and merged to form an arch half as tall as the Archmage's tower. Most Gates of that size required anchor points to open, but with the scores of Masters that stood in the courtyard, there were enough hands to bring it under control. Kytenia shuddered and hugged Marreli close.

The border of the arched Gate buzzed with energy, white-hot and blinding. The sky within seemed to split, falling away in shards that dissolved into shimmering lights before they could hit the ground.

On the other side, the image of a building stabilized into sharp focus. The structure was impressive; its windows revealed four floors, though it did not soar like the Archmage's tower or the palace in Ilmenhith. Banners of the same rich vermillion and bronze Kytenia recalled from Alwhen's palace waved from pointed, copper-roofed gables.

A hot wind flowed through from the other side of the Gate and the Masters moved to either side, until only the Archmage remained before it. Her white robes and snowy hair rippled in the wind. She started forward with a confident stride and behind her, rank by rank, the magelings in their colorful robes followed.

Kytenia reached for her friends' hands and caught hold of Shymin and Marreli. She spared a glance for Rikka, who met her eyes over the top of Marreli's head and nodded back.

They crossed the Gate.

Electric tingles lanced through Kytenia's body. Her skin rose in gooseflesh and her hair stood on end, her heart thumping harder until she thought it might break free of her chest.

And then they were through.

The air that gusted through the Gate had been warm, but this side of the Gate, it hit her like a sweltering wave. The temple was sheltered by the forests near the center of the island; the wind there was gentle, humid. But the trees had been cleared from the land around Alwhen, the earth left bare to the beating sun. Only after Kytenia drew a breath of the warm air did she notice the people.

Onlookers lined the streets. Rows of soldiers dressed in Alwhen's colors held them at bay. Shouts and clamor filled the air, though it was hard to tell if it was jeering or applause that met their arrival.

"See? That wasn't so bad." Shymin moved their group toward the massive building in front of them, step by slow step.

"Children," the Archmage cried as she scaled the stairs and stopped at the building's grand doors. She flung the doors wide, and light spilled into the whitewashed great hall of their new headquarters.

Kytenia's stomach sank, even before the Archmage finished her declaration.

"We are home!"

10

ROLES

Wʜᴀᴛ ʙᴇɢᴀɴ ᴀs ᴀ ᴅʀɪᴢᴢʟᴇ sᴏᴏɴ ɢʀᴇᴡ ɪɴᴛᴏ ᴀ ᴅᴇʟᴜɢᴇ ᴛʜᴀᴛ ʟᴀsᴛᴇᴅ for days. Torrents of rain cascaded down the open column in the center of the inverted tower. No one tried to scale the spiral to the gardens above, the upper walkways slick and the weather too violent for anything to be done outdoors.

Without the gardens to distract her, Firal tried to settle into her little cavern-house. She had no belongings to decorate with, but the time to clean and rearrange things was welcome. Clippings of herbs she'd gathered made cheerful bundles, which she tied with colorful string and hung around the room to dry. The room's previous occupant had bored holes into the wall beside the fireplace. Firal peeled the bark from twigs in the tinder box to make little wooden pegs, which she pressed into the holes to mount her cookware on the walls.

The herbs were not the only supplies she'd gathered. A number of odd, long seed pods she'd found at the back of the garden proved to yield strong fibers with little work. Sheets of coarse paper made from those fibers now dried on scraps of fabric Minna had let her borrow. A jar of indigo leaves she'd set aside on her first day in the gardens would provide ink, sooner or later, and she understood Daemon's wisdom in saving every feather from the chicken he'd brought her after she cut the largest quills into pens.

But after the first few days of rain, Firal grew bored. Daemon was out traveling, according to Minna's husband. Firal spent several evenings by their hearth while Davan was on leave, using charcoal from the fire to draw letters for Tobias to study. She enjoyed their visits, though she hated the war stories Davan told his son before bed. The captain was a warm and fatherly man and didn't strike Firal as the type that belonged in the army, but the men of Core weren't given a choice. If they were sound of body and mind, they were conscripted.

"Was Daemon conscripted, then?" Firal asked as she helped Minna slice vegetables.

"Oh, no. I suppose you wouldn't know, but he wasn't born of us. He joined us later, so our rules didn't apply." Minna chuckled and took another sweet potato. She was nimble with her knife, and her comfort with it made Firal envious. "He volunteered. His service has been a blessing to our soldiers. He has a good mind for military work, they say, and a fair hand with a sword. I suppose he learned it all somewhere, but I couldn't tell you where."

Old suspicions drifted to the forefront of her mind and Firal's brow furrowed with thought. "When did he join you?"

"I was just a child when he came to us. Then again, he wasn't much more than a boy, himself. So it's been a good portion of my life. We ruin-folk don't age like the lot of you. Your magic keeps you young." Minna grinned, but offered nothing else.

Firal grew quiet. During their travels to Ilmenhith, Daemon had confided only a small piece of his history. She had initially dismissed the claim that he'd been born in the temple and that he came and went from Kirban freely as he grew. Perhaps that dismissal had been unwise. She had assumed *coming and going* meant spying or sneaking about; his home within the ruins would have made it easy enough. But if he hadn't joined with the Underlings until he was half grown, that made less sense.

Between that, Daemon's Gift, and his hatred for the temple mages, Firal's thoughts grew heavy. The burden stayed with her for days.

More than once, while she awaited Daemon's return so they could resume their lessons, she ventured through the marketplace beside the river. She still hugged the wall of the tower's walkway when she had to traverse the path, but after her numerous visits to the garden alone, her fears had diminished from raw terror to jangling nerves. Reaching the market was less nerve-wracking, and the cheerful babble of the river was always quick to soothe her.

She had nothing to trade or barter with, but observation of the market proved just as fruitful. Coin had little value among a people so desperate for material goods. Daemon had told her as much, but it was different to see it with her own eyes. In one stall, a blacksmith traded a newly-forged chisel for a live chicken. In another, a woman swapped large spools of fine yarn for a small bale of carded wool. The simplicity appeared pleasant, but it added another layer to Firal's distress. With no trade but her magic, what did she have to offer those who could not learn?

At last, an evening came where the rain tapered off and the stars became visible above the chasm in the inverted tower.

When morning broke, Firal was among the first outside, her new papers, quill pens, and ink in tow. After hours of careful cultivation, the plants thrived with little further care. She walked each row and cataloged the garden. There were so many different plants that she couldn't imagine sending someone to retrieve something fresh without offering a guide. Once the name of every plant was listed on its own page, she gathered a number of leaves and flowers for later reference.

The midday sun soon made the heat oppressive, and Firal took shelter under the trees at the back of the garden to continue her work. Resting her papers against her knees, she drew a careful representation of each plant she'd gathered. She had a neat hand, and she couldn't help but imagine her notes about the size and color of each specimen would do Master Nondar proud. The thought came with an unexpected pang of grief, and she stopped writing.

What was she meant to do without her teacher? Without the temple? She still hadn't found a purpose. She enjoyed teaching Daemon, and she enjoyed the garden, but that was what *he* wished her to do. The notion of continuing north to Ilmenhith still crossed her mind now and then, though she did not know what she would do once she got there. The longer she waited, the less likely it seemed that Ilmenhith's chapter house would aid her, and it wasn't as if she had friends in the capital.

The loss of her friends, too, cut deep. Had she crossed their minds after they'd learned she was expelled? Or had they simply accepted the Archmage's decision and carried on? The memory of all the late nights she'd spent in Kytenia's room with her friends made the ache in her chest sharpen, and Firal squeezed her eyes closed, her pen poised above a half-finished drawing.

"Is that for my benefit?"

The question made her jump and her head jerked upward. Daemon stood above her, his eyes trained on her illustrations.

Firal swept moisture from her eyes before he could see it. "They're for everyone," she replied, masking her sniff with an air of loftiness she hoped was convincing. "You, however, will be learning healing. Should you ever come for lessons, that is."

He made a small sound of uncertainty. "That does seem to be the one thing I just can't do."

"Attend your lessons like you ought?" She raised a brow.

"Healing." The look he gave her was so stern and reprimanding, even with his mask, that she couldn't help but laugh. After the burdensome thoughts that had only just been spinning through her head, the levity was welcome. Those worries could be dealt with another time. Preferably when she was alone.

She gave her eyes one more covert swipe, grateful for the

distraction his presence offered. "I was only joking. But really, Daemon, you can't expect to make progress when you aren't here. Where have you been?"

"Went to check on my men at the northern edge of the ruins and got waylaid by the rain. I'm trying to avoid using Gates, since you said I shouldn't open them alone." He eased himself to the ground beside her and glanced up when the breeze sent a cascade of white trumpet flowers from the trees to the ground.

Firal pointed at them with the tip of her quill. "Do you know what those are? I've never seen flowers like those on a tree before. They grow the oddest fruits—something like a bean. They're not edible from what I can tell, but they make nice enough paper."

Daemon plucked a flower from the grass and turned it between his claws. "Serpent's-tongue. Not good for a whole lot, like you said, but pretty to look at, I suppose." He leaned forward and tucked the blossom into her hair. She blinked in surprise. He didn't seem to notice. "I know we haven't discussed it any more since I first mentioned it, but I wondered if you'd given any thought to what I said about becoming Core's medic."

"It has crossed my mind." She brushed her fingertips against the ruffled edges of the flower and blushed. The heat in her cheeks was difficult to ignore. "I am... open to the idea. For now. I think I'd need more supplies, though."

"What sort of supplies?" He propped his hands in the grass behind him and leaned back. "I can try to find some, as long as it's nothing outrageous."

"Nothing outrageous at all, just the necessities for an infirmary. A table big enough to lay patients on, a few more chairs, shelves for my medicines, that sort of thing."

"I don't think you realize what a commodity furniture is." Daemon eyed her in a disapproving way, the sort of look that always gave her the impression of a frown. "But I'll see what I can find."

"Thank you. I'll need tools and linens, as well." Firal smiled apologetically when his shoulders twitched. She shifted her skirts around her legs and held out her drawings and notes. "Do you have time for a lesson?"

He shook his head as he got up. "Not if I'm to find all the things you need."

"Do you want me to write you a list?"

"You could always just come to the market with me," he suggested. "Maybe you could squeeze in that lesson on the way."

"It'd probably be best for me to sort things at home, first," she said thoughtfully. "I'll have to make room for everything. I suppose the furniture doesn't need to be precisely what I'm used to. I'll make do with what I can."

"How very generous of you." He rolled his eyes and offered her a hand. When she took it, he pulled her to her feet and gestured for her to lead the way.

Firal sorted her papers and tucked her quill behind her other ear, opposite the flower. "The linens and tools, however, cannot be compromised on. I'll definitely make a list for those. After all, if you want me to be a proper medic, I must work under proper conditions."

His eyes narrowed with a grimace behind his mask and for a moment, she couldn't help but wonder at how skilled she'd become at discerning his expressions without ever seeing his face.

"I'll see what I can find," he repeated, noncommittally.

"And when you bring me whatever you find, we should squeeze in a lesson," Firal added as she put her papers into her bag and gave a helpless shrug. "You're good with fire and wind and not a lick else. How do you think you'll improve without practice?"

Daemon mimicked her shrug. "I'll wake up one day and be blessed."

They descended the first few rings of the spiral path. The sound of the rushing river filled the air, and Firal breathed deeper. The underground was pleasantly cool today, though she sometimes found it on the chilly side. Mists floated from the waterfall, scenting the gentle breeze. The smell of the water was as refreshing as the seemingly perpetual updraft that floated through the inverted tower.

"I think we'll both agree that's highly unlikely." A hint of a smile tugged at the corner of her mouth. She resisted.

It was easy to smile around Daemon. He was a different person in Core. She had noticed the change in his demeanor shortly after her arrival, but hadn't been able to determine why it was different, other than that he was simply at ease. He was calmer, slower to frustrate. His increased patience had made their lessons more enjoyable, and she had to admit she found his sarcastic humor enjoyable, too.

Then there was kindness. That one had been a surprise. Firal mulled it over as he moved ahead and bounded up the shallow stairs beside the river. Children played in the water above the small, misty fall. One boy sat on the rocks, cradling a scraped knee. Daemon crouched beside him at the river's edge.

"Found a good lesson, have you?" Firal pushed up her sleeves as she joined them.

Daemon eyed the injury. "I thought you could—"

"Don't be silly." She knelt beside the two of them and slid her satchel to the ground before she reached for Daemon's hand. His scales still felt odd beneath her fingertips, but she'd grown used to them. Or at least, they didn't frighten her anymore. She moved his hand to the child's knee and stroked the length of Daemon's fingers before she let go. Their texture reminded her of leather, softer than the coarse, sharp-edged and unpleasant quality she'd first expected.

The boy stared at Firal with wide eyes. She couldn't help a small sense of amusement. Between the two of them, she still thought Daemon was the odd one. But he was part of these people, whereas she was a newcomer. Perhaps she was the stranger sight.

"Do you remember?" she asked, forcing her thoughts back to the opportunity at hand. "Healing is connected to life. Breathe deep. Feel the ebb and flow of energy within his body. Then see if you can sense the injury."

Daemon's breath caught, but he bit back whatever protest he'd had ready. He closed his eyes and Firal opened her senses in hopes she would feel him at work.

The child's life, like all the others in the underground, glowed in her mind's eye. She felt them on a deeper level, too—something she had never been able to capture in words. They glowed in her senses with a suffuse warmth that touched her very spirit. It was subtle, but still there, like the heat of a flickering candle as she held a hand over the flame.

Injuries, too, hovered within her awareness. The boy's knee, minor as the scrape was, cast the tiniest shadow over the light of his essence. To draw the rest of his energy together and overwhelm it would have taken nothing, but this was not her task. Instead, she searched for Daemon.

He glowed in her senses too, though in a different way. His Gift hummed on the edge of her awareness, like a muted voice from another room. That had always struck her as odd. In the temple, the countless mages around her had borne a clear, bright presence. All she could suppose was that the muddied sensations that surrounded his Gift had something to do with the murky taint in his power. *That* was something she didn't need to feel clearly to identify.

When they'd first met, she'd thought the strangeness she sensed in his power had something to do with his being a wild mage. It was not until they had resumed lessons in Core—where she'd been able to devote her full attention to them—that she realized that hint of wrongness was what had anchored itself to his physical being, twisted him into something that never should have been. She pitied him every time she felt it. But if it was that taint he wanted to overcome, she suspected learning to connect himself to the life force of others was a necessity.

Daemon's low growl of frustration broke into her thoughts. She blinked and willed her eyes to refocus.

"How do you do this?" he asked, exasperated. "It's like trying to hold on to soap with wet fingers." The hum of his magic slid closer, enveloped the boy's presence, and then slipped away without a change.

"Slow down." Firal touched his hand again.

His eyes snapped to her face. Their light flickered behind his mask.

"You shouldn't be holding anything," she said. "It's more of a pulling, or a gentle push. No holding of anything. You're powerful, but there are some things you can't force."

A small grunt escaped him, but he closed his eyes and tried again. His power, still tingling on the edge of her awareness, increased until it burned like an itch in the front of her mind. It tugged at the small shadow that blotted a fragment of the boy's existence, coaxed the edges of wellness to envelop it. The delicate flows of life—the power that ruled over healing—started to move. Then, without warning, they snapped back and escaped his control.

Daemon gritted his teeth and tossed up his hands in defeat.

Having learned how far to push, Firal ended it there. She swept a hand over the boy's knee and a small swell of her power flowed into the injury. The skin wove itself back together, mended without so much as a mark left behind. The boy's mouth fell open as wide as his eyes had been through the whole encounter.

"I can't," Daemon said with heat in his voice.

She shrugged. "Then we move on to something you can do. But don't give up, Daemon, please. Healing is my affinity. I would be a laughable teacher if I couldn't even teach you effective methods for healing."

A wistful shadow dulled his eyes. He turned his head and watched as the boy leaped up and ran to rejoin his friends. "Maybe."

For a moment, she pitied him. There was something charming in his disappointment, though, and the way his shoulders sagged as he watched the child leave betrayed a deeper desire she hadn't realized she understood. It wasn't just control over his power he wanted. The desire to use that power to aid his people burned bright inside him, and she sensed that he saw every misstep as a failure that tried to snuff that flame.

Drawing her fingertips over the wet stones beneath her, she gathered her thoughts. Slowly, she seized control of the water under her hand. It answered her call and she shaped it into a long ribbon. He couldn't be allowed to wallow in self-pity.

Her hand snapped up and the strand of water whipped against his mask.

A shout of pure indignation burst from his throat and he scrambled to his feet.

Firal laughed and stood, too. "You should have sensed that coming. Didn't you feel it?"

The violet glow in the eye slits of his mask brightened and shifted toward red. His right hand moved over the water, his fingers spread.

She mirrored his movements, seizing the water again. It coiled around her ankles like a snake before it lashed at him again. The rope of water struck an invisible barrier and shattered into a thousand droplets. Her mouth fell open. She thought he'd reached for the water. He'd reached for the *air.*

Before she could compose herself, he retreated into the water. The river swirled around his legs, no more than ankle deep, but it would have to be enough. He spread his hands again. She braced for wind and reached for the water at the same time. It surged up around his legs to hold him fast as she scooped spheres from its rippling surface.

No wind came. Instead, thick snakes of water rose from the river beside her, twisting around her waist and dragging her from the river's edge. She squealed with laughter as she stumbled over the stones, her wet skirts clinging to her legs.

The children stopped playing and clustered at the river's edge. Adults soon followed. Firal scooped up more spheres of water, but instead of throwing them at Daemon, she tossed them into the air. They caught on a net of air she wove beneath them, bobbing as the wind rippled and flowed along the river's bed. She'd never noticed the similarity between the two elements before. All energy flowed in channels, but air and water flowed the same way, adhering to known paths. They weren't like the erratic nature of fire or the static nature of earth.

And life, too, ebbed and flowed like a tide.

That's it. She suppressed a grin as she gathered more spheres and tossed them aloft. If he could catch the flow of wind and water, he could grasp healing the same way.

The air shifted and one of her spheres fell. It burst against the crown of her head and doused her. She shrieked at the cold. Another fell, and another. Firal hopped across two large stones in the river to avoid them. The water swelled at her ankles. She spun it into a long tendril and cracked it at him like a whip. It impacted his invisible barrier again and splashed uselessly against its surface. Behind them, a murmur of delight rolled through the growing crowd.

"A mage should always be prepared," Firal called over the hiss of the water that pelted his air shield. "We both know once your concentration's broken, it's hard for you to catch your power again."

"Prepared," Daemon repeated flatly. The light in his eyes flashed brighter. Power surged in him, no longer muddied, but crackling like white-hot static at the edge of her senses. The water rose around her ankles. Then it withdrew, retreating up the riverbed as if the current had reversed. Toward him. Daemon spread his hands and slowly raised them.

The river itself lifted from its bed.

Firal stared in disbelief. The water rose higher and higher above its basin, the quivering sheet swelling and deepening as he held it overhead. Whispers of pure awe rippled through the crowd. Too stunned to continue their game, Firal sank to her knees.

The light of Daemon's eyes softened and lost its red tinge. The water arced over their heads to splash down behind her in the empty riverbed. Spray filled the air as it crashed into the stone. Daylight from the inverted tower danced on the plumes of mist, casting rainbows into the air. The flood unleashed, the river shot over them until the current faded to its normal, placid flow. Slowly, Daemon parted the water above them and allowed it to fall.

The river sank back into its path, mist soaking them both. And then all was normal again.

Small sighs of disappointment came from the watching children. Murmurs of disbelief passed between the adults.

"That's your first mistake," Daemon said. "You think you must be prepared because you might be taken by surprise, without a chance to defend yourself. But who could stand against me without knowing they've come to die?"

Firal bowed her head. Sudden shame washed over her. She was not a powerful mage—she never had been and probably never would be. Surprise was her best weapon. She had nothing else.

His clawed toes came into view and she looked up, startled.

Daemon offered his hand. "Fortunately for you, we're on the same side."

Tentatively, she laid her fingers against his palm. He cradled her hand gently and helped her to her feet. His other hand hovered a few inches from her wet clothing. When he swept his hand downward, the water peeled itself from her clothing to leave it dry.

More murmurs rose from the observers, but when Daemon looked at them, they scattered.

"You've gotten much better with water," she remarked as he helped her out of the river. Her knees trembled beneath her, but he helped her keep her footing.

He passed a hand over himself to dry his clothing the same way. "Well, we have been practicing."

"Moving water from a bucket in my cavern is hardly similar to lifting an entire river." Firal tiptoed to the walkway beside the water and retrieved her bag. "But that was a good lesson, I suppose."

"I have a good teacher." The statement was flat and honest. Not meant to stroke her ego, she decided; simply a statement of fact. Regardless, it should have tickled her pride. It didn't.

She sniffed and turned back the way they'd come. "I have some ideas for how we can approach healing next time. Once the infirmary is set up, perhaps your next healing lesson can take place there."

"Tonight," Daemon agreed. "Have a meal ready when I get there. If I have to drag furniture around all afternoon, I'm going to be hungry." He followed her back to the spiral path that descended into the earth. At the doorway, he offered his arm and positioned himself between her and the chasm.

A hint of suspicion welled within her, but she laid a hand on his arm and allowed him to escort her back to her home. The display earned them curious glances from passersby and more than once, Firal blushed. It must have been odd to see their general with a mageling on his arm. Despite the discomfort that came with those looks, she admitted his presence between her and the pit gave her a stronger sense of security. From the fact he'd offered it without her asking, she suspected he knew as much. She didn't know why she trusted him for protection, but she appreciated it. Especially with the price she knew he'd have to pay for his gentlemanly behavior.

He had quashed the rumors that flared when they first began their lessons, but she saw the way the people watched her, heard the whispers behind her back in the gardens and outside her open door during lessons. There was a touch of respect in the eyes of those who looked at them, though, and a part of her hungered for that recognition. To be respected and revered for what she could do and what she could offer, to be *someone*—was that not what she wanted? What her time in the temple had, in the end, failed to provide? A meaning and a purpose, and the dignity that went with them?

But was obtaining it worth becoming entangled in Daemon's politics and plans? The colonel's well-intentioned words weighed heavily on her thoughts and a frown worked its way onto her face.

She had considered asking Daemon outright about his intentions. Then she had considered seeking Minna's advice instead, but she hadn't bolstered her courage enough to ask the woman's opinion of Colonel Achos.

And what *were* Daemon's intentions? She found herself suddenly aware of his easy stride beside her, the comfortable way he moved with her as a decoration on his arm. She all but shoved him away.

He glanced to his sleeve and then touched it as though he expected to find a spider in its folds. "What's the matter?"

"It isn't proper." A flush rose into her cheeks and Firal silently cursed her fair complexion. "People already speak of us in ways they shouldn't. We oughtn't do anything to encourage it. I wouldn't want them to think there was something unusual between us."

Daemon's snake-slitted eyes fell on her like a weight. "Is there not?"

Her ears burned. "Thank you for your assistance. I can make my way home from here. I'll have food prepared and the room ready to accommodate whatever furnishings you can find." She offered a stiff curtsy before hurrying down the path on her own.

It wasn't until she reached her house and closed the door that she felt like she could breathe again. The heat of embarrassment lingered in her ears and cheeks.

What had he meant by that? Was he trying to rile her? Or was the question genuine? She struggled to recall anything she might have said or done to make him believe she thought of him as anything other than a student.

Did she think of him as something other than a student? The idea hit her like a slap in the face. She couldn't see herself as a real teacher—she was still a mageling, herself—and he certainly wasn't simply a pupil. He was a general, and in bringing her to Core, he'd become something of a savior for her, as well. He was a sound leader. His people respected him. And she did, too.

Not so long ago, she'd blamed him for the temple's ruin and been sure she hated him. How quickly things had changed. Now she saw hints of his honor and integrity, honesty and reliability. A myriad of respectable qualities hidden just beneath the surface. For some reason, he tried to hide them. She'd fallen for it at first, but knowing what she now did, and feeling those glimmers of warmth and respect, how could he be a mere pupil?

And yet, if he wasn't merely a pupil to her, what was he?

A knock at the door made her jump and squeal. It took a moment for her to compose herself enough to answer.

"Everything all right, Miss Firal?" Minna asked with a frown when Firal opened the door. A basket of vegetables rested in her arms.

"Yes, I just stubbed my toe as you knocked." The lie rolled off Firal's tongue smoothly, though she was sure her ears were still red.

"Well mind that you're more careful, miss. Can't have you giving yourself an injury you can't heal." The Underling woman clicked her tongue as she pushed into the room. She left the basket beside the hearth and fetched a tool to prod the banked fire back to life. "I see you haven't even put down your satchel yet. Just gotten back, have you?"

Firal looked to the forgotten bag slung over her shoulder. "Oh. Yes, I was out making notes. I'll have to make all my own reference manuals for healing, now that I haven't got access to Master Nondar's."

Minna's expression shifted to something unreadable. "It's a good space to sit and do it, out under the serpent's-tongue trees."

Firal's eyes widened. After the horseplay in the river, she'd forgotten the white flower tangled in her hair. She freed it from her dark curls and crushed it in her hand. "It's better to be close to the specimens. It'd be hard to draw them accurately if I'm sitting down here in the gloom."

"Of course." Minna chuckled and added another log to the fire. "I imagine Lord Daemon will find your references most useful in his training."

"He's not the reason I'm making the book." Firal tossed her satchel onto the table and moved to help Minna put the stew pot over the fire. "It'll be useful for everyone."

"I didn't mean to say that he was." Minna settled on the edge of the hearth and dusted her hands together. "He's busy enough that his lessons might suffer, in any case. Goodness knows Queen Lumia keeps him on his toes. Davan says she means to have Lord Daemon off on business before long, though who knows what she has him doing. Sometimes I'm not sure the men here have enough duties to justify all their fancy rank and titles."

Firal jumped at the opportunity to change the subject. "How large is the military, anyway? The men of Core are conscripted, but how many of them are there?" She retrieved the bucket of water she kept near the fire and dumped it into the pot. Then she sat beside Minna and reached for one of the paring knives tucked into the vegetable basket. Minna had given Firal many things to help start her new home, but the good cutlery was something she'd unashamedly kept for herself.

"Ten thousand men, perhaps twelve? I'm not right sure. They don't do the best job of divvying them up under the officers, which makes them hard to count. But Davan is in line to be considered for major when they get around to sorting that last thousand." Minna swelled with pride. "I don't know much about how the military works, I admit. But if he's made major,

Davan will spend more nights home with Tobias and myself, and I can't say I don't cherish the idea."

"Best of luck, then." Firal took a sweet potato from the basket and turned to slice it into the stew pot. "Though I'm sure his skill will be recognized. He seems like a good man, and a wise one, at that." And he'd been the one to suggest they send her to Core. She'd never forget that. Silently, she thanked him for the opportunity his choice had granted her.

"I'm sure," Minna agreed. She sprinkled a few herbs into the pot to go with Firal's vegetables. A pleasant aroma filled the room. "You've done a good job with cooking, the past few days. I think I've taught you all I can there. What else do you need from me?"

"I imagine you're a long way off from teaching me all you have to share." Firal dumped the last of an onion into the stew and sniffed hard. "If you have the time to spare, though, I could use your help in moving furniture. I'll need space for new things if I'm to make a proper infirmary."

"Taking the mantle of medic, are you?" A spark of delight lit Minna's eyes. "All of Core will be glad to hear that."

Firal was not so sure. "I hope so. I'm afraid I still have a lot to learn about what's expected of me and what is acceptable. More knowledge about your culture would be helpful. You started to tell me about the chapel the other day, but we didn't speak much before Tobias came in with that skinned knee."

"The chapel it is, then." Minna got to her feet, and Firal followed. Together, the two of them moved the table closer to the hearth. "As I told you, they say the caverns of Core were left behind when Brant pulled up his roots and left the world. Most of our people are quite devout, though the shame of having disappointed the Fathertree weighs on them so heavily that few speak to him directly. They carry their prayers to the priests, instead, who pass them on. The priests and those who are most devout pierce their tongues with silver to prove they're pure enough to speak prayers..."

Firal listened and absorbed as much she could while they rearranged her sparse collection of furniture, but as the woman droned on, her thoughts drifted back to the serpent's-tongue trees and Daemon's arm beneath her hand as they walked through the underground.

The vegetable stew was ready just as a number of men arrived with new furniture in tow. Firal gawked at the assortment of furnishings he'd found, but Daemon did not give her time to stare. He directed the men while she directed the placement of furniture. Minna stayed, serving bowls of stew to the hungry visitors while Daemon paged through the unfinished illustrations and notes Firal had compiled for her new herbal.

With so many hands, the work did not last long. Minna departed with the men, and instead of staying for another lesson, Daemon left with a bowl of food in hand, unwilling to remove his mask to eat. Firal was left alone with a mage-light suspended above her new table. Her unfinished pages lay spread across its surface, a number of dried samples scattered around them. Somewhere in the mess, she found the crushed blossom she had pulled from her hair.

Firal turned it between her fingers as she closed the door. Alone in the firelight, she was glad no one was present to see her press it between the herbal's thick pages.

11

NO EXCEPTIONS

ASH SWIRLED ON THE WIND. KIFEL COUGHED ONCE TO CLEAR HIS throat and pressed his cape over his mouth and nose. The rains across the island had stabilized. They moved in predictable patterns and no longer stirred from nowhere, both of which were good signs. But the temple, strangely, was dry.

The handful of mages in blue-trimmed white who had followed him through the Gate looked up the tower and around the barren courtyard. Most wore expressions of puzzlement and concern. Kifel, on the other hand, showed nothing.

"Should we investigate the tower, Your Majesty?" Temar wrung her hands as she stepped forward. She was a good woman and a good mage, one of few Kifel believed he could trust. He hadn't been the one to appoint her as chief over his court mages, but he was grateful for whatever twist of fate put her there.

"No." He coughed again, the sound muffled by his cape. "There is nothing more to see."

Temar bowed her head and turned to the other mages. Within moments, they had opened a Gate back to the palace.

It was Temar who had suggested he take a contingent of mages with him to Kirban. In that moment, he had known he would find nothing but an empty husk. Temar had been alarmed when the portal to the temple opened. She had not said why, but Kifel suspected the curious power that let one Gifted person sense another worked through Gates as well, and she must have sensed Kirban's mages were gone. But had she insisted he take mages with him so they could open a return Gate? Or had it been concern for his safety?

Both, he decided. Had Temar and her subordinates not accompanied him, he would have been stranded in the empty temple without a way to return. His mages would have come for him eventually, but his temper would have been gone. As it was, he held it by a thread.

Resentment simmered inside him. It had for days. Only half his anger was directed toward the Archmage. The other half burned for himself.

He'd been a fool—a mistake a king could not afford. Lovesick and desperate, he'd tried to placate her, hoped to foster some semblance of the feelings he'd always harbored and she never had. In his efforts to bring peace between the two of them, he'd instead allowed a potential war between the island's two ruling factions to fester.

There was no one but himself to blame.

Kifel strode through the crackling portal and exhaled. His office had become a refuge; he spent more time there than anywhere else. The endless paperwork and short walk to the council chamber meant constant distractions close at hand. He clung to them. Work was all that kept his mind off the perpetual sickness that churned in the pit of his stomach.

His forefathers would have been ashamed.

Ruling was business, his mother had often said. As a ruler, he believed he had done well enough. His people were content, his cities thriving and his borders relatively peaceful. Steady flow of international goods through his ports kept the kingdom's coffers full and allowed him leniency in taxes. He was loved by his people, no mistaking it—yet he was reviled by the woman who should have stood by his side as queen, and his only heir... Kifel cut the thought short and swallowed against the bitter taste in the back of his mouth.

"There will be no more leniency." He unfastened his ash-sullied cape and draped it over the chair at his desk. "Temar, summon my council to my office so they may receive their orders. There shall be no discussion."

The mage curtsied. "As you wish, Your Majesty."

Kifel drew back his chair, but his feet itched with a need to move. Instead of sitting, he paced in front of the tall windows as the mages scattered.

There were only two people he needed to speak with. One was Temar; the other was Ordin Straes, who served as both Captain of the Royal Guard and one of the heads of Kifel's armies. The rest of the council members were to appear only for sake of formality, and they would not be pleased.

He stopped to stare out the windows, his hands clasped behind his back. More than once, he'd considered moving his office to the other side of the palace. The gardens were beautiful, but they were safe, sheltered from the harsh sea winds that swept against the other side of the towers. Tradition had kept him anchored on the safe side of the palace, where imported flowers bloomed in bright swaths of color. He was tired of tradition. Now, he was the sea. Angry, churning, merciless.

The door behind him opened. Medreal's patient voice rose above the storm in his mind. "Your Majesty, your council is in the hallway."

Kifel lifted his chin. "Bring them in."

One by one, the members of his council filtered into the room. Most looked annoyed; Temar alone appeared worried. Kifel locked eyes with her and began before anyone could speak.

"From this moment forward, Temar, all mages on Elenhiise answer to you. You will locate all mages within my territory. They will be taken into custody and questioned. Those who have sworn or will swear fealty to me are free to return to their duties, but shall not interact further with unproven mages. Those who refuse to swear fealty will be imprisoned in the palace and held inside the nullifying barrier. There will be no exceptions. Do you understand?"

Temar's jaw went slack. "Your Majesty—"

"Do you understand?" he repeated.

She bowed her head. "Yes, Your Majesty."

Horror spread itself across the faces of the other councilors. Kifel ignored them and turned his attention to Captain Straes. "Tighten border security. No one passes between the eastern and western halves of the island for any reason. Any group that attempts to force their way through the border from the eastern side shall be treated as a harbinger of war and will be destroyed."

"Yes, Majesty." Captain Straes clapped a hand over his heart and gave a slight bow.

"Majesty," Temar began. "If all mages are to be questioned, your son..."

The word twisted like a knife in his gut, but Kifel did not flinch. He met her eyes, his gaze cold. The councilors watched him, tense and fearful.

"As I said," Kifel replied, "no exceptions."

FIRAL TIPTOED ALONG THE TOWER'S WALL AS A CART RUMBLED PAST on its way to the gardens above. The waterfall bridge was just ahead, but she tried not to look at it. Instead, she kept her eyes trained on Daemon's back.

"I'm not sure I like the idea of lessons involving water anymore," she called, her voice all but lost beneath the sound of people. She enjoyed watching the bustle of the underground city's market, but pressing through it was different. The crowds kept her from visiting often. Since her new duties began, she hadn't visited the market at all.

Word of the infirmary had spread fast. Most days, she propped her door open in the morning and entertained a stream of visitors all day. It cut into her lessons with Daemon, but he hadn't complained. Yet when she'd opened her door that morning, he'd been the only person outside. After the hours of their designated time she'd instead spent treating colicky babies and setting broken bones, she couldn't object when he insisted they carve out a lesson.

He turned to face her, walking backwards, his confidence as awe-inspiring as ever. "Don't worry. I'll leave the river alone. This time, the lesson is for you."

"For me?" She ducked through the doorway that led from the inverted tower to the square, as she'd come to think of the market beside the river.

"A lesson in our history and culture." Daemon paused to let her catch up, then continued ahead at a pace that was easier for her to follow. "Minna's taught you a lot, but you still haven't seen the best part of Core. If you're going to be one of us, it'll help if you participate in community rituals."

"Rituals?" she repeated, doubtful.

He flashed her a look over his shoulder. She was certain he grinned. "You'll see."

They followed the river's edge through the market until the cavern tapered and left only a narrow walkway on either side of the wide river. The water was deeper at the cavern's mouth, and the massive waterwheel clacked overhead. Firal craned her neck to look at it. She had known it was large, but she had never ventured so close. The wooden structure was as tall as the garden's serpent's-tongue trees.

"The waterwheel is the greatest feat of the ruin-folk." Daemon paused beside her and looked up, as well. "Building a similar system would revolutionize life in the surface cities."

She frowned. "They have waterwheels on the surface."

"Not like this." He jerked his head toward the narrow path. "This way."

Firal followed with her fingertips brushing the wall. Eventually, they reached a wide doorway set into the wall beside them. The space beyond was dim, but Daemon waved a hand and lanterns sprung alight along the walls. The display of skill startled her.

"You've gotten quite good with fire," she remarked as he led her up a handful of stairs. It hadn't been that long ago that she'd given him his first lesson. Now he could light a dozen individual flames at once with barely a thought.

"I've had a good teacher," he replied easily.

The air ahead was damp and warm. The corridor turned twice with no offshoots, then emptied into a large room filled with cisterns of carved stone. Thick, rough-spun curtains hung between the basins. A maze of wood slats hung from the ceiling with lanterns suspended between them.

"What is this?" Firal's eyes followed the wood until her chosen slat disappeared into the wall. Narrow channels had been drilled through the stone to let the wood through and she couldn't help but wonder where they led.

"The bathhouse." Daemon waved toward a shelf against the front wall. Jars and bottles of every shape and size decorated it. He transferred a bottle to her hands. "The soaps and bath oils are provided for everyone. Normally, there would be people here, and you'd be expected to share a tub or return later. But it's early. No one comes to bathe until after the morning's work is done."

Firal shot him a glare. "I am not bathing with you."

"Don't flatter yourself." He plucked a bottle from the top shelf and uncorked the top to smell its contents. He grimaced and put it back. "The curtains are for privacy. I always have my own."

"And you bring in water from the river?" She didn't see any buckets. The sound of the river outside was dulled by the solid stone walls, but the noise still reached her ears.

"The water brings itself. Pick your soaps and fetch a towel from that rack over there. Then I'll show you." Daemon stepped up onto the ledge beside a tub and caught hold of one of the curtains. Metal rings in its top rattled against its wooden track as he dragged it away from the wall. He gave it a shake, and then the curtain glided forward to drape elegantly around the far side of the tub.

Firal popped open several bottles to sniff their contents. Most were mild floral fragrances, likely made from flowers grown in the garden. She chose one that smelled sweet with a hint of spice, pulled a worn towel from the rack as directed, and turned toward the tubs.

Still standing on the ledge, Daemon reached overhead and grabbed a dangling cord. She hadn't noticed them before, but two dangled above each basin, high up enough that she would have difficulty reaching them on her own. He pulled the cord taut, then paused. "Go ahead and pour that in here."

"Does the water come from that?" she asked as she opened the bottle and upended it over the empty tub.

"The left cord is hot water. Right cord is cold." He jerked the leftmost cord and a slat in one of the wooden rails opened. Steaming water gushed from the opening, splashing into the tub below. Daemon leaned away.

Firal's mouth fell open. "The water is hot? How?"

His eyes sparkled behind his mask when he looked her way. "The waterwheel. It's made with scoops, not just flat paddles. They pour water into troughs as the wheel turns. Didn't you see it?"

A flush crept into her cheeks. "I suppose I didn't. Where do the troughs go?"

"The water race carries everything from the waterwheel into the boiler room above us. The fires are kept burning so hot water is always available." He pulled the second cord and another spout of water joined the first. Cool water, this time, to offset the heat.

Firal spread a hand over the tub and wriggled her fingers in the steam. "This is incredible. Hot water on demand... I've never seen anything like it."

"It's one of many ideas I hope to take to the surface with us." He stepped back, leaving the water to run as he opened the slats over the neighboring basin.

The space between each cistern was larger than she'd initially noticed. With the curtains drawn, each tub would still boast a wide ledge around it. She assumed it was for clothing and maybe space for someone to sit. Her folded towel fit neatly beside the tub. "What do you mean?"

"Mind the cork at the bottom when you get in. You'll have to put it back in after you drain the water, otherwise they tend to get lost."

Firal leaned forward to peer into the tub. The froth from the soap kept her from seeing anything. "I didn't even notice. It drains, too?"

He pulled another curtain from the wall, halfway encircling his tub. "All of them empty into a channel that runs underneath us. It's a man-sized tunnel that empties into the inverted tower several floors down. You probably haven't gone down far enough to see the second bridge, but that's where the tunnel lets out. From there, the bathwater drains into the waterfall."

"Huh." She dipped a finger into the water as it neared an appropriate depth. Satisfied by the temperature, she climbed onto the slab and strained to reach the cords to shut off the flow of water. The wooden beads at the ends of the cords bounced off her fingertips. "But you didn't answer my question."

Daemon did not reply.

A cold uneasiness crept into her stomach. The only reason he would avoid the answer was if it was unpleasant. The cheerful warning she'd received from Colonel Achos drifted forth from the back of her mind, as it had so many times since their encounter in the gardens. She caught the cords and managed to pull the water slats closed. "You intend to overthrow King Kifelethelas and usurp his throne, don't you?"

He turned toward her, the spark gone from his eyes. "Who told you that?"

The ice in his response made her heart beat faster. She shrugged and feigned indifference as she pulled the curtain on the other side of her tub. It moved more easily than she expected. "I've heard it in Core."

"That's Lumia's intention, not mine." He uncorked his own chosen bottle and poured it into the water. A warm, spiced scent rose to meet the floral fragrance of her own bath.

Firal tucked in her chin and pulled the curtain harder. It slid around to envelop the front of the tub, obscuring the entryway and offering privacy. "Then why go along with it?"

"Because that's politics. You use the tools you're given. If you don't, you're a fool." Following her lead, he closed the curtains between them and shut off the water.

She bristled. "And using people?"

"People are the best tools. You don't have to like it, but when you walk in their circles, you must play their games. If I'm to give these people a better life, that's what I must do."

"Noble," Firal muttered. She untied the bodice of her simple dress and stepped out of her slippers. The latter had become quite worn, but she doubted she'd be able to replace them soon. She'd wished for her lost sandals a thousand times. "If you don't intend to seize the throne in Ilmenhith, then what is your intention?"

"That much should be obvious." A hint of amusement touched his voice. "I want a better life for everyone in Core. I want to reclaim part of the surface. It's been centuries since we were cast out. Things have changed. It's time for things on the surface to change, too."

The soft rustle of fabric on the other side of the curtain made Firal pause. As eager as she was to enjoy her first real bath since Ilmenhith, she hadn't considered that she wouldn't be alone. She toyed with the laces of her dress and looked at the floor. "Should we be here? Together? I wouldn't want anyone to think—"

"That you enjoy my company?" Humor replaced his amusement. "Watching one of our lessons would be enough to clear up that misconception."

Metal pinged on the other side of the curtain and the fabric swayed. On the floor, the corner of his lost mask poked through a gap in the curtains. She stared at it until movement drew her eye upward. A glimpse of his bare back, his bronze flesh so startlingly normal, made her heartbeat pound in her ears. He turned his head, ever so slightly, and she spun away.

Chuckling, Daemon moved his mask across the floor with one clawed foot and drew the curtains closed again. "No peeking."

Heat burned in the tips of her ears and her pulse still thundered, but she swallowed hard and tried to sound composed. "I wouldn't need to peek if you weren't so adamant about keeping secrets." She kept her back to the curtain as she undressed, then hastily slipped into the tub. The water was hotter than she expected and she sucked in a sharp breath as she rose halfway out of the foam.

"Don't take it personally."

Inch by inch, she sank back into the water. "How do you expect me to trust you when you've never let me see your face?"

A pause. "That was part of why I brought you here."

Firal sank chin-deep in the foam. Even with her back turned, his presence made her uncomfortable. "Are you certain this is appropriate?"

"It's a communal bath and the curtains are drawn. But the baths are always empty first thing in the morning, which means I can speak to you for a moment in private." A soft swish of water on his side of the curtain came accompanied by a contented sigh. "I'll be leaving Core soon, traveling to Alwhen to speak to King Relythes. I mean to approach him and negotiate for land."

Despite the heat of the water, a chill stole through her. Was this what Tren meant? Despite Daemon's secrecy, she'd thought him honest. Now, the first glimmers of trickery came to the surface. She braced herself. "Why not negotiate with Kifelethelas?"

"Because the ruins already fall within his territory, but they're useless to him. I stand a good chance of convincing him to relinquish control of the ruins. But if Relythes believes I am allied with Kifelethelas, it will be harder to negotiate with him because he'll see me as an enemy."

"So you'll ally with Relythes, then?" She couldn't keep the heat from her voice, but when Daemon replied, he was calm.

"I mean to ally with both of them."

Firal folded her arms over her chest and slouched in the water. Her dark hair floated on the foam like a shadow. "That's an impossible feat."

"Not impossible," he said slowly, "just difficult. They're both reasonable men, but their feud is older than they are. Elenhiise is fueled by tradition on both sides of the island. But should a third faction rise, on good terms with both, we can finally move forward. I believe it's possible to work with both Kifel and Relythes, but even if they refuse, kings don't live forever. Even Eldani kings. We have the opportunity to become one of the most politically useful countries in the world, but to do that, we have to unify."

"Under your banner?"

"If necessary." The patience in his words was infuriating.

"Why tell me this?" The question spilled out before she could stop it. She was a disgraced mageling, a nobody. Why confide such secrets in her, unless he meant her to become a pawn?

"Because I want you to know our people are not enemies. The Eldani and the ruin-folk can coexist peacefully. You don't have to choose between us and them."

A twinge of hurt pulled at her heart. After all she'd been through, she wasn't sure where her loyalties were anymore. Kifel had done more than enough to earn her loyalty and respect. He had been kind and fair in his dealings with her. She was loyal to her friends, though she had no way of knowing if that loyalty was returned. But the temple that had been her entire life and purpose had rejected her, and the people of Core had welcomed her with open arms. The ruin-folk smiled at her freely, gave thanks for her services readily, and forgave her clumsy missteps as she learned of their culture.

And then there was Daemon.

He didn't have to allow her into his people's city. He would have been justified if he'd never spoken to her again. She didn't dare ask why he had. But they'd leaped right back into his lessons, relying on her understanding of magic to rein in his power—power that was savage enough to corrupt his body, she reminded herself. His interest in learning magic was not altruistic. It was wholly self-serving, and one open, honest moment did not change that.

She closed her eyes. "My people will always come first."

"I understand," Daemon replied softly. "I just hope that in time, you'll come to see us as your people, too."

Water splashed on the other side of the curtain, and Firal listened as he dried himself and dressed. A sucking sound drowned out the rustle of clothing as the water drained from the tub, and then the soft click of his claws trailed out of the room.

Firal drew up her legs and rested her head against her knees. He'd asked nothing of her, yet she felt as burdened as if he had. If it came down to it, could she choose between Daemon's people and her own? The question put a lump of discomfort in the pit of her stomach. She hadn't realized until that moment, but Core had already become her home.

NOTHING MORE

Fragmented beams of sunlight filtered through the skylight and sent dancing rainbows across the floor. One fell across her lap, and Lumia stared without seeing it. She wasn't used to not getting her way. For the third time since the temple's destruction, the nighttime summons she'd sent for Daemon had gone unanswered.

It was not the warmth of his body or the pleasure of coupling she missed, but control. He had been young when she'd taken him beneath her wing and added facets of knowledge to his understanding of politics and royalty. He'd been easy to manage, content to follow her every order simply because she issued it. It was under her tutelage, she told herself, that he'd grown into such a fine young man. Fine to look at, as well, but there were the mages to thank for that. Lumia was not unfamiliar with the forbidden energies that could alter one's form, but that was one thing even she dared not manipulate again.

And yet, despite all her help and all her kindness, he had chosen to wrest his loyalty from her grasp just as things came together. Affairs on the surface simmered on the verge of explosion; there would never be an easier time to supplant the king and claim his lands for her own. She'd thought Daemon an asset to her intentions, but his recent actions had dulled the edge of that plan. She didn't like being forced to revise her strategy.

It would not be impossible to take the throne by herself, but it would be difficult. Much more difficult. Lumia drummed her fingers against the arm of her throne.

Daemon had improved her knowledge of the temple through his experiences within it, and his importance to the Archmage as a failed project gave Lumia an upper hand over the wretched mages. Which was the biggest problem she faced, it seemed. It wasn't Kifelethelas or Relythes that she worried about. It was that infernal Archmage.

The thought of Envesi made her blood boil. Lumia's Gift was formidable, but she was no match for the snowy-haired woman who had ruined her life.

It should have been simple. Pursuing a union had been the most obvious way to cement their alliance and place her in power. With as pretty as she was, Lumia had never expected to be passed over. She, too, was of noble birth, bore the Gift, and hailed from the mainland. But she was not Eldani, and in some places, old prejudices held fast.

Part of her conceded that Kifel's marriage to Envesi had not been his choice. His mother had arranged the whole affair. But blight the man if he'd not simpered and fawned over the dark-haired woman who would become Archmage, ruining the simplest of Lumia's plans, skewing the narrative so she appeared little more than a scorned lover instead of an ally whose trust had been shattered.

Her interference with the Archmage's projects had been labeled petty, but she did not regret it. Her exile from the temple had been worth it. Every effort, every hint of corruption that tainted her power had been worth it to see the horror and despair Envesi suffered when her endeavors were ruined.

She still relished the memory of twisting the energy flows as the Archmage laid them over the child—the memory of Envesi's triumph at breaking down the barriers that created affinities within a Gift, only to see how the tainted power corrupted the boy's body. It had been Lumia's first true success, and she felt no remorse for the hand she'd played in Daemon's creation. The very twists that made him a monster were what had spun him into her grasp, and now he was a precious pawn in her game.

Or he had been.

That he'd begun to slip from her grasp was most troublesome indeed.

She had tried using others for this plan before, but their greed always made them unreliable and a hindrance to her efforts. Even Tren, her last attempt, had gone terribly astray. The man was a strong fighter and decent enough strategist, but he failed to hide his hunger for power. She hadn't been able to keep him collared either, though she'd bound him by blood as she had Daemon.

Even now she could feel them, the two men she'd tied herself to. Tren's presence in her mind was like an ember with all its smoldering anger and hate. She silently cursed the gift of longevity he'd gained by sharing of her blood. Now she'd be trapped with his bitterness welling in her mind for what, two, three centuries? Not that Daemon's presence was much better. His emotions were... Well.

She tossed her head, sighing heavily. She'd hoped taking him to her bed would prevent such immature complications of feeling, but that had proven to be a mistake as well.

Perhaps her approach had been wrong. Trying to rein him in had only driven him farther away. So what if she gave him his head? Granted him a little room to spread his wings and make a few of his own mistakes? He'd mentioned establishing territory above-ground; that was perfect. Let him do as he would for a week or two. It would give her a little time without his emotions echoing so loudly in her head. She couldn't afford to waste much time, but a handful of weeks wouldn't endanger their window of opportunity. She could straighten out her thoughts, then determine the best course of action.As long as they struck while Kifel was weakest, it could still be a deathblow to the Eldani kingdom. And with it, the temple's foundation.

Lumia raised her hands overhead and gave a sharp clap. It didn't take more than a moment for her page to appear from behind one of the grand tapestries that hid the tunnels adjacent to her throne room.

"Summon General Daemon for me, child. Tell him I wish to speak to him regarding his plans to move to the surface." Yes, that would do. Surely he would respond to that.

The boy's eyes widened but he said nothing, bobbing his head in reverence before he disappeared from the room.

Twisting a curl of her golden hair around her finger, Lumia eased back into the worn cushions of her throne. Now the only problem was the mageling.

"LADY FIRAL?"

"I'll be with you in just a moment," Firal called over her shoulder. She bit her lip, determined to finish grinding what she'd dumped into her mortar almost two hours ago. Before Daemon had helped her establish the infirmary, she'd had more time than tasks to fill it with. Now she scarcely had time to breathe, let alone prepare her tinctures. People lined up in the hallway to seek treatment for their ills. Her door never closed, but Minna had fashioned a screen of sorts from an old blanket to allow privacy for exams.

Without Minna's help, Firal would have been lost. The woman had assumed the position of assistant the moment the line had formed, and her help was indispensable. The Underling woman stood across the room, preparing something else. Most visitors griped of minor ailments, best treated by sending them home with a pouch of herbs. Which made the task of preparation all the more important. Firal didn't mind being busy, but a moment to catch her breath and straighten her hair would have been nice.

The soldier at the door cleared his throat. "Queen Lumia demands your presence. You are to appear before her immediately, regarding important business of Core."

Her hand froze on the pestle.

It would have been foolish to think she could live in the underground city without Lumia's knowledge, but after the queen's violent reaction to something so minor as trespassing, part of her had hoped her presence would go unnoticed. She'd been there a handful of weeks and Lumia hadn't seemed to care.

Or Firal thought she hadn't cared. A lump rose in her throat and she swallowed hard as she pushed the mortar farther back on the table. She wiped her hands on her apron and glanced across the room. Minna met her eye with an approving nod, but her face was pinched and uncharacteristically pale.

"Very well." Firal turned toward the door. "Take me to the queen."

The soldier nodded stiffly as she stepped into the hall. Curious faces watched them as she followed the man toward the inverted tower. She mustered a smile for them, though it felt weak. Already, the line murmured with rumors passed down from the front, where patients awaiting treatment had been close enough to hear the exchange.

They passed through the market and into the winding hallways of the underground. The hum of the city faded behind them, but Firal remained quiet, and the soldier did not try to initiate conversation. Her heart hammered in her chest and her stomach tied itself in knots. She couldn't fathom why Lumia might want to see her, but somehow, she doubted it had anything to do with healing.

Eventually, the heavy, ornately carved doors that guarded the throne room loomed before her, a stern reminder of her previous encounter with the queen. Firal tried to bolster her courage.

"My orders are to wait here until your meeting is adjourned," the soldier said as they stopped beside the doors. "Tell me when you are ready to return home and I will escort you."

"Thank you," Firal said as she peered up at the doors. If the soldier's orders included escorting her home afterward, perhaps this meeting wouldn't be so bad. Still, she sucked in a deep breath before she pushed open one door and slipped into the throne room.

Fires in the wrought iron braziers between columns cast a new warmth on a place she remembered as cold, though the room was just as vacant as she recalled. Despite its size, the door made no sound as it closed behind her. The dark throne stood empty on its dais.

Firal hesitated until she caught the echo of low voices at the end of the room. Perhaps this was not meant to be a formal meeting. The threadbare carpet that ran the length of the room muted her footsteps as she crept forward.

Belatedly, she thought she should have changed out of her apron and work dress before answering a summons from the queen. But most of her clothing was work-stained, anyway; she had few outfits to speak of, and she worked every day of the week. Her musing was cut short as she rounded a pillar and saw who the voices belonged to.

"Oh," was all she could squeak out.

Daemon's back was to the column, his shirt open all the way down. He had Lumia by the shoulders, and she had his belt halfway undone in her hands.

"Oh, indeed," Lumia said, a dark look in her blue eyes as her gaze fell on Firal. "You're earlier than I expected." Daemon pushed her back and she gave him a surly pout.

Color rose into Firal's face, though she couldn't make herself look away. Daemon righted his belt, but left his shirt open as he turned to face her. Heat prickled at the tips of her ears and she knew she had turned from pink to crimson. As a medic, she'd seen any number of unclothed bodies. Yet his sculpted stomach and smooth chest were not at all what she'd expected, given his scale-covered hands and peculiar clawed feet, and they stirred something in her that took a moment to name.

Disappointment.

"I can leave if this is a poor time," Firal managed as she tore her eyes away at last.

She shouldn't have been surprised. Lumia was a stunning woman. And yet there was an odd tightness in her chest, spurred by confusing and conflicting emotions she couldn't label. *Foolish girl,* she scolded herself. Daemon was her student. Nothing more.

"You were prompt," Daemon said, as nonchalantly as if she hadn't just walked in on him being undressed by the queen. As if his shirt didn't still hang open. "I appreciate that. I'd prefer to start this expedition as soon as possible."

"Expedition?" Firal studied the carpet underfoot with more interest than it deserved.

Lumia sighed and stalked toward the throne. "In light of the current political turmoil aboveground, it is in our best interest to approach King Relythes as soon as possible to establish cordial relations. Daemon is going as my emissary, and he has requested you accompany him on the trip. You shall go."

Though the queen's words were carefully chosen, Firal noted the ambiguity in the statement. She had not claimed the venture was her brilliant idea, nor had she honored Daemon by acknowledging it was his. Firal suspected it was some sort of test until the queen's final words left her mouth. Gaping, Firal turned toward her. "Why?"

Lumia met her eyes, and her gaze was like ice.

"There are a few reasons." Daemon crossed his arms and shifted his weight to one clawed foot. "Lumia keeps no council. Unlike the surface kings, she has no one to tend Core's needs if she is gone. And soldiers are not an option. It would be one thing if I were a normal emissary, but I'm the general. Should I arrive with soldiers at my command, he might interpret it as a threat."

Firal glanced between them with a frown. "And you think taking me is better than traveling alone?"

He shrugged. "We would be able to continue my lessons while traveling. I would prefer not to miss any more, especially with the unrest between the temple and Ilmenhith."

What unrest? Firal's brow furrowed, but there would be time to ask questions later. "I am not in a position to refuse. As you said, you are the general. And Lumia is the queen. If you expect me to go, then I will go. But I don't..." The words stuck in her mouth and she wet her lips to loosen them. "I mean no offense, but I don't understand why you couldn't give me these orders at our next lesson, instead of calling me here."

"Formality dictates such things," Lumia said with a sniff. "Not that you would know. Daemon departs in the morning and I expect you shall be ready when he comes to call."

Formality? Firal didn't believe that for an instant. Daemon stood beside the throne, his shirt still undone. The message had not been spoken, but it had been perfectly clear. She trained her attention on the floor and curtsied. "Yes, Your Majesty."

"Oh," the queen sighed as her crystalline eyes raked Firal's form, "and do dress appropriately for the trip. You are to appear before a king, after all. You'd shame us if you wear what you apparently think is acceptable attire for such an honor."

Firal flushed again. She willed her hands to be still at her sides, though they itched to remove her stained apron. "Of course, Your Majesty. Is there anything else you need of me?"

"Not at all." Lumia smiled sweetly. "You are dismissed."

Daemon moved as if to escort her to the door.

Firal raised a hand, telling him to stay. "I'll have my things packed and ready to go when you arrive. Thank you, General. Your Majesty."

He tensed, but remained beside the throne. For Brant's sake, couldn't he at least do up his shirt? She gave Lumia another curtsy and refused to look at Daemon again. He was just a student, she reminded herself. Nothing more. Her ears still burned as she returned to the hallway, where the nameless soldier waited to escort her home.

Certainly, now, nothing more.

BUSINESS

TRUE TO HIS WORD, DAEMON ARRIVED AT FIRAL'S DOOR EARLY THE next morning. She hurried to write the last of her instructions for Minna while he waited. She didn't like the idea of leaving her burden on the other woman's shoulders, but she wasn't in a position to refuse Lumia's orders, and the infirmary had to remain open.

Firal still did not understand why she had been chosen for the trip, but she was not convinced it was not some sort of punishment. Continuing Daemon's lessons was important, she agreed, but that hardly made her a suitable escort for a meeting with foreign nobility. But the reason for her inclusion did not change it. Firal tried not to think about it, and instead focused on finishing her notes about which herbs were to be dispensed for what illnesses while she was away.

Minna had insisted on washing Firal's fine black-and-red gown the night before. Though Firal appreciated it—and marveled at the woman's ability to remove the stains from the red silk panels—it only served to remind her of the queen's criticism the day before. She sullenly wished the gown unnecessary as she folded it into the large leather travel pack the Underling woman let her borrow.

The rest of what Minna helped her pack was more reasonable. Spun wool clothing was practical for travel, and a small canvas-bound notebook with a few sticks of wrapped graphite tucked within its pages was sure to be useful.

Firal had just enough time to eat before Daemon insisted they depart. He led her through the market and a number of twisting tunnels at a brisk pace, and none of them felt as long as she remembered. Eventually, some distance from Core, they emerged into the ruins and the weak light of the cloudy morning. It was all she could do to keep from groaning.

"Will we ever travel in anything other than rain?" Firal did her best to keep pace with him, a task made easier by her proper footwear. The sturdy shoes were another gift for which she owed Minna thanks. While the Underling woman had not given them to her, she had suggested them as payment when Firal mended the shoulder of one of Core's few cobblers.

"We won't be traveling in the rain," Daemon said with an edge in his voice. "We don't have time."

"And you think suppressing the rain will be easy?" The last thing she wanted was for his sour mood to set the tone of their trip, yet she couldn't help but ask. She did not mean the question as a negative. So many times, he'd surprised her with what he could do.

He gave her no answer.

The path he cut through the ruins was more convoluted than usual. They zigzagged outward and doubled back, and just when Firal thought they neared the heart of the ruins, the curve of the walls changed. She studied the corridors with a bemused frown. That made no sense. The nearer they were to Core or the rounded rooms that held maluiri trees, with their mushroom tops and egg-shaped fruits, the tighter the curves. These were broad, sweeping arcs, some of them damaged and crumbling.

"The walls looks like we're in the outermost part of the ruins," Firal said, "but we've barely started. Where are we?"

He did not reply.

"Daemon?" she prompted.

Silence.

Bristling with irritation, she hefted her satchel higher on her shoulder and crossed her arms. "Are you going to speak to me?"

"Yes," he said.

Another moment passed in silence and Firal released an exasperated sigh. "Well?"

Daemon paused and held up a small object between his clawed fingers. She extended a hand to take it. He set it in her palm and a wave of energy shot up her arm. Afraid she might drop it, she tightened her grip, though every inch of her skin hummed with its raw power. A shudder coursed through her and she forced her fingers open again to get a better look.

It was only a clear marble. How could it feel so intense?

"What is it?" She pushed it toward him, not wanting to touch it any longer. The flow of such power made her queasy.

"A Gate-stone." Daemon eyed her so neutrally it became uncomfortable. "Since I'm not supposed to open them on my own."

She shook her hand after he took the marble-sized stone. Her fingertips still prickled, and she rubbed her palm against her skirt as if to wipe it clean. "Where did you get a Gate-stone?"

"This was why Lumia raided the temple. She wanted one of these. I found it later. Lumia didn't know how to recharge it, so she couldn't use it." He rolled the stone in his hand. "Watch."

The air split as if sliced with a knife, peeling back to leave smooth, borderless edges beside a wide patch of green that had to be just beyond the easternmost edge of the ruins. Not even the breeze shifted as the portal's edges grew still. The power didn't crackle or seethe like the other Gates she'd seen. Firal gaped. "I didn't even feel it open!"

"It startled me, too, the first time I used it. I guess it's because the stones hold so much power. There's no fluctuation like there is when mages open Gates. You don't feel it open, you don't feel yourself pass through it. You can step right through and never so much as bat an eye." It didn't require the mage holding it open to pass through last, either, as evidenced by the way he strode through ahead of her. Firal eyed the Gate distrustfully before she followed. The lack of sensation as she passed through was downright eerie.

Stones flawless enough to be made into Gate-stones were the rarest of gems. As far as she knew, not even King Kifelethelas himself owned one. "And you knew Lumia intended to steal this?"

"Yes." He turned to face her and, for once, his expressionless mask gave her chills. "Because I needed it, too."

Anger simmered hot under her skin. "Then you're no better than her."

"I didn't say I enjoyed the methods used, but I saw an opportunity and I took it. If my plans are going to work, I need a Gate-stone, and I need to know how to use it." Daemon clutched the little stone tight and stared at his hand.

Firal quieted. *His schemes.* The memory of the colonel's warning made her skin rise in gooseflesh. Her heart warred with itself, torn between trepidation and a deep desire to trust him that she couldn't explain. She tucked her chin into her chest. "If you have a Gate-stone, then why didn't you just Gate us right to Alwhen?"

"Really?" He gave her a skeptical glance. "My teacher asks why I don't Gate us to someplace I've never been?"

Color bloomed in her cheeks, though it didn't lessen her scowl. She hadn't stopped to consider the possibility he'd never been in the eastern lands. Opening a Gate to a place one had never seen with their own eyes wasn't a question of safety; it was impossible.

To her relief, he did not chide her. Instead, he appeared distracted, staring into the space behind her. Closing the Gate, perhaps. "It'll be more useful on the return trip. Right now, I'm still learning how to use it. I can't imagine you'd argue with me practicing."

"No," Firal agreed as she looked over her shoulder. "I believe practice was why you wanted me here."

She had not realized the Gate behind them was visible from their side until she witnessed it sliding closed. It dissipated without so much as a sound, and she shuddered. Firal knew Gate-stones were required to anchor permanent Gates, portals that could be passed through from either side. Perhaps that had something to do with why Daemon could pass through without this one closing behind him.

"You seem practiced enough to me," she said with a nod toward his hand. "Is it difficult to use?"

He shook his head. "Not at all. It's like opening any other Gate, except easier."

Firal snorted softly. "That tells me nothing."

"I don't know how to explain it. It's like... sharing an impression of where you want to go with the power you want to take you there. With a normal Gate, you'd have to hold that power steady, and that's what makes it hard. This steadies itself."

Curious, she inched closer. "Could I use something like that?"

Daemon cast her a dubious glance and slipped the stone out of sight. "You don't have the best record with Gates."

Firal bit back a retort and turned when she caught the sound of movement behind them. A pair of men leading horses emerged from the edge of the ruins. She stiffened.

"Don't worry," Daemon said as he strode toward them. "They're friends. I requested the horses for our trip." He took the reins of the larger horse and inspected its cargo before he swung into the saddle. The black beast was weighted down with several bags of who-knew-what, and it seemed displeased by the added burden of a rider.

Eyeing its large hooves with distrust, Firal shuffled back. "If you can request horses whenever you want, why do we always have to walk through the ruins?"

Daemon snorted. "Considering how often *you* trip in the ruins, do you really think it a safe place for horses? We have few enough of them as it is. We can't afford to have one break a leg. Mount up, you're wasting time."

Uncertain, she looked the second horse over from nose to tail. "I don't know how to ride."

"A leg up for you, then," one of the men laughed. He laced his fingers together and planted them against his knee to make a foothold. "It's a good many miles to the first inn and you won't want to waste daylight. Don't worry, the horses are plenty tame."

Firal shot Daemon a miserable look. His plain mask seemed even more expressionless than usual. With a resigned sigh, she nestled her foot into the sentry's hands and let him boost her to the saddle. She clambered on, none too gracefully, and blushed as she tried to settle her skirts. Despite her best efforts to recover modesty, her legs were left bare to the knee.

The sentries both averted their eyes, though there was no mistaking the smirks of amusement they wore. "Fair winds, General," one said. "My lady." He offered a brief salute before retreating into the ruins with his companion.

Daemon clicked at his mount and moved ahead. Firal glowered at his back as she wriggled in the saddle, awkward and embarrassed. She slapped the reins against her gelding's neck, but the animal did not move.

"Kick it," Daemon called without looking back.

She nudged the horse's sides with her heels. It eased into a walk and she whispered a silent thank-you toward the sky when it followed the other horse without direction. With the beast in motion, she shifted the reins to one hand, as she saw Daemon doing, and attempted to pull her skirts down over her legs again. "Do you know how far it is to the inn?" There had to be something better suited to riding in her bag, even if it was just a pair of woolen stockings to cover her legs.

"The next inn, or the inn we'll stop at?"

"What? How far are you planning on traveling tonight?" Perhaps that was a better question.

Daemon shrugged. "We won't be stopping tonight. From what I hear, the border villages aren't particularly friendly to those coming out of the west. They'll be even less inclined to offer hospitality to a mage and a..." He trailed off, looking down at his four-fingered, green-scaled hand. He flexed his clawed digits and dropped his hand to his thigh. "Well, in any case, I doubt they'd give us a room. We'll ride until tomorrow evening. We should be near a bigger settlement by then."

Firal pursed her lips, but said nothing more. Afternoon and then night passed in relative silence, and she still did not know what she had gotten herself into.

———

THOUGH THEY STOPPED TO REST FROM TIME TO TIME, THEY DID NOT sleep. They rode through the night, despite the weariness of their mounts. Firal grew weary, too, but she knew complaint would get her nowhere. Daemon seemed unsympathetic to those who lacked his strength and endurance, though she hoped he didn't expect her to match a soldier's physical prowess.

When roofs came into view just before sunset, they paused long enough for Firal to stretch her legs and find a place to relieve herself while Daemon pulled bits and pieces of a disguise from his bags. He bound his clawed feet and jammed them into boots, then pulled up his sleeves and wrapped linen bandages around his hands and arms to prevent any accidental glimpses of his scales.

Firal watched with interest as he pulled on his gloves and drew up the hood of his travel cloak. She had grown used to his scales, but she couldn't help envisioning him in the throne room again, his linen shirt undone to the waist. As unusual as his hands and feet were, she couldn't deny the rest of him looked like any other man—not at all unpleasant, with his smooth, bronzed skin and hardened soldier's body. She cringed and tried to shake the thought out of her head. No, she wouldn't let herself think of him that way, no more than she let herself think of Ran's strong physique or dazzling grins. Daemon belonged to Lumia. The same way that, in her mind, Ran belonged to Kytenia.

"Mount up," Daemon ordered, his voice snapping her out of thought.

She pulled herself up into her gelding's saddle with a great deal of effort and fussed with her skirts. Though she had checked her bags, she hadn't found anything more suitable for riding. She'd have to think of something to do with her skirts the next time they stopped. There was simply no way she would ride into Alwhen with her skirts hitched up around her knees.

The roofs they'd seen proved to be little more than a farmstead, though from what Daemon gleaned from the farm hands, they were not far from the village proper. They urged the reluctant horses back into motion and rode on in relative silence as night came. It wasn't long after nightfall that the glow of the little village came into view on the horizon.

"Where are we?" Firal asked as they drew near.

"Halfway to our destination. Maybe a little more." Daemon spared her a glance, the soft glow of his eyes startling in the depths of his hood. No disguise could hide that haunting light. "We've made good time, but the horses can't go much farther."

"I don't believe I can, either," she sighed beneath her breath as they reached the hard-packed dirt of the village main street.

The place seemed altogether more ramshackle than the Eldani villages Firal had seen, its buildings made of rough wood and thatch. The windows glowed with ruddy candlelight rather than the cool luminescence of mage-light she was used to, and though it was dark outside, people still roamed the streets as if they had important business to tend.

The inn stood along the main street, its doors open to the cooler night air. Raucous laughter spilled through the front room as readily as ale, and barmaids swept between tables with a smile and wink ready for those who looked like they still had change in their purses. Firal peered inside and tried not to make a face. The whole place stank of alcohol and unwashed bodies, burnt food and old dust. But the tables were packed with people, a fair number clad in travel cloaks not dissimilar to their own, and she admitted it bode well for the two of them going unnoticed.

Daemon left their exhausted horses with the stable hand and led her inside. The odor was enough to make her gag. Firal covered her nose and mouth with her sleeve. "This place is vile," she muttered. "And loud. How will we sleep?"

"Quite well, if you're really as tired as you've claimed to be." Daemon tugged his hood farther forward, shadowing his mask. He slipped ahead, to where the innkeeper sat behind a desk, and the noise of the crowd swallowed his voice. The innkeeper regarded him with understandable distrust, but a few extra coins placated the man well enough.

Firal brushed close to Daemon's side. "Have they rooms?"

Instead of answering, he rested a gloved hand on her waist and guided her after the portly innkeeper as he moved up the stairs. The display made her cheeks warm.

"Here you are," the innkeeper said as he thrust open a door and stepped inside to light the single tallow candle on the bedside table. "We begin serving breakfast at dawn. It's an extra coin for the meal if you decide to join us." He gave the two of them a curious look, but raucous voices lifted from the room below and he hurried back to his work.

Firal stared past the guttering flame. "There's only one bed."

Daemon grunted and pushed the door closed. "Is that a problem?"

Again, she envisioned him in the throne room with Lumia, the queen's hands on his belt, his shirt undone to the waist. She gave an awkward shrug. He grunted again as he unfastened his cloak and draped it over the foot of the bed. Unbothered by their arrangements, he sat and began to pry off his boots. Firal knelt at the bedside and reached to help. He said nothing, but seemed grateful.

She set his boots aside and carefully unraveled the wrappings that compressed his feet and covered his claws. He flexed his toes and sighed with relief as he tossed his gloves to the floor. That finished, Firal untied the bandaging from his hand and pushed up his sleeve to unwind it. She paused as the last of the wrappings came away.

"What?" he asked, frown evident in his tone.

Firal nudged his sleeve up a little farther, running her fingertips over the scales that decorated his arm. They ended abruptly at his elbow, the transition from scales to flesh far from smooth. His skin appeared blistered where the scales emerged in uneven patches. A thin, black crust of dried blood flaked away when she ran her fingers over them. She'd known it was an affliction, but she hadn't imagined the discomfort his scales must cause. Her fingertips drew over the rough edges again. "I can make a salve for that."

He hesitated. "I would appreciate that."

"How long have you been this way?" An unpleasant knot tightened in her stomach and she couldn't bring herself to let go of his arm. She'd always assumed him more monster than man. It was strange to see just the reverse.

"Forever." Daemon turned his arm in her grasp, studying the rough emergence of his scales. "Since I was born. They... made me this way. I don't really know how."

"Mages?"

He nodded.

Abruptly, she pulled away. "I'm sorry. It's not my place to touch you like that. I shouldn't have."

"No, it's all right." He shifted, awkward. "If you really can make something for it, I would be in your debt. It itches. Always."

"I just don't see how the mages could do something like that to someone. To you. That they could condemn you to a life of hiding." Firal shook her head. For the first time, she was almost glad she had been expelled from the temple. "I suppose that's why you wear a mask, isn't it?"

"No," he said, a distant look in his violet eyes. "But we'll discuss that another time."

"Of course." She moved to the far side of the wide bed and loosened the bodice of her dress. "I'm sure we'll have plenty of opportunities for that."

Daemon seized one of the blankets as he slid to the floor. He wrapped himself in it and settled on his side.

A twinge of guilt tugged at her heart. "What are you doing?"

"There's only one bed," he replied simply.

And they had shared a bed before, she reminded herself with chagrin. He'd always been perfectly decent; gentlemanly, even, though she hadn't known then that such decency was his nature. How had she ever thought him a beast?

"That isn't fair," she said. "You've paid for the room."

"I'm a soldier. I've slept with worse arrangements than a clean floor."

"Well, I haven't. And what if I get cold?" Firal nestled beneath the remaining blankets and drew them to her chin as she wiggled to the edge of the wide bed.

A soft chuckle escaped him. "You play a dangerous game, mageling."

She expected an argument, but none came. Instead, Daemon pinched out the candle's flame before he settled in beside her. Though he was quiet about it, she still heard the rasp of metal as he removed his mask and laid it on the bedside table, and she wondered at how close they'd become.

AFTER THE DARK MORNINGS IN THE UNDERGROUND, WARM SUNLIGHT on her face felt foreign. Firal woke disoriented and blinked hard against the sunbeams that slanted over her eyes. She nestled back into her pillow with a groan and scrubbed her eyes with the back of her hand.

The inn room didn't feel quite so small in the daylight. All their belongings waited in packs and satchels by the door. Daemon sat on the edge of the bed with his back turned toward her, wrapping his arms in binding once again. "Good morning."

She didn't notice his plain metal mask on the bedside table until he reached for it. The leather ties refused to cooperate with his wrapped fingers, and he made a sound of frustration as they slipped from his grasp.

Firal sat up and reached around him to take the mask from his hands. "Here. Let me." Her fingers brushed over his. As thick as the coarse bandages were, it was no wonder the mask gave him difficulty. She couldn't help but think he should have donned the mask first.

He tilted his hand and let the mask slip from his grasp. It weighed heavy in her palm and she curled her fingers around it, exploring the soft buckskin that lined the back. She'd never given the mask's comfort much thought, but now that she did, the lining made sense. Leaning against his back, she lifted the mask into place and arranged the thin straps above his ears. "There?"

His head tilted forward to maneuver it into a comfortable position. "There."

She tugged the straps into a tight knot and let her fingers slip through his hair to ensure it wouldn't tangle on the straps. Then she pushed herself off the bed and smoothed the skirts of her rumpled dress. "You don't have to wear that around me, you know." Across the room, a tray of food caught her eye. From the look of it, Daemon had already taken his share. "I wouldn't think differently of you for how you look."

"Wouldn't you?" he mused. "It would be strange, in any case. I've grown so used to wearing it, I'd feel naked without it."

She wrinkled her nose but said nothing as she selected a coarse piece of buttered bread.

The more she traveled, the more she wondered if inns served anything other than tough bread accompanied by butter, cheese, and cold meats from the night before. As if reading her thoughts, Daemon slipped from the edge of the bed and crossed to their belongings. He pulled an apple from a sack and tossed it in her direction. She opened her hands to catch it, but it bounced from her fingertips and she fumbled to keep it from dropping it.

"We'll reach Alwhen this evening," Daemon said as he settled on the floor. His feet were already bound with linen strips. He pulled on his boots with some difficulty. "Lumia sent word ahead, so Relythes should be expecting us."

Firal studied the apple in her hands. The fruit was not unusual; a number of foreign fruit-bearing trees flourished on the island, brought over from the mainland in decades past. She simply did not want to look at him as she spoke. "I still don't understand why I'm going. I don't know what I'm supposed to do."

"You're a mage," he said, as if that explained everything. She stared at him, and he blinked before he went on. "Mages move freely between the two halves of the island. Both sides recognize them as an asset, but Kifel and Relythes both have court mages who serve them exclusively. Lumia agreed it was best to bring you as one of her emissaries, because it will give the impression we're already on equal terms."

She bristled. "So I'm just another pawn? A tool to be used?"

A soft flicker of light stirred in his eyes. "You're also good company."

"Don't change the subject," she snapped.

The light faded. "Everyone likes to pretend there are two kinds of people—the ones who play the game, and the ones who get played. But we're all pawns."

The lack of denial hurt. She turned away. "And you think you can use me freely."

"No. I think I can trust you for help." Daemon drew up his knees and rested his elbows against them. His feet looked odd in their oversized boots. Then again, perhaps it was just odd to see him with footwear at all. "But I also thought you understood why I would want you to accompany me. I apologize. It seems I was mistaken."

Despite the sincerity in his voice, the words prickled. If she'd stopped to think about it, she might have realized why he wanted her to accompany him. Instead, she'd allowed herself to be distracted. And by what? Whatever his relationship with Lumia was, it was none of her concern. At least, not on a personal level. Professionally—that was another matter. "And who am I here to represent, then? Lumia? Or you?"

His violet eyes darkened behind his mask. "What makes you ask?"

She lowered her eyes and downed as much of the cold and near-flavorless meal as she could. She'd save that apple for later. "I spoke with one of your men. Colonel Achos."

Daemon snorted. "Tren's no man of mine. And as far as I know, he's no colonel."

"Regardless of his rank, he sounded as if he's concerned about your ambitions," Firal said slowly. "I must admit, I didn't realize you had such aggressive plans."

"Aggressive isn't the term I would use," Daemon said. "I don't work the way Lumia does. I see no reason we can't work things out through diplomacy, but we'll hear what Relythes has to say tonight. Come. I've already asked the stablehands to ready the horses." He stood and gathered their belongings from the floor.

Firal glanced around their room again. There was no washbasin. She sucked the butter and crumbs from her fingers instead. "Very well. But we'd best charge that Gate-stone before the trip back home. I don't think my backside can handle a return trip on horseback."

He grunted in response.

Their horses were saddled and waiting when they reached the stables. Daemon fastened their packs behind the saddles and checked the straps twice before he helped Firal onto her mount. The trip held little conversation, though they took turns channeling energy into the Gate-stone after Daemon showed her how. She was amused to see him teaching her for a change, but she'd sensed a shift in his demeanor. He'd grown cold and formal, clearly braced for political chicanery. Despite the moment of comfort they'd shared when she helped with his mask, she held humor at bay and accepted his instruction without comment.

Daemon predicted a fully-charged Gate-stone would open at least a half dozen portals before it had to be replenished. Opening them, he claimed, was what drained its power. The stone could hold a Gate open indefinitely—which Firal supposed was why they were used in the creation of anchored, permanent Gates. She knew woefully little of the artifacts and for a moment, she grieved the loss of the information the temple once held at her fingertips. Yet the feeling was short lived. Even had she been allowed back into the temple, the library no longer existed. What knowledge she gleaned of Gate-stones would have to come from Daemon—and her own experiences.

Recharging the stone proved a challenge. Firal's healing affinity meant she could only draw power from herself or Daemon, and life was a delicate element. Daemon fared better, though now that she thought of it, she didn't know what he drew from. They had never discussed his affinity and it had yet to matter in their lessons, which had revolved around skills all mages were required to learn. Curiosity prickled at her, and Firal watched every time Daemon took the stone.

As they rode through villages and farms, the humming life energy of nearby people gave her more to tap into, but Daemon seemed to draw from everything at once. She tried to open her senses, to feel for the flows of magic that would reveal his source of power.

The air rippled with the energy he funneled into the stone, flows streaming from the wind, the earth underfoot, even the sun. She couldn't help but marvel, despite the uneasy chill his display of power gave her. A mage with no affinity was unheard of. Even the Archmage was bound, limited by the energies she could control. If Daemon really was able to draw on everything around him, his strength would be unmatched. The memory of tying her energies to his in order to open a Gate together stirred in her mind, and her skin rose in gooseflesh.

She'd assumed it was the power of the Gate that had burned through her, so white-hot she thought she'd be seared away. But what if it had been him?

Firal was now certain it was best to give him knowledge and control. He outstripped her in raw power, but she won in matters of skill. Beneath her guidance, there was no chance of his power sources coming unmade.

When at last they reached the eastern capital, a ruddy tint colored the sky. They stopped some distance from the palace—a great, squat building that lacked all grace. Daemon left his horse with Firal on the main street and disappeared between two buildings. When he returned, he had changed into the finery he'd brought in his bags. He made an imposing figure in the silver-embroidered blue coat he pulled on, though Firal frowned at the choice of color.

Though the Underlings had no color or standard, Lumia favored red and black. It was an odd coincidence Firal's ballgown sported those colors. Yet Daemon chose to represent Lumia's people while wearing the colors of the Eldani king. The thought put an odd tingle in the back of her head and she shook it loose as he pushed her bag into her arms with orders to change.

Firal blinked at her belongings twice before he directed her toward the stable he'd used. Unwilling to prolong their travel, she crept into an empty stall and tried not to sneeze. Grateful as she was to shed her dusty travel wear, she couldn't help but feel odd putting on her best finery in a stable. She supposed she ought to be grateful she had somewhere to change at all. Straw clung to the hem of her skirt and her discarded clothing. Unsure what else to do, she turned her worn clothing inside out and stuffed it into her bag before she rejoined Daemon in the street. He gave her little more than a cursory glance, nodding his approval as he helped her back onto her mount. Together, they continued to the palace in the same sullen silence that had dominated the day.

The full skirts of her ballgown did a better job of covering her legs than her work dress, and Firal allowed herself to relax. She raked her fingers through her hair to put it into some semblance of order while they rode, and by the time they reached the front of the palace, she had herself mostly presentable.

The portcullis was raised, allowing anyone in and out of the courtyard. Clearly, Relythes wasn't a king who worried about enemies infiltrating his castle.

"Different sort of world, out here," Daemon murmured, as if in answer to her thoughts.

Peasant men and women in the courtyard paid them little mind as they rode through and the front doors of the palace came into sight. The doors stood open to the pleasant day, guards lounging against the walls beside them. One or two of the men tensed at their approach. They stood straighter and their hands went to their sword hilts, though the rest of the guards watched in disinterest.

Daemon dismounted his horse in front of them. "I trust King Relythes is still in his receiving hall?" The words rolled off his tongue with a note of boredom.

"Aye, that he is," the nearer guard replied, eyeing Daemon dubiously. "You are... of the Underlings? His Majesty is expecting you." He took the reins of both horses. Another man appeared at Firal's side, offering a hand to help her down. She gladly accepted.

"Good. See that our animals are brushed and fed. We expect them to be well refreshed when we return." Daemon carried the lordly attitude to perfection, down to the careless way he flicked a square copper coin to one of the men. He slipped past the rest of the guards and into the castle without so much as another word, adjusting his collar on the way. Firal brushed a wisp of straw from her skirts and followed.

Compared to the soaring palace of Ilmenhith, Firal found Alwhen's palace clumsy and cramped. Worse, the air inside was thick with the sour smell of wine and ale, and clogged with the smutty haze of torch and tobacco smoke. Though the sting in her lungs put tears in her eyes, she only let out a single cough.

A narrow fire pit ran the length of the hall. Long tables framed it, all but overflowing with people attending the daily feast. Commoners and nobles alike sat rubbing elbows and not seeming to notice the difference in their rank. If not for the crown upon his head, Firal might not have noticed Relythes at the center of the table at the far end. The throne on the dais behind him stood empty.

Despite the searing heat of the fire within the crowded room, Relythes wore a long-sleeved vermillion coat, its collar and cuffs trimmed with tawny fur. He wasn't at all like Kifel in appearance or mannerism, though Firal wasn't sure why she expected him to be. Wine sloshed from his goblet as he slapped someone on the back and roared with laughter.

"Relythes," Daemon said in greeting, his tone less cordial, less formal than it should have been.

The king eyed him over the rim of his goblet, mirth fading from his face. "Never spoken to a ruler before, have you, boy?" His words were gruff, but not quite angry. He glanced between the two of them before his gaze settled on Daemon's mask. "Who are you supposed to be, the new court jester? I've enough entertainment already."

"I'd have to agree. Your palace proves quite the spectacle. I am Daemon, general to Lumia, queen of the ruin-folk. The Underlings, as you call us. This is my court mage." He gestured to Firal. She dipped in a curtsy, unsure whether or not she was expected to address him. Relythes spoke before she had a chance.

"I don't care who she is, boy, and I don't care who you are. I don't like the tone your lady used in writing to me, and as a result, I don't much like you." The human king's eyes narrowed. He sipped from his goblet without looking away or even so much as blinking. "What makes you think I'd parcel off some bit of my land to a band of troublemakers? Your lady, *Queen* Lumia as she calls herself," he snorted as if it were some sort of joke, "clearly intends to found her own nation right there on my border. You don't plan to pay taxes, you don't plan to respect my authority, you won't even show your face in my court! Why should I sell you any of my land?"

"Are you really so concerned about having a small group of weary people at the edge of your territory?" Daemon kept his tone cool, though Firal caught the way his shoulders stiffened. "The land we're most interested in is that which borders the Kirban Ruins and runs south to the coast. Your people are too superstitious to set foot anywhere near the ruins, even to graze livestock. Wouldn't it be wiser to sell it and profit? To use us as a buffer between you and Kifelethelas? I know Lumia stated what she is willing to pay."

Relythes stared at him for a long moment. He put down his drink. "If it's the ruins you're so interested in, why bring this bid to me instead of the Eldani king?"

Daemon hesitated.

"Brant's bark, boy, take off that bloody mask!" the king snapped. "I refuse to deal with a man whose features I can't even see."

"Then we shall speak in private," Daemon said. "Send away your visitors. My mage will wait outside."

Firal's brows shot up. She hadn't traveled all that distance alongside him just to be sent away. But Daemon gave her a sidewise glance, and the shadowed look in his normally vivid eyes made her bite her tongue.

"Fine," Relythes said. "They will wait in the courtyard. This had better be worth my while." He raised his hands and clapped twice to make it an official command.

People rose from the tables and bowed, one at a time. The crowd swelled like a rising tide before the tangle of people separated and those gathered made their way to the door. Only Firal lingered.

"Go," Daemon ordered.

She bit her lip and bowed, too. "I will be waiting in the courtyard, my lord," she said, careful to layer her tone with respect. Her feet felt like lead and a strange sensation prickled between her shoulder blades, but she crept toward the door. The last of the revelers disappeared as she glanced back and caught one last glimpse of Daemon from behind. He reached for his mask and she tore her eyes away.

"You?" Relythes breathed, almost in disbelief. "Well now, that does change things."

Firal forced herself to go on without looking again, leaving the two men to their business.

Most of the county hall's inhabitants now stood in the courtyard, uncertain of what to do with themselves. Several were clearly drunk, unable to remain on their feet. Firal gave them a wide berth as she searched for somewhere to sit. It didn't take long to locate a stone bench beneath a well-pruned tree, and she settled on it with a sigh. The sound of her name, spoken as a question behind her, made her jump.

"It is you! Brant's mercy, child, what are you doing in a place like this? It's been weeks, I would have thought you'd be settled safely in Ilmenhith by now!"

Firal's heart leaped at the warmth in the familiar voice and she spun to face her mentor. "Master Nondar!" The sight of the elderly mage leaning on his cane made tears brim in her eyes. Unable to restrain herself, she darted forward and flung her arms around the Master's shoulders. "I thought I'd never see you again!"

He stroked her hair with a gnarled hand. "And if all was right in the world, you wouldn't have."

Firal held tight to his white robes, but leaned back to look him in the eye. "What are you doing in Alwhen? Shouldn't you be home, helping rebuild the temple?"

Nondar's face darkened. "Much has happened since you were sent away, child. Far too much. The Archmage has abandoned the temple for ruined. All of the mages stationed in Kirban are now in Alwhen."

"What?" She swiped tears from her eyes with the back of her hand. "Why? Why here? Surely one of the chapter houses in Ilmenhith—"

"The temple no longer has any association with Ilmenhith," Nondar interrupted, his frosty eyes narrowing until they all but vanished among wrinkles. The grim set of his mouth said far more than words. "The Archmage has seceded from King Kifelethelas's rule. She had us abandon Kirban Temple and she acts now as adviser to Relythes."

"And what of the Masters?" Firal asked, wiping her eyes again. "Do they agree with this?"

He shook his head. "I cannot speak for the other Masters, or for any of the mages. I cannot begin to speculate how they feel about this action."

"How do you feel?"

He eyed her. "Glad you are safe, my child. That is all I can say."

"But there are mages all across the island! Surely the Archmage hasn't called them all? Without the mages, Kifel's armies will—" She stopped short and the color drained from her face. Kings don't live forever, Daemon said in the bath. Was this what he meant? A collapse of the western kingdom? Her stomach sank. Had he known?

"I know, child," Nondar murmured. "I am as concerned as you. But I cannot do much on my own. I have taken what measures I can. But you mustn't speak of this matter, should you encounter other mages."

"Who's on your side?" she asked quietly. "Is anyone?"

"It would be safer if we not discuss this." He cast a wary glance to the people who lingered in the courtyard. "All will come together in time, rest assured of that."

"Firal."

The sound of her name made her jump again. She turned toward Daemon half in surprise, half in disappointment, then gave Nondar an apologetic glance. "I have to go."

The old Master looked between the two of them, his brow furrowed and his face clouded with something that wasn't quite worry. "Who is this?" he asked, though the tone of the question implied he already knew.

"Business here is done." Daemon's eyes weighed on the wizened mage with none of their normal expressiveness.

Firal smoothed her skirts as she faced Daemon. "Did he agree?"

"We will discuss that on the way home," he replied.

Nondar frowned, the lines of his face deep with concern. "So this is the path you've chosen."

Firal's cheeks reddened, though she wasn't certain whether Nondar had spoken to her or to Daemon. Unable to bring herself to look at the Master mage again, she clenched her hands to fists and moved to her place at Daemon's side. He rested a clawed hand against her back and guided her toward the gates, where their horses waited.

As they retreated, she felt the weight of Nondar's stare like a burden on her shoulders.

CELEBRATIONS

"THAT IS ENOUGH!" NONDAR ROARED. THE THUNDER OF HIS VOICE brought the room to silence and the other Masters stared at him in a mix of surprise and shame. He shook his head and eased back into his chair. Mages, all of them, with hundreds of years behind them. Yet they still managed to squabble and fuss like children.

For the dozenth time, he checked the ward he'd erected around their meeting room. It stood secure, shielding them from spying eyes and listening ears, keeping even their heated shouting silenced beyond the room's four walls.

Unsurprisingly, Anaide was the one to break the silence. "Would you assume the position yourself, then?" she asked, tone as venomous as the look on her face.

"I would have us refrain from wasting our breath discussing the matter now." Nondar rested his arms on the edge of the table. "We haven't even parted from the temple yet, and you already seek to fragment us more."

"Then how would you see us led?" A younger Master, a woman Nondar didn't know, mimicked Anaide's tone.

"By council," Nondar said. "None of us should lead

absolutely. We would do best without an Archmage. Each Master's word should hold equal weight."

The room fell silent again, but this time it was with an air of agreement. Nondar allowed himself some slight relief. The greater his burden grew, the more often he had to remind himself to unclench his jaw and let tension seep from his shoulders.

"And what of the problem of the king's son?" Edagan asked, the question adding another weight to Nondar's mind. She leveled her eyes with his, her expression stony. "After all, we've never stripped a mage of Master rank before. We all know he wasn't ready. He is a tool to her, nothing more. A way to control Kifel."

"He is more ready than you may think." Nondar smiled grimly. "Envesi cannot use him. She cannot control him, so how would she use him?"

"Unless his allegiance lies with his father, he is a threat to our cause," Anaide argued. "Or do you claim to know his loyalties?"

Nondar hesitated, his gaze drifting from the table.

"Yes or no, half-blood," Edagan said. "It isn't a hard question."

"But the question assumes there are only two sides contending in the matter." He stared at the wall beyond his two peers and the slew of unfamiliar mages they'd brought with them. "He does not oppose his father, but he doesn't oppose Relythes, either. However, it isn't hard to see his resentment toward the Archmage. That is all that concerns us."

"The enemy of our enemy is not always a friend," Anaide murmured.

"And a friend is not always enemies with our foe." Nondar tried to sound indifferent. "Regardless, the boy is the least of our concerns now. If he takes a side, it will surely be at the behest of the mageling we lost to Lumia's faction. That woman may think she operates in secrecy, but she hasn't been forgotten. Her attempts to manipulate events do not go unnoticed."

"That woman should have been silenced by the temple a long time ago," Anaide said, rubbing her temples. "The abominations she performs with her magic never should have been allowed."

"And who are we to speak of abominations?" Edagan laughed bitterly, rising from her chair. "Had we not assisted Envesi at the very beginning, none of this would have happened. I agree with Nondar in that we should be led by council, at least until the dust settles, and that a faster split is better. I've had enough for today. I will organize my students and be ready for the Gate at moon's zenith. I suggest all of you organize your mages, as well." She cast a meaningful eye over the Masters present. Her gaze lingered on Nondar and then shifted to Anaide, and she sniffed in displeasure before she left.

Nondar mulled over her suggestion and the number of mages who answered to him. As Masters of their Houses of affinity, Nondar, Anaide, and Edagan held more rank than the other white-clad mages in the room, but only under Envesi's rule. It was hard to predict how power would shift among them once they split from the temple. Nondar suspected each affinity would still need to be led by an individual. A council was best for the mages as a whole, but how could a mage with an earth affinity speak for matters of healing? The Houses would have to remain self-governing, even beneath a council.

"Edagan is right," Nondar said, checking the wards yet again as the door closed at the woman's heels. "We should be preparing. All of you, organize what mages and magelings you know can be trusted. Have them ready themselves. As planned, we depart at moon's zenith tonight, and not a moment later."

There was a murmur of assent among the gathered Masters, and he released the wards as they left. He did not look to see when Anaide excused herself from his company, unwilling to subject himself to the glowers he expected she threw his way. He did not need to borrow trouble; there would be plenty after the fracture. The mages would be looking to the three of them—Anaide, Edagan, and himself—for guidance, and he did not look forward to determining who among them was best suited to give it. But he was given little time to brood over it, as a knock sounded at the door only moments after the last of the Masters took their leave.

"Excuse me, Master," Rikka said, peeking into the room. "I don't mean to interrupt, but I was hoping to speak to you. It's about my family in Ilmenhith."

Nondar waved the mageling girl in. "Of course, child. Your needs are never an interruption." He set new wards in place as Rikka stepped into the now-quiet meeting hall and shut the door. It was fortunate the girl really did have family in Ilmenhith. Aside from the phrase being an ideal code, the existence of her family meant the frequent letters she received from the capital were unlikely to raise suspicion.

"So, tell me," Nondar said. "What did today's letter say?"

He sensed her prodding at the wards before she spoke. Her caution pleased him, but he'd woven them carefully, creating a bubble around the two of them that shrank as she came closer. Even aware of its presence, she kept her voice low.

"I didn't read it yet. I wasn't certain it was my place to open it." Rikka pulled back a chair and settled beside him at the table. She held out the folded letter, the wax seal on its surface intact.

"Of course it's your place." It had been her place since he'd caught her in the dovecote, the night the Archmage had announced the temple's secession. Rikka and her friends had begged forgiveness, but Nondar had been there for the same reason, a message for the king in his hand. "You have been an excellent confidant and messenger throughout this ordeal. We trust you, though I appreciate your concern for secrecy." He turned over the letter and broke its seal. It hadn't been tampered with, the paper's folds still as crisp as when the king's fingers pressed it.

"Do you still mean for us to leave the... the temple tonight, Master?" Rikka faltered over the words, though he couldn't blame her. They had not determined what to call themselves now that the physical temple had been left behind, a ruined husk of its former glory. There were times he felt their congregation was little more than a husk, itself.

"Yes, and you'd do well to be prepared for it. I trust you and your friends will be ready?" He did not look her way again, his mage-blue eyes skimming the simple letter. It was little more than a quick note, but its contents were a relief. The chapter house in Ilmenhith was ready to receive them, Kifel's loyal court mages having made all preparations. It would be easy to rebuild there.

"We are ready now, Master." Rikka clasped her hands in her lap. "Though I did have a question."

"Ask away, child. We mean to keep no secrets from the mages who come with us. We are not like the Archmage in that respect."

She studied his face for a long moment before she spoke. "What will happen to mages like Firal? Those that left the temple or were sent away? Will they be welcomed back, or will they still be exiled from both halves of the temple?"

Nondar pursed his lips. They'd not discussed the possibility of rogue mages returning after the fracture, and he was reluctant to give an answer that might be taken as committal. "Their choices are their own," he said slowly, testing the words. "We will address each situation as it arises, but no one can or will summon them back to the flock. If they are happier as free mages, living without bonds to the temple, then so be it."

Rikka seemed satisfied by the answer, or at least, she did not press the matter. But she did lean against the table, wringing her hands. "I'm worried about how many mages are going with us, too. I know so few of them, and even some of the Masters are people I've hardly seen before. How are we to know if we can trust them?"

"I would not worry about that, my child. They risk much in being a part of our rebellion, especially the Masters. If they did not want to be a part of us, they would not be moving with us."

He offered a soothing smile and waved a hand. "Now, get on, then. I shall see you tonight when the Gate is opened. Until then, it's best for you to carry on with your duties. The longer you are here with me, the more likely it is that something will be noticed."

"Yes, Master." She gave a stiff curtsy as she rose from her chair and smoothed skirts on her way out of the room.

Nondar turned over the letter in his hands until the door closed behind her. Alone, he allowed himself to frown. The capital was ready to receive them, perhaps, but there were still many issues to be resolved. It was well and good that the magelings thought they would steal away in secrecy, but a part of him felt shamed that would not be the case. He wore a brave face for the magelings, but inwardly, he thought of the onslaught they were sure to face and prayed they had enough Masters to hold the barrier.

TENSE, FIRAL CLUTCHED AT THE POMMEL OF HER SADDLE AS THE Gate opened. Though she had passed through Gates only a small number of times, the sensation had been unique enough that it embedded itself in her memory and stirred every time she stood before one of the portals. Despite knowing the Gate-stone made this one different, she couldn't help that instinct. Still, a sense of wonder stole through her when they crossed the Gate without so much as a tingle.

Their ride through Alwhen had been quiet, the city's people uninterested in more travelers. Solemn and silent, Daemon's sour mood had kept Firal quiet, too. Not far past the city's edge, he had reached for the Gate-stone, signaling the end of their journey.

The outermost walls of the ruins now sprawled ahead of them, so similar to those just outside the temple that for a moment, homesickness stirred in her chest. The Gate slid closed behind them without a sound. Daemon didn't seem to notice, but Firal craned her neck to look over her shoulder.

"I'd still like to know how that works," she murmured. "It stores so much energy for such a small thing, but it's so much more stable than any energy source I've ever seen."

"If it was something that easy to explain or understand, the temple mages probably would have made more of them." Daemon rolled the Gate-stone in the palm of his hand before he put it in his pocket. "As it is, I don't know that the mages themselves understand how they work. Some artifacts the mages possess came from the mainland. Who knows how old they are."

Firal nodded thoughtfully. She had read about some of the temple's artifacts and was inclined to agree. She'd never encountered the Gate-stones in the books she'd read, but many of the artifacts the temple held were ancient. Many struck Firal as useless trinkets, too, but perhaps she would have thought the same of a Gate-stone if she'd come across it and not realized what it could do. Which planted a new question in her mind. Daemon had not explained how the stone had come into his possession, or how he recognized what it could do. Her worries churned up anew.

"Come." Daemon said as he started into the ruins. "We have to return the horses."

Unlike the corridors nearest the temple, this part of the labyrinth was clean and well-maintained, but the twisting path was narrower. The horses couldn't walk side by side, so she let her mount follow a few paces behind. Perched in the saddle, she could just see over the tops of the crumbling walls. The maze sprawled to the horizon. For the first time, she realized how futile it was to try and make a map.

"You have questions," Daemon said softly.

The observation brought her up short. She couldn't refute it; her mind had been turning since they parted ways in the king's receiving hall. "Yes."

"You're allowed to ask."

A thousand questions burned on her tongue, but she tempered her desire to unleash them all. "Asking just doesn't guarantee an answer."

"No," he agreed. Yet the calm way he voiced the single word seemed amicable, almost inviting. Perhaps this was what she'd hoped for—a sign of trust.

Firal stifled the questions that first came to mind and dug for something less intrusive. "How long were you at the temple? You seem to know a lot about it."

"I was born there. Spent the first few years of my life there. They kept me close for study. I was useful and interesting, until they realized they couldn't fix me."

"When you were born, were you...?" She trailed off, unable to finish.

"Normal?" He flexed his fingers, his horse's reins between them. He still wore his gloves, hiding the strange, vivid green scales she'd grown accustomed to. "I've never been that."

Firal shook her head. "I lived in the temple my whole life. I never saw you there."

"Maybe you just didn't know what you were looking for."

Maybe she didn't. The mystery of what hid behind his mask still needled at her. Relythes had recognized him. As her jumbled thoughts drew together, a painted image prickled at the back of her mind, etched into her memory by the boy-child's vibrant eyes.

"You're him, aren't you?" The words tumbled free before she could stop them.

Daemon stopped his horse and turned his head until she saw just a sliver of his mask. One violet eye watched her, its luminescence eerie in the daylight.

She swallowed and went on. "The boy in the painting, the one in Kifel's palace. The child in the stories. The child he lost. That's you, isn't it?"

He nudged his horse forward again.

A thread of ice ran through her and she bumped her heels against her mount's sides, desperate to get closer. "Daemon?"

"You don't know as much as you think," he murmured.

She steeled her resolve. "Take off your mask."

"Not now."

"Why? Because the king's scouts would recognize you?" Her heart thundered in her chest, her pulse loud in her ears. "Is that what you wanted to speak to me about the other day?"

"Not now," he repeated, sharper.

They rounded a corner into a circular room with a fire pit in the middle. The handful of men crouched around it all but leaped to their feet. A few tents stood at the edges of the space, several horses grazing contentedly on the thick grasses between them.

Firal's racing heart quieted as it sank. The last time she'd heard Daemon angry had been their confrontation after the temple burned, what now seemed an eternity ago. The heat in his voice now left her uncomfortably cold.

One of the soldiers—sentries, Firal realized, as she recognized one of the men who had brought the horses before—came to take their mounts. "News?" the man asked with hope clear on his face.

"News," Daemon agreed. He swung down from his horse and cast a look in Firal's direction. One of the other men hurried to help her down. "I trust Core is waiting to hear it?"

"Yes, sir. Half the city will be gathered in the great hall as soon as you get there, I'm sure."

Firal smoothed her skirts as she reached the ground, murmuring thanks to the soldier who aided her dismount. Out of the corner of her eye, she caught the shadowed glance Daemon sent her. She raised a brow in response.

"Make sure the horses are seen to," Daemon said as he removed his bags from the saddle. He jerked his head in the direction he was headed, indication Firal should follow.

The soldier beside her offered her bags. She snatched them

from his hands and chased Daemon around a corner. "Are you really going to make these men wait to hear what happened?"

He shrugged. "I'm making you wait, aren't I?"

"They won't be able to reach Core before we do," she said. "They won't be there to hear the announcement."

"Word travels. They're sending word to Core that we're coming. Their messenger will carry word back."

She pursed her lips, though she chose not to press any further. Instead, she watched his back and walked, and wondered at all the pieces that began to fit together.

He wouldn't answer her question. That, in itself, told her enough. The history between the temple and the royal family was murky, bathed in secrecy and protected by the way the Masters treated it as taboo. But the king had commissioned the temple for *something,* and as she walked a handful of paces behind Daemon, she began to suspect what.

They'd always emphasized the strength of mages in numbers and pushed to train as many as possible, though few bore the power necessary to qualify for complete training. The Masters bore a mission, a responsibility to the king, and while no one was allowed to speak of it, the quiet grudge between King Kifel and the Archmage had always been palpable.

Firal shifted her bag to keep it from sliding off her shoulder. Daemon blamed the mages. They'd made him into what he was, then failed to restore him to what he'd been. Try as she might, she couldn't recall the hands and feet of the boy in the painting in Ilmenhith. The child in the image had been tucked between his parents, where the folds of his father's cape and his mother's skirt hid his limbs.

And oh, his *mother.* Her ice-blue eyes burned in Firal's memory. Mage-blue, she'd been sure of it. Yet she hadn't stopped to consider what that meant. Mages were warned against practicing their craft while pregnant; it was a lesson all magelings were taught early. An unborn child was fragile, its delicate strands of life too easily disrupted by the flow of power through its mother's body. She had assumed the risk was miscarriage. What if it was corruption, instead?

Firal rubbed her temples as she tried to put her thoughts in order. So many things she'd been taught seemed trivial until this moment. Now, she questioned everything.

Despite the Gate-stone in his hand, Daemon chose to walk most of the distance back to the heart of the ruins. Firal didn't argue, nor did she try to converse. Tangled possibilities spun in her head and she struggled to catch and unravel them. The solid ground beneath her feet offered needed reassurance and stability. And the exercise helped her stiff legs and aching backside. A single night in an inn wasn't enough to let her recover from the long ride. After a good night's sleep, perhaps the puzzle wouldn't be so difficult.

The sun hung low in the sky by the time Daemon pulled the Gate-stone out for one last use. "Most of Core's people will be gathered before the throne by now," he said, answering her unspoken question.

She frowned. "Does Lumia know what news you bring?" Though she hadn't seen him slip any notes to the sentry when he'd passed over his horse's reins, she wouldn't discount the possibility.

"She'll know soon enough." He led her through the portal and into the familiar clearing surrounding the spiral path that led down into Core.

The underground city's marketplace was strangely quiet, no one present but the merchants who wouldn't leave their stalls. Firal watched them as she passed. As they walked, Daemon once again adopted the stance and air he'd carried when they stood before Relythes. It reminded her of the first time she'd seen him display such elegance, leading her through dance steps in the king's ballroom. She'd wondered at his grace then. Now, she couldn't believe she'd missed the obvious air of nobility he'd tried to hide. Seeing it now cemented what she was already sure she knew, and with that certainty came a hint of shame.

He'd treated her as an equal since her arrival in Core, but they'd never been on the same footing at all.

She followed him through winding tunnels into hallways she recognized, the pathway packed with people who shuffled to make room for the two of them to pass. They bowed to Daemon and offered her respectful nods. Firal nodded back and held her skirts close so they wouldn't be stepped on.

Ahead, the din of voices flooded the great hall. People filled the vast room from wall to wall, perched atop the unlit iron braziers and held back tapestries that hid more corridors, where yet more people waited for the announcement to come. The crowd stepped aside for Daemon, letting him move toward the throne where Lumia waited. But the crowds closed up behind him, swallowing Firal and trapping her in the crush of bodies as he swept forward.

"Daemon!" she called. The rising roar of the crowd drowned her small voice. She strained on tiptoe to see him. He came into sight again when he stepped onto the throne's dais to stand beside Lumia.

The Underling queen's face twisted with displeasure and she obscured her mouth with her fingers, hiding her lips to match the way the crowd hid her words. Daemon whispered something back before he turned to face the great hall. A hush swept over the room.

"Children of Elenhiise!" His voice was strong and clear, carrying throughout the room and silencing the last murmurs of those gathered. He drew himself up as Lumia reclined in her throne. He was a tall man, and the way he stood with his chin held high made him look like he, rather than Lumia, was leader. Firal rubbed her arms as if to ward off a chill.

"The years you've spent underground have been harrowing. The struggle for survival reaches back farther than anyone here has lived." His luminescent eyes skimmed the faces before him as he continued. "But those struggles will end. It will not be an overnight process. It may take years. It may not happen in your lifetime. But they *will* end, and the time for change is now. Tonight you may sleep in caves, but tomorrow, a treaty shall be signed. With it, we regain our right to the surface."

The sound that rolled through the crowd was an unsettling mix of cheers and startled murmurs, excited faces paired with just as many thoughtful frowns. Firal's stomach twisted at the idea of dissent. She folded her arms tight across her chest and swallowed against worry as Daemon went on.

"This is the first of many strides we must take to reclaim what is rightfully ours, but it begins our journey. The peace treaty with King Relythes has already been drawn, and with it, a contract to buy a parcel of land bordering the eastern ruins. These agreements only await confirmation from Her Majesty, Lumia of the people who shall no longer be called Underlings."

Snorting a laugh, Lumia rested an elbow on the arm of her throne and propped her chin on her fist. "What, then, shall we be called? Ruin-folk? The ruins do not yet belong to us." The biting edge in her words drove the room to dead silence.

"Why should we name ourselves anything?" Daemon let his gaze rove over the great hall. "We are people like any others on this island. Children of Elenhiise, people of the earth and sea and sky. Why should we be made to distinguish ourselves?"

Lumia's crystalline blue eyes weighed on him for a moment before she smiled, though a shadow ghosted over her features. "So those who have wronged us know who seeks revenge. Tomorrow, we take back the edge of our ruins from Relythes. Afterward, we will take back the rest from Kifel. But for now..." She rose from her throne and spread her arms wide. "Let us revel in what we have accomplished. We have cast off the shackles of the surface. Our freedom begins now!"

This time, the people roared with enthusiasm. The excitement rolled through the crowd like a wave as people spilled through the doors in a rush to spread the news.

Firal hugged herself and let the movement of the people carry her; it was easier than fighting to stay in one place. More than once, she looked over her shoulder in vain hope of catching a glimpse of Daemon. Instead, she saw the faces of hundreds of strangers, and not everyone glowed.

Lumia herself did not appear thrilled, though the queen's somber face grew harder and harder to see as the throng pushed Firal to the door.

The news was unsettling. Though the greater response was clearly joy, not everyone shared in the delight of their newfound freedom. Stormy faces dotted the crowd and arguments broke out beneath the sound of celebration. Firal couldn't blame them. Core had a distinct culture, a way of life that still seemed odd after her lifetime on the island's surface. The underground city was calm, placid, warm. There was structure. Everyone knew their place and what was demanded of them, and the benevolence she saw toward children and the infirm was heartwarming after the cold mentality at the temple, where everyone was disposable. It hurt to be cast aside. Leaving Core would mean an upheaval of their traditions.

There were other issues with leaving the underground, besides. As Core's newfound healer, she was not certain all the city's inhabitants were equipped to be moved. Re-integration with the surface meant exposure to unfamiliar illness, and Core's inhabitants had been all but isolated. Though she was confident in her healing skills, she was only one mage. She could not hope to contain an outbreak of disease on her own. Had she been given time to consider such difficulties, she could have discussed it with Daemon before all this. Instead, she'd been caught up in her own selfish concerns and her fears of becoming entangled in someone else's web.

The crowds spilled into the wide marketplace cavern and thinned enough that it became bearable to walk among them. The distant sound of music already flowed from the spiral pathway that led to the heart of the ruins. Firal turned toward it, the pulse of the drums beckoning her as it did so many others.

She climbed to the clearing where the herb garden grew, and the rhythm hummed in her bones.

Bonfires flared to life all around the mouth of the inverted tower. Embers twirled and shimmered in the air over the heads of those who gathered to celebrate, the glittering light reminiscent of stars. Musicians perched beside the growing flames, the earthy sounds of their instruments joined by dozens of cheerful voices in an unfamiliar folk song.

The excitement in the air didn't touch her. Instead, the cadence of the drums turned her heartbeat into an uneasy rhythm and put a nervous flutter in her throat. Firal's feet carried her toward the open space at the far end of the herb garden she'd come to love, toward the fire that blazed beneath the serpent's-tongue trees. It was quieter there. People circled the fire in graceful dances and Firal watched their steps until she grew dizzy. She eased herself to the grass a few paces away from the dancers and their fire, and watched instead as women wove the white tree blossoms into their hair. The sight reminded her of the flower left to dry between the pages of her herbal, the way Daemon had poked it into her hair with gentle claws.

She forced the thought away and instead focused on the heavy, almost primal rhythm of the music. The movement of the dancers and the flickering of the fire beyond them was mesmerizing, and Firal was happy to draw her knees to her chest, drape her arms around them, and let herself be hypnotized.

"You're welcome to join the dance, you know."

Firal glanced up as Daemon sat beside her. His sleeve brushed her arm, the warmth of his skin radiating from underneath the coarse fabric. She turned away and shifted to put a few more inches between them. "I'm not so good at dancing."

"You did fine in Ilmenhith." He picked a fallen flower from the grass and twirled it between his claws. "Or is it that you don't have a partner?"

"It's that I don't feel like dancing," she said, a little more hotly than she intended.

His gaze seemed as devoid of expression as his unadorned mask. "I see."

Music filled the silence that fell between them. The joy in the sound seemed distant now; separate, not for her. No matter how welcoming the people of Core had been, the sense of being an outsider still lingered. It grew worse in Daemon's presence. This triumph was his, earned through means she couldn't pretend to understand. Exiled or no, a mage had no place here. She'd thought she was supposed to be Core's healer. After their trip together, she no longer understood her role.

She plucked blades of grass from beside her feet and picked them into pieces as she broke the uncomfortable still. "So you'll escort Lumia to Alwhen for the official treaty to be signed?"

"I must," he replied. "The treaty isn't just with Lumia. It's also with me. She just doesn't know that."

"How long do you expect the two of you will be away?" She tried to sound nonchalant. A white flower lay close by. She picked it up and slid her fingertips over its ruffled petals.

"Why, will you miss me?"

"I just wanted to know how long you plan to shirk your lessons." Firal sniffed. "You can't neglect your studies for long. Your skills are not yet refined enough to allow you to neglect them."

"I think I'd prefer it if you missed me," Daemon muttered. "We won't be gone long. Now that I've been to Alwhen's palace, I can use the Gate-stone to get us there and back. But I can't say how long our conference will take, or how long it'll take me to get Lumia to agree to everything I've worked out. She didn't agree with all of this plan to begin with."

"Then why pursue it?" She cast the rumpled flower back to the grass.

"Because it's the right thing to do. All of the ruins should belong to these people, not just what's underground," Daemon said. "I know it will stir some dissent at first, but it won't be that way forever. We'll eliminate my people's fear of the surface world as we establish cities. Our settlements up here will slowly merge with Core, underground. One home, one people. It will just take time."

She frowned. It made sense, though there was always the possibility the adjustment would be harder than he thought. "I don't see why you don't just claim the ruins and build here anyway, regardless of who owns the land. No one comes in here."

"Aside from you," he said.

"Regardless," she replied, ignoring the flush that rose into her cheeks, "I'm not sure I follow your plans. You say you want to give the ruins back to your people, but you also want to ally with both surface kingdoms. What if Kifel refuses to part with the ruins? It won't matter what Relythes has given us, you'd be stuck with half of us here and half of us there."

Daemon shook his head. "Kifel won't care if I take the ruins, as long as we pose no threat to the rest of his kingdom. This land is useless to him. Relythes was the hard part. That's why we started with him." He reached for a flower in the grass. "But now he thinks he can play us off against Kifel."

"Because he knew you." Firal studied the way the firelight glinted on his mask.

He hesitated. "It's good for one involved in politics to be familiar with leaders they may, at some point, do business with."

"I mean the real you," she said. "The one who isn't hiding."

"Masks come in many varieties. What I wear sets me free."

She bridled her irritation and struggled to keep her voice calm. "But if he already knew you, there was no need to do things this way. You could have gone with Lumia instead of me, signed all your contracts and treaties ahead of the announcement. You could have gone alone. He already knew you. He'd know all about your court mages or what have you,

175

too. So why was I there? Why, really? I would have been more useful here in Core."

"I told you. I enjoy your company." He studied her with a level gaze, his violet eyes bright in the eventide.

The answer was so calm and simple that she couldn't believe it genuine. He'd taken her because he wanted something, she was sure of it. Yet the only reasons that came to mind skirted answers he refused to give. There was a reason he'd removed his mask before she left the room. He'd allowed her to hear the surprise in the king's voice. He'd allowed her to wage her speculations, and he had not denied them. But his mask was still on, and the metal mask that shielded his face was not the only one he wore.

Firal pushed herself up from the ground. "Well, I apologize that I must deprive you of my company now. The trip has left me rather worn out. I believe I will retire for the evening. We shall resume lessons upon your return."

Daemon rose to follow her. "I won't be absent long. A few days, at most."

"I can find my way back to my house on my own, thank you. Or is my company so enjoyable that you're compelled to follow me?"

"Is mine so deplorable that you're eager to escape?" His tone was only half jest.

Firal didn't reply. She cut through the gardens and down the spiral pathway into the underground. Daemon trailed not far behind.

"Why is it you suddenly won't speak to me?" he asked, exasperated.

"Why is it you're suddenly so determined to speak to me?" she countered.

"You've been my mentor for weeks. I thought we'd established enough of a relationship that speaking would be easy."

She hurried down the corridor, anxious to reach the shelter of her home. "I'm not sure we should have a relationship at all."

Daemon quickened his step, closing the distance between them. "What do you mean?"

The doorway to her house waited just ahead. Reaching it gave her no relief. "I can't imagine Lumia appreciates you spending so much time with me. The last thing I want to do is end up on the wrong side of the queen." She heaved back the door. The stiff hinges gave a long groan of protest.

He snorted. "What does it matter what Lumia thinks?"

Though he didn't block the door, Firal lingered in the hall, unable to make herself cross the threshold. Her feet refused to move, weighted down by her heavy heart. "Before the trip, when you called me to the great hall. I didn't intend to interrupt you. I don't mean for Lumia to misunderstand. You're a good student. I enjoy our lessons, and I've become quite fond of you, Daemon. But I don't mean to come between the two of you."

"Is that what this is all about?" he asked incredulously. "She is my queen, nothing more."

"But you are her lover." She slipped through the shadowy doorway of her dark, quiet house.

"Not anymore."

"That's not what it looked like," she murmured.

"But I wasn't—you think that—" He cut himself short with a growl of exasperation and stepped inside after her. The door slammed shut behind him, darkness enveloping everything but his eyes.

Firal opened her mouth to protest, and her voice failed her as he cradled her face in his hands. His mask dangled against her shoulder with its strings looped over his fingers, and when he turned her face upward, the brush of his lips against hers drove all words from her mind.

Warmth blossomed in her cheeks and chest. His fingers curled in her hair to draw her closer and she melted into his touch as he kissed her again, so desperate and deep with passion that it left her weak in the knees.

"You have no idea what it's like," he whispered when he finally pulled back, "spending every day wanting something you can't have."

She struggled to find her breath as he slipped away, his claws a tender caress on her cheek. Stunned to silence, she reached after him as he opened the door again. Her fingertips brushed his sleeve as he settled his mask in place once more.

Then he was gone.

1 5

UNMASKED

IF A BETTER WAY TO MOVE THE LOYAL MAGES FROM ALWHEN EXISTED, Nondar was sure he would have thought of it by now. The building they'd been given was impressive by the standards of eastern architecture, but its grounds lacked the open air courtyards they were used to. They could have opened a Gate in one of the offices, but it would have been small and harder to defend.

They'd tried to make their gathering as inconspicuous as possible, the Masters conversing lightly about that night's drills and practices to disguise their intentions. No one would know what was happening until—hopefully—it was too late to stop them.

Casting one last look around his quarters, Nondar found himself somehow relieved that the temple had burned. He had little left in the way of possessions, which meant there was no need to transport *things* in addition to people. All could be replaced—and would be, once they settled in Ilmenhith. He closed his door and resigned himself to the fact he would not see the room again.

The last of the loyal mages trickled past him in the hallway and slipped out the front door with solemn faces. The magelings had been divided into groups, each group paired with a Master to lead them.

Their gathering had not gone unnoticed. Nondar saw a number of Masters he knew were not on their side. None attempted to join the groups, but plenty lingered and watched. Anaide stood with a Master he didn't recognize, tittering something about not having room indoors for proper exercises. They weren't fooling anyone, but if nothing else, at least they hadn't drawn the attention of the Archmage.

"Are we ready?" Edagan fell in step beside him, her stride smooth and graceful, a sharp contrast to his limping gait.

"As ready as we ever will be," Nondar sighed.

Edagan lifted her chin as they moved into the gathered crowd. Anaide murmured some sort of parting excuse to the Master beside her and joined the two of them at the front steps. Her group of magelings clustered at her heels.

"Is everyone present?" Nondar glanced across the crowd. Some carried mage-lights and in the dead of night, the illumination drew more attention than he liked. The glare hurt his eyes, but his vision slid out of focus as the strange, prickling sensation of the Calling rolled through him.

"If those expected aren't here already, they will be shortly," Anaide said as she released the power and let the Calling fade.

Edagan sniffed. "I'm sure you haven't memorized everyone who's a part of this."

"Only the Masters. Magelings aren't my problem." Anaide glanced up as the Masters she'd summoned moved toward her.

Nondar mentally counted them, his lips pressing tight with his frown. "Yes, that's all of them."

"Then we begin now." Edagan raised her hands overhead and clapped once before snaring the flow of energy in the disrupted air. She spun it into a rippling, shimmering shield and spread it with her arms. Anaide caught the edge of it and twisted the flows farther, pushing a thread of energy toward Nondar so he could do the same. One by one, the gathered Masters caught hold of the barrier, spinning it out and pushing it farther with their own energies. Nondar pushed as far as he could reach. Alone, a mage could hope to create enough of a shield to encircle maybe a half-dozen people. Together, they'd have to shield hundreds.

"Push the others out!" Anaide shouted. Several blue-robed magelings broke away from her group to seize magic of their own. They wove the flows together into a force that shoved the unwelcome Masters beyond the edge of the shield.

That's it, then, Nondar thought. *Now we've made our enemies.*

"Traitors!" someone screamed from the other side of the shield as they brought the barrier to the ground. "Rebels!"

Without warning, a gout of flame impacted the shield. The barrier rippled, but held fast.

"Well, look who it is," Edagan murmured. "Can't say I'm surprised."

Alira ran down the steps, shouting orders to the Masters outside the shield's wall. They moved into formation and lashed out against the barrier with controlled bursts of magic.

Nondar set the flow of the shield's energy into a cycle. It would consume all its given power and spin itself out soon enough, especially with how large the shield had grown, but it didn't need to hold for long. Mages all across the crowd followed his lead. Some of the magelings had even joined the effort, though most looked too frightened to move.

He waited until he felt his last ties to the shield give way to the loop, then raised his hands. His power freed, he traced the shape of the Gate and bordered it with his own energy to form the crackling, lightning edge of the would-be portal. Anaide joined first and the rest of the Masters followed, lending their strength in a unified wave.

White-hot streaks sizzled from edge to edge across the opening Gate and blossomed into a portal that led to the courtyard of Ilmenhith's palace. The image wavered, and for a moment Nondar thought they'd opened it too wide. Then the ripple stilled and the portal anchored itself to the ground.

"Stop them!" Alira screeched as she threw her magic against the barrier, searching desperately for the looping power that sustained it. "Untie the flows! Do something!"

"Let them go," the Archmage barked behind her.

Nondar's head turned. Envesi stood in the doorway, her white hair and robes lashing in the wind their Gate had created.

Alira grew pale as she turned to face the older woman, but the Archmage's eyes weighed heavy on the Gate. "If they're that eager to escape, then they are of no further use to us."

"But—" Alira started, but the frosty look Envesi gave her made her jaw clamp shut.

"Everyone, move through the Gate!" Anaide ordered. The mages beneath the shield snapped to attention. The magelings went first, funneled into the Gate by the Masters behind them. Edagan and Nondar posted themselves at the back of the group as a handful of other Masters drew the shield close to their heels. The barrier shrank as the crowd moved into the palace courtyard.

Nondar kept one hand outstretched toward the portal he supported, and the other clutched his cane in a white-knuckled grip. Between the cost of the shield, sustaining the Gate, and moving forward, it was all he could do just to walk.

"Keep it up, old man," Edagan said. He half expected her to offer her arm. To his relief, the insult didn't come. One after another, the mages passed through the Gate, the shield and Gate both dwindling with the crowd.

"How can you let them leave?" Alira cried. Nondar turned his head and strained to listen over the Gate's powerful hum.

"Foolish child." Envesi gave the younger woman a dark look, though a smile wreathed itself upon her features. "They're more useful to us there than they are here."

Alira's mouth fell open.

Brow furrowed, Nondar tore his eyes away. The last of the

Masters moved through the portal. Anaide paused to look back. Then the three Masters of affinity crossed into Ilmenhith, and the Gate and shield shattered into a haze of shimmering white motes.

———

WITHOUT ANY CLOUDS TO OBSCURE IT, THE DEEP BLUE THAT stretched overhead from horizon to horizon felt like it could swallow the world whole. The clear weather put everyone in good spirits. The fifty-something men at Daemon's back laughed, and even the horse he led pranced. He didn't like to ride when his men were without mounts of their own, a preference the bay gelding didn't seem to mind. He would have left the animal in the safety of the ruins if there weren't appearances to keep. Horses were too valuable for average expeditions, but if luck held, this wouldn't be average.

They'd left the ruins early that morning and pushed northwest. It took them closer to Ilmenhith than Daemon liked, but it would be worth it. The location he'd selected was important for his intentions. Today, they carried news, and its delivery was every bit as important as the trade they hoped to accomplish.

Dealings with Relythes had gone better than expected. The treaty signing had been fast, simple, and painless. The new alliance recognized the ruin-folk as their own faction and granted them sovereignty over their new land, small as the sliver may be. Lumia signed with minimal complaint, then the Gate-stone carried both of them home. She had rejoined the festivities in Core. Daemon threw himself into his work instead.

He'd never excelled at self-discipline. Most of the time, his position sheltered him from the repercussions of his rash behavior. This time, he didn't think the repercussions could be avoided.

Nor did he think he wanted them to.

But his role came with responsibilities and obligations. No matter what he wanted, that didn't change. Giving in to a moment's impulse had been a mistake. He'd worked too hard, too long, to make such mistakes. If he was to unify Elenhiise under one banner, it could not happen again. He didn't dare return to Firal for the lessons he'd grown to treasure, not after what he'd done. And so he worked.

Negotiations with the last village had gone well, but the ruin-folk hadn't held their own territory then. It had been violence, not respect, that convinced the village to cooperate. Daemon anticipated more trouble this time, though he hadn't shared that concern with his men. Barter was less important than letting word of their newfound power permeate the island, so even if negotiation went nowhere, they would still accomplish something.

It was a simple proclamation. *We are here. The island will not be taken from us.* A brazen warning from people so small, but it made things clear, and King Kifelethelas would hear it most clearly of all.

I will be recognized.

The shrill cry of a warning bugle cut through his thoughts.

Daemon spat a curse as a fleet of horsemen with blue and silver banners crested the western horizon. Riders from Ilmenhith. What were they doing here? They'd ventured northwest, but not that close. Behind him, weapons rasped as they left their sheaths. Daemon cursed again. "Hold your positions!" The riders did not slow. "Brace and prepare for potential combat!"

Shouts of compliance echoed from the men behind him. He'd brought few soldiers; too many would have given the impression of an invading army. Now it seemed they hadn't escaped that interpretation. Horses surged toward them in numbers so great, they couldn't hope to withstand a skirmish.

"I think we've been mistaken for eastern raiders," Davan said at his side.

Daemon grimaced behind his mask and released his horse's reins. "I get the feeling they're not coming to negotiate." He positioned himself in the center of their shallow formation and grasped the hilt of the sword strapped at his side. "We are not enemies. Remain defensive. We wait for them to make the first move. The moment they draw weapons, retreat."

At the head of the oncoming cavalry, a knight shouted, his words lost in the hoof beats of his army. Tension mounted.

In fluid synchronicity, each of the horsemen drew their swords.

Daemon drew his own. "Go!"

The wave of the king's cavalry crashed down on them. Daemon braced himself and his sword rang against the lead knight's blade. He staggered as he deflected the strike.

Beside him, Davan defended against another blow.

"Take the horse!" Daemon ordered. "Break past them and get back to the ruins!" Blight it all, why hadn't he thought to bring the Gate-stone? He couldn't focus now to open a Gate without its aid.

Davan seized the reins and spun to lead the retreat.

Half the army swept around them. The horses outpaced Daemon's fleeing men easily and spiraled them back into the group. Eldani in armor dismounted and pressed forward with weapons bared.

Something was wrong. Kifel was a patient, lenient king. His armies never bore such force against simple raiders.

Daemon held his sword at his side and raised his other hand, palm out, clawed fingers spread. "Stop this!"

A soldier advanced on him instead.

The tip of Daemon's sword raked through the dirt as he brought it up to meet his opponent in combat. His men clustered behind him and readied their weapons for battle. Loyal, every one of them. Daemon cursed them for it as battle erupted around him.

No negotiation. No warning. Just war. Daemon gritted his

teeth and pushed his enemy back with a flurry of blows. He was not as experienced as Kifel's cavalry, but he was just as skilled, and he had more than just his sword.

The soldier's swing went wide. Daemon swept forward and drove his blade into the man's chest, the soldier's death cry lost in the rage of sudden battle. Blood spattered silver armor and dusty ground as Daemon freed his sword.

Steel against steel created a chaotic melody that reverberated in his head. His breath burned in his chest as he heaved his sword overhead to meet a charging rider. The blade plunged between plates of armor in the horseman's side and drove him from the saddle, the man dead before he ever hit the ground. Only vaguely was Daemon aware of his band dissolving around him. He didn't see Davan or his horse. Silently, he prayed it meant the captain had gotten away.

Concentrate. Firal's lessons echoed in his mind. Bodies fell, the glimmer of life energy within them fading. Power burned in the air and earth around him. Magic was his only hope to save his men. Daemon tried to shut out the noise and reach for it.

"What are you doing here?"

The familiar voice shattered his concentration and the flows of power slipped away. Daemon held his sword, ready to strike. He didn't remember raising it. Beside him, an Eldani soldier cast his helmet aside.

"I could ask you the same thing!" Daemon spun to deflect a blade.

Vahn knocked an Underling to the ground without killing him. "Stop!" He raised a hand in vain attempt to stop the onslaught. "Weapons down!"

No one listened. His lips moving with an unheard curse, Vahn pressed back to back with Daemon and parried another attack.

"Why aren't you in Ilmenhith?" Daemon barely caught a strike from the side. Their swords clashed hard enough to send a shock up his arms, but his strength won out, and the weapon spun from his opponent's hands.

"We carry orders to mages on the border. One of the scouts saw you and thought you were raiders." Vahn grimaced and jerked an elbow into Daemon's back when another Underling came at him.

They spun together and Daemon held out a hand. The Underling soldier froze, eyes wide with confusion.

"Stop fighting and retreat!" Daemon snapped. "Vahn, can't you stop them?"

"I'm trying! Take off your mask!"

Something flashed past him and Daemon flinched. Arrows. The last thing they needed.

"Stop!" Vahn shouted. This time, he turned toward his commanding officer, arms raised, beseeching. "We've made a mistake!"

The whistle of a blade didn't register until a moment too late. The impact against his shoulder knocked Daemon to the ground. Vibrations rang through his armor and turned his limbs to jelly. All but paralyzed, he thrust his hands against the dirt and rolled to his back just as the blade struck the ground where he'd been. He deflected a second strike with his gauntlet. Sparks flared and dimmed his vision. Pain burned in his arm. He planted a foot in the stomach of his attacker and knocked the man off balance just long enough to get to his feet.

"Watch out!" Vahn cried behind him.

Daemon spun and an armored fist plowed into his steel mask. He stumbled backwards, struggling to regain his balance. The sparks still danced in his eyes, dark spots that swirled across his vision. Blinded, he couldn't defend. Searing pain exploded in his side. He staggered. The knight swept his legs out from underneath him and he went down hard.

Stars flashed and swirled around the distorted image of the knight above him, who shook black blood from his sword and stepped over Daemon's body to continue the fight.

Numbly, Daemon's hand found its way to his side, to the break in his armor and the wound beneath. Warm ichor seeped into his gauntlet. Pain throbbed with each beat of his heart. His breath quickened and he struggled to roll onto his side. Agony shot through him, blurring his vision even more, fading the screams and shouting voices to a dull hum in his head. He tried to find his feet. His legs failed beneath him.

"Stop trying to move, you bloody idiot!" Vahn pushed him back into the dirt.

Daemon choked back a cry and gasped for breath. Sweat rolled down his brow behind his mask, though an icy chill washed over him.

Vahn tore a piece from his tunic and stuffed the cloth into the break in Daemon's armor. "Hold still. I'll get you out of here."

His breath grew labored, his mouth dry. Daemon's words failed him as his head sank to the earth.

"You hear me?" Vahn said. "Just hold on."

Daemon swallowed, and the world faded to black.

Firal blinked and brushed dirt from her hands as Tobias called her name again. Children did not often visit the garden above Core, despite her insistence the sun would do them good.

"I'm here." She pushed herself up from the warm earth. The weather had been strangely pleasant after Daemon's grand announcement, as if the island itself rejoiced at the news. A number of people sat under the serpent's-tongue trees, building high-wheeled wagons to transport things through the ruins and into their new territory. But the children, it seemed, preferred to play near the underground river.

Tobias stopped on the garden path, a look of bewilderment on his face. He braced his hands against his knees and panted. "Miss Firal, you have to come right now!"

"Come where?" She wiped her hands on her apron as she met him on the wide pathway. "What's the matter?"

"Mama said there was a big fight and soldiers got hurt. You have to come right away!" Tobias wiped his brow and wrung the hem of his shirt between his hands.

Firal frowned. Soldiers had been posted on their new land just the night before, after Lumia returned from negotiations. Surely there hadn't been a conflict already. "Catch your breath, then you go find your mother and keep out of trouble. I'll see to this right away." She patted his head as she walked past, keeping her pace as even as she could until she passed out of the child's view. The last thing she wanted to do was frighten the boy, but if Minna sent him all the way to the gardens to retrieve her, it had to be severe. When she no longer felt Tobias's eyes on her back, she sprinted ahead.

Anxious voices flowed up the inverted tower, drawing her toward the avenue that led to her infirmary. A handful of men clustered outside her door, Minna beside them. Dark droplets marked the floor of the long corridor. When she saw them, she lifted her skirts above her ankles and ran. The men at her door parted to let her past.

One rough-hewn table had been dragged to the center of the room. The prone form upon it made her heart skip a beat.

"Daemon," Firal breathed. Of all the people it could have been, she'd never expected him.

Black ichor flowed from the gaps in his armor, dripping from the side of the table to pool on the floor. A handful of soldiers stood around him, holding him down, though he did not move. Her eyes flicked to one of the men at the head of the table. "What happened?"

Minna's husband stepped forward from the group, twisting one of his gloves in his hands. "Sword to the side. Don't know how bad it is, seemed unwise to play medic when we're not. We were out to negotiate trade with another village. The Eldani king's men caught us by surprise. They initiated battle. They've never done that before. He ordered us to run, but he didn't try to get away, himself."

Firal hurried to her washbasin and lathered her hands and arms. She tried to put on the cool, collected front she knew a medic ought to wear, but fear knotted her middle and churned it with ice. Her hands shook. "Minna," she called, willing herself to focus. "Run a knife over a flame and get the antiseptics."

"Yes, Miss." Minna fetched a satchel from where it hung on the wall and spilled its contents across a counter.

Drying her arms on a clean towel, Firal tried to collect herself. "Unfasten his armor. His breastplate needs to come off, now."

Davan made quick work of the latches and straps she wouldn't have found on her own. When the breastplate came away, Daemon groaned.

Her stomach lurched at the sight of the black blood pooled inside his armor. "How long has he been bleeding?"

"I don't know, Miss," Davan said apologetically. "We got him here as fast as we could. If not for that Eldani boy that helped us, we'd not have gotten him out of the skirmish at all."

"Eldani boy?" Her brow furrowed, but she shook her head. "No, never mind. Minna, get me a cloth and cold water. He needs painkillers, too. Davan, help me with the rest of his armor." Her eyes went to Daemon's mask. The only analgesics she'd been able to make had to be imbibed.

She swallowed hard and reached for his mask.

"Don't touch it!" One of the soldiers slapped her hand away. "The general's mask is never removed."

Firal glowered, her composure gone in an instant. "Get out! Go! Minna, get them out of the way!"

Minna deposited supplies at Firal's side before she waved the men back. Together, she and Davan herded them out of the room. Growling and shaking her head, Firal thrust an abandoned piece of armor off the table and let it land with a clang. She loosened the ties of Daemon's mask and thrust it back. Her eyes fell on his face and her stomach dropped to her knees.

The plain steel mask clattered to the floor.

A strong hand grasped her elbow and steadied her. "Stay on your feet now, Miss," Davan said, his expression solemn. "Can't have you taking ill when the general needs you."

Her head spun and her knees felt as firm as water. "Daemon," she choked, laying hands on his face. "Hold on. Stay with me!"

Sweat beaded his brow, his skin scorched with fever. His eyes rolled back in his head.

"Ran!" Firal cried, tears brimming on her dark eyelashes. He looked at her then, snake-slitted eyes hazy, but focused on her face. "Stay with me," she repeated, brushing back his dark hair.

Her stomach lurched again as Davan removed more pieces of armor. She sliced open the bloodied tunic and exposed the deep wound in Daemon's side. The blade hadn't fully skewered him, at least, though that was a small consolation. She wrung water from the cloth Minna left in the bowl and put the rag over his brow with one hand, the fingers of her other hand curling over his wound.

Little strength pulsed within him. The thinnest trickle of life energy answered her call. It had to be enough.

She snared it and bent it to her will, rerouting its flow through his body. Focusing on his hot skin beneath her fingers, she called forth her own energies. Her fingertips tingled as the flows of her life force interwove with the feeble threads of his. They brightened in her senses, even as weakness washed over her. Warmth filled her shaking hands as she manipulated the energies, working power into his torn flesh, willing it to mend.

It fought. A shadow pushed against her, a deep, bitter flow of power that welled from within the wound. New fear lodged itself in her belly. He had too little strength for her to use. The shadow surged beneath her efforts, thin veins blackening beneath his skin to mark its path.

Firal couldn't fight long. She'd have to cut corners. Stave off infection, stem the bleeding, seal it over. Before the soul-deep poison of corrupted magic spread.

A thin sheen of sweat formed on her brow as she labored. Without another mage to aid her, there was no way she'd be able to repair it fully.

Fingers brushed her arm. Minna pressed close to her side, her strength a soft beacon at the edge of Firal's senses. She turned her head. Davan crowded at her other side. Stronger, deeper, the life essence of a man in his prime. They weren't mages, but their presence was power—precious power—in the only vein of magic she could tap.

A gentle claw rasped against her hand and she gripped his cold fingers with all her might. Magic surged through her, one last, forceful thrust fed by the presence of the Giftless people at her side.

The shadow gave way and Daemon's life force flared. Firal gasped as her knees buckled beneath her. She clutched the edge of the table for balance, her fingers sliding in the sticky ichor. Strong hands caught her before she fell.

"That'll do, Miss," Davan said as she sank into his arms. "That'll do," he repeated, the soothing note of his voice all she needed to let go. Tension slipped from her shoulders and she let herself succumb to exhaustion.

16

KNOWN

"SO WITH HALF OUR MAGES GONE, AND THE REST OF US TRYING TO hide their absence from Relythes, what's your plan now?" Melora folded her arms over her chest as she leaned back in her chair.

None of the Masters left in Alwhen were happy with Envesi's decision to let the traitors go, though few were courageous enough to voice their objections. Melora, on the other hand, had no qualms with letting the Archmage know exactly how she felt. Alira sat beside her and nodded.

"Please," Envesi sighed. "Our numbers are reduced, but things are not out of hand."

"If you've already decided how to handle this, you should have told us sooner." Alira tried to look calm and neutral, but anger and fear still flashed in her eyes. Melora couldn't stand the girl, but the two of them were the highest-ranking Masters who remained, second only to the Archmage. It wouldn't do to show dissent in front of the lesser mages.

Envesi eyed the empty chairs at the table's sides, seats previously reserved for Edagan, Nondar, and Anaide. Despite the obvious fact they would not return, the lower-ranking Masters present refused to fill their seats.

"There are bigger things to worry about than their defection," the Archmage said at last.

Melora raised a brow. Little escaped her notice, and she was irritated enough at having failed to see the festering divide among the mages until it came to fruition. If she had missed something else, she was going to be angry. "What, for example?"

Envesi rested her elbows on the arms of her chair and laced her fingers together. "The other day, one the mages attending our new king mentioned an unusual visitor. A young man who introduced himself as 'General' Daemon, and entered negotiations to purchase land near the ruins."

"Well, he's certainly grown bold, hasn't he?" Melora rubbed her mouth as if to wipe away the look of displeasure that twisted her lips.

"Naturally, Relythes made the mistake of indulging him. Even after he demanded the so-called general remove his mask." The Archmage shook her head in disgust. "That little problem will need to be nipped in the bud as soon as possible."

Alira's brow knit as she looked between the two of them. "One of the Underling pests? I don't see why that would be a problem for us."

Melora shot her an incredulous stare and then glanced to Envesi. "Doesn't she know?"

"She is a bit younger than the rest of the Masters who were on my council," Envesi said, though a wry smile twisted her mouth.

"She *doesn't* know!" Melora almost crowed with laughter when the younger Master's face crumpled into a scowl. "How long have you been Master of your House? You poor, ignorant child!"

Alira's face grew red. "What haven't I been told?"

Melora cackled. "This general, the leader of the Underling army, is the Eldani king's son!"

Alira's mouth hung open a moment before she produced words. "But I thought his son—I mean, wasn't he—"

"A student at the temple, yes." The Archmage shrugged. "He's played at being one of those pitiful cave-dwellers for some time, but if he's started to carve out pieces of land from eastern holdings, that's a new problem."

A sneer worked its way onto Melora's face. The Archmage demanded respect, but this chain of events was too rich. "A problem, or another weapon for you to wedge between yourself and your estranged king?"

Envesi made a small sound of displeasure. "I had hoped allowing him to run with those outcasts would keep him close when I needed him and out of my hair when I didn't, but if he's begun to claim land, the issue must be handled. Should he make a stand against Kifel, you know the blame would be put on us. We sit in a precarious position and could easily fall. I have worked too hard to strengthen the influence of magic to fail now."

Alira chewed her lower lip and stared at the table. Embarrassment still colored her cheeks, but she had regained her composure. A small surprise, given the girl's impulsive nature. "But if he chooses to stand against his own father, wouldn't that present a strong opportunity for us to sever ties completely?"

"Are you suggesting we ally ourselves with the wildling's forces?" Melora asked.

"The wildling," Envesi interjected, her nose wrinkled with disdain, "is a problem that should be eradicated, not encouraged. I have no desire to be involved with politics beyond those which influence mages. My goal is to advance and preserve the existence of our Gifts. Kifel's support was vital to the establishment of the temple, but he expected use of our power for his own desires. I cannot allow the expectations of outsiders to interfere with our goals."

Melora drummed her fingertips against the table. "Yet if interference is what we wish to avoid, perhaps the best thing we could do is encourage the situation to fester. It's bound to remove Kifel from power, or eliminate proof of our shortcomings if the wildling is eradicated. But we also cannot assume the boy will meet Kifel with animosity, as Alira suggests. The last thing we need is two nobles with vendettas against us."

Alira frowned at her. "So, what, you think we should instigate a war?"

"The word 'instigate' seems rather childish, but yes." Melora shrugged. "Stir them up, convince them to fight one another, and it will leave us with only one opponent. Assuming, of course, the girl isn't involved."

Alira glanced between them. "What girl?"

Envesi ignored the question. "Our incoming mages claim the girl never arrived in Ilmenhith or any of the other chapter houses. I expect the boy has added her to his collection. It is the best possible outcome, given the current situation."

"Unless he means to use her," Melora said. "She would make a powerful weapon. The last thing we want is for the wildling to have the whole western kingdom behind him."

"Please," the Archmage scoffed. "He is a Master in name only. What he knows is limited. Regardless, whatever his intentions, it is better to leave that pawn for him to toy with than to have her stoke Kifel's anger toward the temple. All I expect is for the Masters here to continue to serve as my eyes and ears. It is not yet time for us to act."

"Very well then." Melora didn't agree, but she didn't think an argument would change the Archmage's mind. "When you are in need of our assistance, let us know. If all we are to do is wait, then there is nothing more to discuss."

"Indeed. I will summon you when I am in need of hands. In the meantime, watch for events to unfold. You are dismissed." Envesi flicked her fingers toward the door.

Melora stood and bowed. Alira and the rest of the mages in the council chamber did the same. As the mages filtered from the room, Alira made her way to Melora's side.

"May I speak with you?" Alira asked, voice low.

"You are already speaking with me, child, but you may continue to do so."

A sullen look remained in Alira's eyes, but she quashed her pride. "What the Archmage said, about the king's son and a girl..."

Melora crossed her arms as they strode down the hall. She couldn't help a smirk, delighted at the notion a Master of affinity could be so clueless. "You wish to know the rest of that story, eh? Very well. As Master of the House of Fire, it is your right." She cleared her throat as if beginning a well-practiced recital. "It was back at the founding of the temple. Before the council saw fit to denounce the Archmage's marriage to King Kifelethelas and forbid mention of her throne. You would have been a child then. The wildling was our first real project, our first major undertaking. The temple was made for creating weapons like him, you see. It deviated from that plan over time, but that was the reason for its founding. The creation of powerful mages to restore glory to magekind."

Alira nodded, but remained silent. Melora slowed a shade to allow the other mages to outpace them before she went on. "Mages like you and I are limited in our capabilities. Not only are we restricted in what energies we may draw on, but we can only wield so much of our own strength without the risk of unmaking ourselves. The idea was, since all natural things are limited to preserve the balance of things, we would make an unnatural thing, and its power would be unlimited."

"And you were a part of this project?" Alira asked in a murmur.

"You are the only Master of an affinity who was not." Melora smirked. "Of course, the magic went horribly awry. I suppose such things happen when you attempt matters best left to the divine. We meant to create a child in the shape of a man. What we created was a monster. Had the Archmage been involved through the end, perhaps it wouldn't have happened. But she was with child, and as such, she was unable to safely wield magic. She could not risk the king's unborn child. Without her expert hand guiding the flows, Lomithrandel was the result."

"I don't understand." Alira shook her head. "If he was—is—some sort of magic construct, how did he come to be Kifel's son?"

"Ah, yes. The king knew of his unborn child, but he did not know when it was expected. Kifel was desperate for a child, and Envesi needed his financial support for the establishment of the temple. When the Archmage saw how her experiment had gone awry, she gave the creature to the king in place of the child she'd never let him have."

"And the child?" Alira asked.

Melora sniffed. "Gone."

The younger Master was quiet for a time. They strode into the main living hall together before Alira spoke again. "When you say you planned to make his power unlimited... How powerful is he?"

Melora considered the question for a time before she decided where to start. "As you're well aware, there are few mages born without an innate affinity. But once they choose an element to first draw upon, whether consciously or unconsciously, that becomes the element they are restricted to for the rest of their lives."

"Of course," Alira said, irritated.

Melora resisted a smile. A lecture on something taught to magelings was unnecessary, but she enjoyed ruffling the girl's feathers. "He is free of those bonds. He bears no affinity. None. He can draw from anything, anywhere. I couldn't say how powerful he is. I don't know how much energy there is in the world."

Dumbfounded, Alira stopped in her tracks. "If that's the case, shouldn't the Archmage be afraid of him?"

"Dear child," the elder Master laughed. "I don't know that he's aware of the extent of his own strength. But that's not our concern. Finding how to make more like him, mages who know no limits, but without the corruption? That is what the temple stands for." She patted Alira's shoulder and slipped away between the long, narrow dinner tables, silently gloating at the young Master's dismay.

———

THE RATTLE OF A SPOON AGAINST THE SOUP KETTLE STARTLED FIRAL awake. Her head pounded, the weak light of candles and the fire on the hearth enough to make her groan.

"Easy now," Minna cautioned, her voice soft. "Don't be stirring around too much, neither one of you."

It wasn't until Minna spoke that Firal realized she wasn't alone in the bed. She rested against another body, thick blankets pulled over both of them. She wrenched her eyes open and her stomach gave a heavy flop at the sight of Daemon by her side. Or could she think of him as Daemon now? With darker hair and his peculiar eyes, not to mention the claws and scales that decorated his hands and feet, he did look different. Just not different enough. His face showed nothing but weariness, but when their eyes met, her nausea stirred into rage.

She thrust herself back and slapped him with all her might. "Liar!"

"Now now, Miss Firal!" Minna clicked her tongue and scuttled across the room with bowls of soup in hand. "The two of you have been through enough without any of that."

Firal ignored her. Angry tears brimmed on her eyelashes, but she did not dare blink them away, lest they fall. "How could you? All this time, you were lying to me!"

His eyes closed, his brow knit with emotion. "Firal—"

She slapped him again.

"That is enough!" Minna thunked the bowls onto the bedside table and caught Firal by the wrist. "Behave yourself! After everything you did yesterday, you need to rest. That goes for Lord Daemon, as well."

"Ran," Firal said as she cast him a shadowed look. "His name is Lomithrandel."

"It's what I answer to that counts." Daemon's—Ran's—voice was weak, defeated, betraying the weariness of a man pulled back from the brink of death.

"Well, I don't care what he's called or what he answers to." Minna looked between the two of them, frowning. "It sounds like the two of you need time to speak. If you'll not hit him any more, Miss Firal, I'll leave you be. Otherwise I've a mind to bundle you down the hall and stuff you in bed with Tobias."

Firal pushed herself out from under the blankets, silently relieved to see she still wore her dirty work dress. Her cheeks were hot enough without the addition of shame. "We'll be fine, Minna, thank you." She managed to keep her voice level as she swung her legs over the edge of the bed, though she shook with a mixture of anger and fatigue. She clutched the bedding for support and stared at her feet. Her anger hadn't distracted her from her churning stomach; she thought she might retch. "I will call for you if I need you."

Minna gave her a reprimanding look but said nothing more. As she departed, she left the door open a crack. The silence that followed grew uncomfortably thick.

"I know you're angry with me," Ran—Daemon—said at last, watching her with a placidity that made her seethe.

Firal snorted. "Angry with you? All these years, you hid this from me. You tried to make me think you were two different people!"

"It's not like that."

"Then what is it like?" She glowered at him over her shoulder. Her hands felt numb, curled to fists in the blankets. The rush of anger and betrayal that burned inside her left her cold.

"You have no idea what it's been like. I've wanted to tell you, Brant knows how badly. Can't you understand how hard that is?" Daemon tried to sit up, but his face twisted with pain. He groaned and clamped a clawed hand over his side. Firal knew the surface wound was gone, not a mark left to show it had been there, but the lingering effects of the damage would take some time to heal. He sank back into the bed and licked his lips before speaking again. "I lied. I know. I'm sorry. But it was never supposed to go this far."

Firal crossed her arms to try and stop herself from shaking. After he'd kissed her and left her in the dark, she hadn't known what to say. She hadn't even known what to think, but part of her had remained aflutter, desperate to feel his lips on hers again. Now, the tumult of that memory threatened to make her ill. "And how far was it supposed to go, Ran?"

He grimaced. "Don't call me that. Please."

"Why not?"

"Ran doesn't exist," he said, exasperated. "He never has."

She crossed her arms tighter. He studied her for a time before he spoke again.

"I thought... I thought it would be better that way." He bowed his head and rubbed his hands together. She hadn't noticed that he held them clasped before him, rubbing his clawed fingers as if to wash them clean of his mistakes. "If you didn't know. If you never saw what I really was. I spent so much time trying to push you away. Teasing you, tormenting you, because I was afraid of what would happen if I didn't. And then you found me in the ruins."

She stared at him in silence, then bit her lip and forced herself to look away. She didn't want to hear it, but she couldn't bring herself to stop him. No more than she could stop the queasy feeling in her stomach.

"I thought I could scare you away," he admitted. "So I tried. But Brant blight it, you aren't afraid of anything. No matter how hard I tried, you kept coming back. And then I thought that...

maybe, if you knew me—the real me, not the disguise I've always worn—maybe there was hope."

Hope? The word landed like a blow. Yet, looking back, beacons showing just that feeling stood out among her memories. Daemon putting flowers in her hair. The way he twirled her on the dance floor in the king's ballroom. The tenderness and desperation of his kiss. She couldn't meet his eyes. "I don't even know how you do it," she murmured. "You look so..."

"Different?" He smiled hesitantly. He shifted to free an arm, but his strength faded. He closed his eyes a moment, then nodded toward his armor, stacked against the wall. "Over there. The pouch I had on my belt, get it for me?"

She eyed him distrustfully. "Why?"

"I want to show you something."

Her mouth tightened, though she complied. She rocked on her feet when she stood, but her hands found the edge of a table and offered some stability. She clung to whatever she could for balance as she crossed the room, her eyes trained on the floor.

The bloodstains had been scrubbed away. She'd have to thank Minna for cleaning up. His armor, too, had been cleaned, as she saw when she reached the stack at the far wall. Firal studied it for a time. What remained of his shirt lay folded inside the hollow of his upside-down breastplate, the pale fabric stained black with old blood. His belt sat coiled beside it. Several pouches decorated the belt and she hesitated before taking the whole thing.

Daemon dragged himself upright, though he clutched his side and gasped for breath. She passed him the belt and perched on the far end of the bed. Her head spun and weakness rose in her like a tide. In the temple, Masters had always monitored her for overexertion when she worked. They had stopped her more than once, though she had been a less practiced healer then. What she'd been through in the temple now paled in comparison to the experience she'd gained in Core. Nothing had ever left her so faint as this.

He opened one of the pouches and removed something. "When we were in the ruins together, waiting out a storm in a cavern... do you remember?" He turned to put down his belt and gasped when the simple motion aggravated his injury.

Firal rose halfway to help him before she caught herself and returned to her seat. As angry and hurt as she was, the urge to help overshadowed her feelings. She fought it down. Why should she care if he suffered? It was the least he deserved for what he'd done. Yet worry gnawed at her, and even seeing him relax into the pillows Minna had propped him up with offered no relief. Firal laced her fingers together in her lap and convinced herself it was her concern as a healer, nothing more.

Daemon's breath steadied and he went on. "While we waited, you said you were looking for your journal because your pendant was in it, and I told you I had something similar."

She cringed. She recalled their conversation about Ran's bloodline—his bloodline—too, and how she'd thought herself honored by the secrets he'd confided. Now she looked at him and wondered at how foolish she'd been. "I remember," she said at last.

"This is what I was talking about." He unfolded the cloth to reveal an amulet on a silver chain. Shades of blue and green swirled to the surface in the dark stone. Candlelight danced within it in streaks and shimmers, and he tilted it to catch the light before he picked it up.

The moment he touched the amulet, his arm seemed to ripple, claws and scales vanishing to leave smooth skin in their place. Firal's hand clapped over her mouth. His hair faded to the tawny color she was used to, the rich violet of his eyes masked with familiar blue. On impulse, she reached for his arm, then hesitated. He didn't pull away, and she drew her fingertips over his forearm.

"I don't understand," she murmured as she studied the veins in his hands. "This feels like... I mean, it changes you entirely."

"It's an illusion." He ran a thumb over the stone. "You feel what you see because your mind would reject anything else. For me, it feels no different."

"There haven't been any mages powerful enough to create illusions for hundreds of years," Firal said. "Never mind gems imbued with magic. They're worth a king's ransom."

"Well, a king's pockets are as deep as his shame. Nothing is outside his reach. Nothing but fixing what's wrong with me." He turned the amulet between his fingers and rubbed its surface like it was a nervous habit. "So you see, this is the me that never existed. Nothing but a mask."

Tears stung her eyes and she tried to will them away. "It's not a very good mask. It doesn't change your face."

A hint of a smile pulled at the corners of his mouth. "This changes enough to convince people I might be Kifel's blood, maybe an illegitimate son he hasn't admitted to siring. But it wasn't enough. Trying to mind the way I moved and the timbre I spoke with while I wore the stone helped, but eventually, the people I know recognize me without it. That's what the other mask was for."

"So you could hide from me?"

He looked away. "So I can hide from everyone. Even here, I can't be free. The older soldiers know my father. They've been raiding long enough to recognize him, or know him by description, if nothing else. If they recognized me as their enemy's son, they would never follow me. They'd be suspicious of every action, question every motive, even though all I ever wanted was to make a difference."

"You weren't known as the king's son at the temple," she said. "No one recognized your face."

"The Masters did, but they already knew. They were ordered to keep quiet. But the temple is also isolated. Most magelings will never see the king, or the portraits of his adopted son, so they'd have no way of knowing what I looked like. The temple is the only place I've ever been where my face wasn't known. It's the only reason I kept going back." He paused, his eyes weighing on her. "Or, one of the only reasons."

Wordlessly, Firal pried his fingers open and took the amulet from his grasp. The complex magic that held the illusion slipped away and the image dissolved like scattering grains of sand. The power-imbued stone hummed in her palm, prickling like static electricity, older and more terrifying than the Gate-stone she'd held before. She let it fall to the blankets and took his hand instead. He was real, solid, raw and exposed. His scales, smooth and glossy, were familiar and yet somehow now foreign beneath her touch. A deep ache stirred in her chest.

He drew his fingers from her hold and turned away. Pain etched itself in the furrow of his brow and the twist of his mouth. For once, his otherworldly eyes held no light. Firal had to stop herself from probing his energies in search of the cause. It was nothing she could heal.

"I can't imagine how much of a monster you think I am," Daemon murmured.

She forced herself to look away. "You're right. You don't know what I think." The bowls of soup on the bedside table caught her eye and she leaned forward to take one. The clear broth it held was disappointing, but it was better than nothing. She tried to push the bowl into Daemon's hands. "The soup's getting cold. You'd best get something in you, or you'll never heal all the way."

The soup was not cold. Thin curls of steam still hovered over its surface. Daemon stared at it for a time, then pushed it away and turned toward the wall.

Firal struggled not to sigh. She wanted nothing more than to be angry. After everything that had happened, she deserved the right to anger. Yet the way he curled into himself in the bed beside her wrenched her heart and sapped her will to argue. Hurt as she was, she was a healer, and that empathy shone through at the most inconvenient times. His hurt ran deep, an old wound that festered beyond what she could help. Magic could do many things, but it couldn't mend an injured soul.

She cradled the bowl to her chest and spooned broth into her mouth. "You could have told me, you know."

He laughed bitterly. "Told you? I've spent almost every day of my life hiding what I am, struggling to be just like everyone else. And knowing that no matter what I do, no matter how I try, I never will be."

"Because hiding helped you so much," she muttered. "Even Relythes knew you."

"Relythes has business with my father's court. Of course he'd recognize me."

"Which implies you think I have no business knowing. Did you decide that before or after you kissed me?" She raised a brow.

He opened his mouth as if to say something, then clamped it shut a moment later.

"That's what I thought." Firal lifted a spoonful of broth and sipped from its edge.

Again, he curled smaller on the bed, his chin tucked into his chest and his knees drawn up. She'd never seen a man so vulnerable. Truthfully, she didn't feel much stronger.

"You need to eat," she said.

"I'm not hungry."

"That wasn't a suggestion." The broth had cooled enough to drink without discomfort. She caught his jaw in one hand and twisted his face toward her so she could press the bowl's edge to his lips. A glimmer of ruddy light flashed in his eyes. Good; anger was preferable to the miserable wallowing. She forced his mouth open and poured the broth past his lips before he could protest. He managed to swallow once before he choked.

His eyes flared red as he coughed and sputtered, their light vanishing just as quickly. Groans interspersed the coughing and he clamped a hand over his side, his face twisted again with pain. A flutter of guilt occupied Firal's thoughts for a moment, but she brushed it away.

"Drink," she ordered. She put the bowl before his face again, but this time, she didn't try to force him.

Daemon glowered at her, but guided the bowl to his lips and drank from its edge. When he'd swallowed all he could, he pushed her hands away.

Satisfied, she put the bowl aside and nudged his bare shoulder to encourage him to rest. He sank back into the pillows without much coaxing. His eyes fell closed, and for a moment, she thought him asleep. As appealing as sleep sounded, she was unlikely to rest so long as he occupied her bed. Enough shame needled at her for having woken beside him, though she knew Minna must have tucked them in. Her makeshift infirmary had no beds but her own. When patients were too ill or injured to leave bed, she simply traveled to them.

"Davan will have to move you," she murmured, more to herself than Daemon, but his eyelids fluttered open just the same. She frowned at him and tugged the blankets upward until they covered his bare shoulders. He was fine to look at, despite the scales and claws that marred his extremities, but she'd seen more than enough of him for one day.

"There are plenty of women who would be thrilled to have me in their beds," he said.

The attempt at humor should have been reassuring, but it was irritating, instead. Firal huffed. "Then they're welcome to retrieve you from mine."

"I wouldn't want to be anywhere else." He paused, and a hint of a sheepish smile flickered across his face. "I mean, you're the healer. I'm less likely to die here."

She made a soft, skeptical sound and retrieved her cooling broth. It wouldn't have been hard to warm it, but even grasping that much power sounded taxing beyond what she could bear. As it was, she didn't know how she managed to stay upright. So she ate as it grew tepid, and still savored every spoonful.

"Why didn't you let me?"

Firal glanced down at him with a frown. "What?"

"Die." His brows drew together in a combination of puzzlement and worry. "Why did you heal me? After you saw me?"

"It's my responsibility." She shrugged. "Regardless of what you've done, letting you die when I have the power to stop it would be terribly inhumane."

"Duty," he said, a note of disappointment in his voice.

"And that I was terrified I might lose you." The thought made her chest clench. "I've never seen anyone so close to death. If not for Davan and Minna, I... I don't know that I could have brought you back. I don't know you anymore. I don't know who you are, what's real, what's lies, but if I'd let you slip away, I'd never find out."

He slid a hand from beneath the blankets and brushed the backs of his fingers against her arm. "But you didn't." His hand dropped. "I owe you a debt of more than just gratitude. I owe you my life. And I owe you an apology."

Firal twitched away from his touch.

"I am sorry," he said. "And I know my word's not good for much, but I promise you I never lied about anything, except maybe by omission."

"Dishonesty by any means is still dishonest."

He made a placating motion. "Which is why I acknowledge you have every right to be angry."

"You're right," she agreed. "I do." She put her bowl aside and pushed herself from the edge of the bed. "You stay here and heal. The sooner you get out of my house, the better." Though weak and weary, she needed fresh air. *And time to think,* she added mentally on her way to the open door. She expected eavesdroppers, but to her surprise, the hall beyond her doorway was empty.

"Firal," he called after her.

She paused with one hand on the doorframe and looked back.

"When you come back, bring me something to wear. I doubt you want me leaving your house like this." He drew back the blankets just enough to expose his bare hip.

Firal gasped and turned redder than ever before. She darted into the hallway and slammed the door behind her.

17

RETURNS

Kifel didn't bother trying to hide his exasperation when his office door opened for what seemed the hundredth time. "What is it now?" he all but snapped as his stewardess led in a familiar mageling.

Shymin offered a stiff bow and an apologetic glance as Medreal closed the door behind them. She turned to the older woman as if seeking permission and waited for Medreal's nod before she spoke. "A missive from the border, sire. There's a group of men moving near your territory. The mages stationed nearest the border believe they are either scouts or scavengers. The mages have requested soldiers be sent to aid with investigation and, if necessary, to turn the group away." The mageling stopped in front of Kifel's desk and held out the letter.

He took it and frowned. Whoever had broken the wax seal had done so shamelessly. "Who opened this?"

"Master Anaide, Sire." Shymin lowered her eyes. "The missive was sent to her. She asked me to deliver it to you."

Kifel sighed, leaning back in his chair. He unfolded the letter, skimmed it, and tossed it to his desk. "And Anaide only asked you to deliver it to me because she can't order soldiers to the border by herself, I imagine?"

The girl shifted on her feet and fidgeted with her skirt as she floundered for words. Kifel almost felt sorry for her. He held up one hand and rubbed his eyes with the other. "No, you don't have to speak, I don't expect you to answer. But everyone wants something, and I find myself very short of help these days." He drew a fresh sheet of paper from his desk's drawer and took his pen, tapping it against the mouth of its inkwell. There was no need for a lengthy order; a command for a band of soldiers to move east was enough. He surveyed the note for a moment before he added instructions for the border mages to return to Ilmenhith after the problem was settled.

To say he did not trust the mages would have been an understatement, but it had been impossible to refuse them when half the temple arrived at his doorstep. Backed into a corner as he was, he had allowed them a refuge in the capital, but only after Temar and the rest of his court mages had interrogated each and every one of the Masters. The magelings, too, deserved questioning, but the line had to be drawn somewhere. The magelings would be tested for loyalty in the days to come. For now, that they answered to loyal Masters would have to be enough.

"I apologize for the inconvenience, sire," Shymin murmured, the fabric of her skirt still bunched in both hands.

"Inconvenience is something I am, sadly, quite used to." He sprinkled sand across the page to dry the ink. Curving the paper, he jostled the dust back into its bowl. There had been a time when his need to sign and stamp documents had been all but nonexistent. Now, the pounce bowl sat filled with ink-stained clumps and the box of sealing wax in his drawer was all but empty. He folded the letter, sealed it, and stamped it with the royal crest. "That should suffice. Anaide may present that to any officer in the city guard to receive the assistance she needs. And the next time Anaide desires something, remind her that she is welcome to visit me herself."

The mageling swallowed and offered a nervous smile. "Of course, sire. Thank you." She took the letter when he offered it and dipped in a curtsy before she turned to excuse herself from the office. Medreal let her out as quietly as she'd let her in.

Kifel eyed the old woman as he dropped his pen back into the inkwell. "How many mages are stationed near the border?"

"Not many, Your Majesty." Medreal shrugged. "There are few cities large enough to warrant them."

He nodded, settling back in his chair. "How many chapter houses sit along the border?"

"Two, I believe. Why do you ask?"

"Because I've never paid much mind to the affairs of mages. It's clear that was a mistake." He laced his fingers together and gazed down at the discarded letter. "How many mages are there on Elenhiise? Where are they? How many of those who haven't yet answered my summons are on my side, and how can we tell?"

Medreal raised a brow. "Those are questions I cannot answer, my king."

"Precisely." He rubbed his temples with his thumbs. "And who can? The Masters? The Archmage?"

"The chief of your court mages does a well enough job," she said.

"Not good enough." Kifel tapped a finger against the edge of the desk. "There are a number of mages still missing."

"Including your son?"

He hesitated.

Medreal joined him at his desk. "I see." She moved documents until she uncovered a silver teapot amid the papers. Her fingertips brushed its side to check its temperature. He'd forgotten it was there, but when she refilled his cup, the tea steamed. "Well, Majesty, another option is traveling the borderlands on your own and counting the chapter houses for yourself."

213

"I've been to the borderlands before," Kifel said, sighing in exasperation. "At some point or another, I've visited every mage's station on my lands. There were so many of them I can't recall the number. I couldn't possibly make that trip now."

A heavy silence presided over the room as he watched her add sugar and cream to his cup. At last, he reached for the tea and spoke again. "I gave her everything she asked. How could she turn my own mages against me?"

Medreal idly turned the teapot's lid to line up the engraved pattern. "Not all the mages are against you, my liege."

"I know." He smiled, not an ounce of mirth in the expression. "That's why the city is full of them."

"Do you regret the decision to grant them sanctuary?"

Did he? Kifel watched the cream swirl and settle in his cup. "No. I just wish I was certain that all the mages in my lands were loyal. Until the rest respond to my summons and swear themselves to me or else defect to join Envesi, I can't trust any correspondence that comes in." He drained his cup in a few swallows as he pushed himself up from his desk.

Medreal pursed her lips, a look of displeasure he'd learned to recognize long ago. "Will you be taking leave for the afternoon, sire?"

"Perhaps longer." He brushed wrinkles out of his coat and deposited his empty cup in her hand. "I intend to have several mages accompany the handful of men I'm sending to investigate the situation at the border. I will select them myself." He took his sword from beside the desk and strapped it at his hip.

She bowed her head in understanding and stepped aside.

No matter how unsure he was about the loyalties of the mages in the capital, Kifel was glad their headquarters was near the palace. It made them easy to monitor. The proximity of their chapter house meant Temar and the other court mages could sense the Masters as they came and went. They continually left new reports on Kifel's desk, notifying him that new groups of mages had arrived. So far, every Master who had reported to the chapter house had appeared before him and sworn allegiance. He hoped that would remain the case.

Kifel walked the halls of his palace in solitude, but two guards took up his flank as he crossed the courtyard. He didn't like taking them, but he wasn't certain he liked the idea of going alone. It was strange how quickly things had changed, how fast he'd become uncomfortable with the mages after so many years of walking freely in the temple's gardens.

The chapter house had no need for guards, its doors open to the breeze. The front room was something like a parlor, filled with couches and small tables. A single desk sat near the entrance, the young woman behind it scrawling something in a book. A receptionist seemed unnecessary, but if there were still mages filtering in from other chapter houses, he could understand the desire to have someone present to greet them.

The woman glanced up, startled by their appearance in the doorway. She leaped to her feet and smoothed her blue mageling's robes. "Your Majesty! I—I beg your pardon, had we known you were coming, there would have been a Master at the door to—"

"No need," Kifel interrupted with a wave of his hand. "Just direct me to Master Anaide."

She winced. "Master Anaide is indisposed, arranging travel accommodations for a number of mages traveling from Wethertree."

His jaw tightened. It seemed Envesi wasn't the only mage who had grown inconsiderate of his rank. Anger simmered inside him, but he tamped it down. Establishing control over the mages in Ilmenhith was important, yet everything had to be managed with a gentle hand. Who knew what would drive them back to Envesi's flock? "I see."

The mageling averted her eyes. "Master Edagan is present, if you would like to speak with her in the meantime? Her office is at the far end of the hall, on the left."

"Of course." The words came out sharper than he meant, but

Kifel didn't wait for the mageling to react before he delved deeper into the chapter house.

Most of the doors in the hallway were closed, but the door to Edagan's office stood wide open. The white-haired and sour-faced mage sat at her desk, sorting through piles of paper. He stepped inside and his men posted themselves on either side of the door.

"Ah, my liege. King or not, I would prefer if you knocked." Edagan never looked up from the papers in her hands. "I don't imagine you've come to discuss what we were able to retrieve from Kirban's abandoned storerooms. How may I assist you, Majesty?"

Kifel raised a brow. The woman had a brusque way of speaking, he was used to that. She knew her place well enough and had never challenged him, but he had grown tired of the casual manner the Master mages had begun to take with him. Still, he set the thought aside for later. When he corrected them, it would be before his council. A scolding before Ilmenhith's elite would sting more than a private reprimand. "A mageling just brought news from the borderlands. The letter she carried requested support, so mages could investigate reports of trespassers in my territories."

"Ah, Anaide sent a messenger already, did she?" Edagan set the papers aside and gave him her full attention. "I apologize for requiring your involvement so soon, but with the temple now divided, we can no longer operate autonomously. We do not have the numbers or the ability to defend the border on your behalf."

"You defending the border was never required," Kifel replied, bridling his annoyance. "It was also never necessary. All I asked was that you keep watch. Relythes and I have long held a quiet disagreement and have been content to keep to our own lands."

Edagan smiled sadly. "I'm afraid Envesi has changed that."

"So it would seem." He rested a hand on the pommel of his

sword and drummed his fingertips against the hilt. "Who will be carrying out this expedition?"

The aging Master shrugged. "Your response will have been left on Anaide's desk, I'd imagine. Did you not mean for her to lead the group?"

"She was not here to meet me, so you will be taking over." He fixed her with a hard look. "You'll get your soldiers to support the expedition, but I will select mages from my court to accompany you for the investigation. Once the matter has been seen to, you will collect all mages from this remaining border outpost—as well as those who have not yet answered my summons—and recall them to the capital at once. They will remain within Ilmenhith. No more village outposts, no more chapter houses."

She half rose from her chair. "But sire! If there are no mages in villages, they—"

"That's an order, not a request," Kifel snapped. "Once all mages are present here in Ilmenhith, you will scour your ranks to find those who may dissent or oppose my rule, and they will be excommunicated from your order."

A pained look twisted Edagan's face. "But there are so few of us left." It was more a lament than a protest.

"And I would rather have a handful of mages I can trust than a country full of them I cannot. Understood?"

"Yes, Your Majesty." She sank back into her chair and lowered her eyes to her desk. "It will be done."

"Good. When my mages come for you, you may depart." Kifel gestured for his men to precede him into the hallway. He said nothing more to the Master mage, and she didn't try to stop him as he took his leave. The two soldiers fell in on either side of the king.

A mageling girl stepped from an office and started when she saw them coming. She closed the door and pressed her back to the wall as they passed. Kifel spared her a sidewise glance, his emerald eyes narrowing when he recognized her. Then they moved on, and he found himself resting a hand on his sword again as Shymin's eyes followed him out.

———

VAHN GRIMACED AS ANOTHER MERCHANT SNEERED AND TURNED away with a look of pure disdain. He couldn't blame the man, though the reaction grated on his nerves. The road back to Ilmenhith had been unforgiving, and he was a little worse for wear. Or perhaps that was a gentle way to put it. He was certain he looked haggard, his face smudged with dust and sweat and his clothing stained with dark spatters from the encounter more than a week before. Nothing sounded better than a good bath. His travels back to the capital had added a coat of dirt and caked mud, and the boots on his feet had given him blisters some time ago, so he walked with an uneven gait.

The merchant seemed content to pretend Vahn wasn't there. For the most part, no one looked at him twice. He couldn't decide whether he appreciated that or not. With his shambling walk and dirty uniform, he knew how he looked; it wouldn't have been the first time he'd dragged himself out of an alley behind the cheap taverns at the edge of town. Even the city guards, men whose names he knew well after their years of service beneath his father, nudged each other and pointed at him as if it were some grand joke. Others turned up their noses as they would if he were a drunken beggar. But beggars didn't carry the king's steel.

Ilmenhith had grown soft. Vahn had never realized how ill-prepared the city's defenses were. But Ilmenhith didn't know struggle; the city didn't know war. In the eyes of its inhabitants, a dirty and limping cadet meant drink, not danger. He supposed it was for the best. The news he carried could not be delivered to just anyone.

The towers looming over the palace wall were a welcome sight. Vahn hurried past the bustle of the market and into the open streets that ringed the palace. He'd gone half a dozen steps before he stopped dead in his tracks and blinked at a handful of robed figures in his path. He rubbed his eyes and looked again, almost positive he'd seen wrong.

He had not. A woman in Master white stood beside the large building he recognized as the capital's chapter house—a sight that wasn't unusual on its own. It was the magelings in their colorful robes that filtered in and out of the building at the Master's behest that caught him off guard.

What were they doing there? The solstice had been the first occasion in the temple's history where magelings traveled so far from the temple's grounds. They certainly had no business in the chapter house. Only those who had graduated to the rank of Master were stationed in the cities. He turned away and gave a startled shout when he collided with a girl in a yellow robe.

She stumbled backwards with a scowl on her face. "Careful!"

"I'm sorry, I didn't mean to—" He stopped short when he saw her face and took a half step back, unconsciously smoothing his dirty shirt. "Kytenia?"

The mageling's brows rose. "Vahn?" Her hazel eyes darted up and down his disheveled frame. "What in the world happened to you?"

He grimaced for what seemed like the dozenth time since entering the city. "It's a long story."

Kytenia folded her arms over her chest. "I imagine stories should wait until after you've bathed."

"Is it that bad?" he asked, looking down at himself.

Her expression indicated it was, though she avoided answering the question. "Where are you going? Not to the palace, I hope. Not looking like that."

Vahn hesitated. Where was he going? The barracks would be all but empty this time of day. He didn't know where his father would be, and he wasn't sure who else he could report to. He'd want to speak to the king, of course, or at least send him a message. By now, Kifel may have heard about the unexpected brawl, but not that his son had been involved—or that he'd survived. But Vahn wasn't an officer. He barely scraped the bottom rung of the military ladder. He couldn't possibly report directly to the king. "I'm sure my commanding officer will want to speak with me."

"Well if that's the case, it'll probably have to wait. A huge contingent left this morning, traveling with Masters to gather the mages still scattered across the island. Each Master was to be escorted by an officer." When he frowned, she eyed him and tilted her head. "How long have you been gone?"

"Too long, evidently." Why would the mages be recalled? They provided a vital service, supplying healing for both soldiers and peasants across Elenhiise. He blinked twice, suddenly reminded of the reason for Ran's ensured survival. "Firal!"

Kytenia's eyes went wide. "What? What about her? Do you know where she is?"

"What was she doing out of the temple? What are *you* doing out of the temple?" He paused and then added, "You mean you knew she was gone?"

"She was expelled just as the lot of you were given orders to leave Kirban. I thought she'd come to Ilmenhith, but..." She glanced over her shoulder, wringing her hands until her knuckles turned white. "Why don't you come inside and clean up? If you know where she's gone, we want to talk with you."

Vahn breathed a sigh and his shoulders sagged. "I wouldn't refuse a bath and change of clothes." Perhaps he could speak to one of the high-ranking Masters while there. They were privy to Ran's circumstances, and surely they would pass word to the king. Besides, he hadn't yet worked through what he would say to the officers when he did report. While he was certain the rest of his unit had continued on to the chapter house they'd been ordered to visit, Vahn did not know when the officers in Ilmenhith would receive word he had deserted the group—if they hadn't already. His father's reputation would allow him to unravel a good deal of the damage, but addressing his father was another concern.

"Good. This way." Kytenia jerked her head toward the door and led the way. She paused to say something to the Master at the entrance, her voice just low enough that he couldn't hear. The two women looked back at him before the Master nodded and motioned them inside. Vahn gave the Master a respectful half-bow before following Kytenia's lead.

He'd been inside the chapter house several times to deliver messages before he'd gained a real place in the military. He saw a few faces he recognized from those days. They eyed him strangely, but he inclined his head in greeting anyway. No one looked particularly happy, though if the Masters really were recalling all mages to Ilmenhith, he understood why.

Kytenia led him up a flight of stairs and down a narrow hallway. They stopped in front of an unmarked door. He didn't know how the mages kept their bearings. At least in the palace, there were paintings and distinct vases that helped differentiate each hall. The chapter house was bare, sterile.

"In here," Kytenia said as she pushed open the door and stepped inside.

There were no windows, but a handful of mage-lights floating near the ceiling gave the room the same bright cast one might expect from daylight. A large bronze tub stood in the center of the room, already filled with water. A shelf with towels and soaps waited against the wall. Vahn glanced over his shoulder. "Ah... Maybe before the bath, I should—"

Kytenia snorted. "Oh, no you don't. You're a mess, not fit to present to anyone." She put her hands against the edge of the tub and a flicker of concentration crossed her face. "There. The water is warm now. You go ahead and clean yourself up. I'll have someone find a change of clothes and bring it up for you. I want to speak with you as soon as you're done."

"Thank you," Vahn murmured as she brushed past him and

slid out of the room, closing the door behind her. She wasn't going to let him object, so he might as well do as he was told.

Steam rose from the water, filling the room with stifling humidity. Being around mages wasn't new, but he never got over the odd discomfort of seeing them practice their craft. Giftless as he was, he never knew what to expect.

Vahn waited until he was certain Kytenia wasn't returning before he undressed. His clothes were likely ruined; he didn't have much hope for getting week-old bloodstains out of his uniform. With fortune, he wouldn't be expected to pay for its replacement. Still, he folded his clothes as neatly as he could and left them on the floor beside the tub.

His toes touched the water and he sucked in a sharp breath. It was almost too hot, but he pushed his foot down into the water anyway. Then he sank into the tub, groaning in relief as the heat seeped into his muscles. He hadn't realized how sore and tired he'd been, too driven by the need to return and report.

As low in the ranks as he was, Vahn hadn't been privy to the reason they'd been ordered to ride for the border. The more he thought about it, the more he was certain the orders his unit carried had been orders of recall for the mages. If that task was important enough for Ilmenhith to send Masters and officers to ensure those orders were received, his unit would have continued on without sending anyone back to look for him. Convenient, he supposed, but his name would still be listed in the report of absentees sent back to the capital.

The skirmish had become a blur. He didn't remember what he'd said or done after his friend had fallen. He thought he remembered begging—pleading for the rest of the cavalry to stop and listen—but he didn't recall what was said, or by whom. Some of Ran's group had escaped, a miracle he'd thanked Brant for a dozen times during his week of foot travel. Vahn had asked his commanding officer to let him stay, to move the dead into the outermost rings of the ruins where they would be undisturbed. The captain had ordered him to catch up when he was finished.

Instead, Vahn had helped the enemy rescue his friend and then turned toward Ilmenhith. The Underlings had sworn Ran would survive and forbidden Vahn from accompanying them into the underground. He'd insisted until they'd named Firal as their healer.

The door banged open. Vahn shouted and scrambled to cover himself.

"Oh please, boy, you've nothing I haven't seen before." Edagan swept into the room, the skirt of her robes swirling about her ankles. She closed the door as forcefully as she'd opened it, dragged a stool from the corner and stood it at the foot of the tub. The old mage dropped onto it with a thump.

"What are you doing in here?" Vahn drew up his knees, still shielding his nakedness with both hands. He sank into the soapy water until it covered his shoulders.

The white-robed woman sniffed. "No one enters or exits our headquarters without the Masters knowing. Anaide and Nondar are both out. That leaves me to deal with the matter." She pursed her lips. Her face looked like a withered prune. "I understand you know the whereabouts of one of our lost magelings?"

His eyes darted from her to one of the folded towels on the shelf. "Firal? Kytenia said she was expelled. I assume that means she's no longer part of the temple?"

"The temple is no more," Edagan replied dryly. "She was expelled by an Archmage we no longer serve, and it was done without input from the Masters of the Houses of affinity. We wish to recall her immediately."

Vahn struggled to absorb everything he'd just heard. The nonchalant way she spoke was startling enough, never mind the information she'd shared. They no longer followed the Archmage? If the temple had dissolved, that explained why Ilmenhith's chapter house was bursting with mages. He drew a long breath and spoke slowly. "There's a colony of people inside the ruins."

"Yes, yes, the Underthings, or whatever it is they call

themselves. We know about those." Edagan waved a hand, scowling. "The girl. Firal. Where is Firal?"

"She's with them," he said. "Acting as their healer." How long had the Masters been aware there were people living just beyond the temple's grounds? If Ran hadn't told him, he never would have known.

"And was Lomithrandel with her?" The question came as though she'd heard his thoughts. His mouth worked without producing words for a time before the old mage added, "I was present when the poor wretch took his first breath, boy. We know where he goes and who he sees."

"Yes." Vahn winced at how fast he answered. "He was injured. Before they turned me out of the ruins, I was told Firal would see to his care. The king will want to know he—"

"The king will be told. And you're right, he'll certainly want to know the whereabouts of his child. They've been apart for far too long." Edagan stood with a surprising grace, given her elderly frame. "Good boy. Clean yourself up and stop blushing."

He grew redder at the suggestion and sank until his nose nearly touched the surface of the water. The moment the Master was gone, he scrubbed as fast as he could manage. He'd only just stepped from the water and wrapped a towel around his waist when someone knocked.

"There's no peace in this bloody place," he grumbled, slinging another towel around his shoulders. He braced himself for another onslaught of questions and opened the door.

At sight of his state of undress, a flush rose into Kytenia's cheeks. "Ah," she breathed, looking away, though he was modestly covered. "I brought you a fresh outfit. It isn't much, but it ought to fit." She held out the folded clothing for him to take, her eyes exploring the ceiling as if she'd never noticed it before.

Vahn sighed. "Thank you." He inspected what she'd brought as he took it from her hands. "I'll be right out, if you'll give me a moment to dress."

"Of course," she said, her eyes still turned toward the heavens.

He pushed the door closed and dressed. The clothing she'd provided wasn't much, but even the coarse cloth of the dark trousers and ivory shirt seemed fine after his filthy uniform. She hadn't brought fresh socks. He considered his for a moment, his nose wrinkled. Deciding he was better off without them, he gathered his soiled clothing under one arm, his boots under the other, and stepped barefoot into the hall.

Kytenia glanced over her shoulder and offered a faint smile when she saw him. "I suppose Master Edagan's already wrung everything out of you?"

"Did you tell her why I was here?" He turned to look down the hallway. There wasn't another soul to be seen.

"Not on purpose." She ducked her head. "I was so excited. I ran into Rikka in the hall and told her you were here and had news. I didn't even know Edagan was listening until she shook the rest out of me."

"When did the mages break away from the Archmage?" The question made something prickle unpleasantly between his shoulder blades, though he felt better for having it out. The look Kytenia gave him was guarded at best.

"We haven't been in Ilmenhith long, but we're not supposed to talk about it." She kept her voice low, as if she expected to be scolded for speaking at all. "Did Master Edagan...?"

"She told me a little, but I got the sense the Masters don't want anyone to know much."

Kytenia offered a halfhearted smile. "They haven't told us much more. Here, this way."

Vahn nodded, letting silence fall between them. Kytenia led him back to the entryway of the chapter house. It was a comfortable sitting room, where a handful of familiar-looking magelings waited on the couches. He recognized them as the group of girls he'd seen Firal and Kytenia with, but he couldn't recall their names. A small girl with her hair in dark braids was the first to rise, the redhead short to follow. The third girl did not stir, merely looking at the two of them expectantly.

"Well?" the redheaded girl asked. What *was* her name, again?

"Well what?" He frowned.

"Where's Firal? Can you bring her to us?" The girl with braids clutched the ends of her hair and stared up at him with hope in her eyes.

Vahn glanced between them, uncertain. "I don't know if I should say. I've already spoken with one of the Masters, and—"

"If Edagan didn't want you to talk about it, she'd have said so," Kytenia said.

He inched toward the couch across from where the oldest girl sat with her arms crossed. Her eyes weighed on him, sharp and serious, and he decided he couldn't refuse. He cleared his throat and sat, his belongings still in his arms. "She's safe, I can tell you that much for certain. She's with... an acquaintance of mine," he said, neatly skirting any real mention of Ran. "They're in the ruins."

All four of the girls regarded him with blank expressions. Finally, the mageling with the braids sank into her seat, her eyes round as saucers.

The girl with red hair plopped down on the couch and kicked up her heels. "Oh, this is going to be quite a story."

"And he's going to tell it all. Right, Vahn?" Kytenia gave him a stern look.

"Of course," he agreed. He wasn't likely to escape, anyway. He put his uniform and boots on the floor and rested his elbows on his knees. "I guess it started when we received those orders telling us to leave Kirban Temple. I thought it was odd, but it wasn't my place to question it. It must have been a sudden decision, or my father would have sent me word. In any case, we stopped in Wethertree for supplies. While we were there, we were told to carry orders to mages stationed near the border. On our way, one of the scouts spotted a band of armored men..." He continued the story in as dry a fashion he could manage, mindful not to use Ran's name.

Kytenia hung on every word and as Vahn spoke, a light grew in her eyes. He tried to pay her no mind, his gaze drifting to the ceiling as the rest of the story flowed. He didn't dare meet her eyes. For some reason, the way she looked at him made a flush rise into his cheeks.

SEVERANCE

DAEMON READ DAVAN'S NOTES A THIRD TIME BEFORE HE PUT THEM aside and forced himself to his feet. His men had long since left him in Lumia's meeting rooms and he was grateful no one was there to see him struggle. More grateful to have a positive report on his friend's whereabouts, but he hadn't thought Vahn would be mistreated. Davan had personally escorted him to the edge of the ruins and made careful note of the travel supplies they'd sent with him. Daemon would have to remember to pass along his thanks.

For Vahn, thanks hardly seemed enough. How many times had Vahn saved his hide? Daemon didn't remember, no more than he remembered what started the fight when they'd first met. He remembered that first shove and the way he'd answered with fists. They'd scrapped and tumbled in the palace gardens for some time before the chain holding his amulet had snapped, and when Vahn saw the scales and claws for the first time, the fight stopped.

Vahn hadn't said anything. He hadn't shrieked like the few nursemaids who had seen him, hadn't fainted or tried to run. He'd simply stood there, mouth agape, until Medreal whisked Daemon back to his quarters in the upper floor of the palace.

The following day, the boy appeared outside the royal living quarters, looking for a playmate. From that moment forward, Vahn had been there. Present. Dependable. The only friend he had—at least, until the temple.

Daemon grimaced at the thought of Firal. There were bigger things to worry about than whether or not Core's healer was still angry at him. That was all she was, he reminded himself. All she could be. Even if she forgave him, what future could they have? He tried to force her from his mind as he departed the meeting room and crept through the dark corridors toward more private spaces.

He'd planned to visit his office near the barracks, but when he reached the top of a flight of stairs, he reconsidered his destination. He'd been back on his feet for a single day and the long tunnels ahead seemed an insurmountable distance. Instead, he turned toward his chambers.

Exhaustion weighed heavy on his shoulders by the time he reached his door. Though the wound in his side had been healed, he could have sworn it was still there. That was normal, Firal said, and it would take time for the afterpains of healing to subside. He pushed open his door and paused. The tallow candles were already lit.

"You look tired." Lumia slid from behind the door with all the grace of a viper, a gleam in her eyes.

"Recovery tends to take a lot of energy." Daemon rested a hand over his side and let out a hissing breath as she glided behind him. The door clicked shut, the snap of the lock reverberating in the room like the closing of a prison gate.

Lumia frowned. "Yes, I heard you were injured. I couldn't bear to see you in such a state. I've missed you, my pet."

"How did you know I'd be here?" He forced himself to lower his hand.

"I didn't." She shrugged. "I was just going through your things."

Daemon made his way to the bed and leaned against a

bedpost as he scanned the room. His quarters in the underground were well-furnished, with the desk, chairs, bed and wardrobe carved from fine, dark wood. Thick furs on the bed served as blankets, and colorful rugs lay spread across the cold stone floor. Nothing looked out of place. "Find anything interesting?"

"Yes." She smirked. "I found you."

He unfastened the ties of his mask and dropped it to the bed beside him. He said nothing, knowing the silence would agitate her.

"Is there a reason you never came to tell me what happened?" Her tone was deceptively calm, her eyes cold. She moved toward him with a predatory step.

"I wasn't in much of a position to go anywhere. I'm only just now able to walk." He pushed away from the bedpost and straightened, grimacing at a stab of pain in his side. "And not very well, at that."

Her eyes narrowed. "Where were you?"

"Jealousy is unbecoming, Lumia." He didn't have to look to know the response angered her. He might have sworn the air grew colder.

"Jealousy!" She laughed bitterly and shook her head. "Not jealousy. Anger, and it is rightly deserved. You forget yourself. You think it coincidence the mageling ended up here? You're indebted now. The mages will sink their claws back into you any way they can."

"She's the best healer we have. If it had been up to you to save me, I'd be dead."

"Better dead than a slave to their cause," she said. "Do not forget all I've done to free you from the temple."

Daemon's gaze darkened. "Leave. Now. I'm tired and I wish to rest. I don't have the energy to deal with you tonight."

Her blue eyes flashed fire. "Remember who you're speaking to. I am your queen!"

"In name only," he replied. "What have you done to lead

these people? In all the years I've been here, I've never seen you lift one finger to ease their struggles. They finally have enough food, a trade economy that's beginning to thrive, a parcel of land to help them grow more self-sufficient, and none of it was your doing."

Lumia's hands clenched to fists. "I signed the treaty to give them that land."

"Only because I didn't have the authority to do so."

Her eyes widened, then narrowed to slits. "What are you saying?"

"That you don't lead these people," he said coolly. "I do."

A growing scowl shadowed her face and her fists tightened until they trembled at her sides. The candles flickered as a surge of energy rippled around her. "How dare you? After everything I've done for you, after all the promises I've made to give you power—"

"I don't need you to give me power," he interrupted. "I already have it."

Golden curls spilled forward over Lumia's shoulders as her jaw clenched and she tucked her chin into her chest.

The sensation started as a prickle in the back of his hand and grew to a low, pulsating heat in the lines of the scar she'd given him. His fingers twitched; he curled them into his palm. The heat intensified, pain lancing through his scarred left hand. "What are you doing?"

"You swore yourself to me," she hissed. "I own you."

The scar burst, shooting searing heat up his arm. Black ichor welled in the open wounds, smoke rising as it began to sizzle on the back of his hand. Daemon spat a curse and scraped frantically at the oil-black blood that scorched his scales, sending spatters across the furs and floor. Plumes of smoke spiraled from the edges of each drop as they began to glow red-hot and eat into everything they touched.

"Stop this!" He clutched his arm as the heat moved upward.

The veins in the tanned flesh of his upper arm and shoulder swelled beneath his skin, forming dark lines that traced the flow of foul magic.

"I own you!" Lumia screamed, the air around her crackling with power.

Daemon gritted his teeth, his snake-slitted eyes flaring with reddish light. He lashed out on instinct and grasped at the air beside her head. He felt the catch of energy flows in his hand and snared them unconsciously with his own. He turned his hand, let the gesture guide his power, and twisted the flows tight.

She squealed and struggled to take back her power.

He wound the energy tighter, pulling hard against her influence. The black pollution in his veins receded, the blistering ichor rolling freely from his hand suddenly cool.

"Stop!" she shrieked, grasping desperately at his outstretched arm, clawing at his hand as tendrils of her energy battered against his hold on the flows.

"You own nothing," he spat. The ties to her power drew tight and strained against his pull. Then, one by one, he tore them away. The strands of energy snapped like threads.

Lumia screamed. She fell to her knees and lifted trembling hands to cradle her head. The air around her went dead, the tingling presence of her Gift extinguished like a candle's flame. Power snapped back to him and Daemon staggered. It surged into him, restoring, replenishing. He grabbed the bedpost for support. The black blood that trickled from his wounded hand grew icy on his scales. His head spun, but not from weakness. The pain and exhaustion was gone. He straightened and looked down at her, though it took a moment for his eyes to focus.

"And you cannot control me," he rasped. His legs grew steady beneath him. He let go of the bedpost and made for the door, leaving her crumpled on the cold stone of the floor as her agonized screams echoed through the endless hallways.

KYTENIA SAT AT THE EDGE OF THE STREET WITH HER CHIN CUPPED IN her hands and her elbows propped on her knees, watching the workers go by. Expansion of the chapter house was well underway, merging the new headquarters for Ilmenhith's mages with what used to be a noble's home next door. She and a handful of other magelings watched idly through the day.

Things hadn't settled enough to let classes resume. With all the construction afoot, she doubted it would settle soon. The changes were necessary, as the chapter house was not equipped to hold the number of mages that now occupied it. Things would only get worse as mages trickled in from the countryside.

The new construction would double the size of the chapter house. Kytenia imagined it had cost the Masters a considerable sum to oust the nobles from the tall stone building next door, though the king had probably offered leverage. It would be good to have better sleeping quarters but, with luck, the first thing they built in the new addition would be a proper dinner hall. If they couldn't have lessons, Kytenia at least wanted a decent meal.

She kicked a pebble as she rose and put a hand to her grumbling stomach. The mages didn't go hungry, but sharing a dinner hall with the king's military was not the best arrangement. With strict shifts to keep, the soldiers and city guards couldn't afford to defer to hungry magelings, which meant mealtimes for mages always came late. It was closer to evening than midday, though, and she was unwilling to wait any longer for the crowds to thin. If she had to compete with soldiers for food, then so be it.

Kytenia fixed her skirts and smoothed her hair, stealing a glance at her reflection in the plate glass of a shop window before she ducked inside. Sharing the dinner hall wasn't all inconvenience, at least. There were some advantages to sharing tables with the king's men. She'd been excited to spend time with Vahn after the letters he'd left when he departed the temple, and she was relieved it had been easy to find the opportunity. He sat in the same place every day, though today her friends had beaten her to joining him. Rikka sat beside him, Marreli across the table. Shymin rarely joined them, but she'd been busy running errands for the Masters, so Kytenia understood.

"Starting without me today?" She planted her hands on her hips and gave the three of them a stern look.

Marreli patted the bench beside her. "Rikka and I just finished, and Vahn just got here. Sit down, I'll go get you a plate."

"Thank you. Oh, and get an extra sweetroll if they have them today!" Kytenia called as the gray mageling disappeared.

Vahn leaned forward to offer the sugar-frosted roll from his plate. "To hold you over?" He grinned.

Kytenia took it with a coy smile. The sparkle in his eyes made her cheeks heat.

Rikka looked between the two of them and made a sound of amusement. "I'll go help Marreli. She almost dropped her tray walking through the crowd earlier." She got up before anyone could protest.

Vahn glanced after her and stuffed something in his mouth. His shoulders lifted in an exaggerated shrug. "Guess we're alone now," he mused. There was a hint of something in his voice Kytenia couldn't put a finger on, but his expression was sly.

She tore off a piece of her roll and gave him a suspicious look. "Did you tell them to leave?"

"Of course not! I just suggested it might be nice to speak to you alone, if you were to show up."

She blushed. They'd eaten with him often since his return to Ilmenhith, though at first it was just so he could teach them about the city. But it hadn't taken long for all of them to speak of him as a friend, and with his bright smiles and playful demeanor, this wasn't the first time she found herself blushing over him. He seemed to have that effect on all of them. "What would Firal think if she knew?"

He raised a brow. "I don't know. Why?"

She pursed her lips. Gentle probing hadn't worked in the past. She didn't know why she'd bothered to try again. "With how much time you two spent together in the temple, I thought maybe you were close."

Vahn shrugged again. "Thought I ought to help her, since she was a friend of Ran's. Thought that made her a friend of mine, too, but Ran didn't seem to like the idea."

There had been rumors about that in the temple, something about Ran and Vahn fighting over a girl before a Master stepped in. Kytenia hadn't thought much of the story true, but the way Vahn shifted when he spoke made her reconsider. She chewed her sweetroll thoughtfully. "He liked her, didn't he?"

"Oh, he was crazy about her. There were always girls in Ilmenhith who made eyes at him, but I don't know that he even noticed them chasing his boots. It was always Firal this, Firal that. I thought he needed some prodding to get him to move, but he didn't like that, either."

Kytenia made herself smile. She'd always known she had little chance with Ran. Whatever glimmer of hope she'd held faded after she'd heard he was made a Master. "Did you like her?"

Vahn blinked. "No," he said after a time. It wasn't hesitance, exactly. He seemed more surprised that she'd asked. "Not like that."

She wet her lips with her tongue. "What about me?"

He gave her a startled look, though the corners of his mouth twitched into a smirk, a sparkle in his eyes.

Kytenia jumped when Marreli put a plate of food in front of her, yielding a strange look from the younger girl and a calculating frown from Rikka.

"I couldn't get you a second sweetroll," Marreli said,

glancing between Kytenia and Vahn, "but it looks like you got one already."

"Should we leave you alone?" Rikka didn't sound unhappy, but she didn't look impressed. Belatedly, Kytenia recalled Rikka at Vahn's side and wondered if she'd missed an undercurrent. Rikka was rather fond of men, after all, and she would have to be blind to miss the way Vahn flirted with everyone.

Vahn's voice drew Kytenia's attention. "It's always nice to visit with you girls. You don't have to go anywhere."

"Oh, but we haven't got a reason to stay. We've already eaten. Besides, I haven't had a chance to see what the builders are doing today." Marreli twisted one of her dark braids with both hands, her face taking the sweet, dreamy look it did whenever her imagination was at play. "Won't you go with me, Rikka? I hate to go alone, I'm always afraid I'll be run over in the street."

"You probably would, walking around with your head in the clouds all the time." Rikka mustered a smile. "All right, we'll go. I'll see you back in our room tonight, Kyt."

Kytenia's forced smile faded as soon as her friends slipped away. She bit her lower lip and turned back to her food.

"She's sweet," Vahn said.

"Marreli?"

"Rikka." He wiped his mouth with the back of his hand and reached for his mug. The dishes were plain earthenware, functional but rough, though Kytenia supposed soldiers had no need for anything fancier. "She's feisty, but so nice to Marreli. Even though she's a good few years older, isn't she?"

"She is, but I think that's why they get along," Kytenia said. "She and Rikka are childhood friends, but really, Marreli is like a younger sister to all of us. I think she'll be lost if Rikka ever finds the husband she's after."

Vahn squinted at his water and then gave her a weighted look. "I think she has a little growing up to do before that happens. I like girls who are more mature. Like you."

Color rose in her cheeks again. His tone was playful, like always, but his expression was so serious she didn't know whether he was teasing or not. "Firal's a lot more mature than I am."

"Ran's a lot more mature than I am, too. They must be a good match." His expression didn't change. She looked away.

"It's strange," she murmured, picking pieces from her half-eaten sweetroll. "When we were growing up, Firal always said she felt like she was second to me. But she's smarter than I am. More serious, more adult, more talented, more liked by the Masters. I never told her, but I think she had it backwards. She doesn't think much of herself, but I'm the one who's always come second."

Vahn laughed and leaned against the table. "How do you think I felt growing up with Ran?"

Sheepish, she ducked her eyes with a smile. "I guess you understand, don't you?"

"Better than you could imagine. No one gives the prince's best friend a second glance."

Kytenia's mouth dropped open. "The *what?*"

His face fell. "Firal didn't tell you?"

"You mean she knew?" she cried.

"Ah, I thought she would have..." Vahn trailed off with a grimace, rubbing the back of his neck. "Forget I said anything. He'd wring my neck if he heard I was blabbing his secrets. I just thought that with how close you and Firal were..."

Her head spun with the revelation—and disappointment Firal had kept it from her. "I would have thought so, too," she murmured. The prince. A thousand mysteries collided in her head and resolved in a moment, leaving her dazed.

"In any case," Vahn said, settling back into that casually cheerful tone as if he weren't changing the subject, "I know just what you mean about playing second. But I promise you, Kytenia, you'll never be second to me."

Her heart skipped a beat and, startled, she met his eyes. There was honesty in his gaze, and just a hint of shy uncertainty.

Her lips drew into a smile. It was as good as any admission she could have hoped for. Maybe better, with the earnest timidity in his gaze. She thought he wanted an answer, but her tongue wouldn't move. She let her smile speak for her.

She believed it.

TRUTH

A shadow at the window made Nondar look up from his work. He rubbed his forehead and adjusted his spectacles as the crow settled on the ledge, cawing and batting its wings in a way he dared say was impatient. Grumbling beneath his breath, he pushed himself up from the desk he'd occupied for hours and hobbled to the window to claim the note in the tube fastened to the animal's leg. He never had cared for the use of corvids as messengers. It wasn't that he believed in omens, but the creatures were terribly unpleasant to find in one's room.

The color of the seal on the thin roll of paper indicated no need for response. His hands trembled as he waved the bird away, reminding him again of how frail he'd become. Grumbling over that as well, he crept back to his chair and sat down to cut open the seal and read.

The child has been found. Notify the king at once.

E.

Nondar sighed as he let the paper drop to the mound of

others on the desk before him. If Edagan had heard, there was no longer any way for him to keep it secret. Had she or Anaide discovered he was aware of where the king's child had been, they might have flayed him for not sharing the knowledge. Twisting his narrow white beard, the old half-blood leaned back in his chair.

His party hadn't been in Wethertree for long, certainly not long enough to make any real progress. They'd started by riding along the northern coast, sending mages from their various stations back to the major cities. From the chapter house in Wethertree and those in the other large settlements, they could be Gated back to the capital.

The mages at the chapter house in Wethertree kept excellent records of where more mages were posted. If they hadn't defected, that was. Most of the mages listed in the records were Masters, though there was a handful of magelings who served as apprentices or assistants. They had kept track of several wild mages as well, which surprised Nondar considerably. He'd gone over that list at least a dozen times before he decided to send a notice to each of them, asking they report to the new headquarters in Ilmenhith. All but one.

He'd been stunned to see Lumia's name on the list; it was one he'd not read or heard spoken in years. Why the mages here had chosen to keep track of her, he didn't know, though listing her with wild mages had been clever. The Archmage cared little for wildlings and claimed they had no real potential. With her name on that list, the Archmage would never have known Lumia was still being watched.

"And now I'm to send the king straight to you," Nondar murmured thoughtfully, giving his beard another twist before he reached for his cane. It was better not to waste time. After that note, he knew Edagan would be watching.

Wethertree was a pleasant city, if a stark contrast to the tall structures of Ilmenhith. Nondar had always enjoyed visiting, though it had been a while since he'd last stayed for any real amount of time. The second-largest city in the western territory, Wethertree sprawled like an unkempt hedge. The squat shops and houses were built of weathered gray wood, some with dark wooden shingles still visible, others covered almost entirely with vines.

The city sat in the midst of sparse woods, though thick tropical forest grew just a little farther south. The residents hadn't bothered to cut down any trees, opting to let the city grow around them instead. Neat cobblestone streets wound their way between the buildings, interrupted here and there by tall trees with stone rings at their bases.

The mossy avenues were all but empty this early in the day, most village folk already at work in the forests to the south. It was well there was no one else about. It made it easier to find the cluster of armed guards he was looking for, their group visible from the doorway of the chapter house. They lounged outside the door of the inn, its roof gray with lichen and just brushing the branches of the trees overhead. Nondar had not been pleased with Kifel's choice to stay there, but with a cluster of mages and soldiers surrounding him, it was unlikely the king would encounter trouble. Still, the old Master would have felt better if Kifel had agreed to stay in the chapter house, as was customary. At least there he could ward against prying eyes.

A few of the soldiers regarded Nondar with disinterested glances as they moved aside to let him through the door. None of them offered to help him, however, and he grumbled as he hobbled inside. "You really ought to teach your boys some manners." He raised his voice over the murmurs of the few mages that clustered in the corner. Their group grew quiet.

Kifel sat at his own table, a guard over either shoulder, but no one sat with him. Maps covered the tabletop, all of them marked with colors. The king set aside a piece of chalk and rubbed his chin, leaving smudges of blue. He didn't look up from the maps. "I tried that with Lomithrandel. You can see how well it worked."

Nondar settled on the bench across the table from the king and studied the maps with a neutral expression. Each outpost had been circled in black ink. Different colored chalk marks beside them indicated whether or not they'd received a response to their recall orders. He wasn't certain what all of the colors meant, but the number of red marks made him frown.

It had been a distant hope that all the mages they sought would side with them. While the response had been more favorable than Nondar expected, at least a third of those they spoke to packed their things in the night and departed for Alwhen before they could be imprisoned. He couldn't fault them for their loyalty to the Archmage, though he etched the face of each mage that turned against them into his memory. He would see them again, he was sure, and not likely on good terms.

"Sire," Nondar said, still gripping his cane as though he needed the support. "I received a crow only moments ago. Master Edagan has located your child."

Kifel reached for another piece of chalk. "Where?" No doubt the king assumed he meant Lomithrandel. The boy had been missing for weeks. It wasn't unusual for him to disappear for a few days here and there, but he'd vanished just as the temple fractured, now almost a month prior. The king would not admit it, but the Masters saw how it tore at his heart.

Nondar hesitated. "I would speak to you of this matter in private, if possible."

One by one, more red marks shaded the maps. "Spit it out, Nondar. There's no one here who can't keep secrets."

The Master pursed his lips. "She currently resides in the underground portion of the ruins. I believe you will find your son there, as well."

The king's chalk stopped mid-stroke as he looked up, his eyes weighing on the mage in front of him. Obviously, he wasn't quite sure what he'd heard. "What?"

"There are many things the Archmage thought to hide, my king," Nondar said.

Kifel's brow furrowed, his voice dropping so the other mages could not hear. "What have you kept from me, all these years?"

"A daughter." Nondar leaned against the table. "I have kept her safe, to the best of my ability. She knows not of her parentage. Your wife laid no claim to the child after she was born, obsessed with her experiments and convolutions of magic. We thought it best that she did not know. Every child wants to feel loved by their mother. It would have been cruel."

Kifel squeezed his eyes closed and his face twisted with pain. "Then, my son?"

"If there was ever a doubt, we would have told you. I was there when he was born, sire. You have always known Lomithrandel was not your child. I know you accepted my word as I gave it, no matter what Envesi told you." Nondar's shoulders sagged along with his thick eyebrows. "That you chose to raise him despite that always was admirable."

"Who is she?" Kifel asked.

The old Master eyed him. "I suspect you already know."

The king bowed his head and released the piece of chalk he'd held in a white-knuckled grip. "Does Ran know?"

"He does not," Nondar replied. It was strange to see his king struggle with emotion. He struggled with it himself, fighting to keep the knot in his stomach, lest it come up with his morning meal. "We thought that best, as well. He always was charmed by the girl. Imagine the jealousy it would have spawned between them. Him knowing he could never replace a blood child, her knowing you raised a foundling in her place."

Kifel clasped his hands together and rested his brow against them. "How many know?"

"Anaide, Edagan, the Archmage Envesi, Melora, and myself." Nondar paused and then added, "And one other, long excommunicated from the temple. It's possible she chose to harbor the girl for that reason, to keep her from returning to Ilmenhith. To keep her from you."

A long, quiet moment passed before Kifel nodded again. He

pushed himself up and took his sword from where it rested against the table. He strapped it to his side in silence, but his fingers shook.

Nondar frowned. "Sire?"

Kifel motioned for him to remain seated. "Stay in Wethertree, continue to speak to the mages that answer their summons. Screen them without me. I trust your judgment. You have enough mages present to open a Gate?"

"Yes, sire, but—" Nondar started, silenced by a gesture from the king.

"Good. I will not need your assistance." A steely look set itself in Kifel's eyes as he strode out the door with his entourage of guards on his heels.

Nondar bowed his head and exhaled deeply. Not for the first time, he questioned the wisdom of his fellow mages.

"AND YOU ARE POSITIVE THAT IS WHAT THE MESSAGE SAID?" ENVESI pressed, scrutinizing the mageling that stood before her desk.

The girl kept her head bowed, perhaps out of respect, perhaps out of fear. "Yes, Archmage. Master Edagan herself asked me to deliver it to the aviary."

"You must be quite good at opening seals without being noticed," the Archmage said, leaning back in her chair.

The mageling twitched. "I am not, Archmage. I took some of the colored wax from Edagan's desk when I was cleaning. None of the Masters in Ilmenhith use signets or crests any longer, just colors. I softened and peeled the old wax and resealed it with new."

"Clever enough." The concession came in a tone that gave it little worth. Envesi stroked her jaw with her forefinger and thumb. There was no real backlash she could receive from the child's discovery, now that she'd already distanced herself from Kifel's rule. But it did add the possibility of complications. She had counted on damaging the chances of Kifel having a viable heir when she'd elevated Lomithrandel to the rank of Master. Having a daughter in line meant any number of young men could now compete for the rank that came with marriage, and behind them, there would be the strength of countless noble houses in Ilmenhith.

"Archmage, if I may be so bold as to ask..." The mageling girl dared to lift her eyes.

"Ask what, child?" Envesi could humor a question or two. The girl brought her useful information.

The girl shuffled her feet. "I think I know who the letter was about. Why is she important to the king?"

The question wasn't what she'd expected. The Archmage lifted one white brow. "What was your name again, girl?"

"Shymin, Archmage," the mageling supplied.

"Of course. Tell me, Shymin, does it bother you to know that you stand on the side opposite your friends?" Envesi leaned forward and rested her elbows on her desk. "What drove you to seek me out?"

Shymin swallowed. "We disagreed. My friends and I, I mean. I learned one had done something she shouldn't. Well, several things she shouldn't, really. Later, I learned that a Master was aware of what she'd done and had worked to hide it. What she did was wrong. Regardless of which side I'm on, it was wrong. What changed things was which side that Master was on. I don't feel I can follow a Master who can't abide by their own rules."

"I see," Envesi murmured. "So you side against a leader, not a friend."

"Yes, Archmage." Shymin bowed her head again and clasped her hands together so tightly her knuckles turned white.

Envesi rested a finger against her lips and eyed the mageling, thoughtful. A useful girl, if transparent. It was a wonder she managed to maintain such secrecy in the chapter house in Ilmenhith. But there was nothing wrong with humoring her, as long as she remained useful. Envesi gathered ink and paper and reached for a quill. "The girl may be of use to Kifel because her connections give her potential influence over the throne. I don't know if he'll be rash enough to make use of those connections, but knowing her whereabouts may be perceived as important. Now, as for you."

The Archmage took a piece of colored sealing wax from a box on her desk. She'd made sure to keep the right colors on hand. She penned a short missive while the wax heated. The paper Relythes supplied her with was of fine quality; the ink dried quickly and did not feather. She folded the note and stamped the wax with a seal from another box. "See that this message is given to Edagan. Tell her it is from one of the chapter houses on the border that has not yet been recalled. She will recognize the colored wax. They send word that a band of rebels attempt to claim land just outside the ruins."

Shymin took the offered letter and stepped back. "Yes, Archmage."

The Archmage nodded in approval. It took little prompting to get the girl to understand. That would be worth remembering, when everything was over and it was time to raise magelings through the ranks. She waved a hand. "Off with you, then. You will report to me again when you feel me Calling for you."

"Yes, Archmage." The girl bowed and hurried off. Outside, a handful of Masters would be waiting to Gate her back to Ilmenhith.

After the mageling had gone, Envesi allowed herself a frown. Had she more Masters positioned on the other side, transporting spies with information from the capital would be easier. She'd have sent her Gate-stone back with the girl for the sake of convenience, if she'd been able to find it. It hadn't been among her things when they settled in Alwhen, though she didn't suspect any of the Masters that defected had known to take it. Chances were, some soldier found it in the tower and kept it, thinking it a pretty marble. The idea left a sour taste in her mouth.

At least there was still the option of Gates. It was foolish of Kifel to place the mages in their old chapter house, a place any of Envesi's mages knew well enough to Gate to, but she'd expected nothing else. Keeping him distracted was a simple task. Feeding false information from various outposts would keep his head spinning until she'd determined the best way to bridge the temple's divide.

There was always the option of tying herself completely to Relythes. It was an idea worthy of consideration, no matter how distasteful she found it. His latest wife had recently been lost in childbirth. The mages were formidable, but after Kirban's destruction, the temple lacked resources of its own. Relythes had been generous, but her work demanded more than mere generosity would provide. She needed the power a *throne* could provide.

Envesi laid a fresh sheet of paper on her desk. If that was the angle she was going to play, she'd have to become much more cordial, and quickly. She dipped her quill and carefully began to pen the invitation for Relythes to join her for a formal dinner with her mage council.

BY BLESSING OF BRANT

D<small>IM FIRELIGHT DANCED OVER THE CURVES AND ANGLES OF THE HIGH,</small> vaulted ceiling. Lumia's head lolled as she watched the shadows move. She tried again to feel it, hands extended toward the flame cradled in the iron brazier before her. It warmed her flesh, heat wafting in gentle waves, but she felt nothing else. Her blue eyes slid shut.

The throne room was empty except for her, kneeling beside the only lit brazier in the great hall. More than one servant had offered to light the rest, but she rebuked each of them and sent them away. They had no idea why she was distressed and she did not intend to explain. She should have been able to light them on her own. She should have been able to feel more than the warmth of the flames.

Head hanging, she opened her eyes and looked at the bleak space around her. She'd never found the underground portion of the ruins oppressive before, never wished for the daylight she'd been driven from so many years ago. Of course, she'd never been without the ability to sense her surroundings that came with her Gift, either.

What had he done? All magelings learned the risks of magic. A mage who used too much energy risked burning out and losing their Gift. Drawing too much energy from one source risked unmaking it. But she'd never heard of this. Even after she'd earned the right to wear the white robes and eye markings that proclaimed her Master of the House of Fire, she'd never heard of this.

Gazing down at her hands, Lumia ran through the memories again. It had been like nothing else. The odd impression of being snared, the stress of being wound tight, the snapping sensation that made a painful heat blossom in her chest and head. That was the moment she'd stopped feeling it. The moment she'd stopped feeling him.

Tren's presence, too, was gone from her senses. Just like every other trace of energy. She'd never thought such a thing possible, but she couldn't deny she no longer felt any of the flows around her.

Her magic was gone.

And what would her people say when their beautiful, immortal queen began to age? She buried her face in her hands and willed herself not to cry again. She forced herself to rise from the cold, black stone floor. To hold her head high. Her eyes were still swollen, her throat raw. Step by step she returned to her throne to perch upon it as regally as she ever had.

It was not insurmountable, she reminded herself. Difficult, but not insurmountable. It presented a new set of challenges to overcome, nothing more. She could no longer sense Daemon and, without the ability to manipulate the flows of power, she couldn't control him that way. But there were options. The girl, for example. That bloody, blighted girl.

"I'd say sulking doesn't suit you, but you take to it so well." Tren's voice from behind the throne caught her off guard.

Lumia gritted her teeth and glowered at him as he moved from one of the tapestry-covered doorways. "If I wanted you in my throne room, I would have called for you."

The weight of his stare made her uncomfortable. Again she felt a pang of distress. She'd never been able to read thoughts, but the blood-bond had given her a sense of his emotions, which was just as good. She didn't like the way he studied her, his face as unreadable as stone, his eyes sharp with a predatory gleam. She gave a start when he finally spoke.

"You aren't unaffected, I see." He paused before her. "I shouldn't be surprised that you already know. You did it to him too, after all."

The reference to their lost link made the hair on the back of her neck prickle. He had no way of knowing it was gone, of course; without a Gift, he wouldn't have sensed any change. But what did he expect her to know? She bit her tongue to keep her expression still and forced her breath to stay even. "You've always struggled to hide your jealousy," she said, choosing to focus on the one thing she was certain of, the emotion he'd never been able to quash. "You never have been able to reconcile with the fact that you simply were not as useful as him."

Tren's eyes narrowed, though he said nothing at first. His hands clasped behind his back as he paced around her in a slow circle. A predator indeed. One she'd riled. One she no longer had leashed.

"What's it like?" he asked. "Feeling all those emotions that come from him? All the sensations that come from him being in another woman's arms?"

She bristled.

He smirked. "Struck a nerve, did I?" He paused mid-circle and stared into the shadow of the throne room. "Surely you never believed you'd be able to keep him."

Heat rose into her cheeks and she jerked her head to the side, refusing to let him see that he'd gotten to her. So that was what he thought she knew. She clenched her teeth so tight it made her jaw ache. Her fingers dug at the iron arms of her throne. How had it come to this? "He is still of use to me," she snapped.

"How?" Tren folded his arms and stared at her.

"If he fancies the girl, let him have her. It will cement his claim to the throne and only adds a single obstacle to our path."

She added careful inflection to the last words. It had been so easy to discard Tren when Daemon came along. Now she found herself silently praying she'd be able to reel him back in. "It wasn't how I planned things, but she has her uses, as well. I've allowed her to stay for that reason. Or did you think her presence was beyond my control?" She settled more comfortably into the cushions of her throne as she regained composure.

He avoided meeting her eyes. "Given your predisposition toward jealousy, I wondered." It wasn't quite an admission, but the question put him on his toes.

Lumia scrambled for a way to tie things together, careful to keep her face serene. She always had been good at thinking on her feet. "Daemon is a headstrong boy, always has been. So let him believe he has power for now. He believes he can use it to get what he wants. All we have to do is point him toward our goals—what we've made him think he wants. He thinks he has control of the army, so we let him use that to take a kingdom."

"And then?"

"Simple," she said, batting her eyes. "You take back your armies and we remove the pawns from the chessboard. One way or another, the mages will be destroyed. But for now, my general, let us talk about you."

Tren blinked at the title and straightened where he stood.

A smile twisted the corners of her mouth as a new strategy began to weave itself in her mind. Not all the details had come together, but there was time for that. With Tren at the edges of her web again, all she had to do was entangle him before he realized just who the pawns were.

———

THERE WERE FEW PASSAGES IN THE RUINS WIDE ENOUGH TO accommodate the supply wagons. Firal stepped into a side passage to watch one pass. The wagons had been coming and going between Core and the new outpost for days, wearing a path into the thick grass. Following the tracks through the ruins meant slow going, but she appreciated the clear trail.

With as few beasts of burden as the ruin-folk owned, most of the high-wheeled wagons were pulled by men. More than a few had stopped to ask if she wished to ride, but the flatbeds were loaded down with tools, building materials, and other supplies, so she politely declined and waved them away. They needed no additional burden, and walking did her good. The weather had been fair and everyone seemed to enjoy the time outdoors. With the sun on her face, Firal understood why. She had missed her long walks in the ruins, though revisiting them now stirred the ache of homesickness in her chest. She tried to pay it no mind.

From talk in the marketplace, the new village south of the ruins was coming along nicely, though Firal hadn't yet made her way out to see it. She hadn't planned to visit so soon, but Minna had suggested she visit the construction site while the men worked, just in case there were more injuries. There had been a few. Cuts from mishandled saws or the occasional broken thumb from a misaimed hammer were not concerning, but it slowed things down when the men had to return to the underground for healing.

Beyond the edge of the ruins, the trail stretched on another mile or two before the pale wood of new buildings came into view beneath the forest canopy. People dotted the landscape, exploring their new territory or scouting for provisions among the trees, their clothing a bright ivory against the lush green.

The land they had claimed was unlike anything Firal had seen. The eastern half of the island was higher in altitude, if slightly, and grasslands spread from the northern cliffs to the rolling plain where Alwhen stood. The western half was manicured, its forests pushed back to allow tidy fields for agriculture. But this—the narrow strip of land that ran past the temple and on to the southern coast—was untamed. Copious trees and ferns sprang forth from fertile ground, though the path she followed cut a wide swath through them. It had been a roadway, though rarely used, needed only for Relythes to patrol the border.

The ruin-folk had chosen a large clearing in the forest to establish their first outpost. Eventually, they would move farther south and build on the coast. Such was first step in Daemon's plan to unify the island, but as she walked the trail that seemed to split the east from the west, his cause seemed more far-fetched than ever.

Yet he had leverage in the east, she reminded herself. With knowledge of his true identity, it became easier to understand why Relythes had parted with this strip of jungle, and Firal cursed herself for having missed it before. Ran—Daemon— pushed against his father's rule, and Relythes thought he was propelling the rebellion. A subtle way to jab at Kifel without bringing retaliation down on his own borders. It was petty, and Firal suspected that was exactly why Daemon had known it would work.

Firal fidgeted with the strap of the satchel slung over her shoulder. She tried not to think of Daemon more than she had to. Beyond that first deep conversation, their communication since his injury had been stiff and formal, but not because she didn't wish to speak to him. He pushed her away, just as he had before, keeping her at arm's distance instead of addressing whatever he thought kept them apart. After he had recovered enough to walk with assistance, he'd gone somewhere else to recover, and she hadn't seen him since. Minna insisted he would warm up after his wounds healed—both physical and emotional. Firal hoped she was right. No matter how his deception had hurt, she did not wish him ill. And though her feelings for him had grown confusing and conflicted, they had not gone away. She suspected life would be easier if they had.

Hammers rang in the air and cheerful voices echoed from the village site ahead. Firal picked up her pace, refreshed by the sound. She'd packed a few useful things, her bag filled with gauze and bandages, along with a few bottles of painkilling tinctures and antiseptic salves. And the herbal volume, of course. If it ended up being a slow afternoon, she could always work on her notes.

Working men paused to offer greetings and respectful nods as she reached the edge of the would-be city. She smiled in return, surveying their work as she searched for a place to settle. The village was little more than a main street now, with buildings of all shapes and sizes being erected on either side. A stone-walled well stood toward the end of the street; it had likely been the first thing they'd built. A handful of buckets sat beside it, as well as a few cut logs to offer a resting place. Firal made her way toward it.

Tree stumps ringed the south side of the clearing. A narrow avenue wound between the trees beyond the well, clogged with tall grasses and small saplings. She imagined the rest of the road had looked much the same before construction began.

Dust coated the logs beside the well, but Firal sat anyway and eased her satchel to the ground. She recognized a few nearby faces from the market, though more were unfamiliar men she assumed were part of the army. More familiar women and children roamed the edges of the clearing, but the main street was clear, giving the ruin-folk room to work. They'd established an efficient method. A handful of men rolled logs from the wagons, while others moved them to a sawdusty space where a group of workers cut them to usable lumber. Her eyes lingered on the men working the axes and she frowned. Her healing might be necessary sooner than she thought.

"You should be resting." Firal raised her voice as she approached. "That's too much for you to be doing with that injury."

Daemon spared her a glance on the downswing of his axe. He let it rest where it buried itself in the log. "I took care of that," he replied, a little breathless, but not strained.

She crossed her arms. "You took care of what?"

"The injury. I'm fine, thank you, Miss Healer." He planted a clawed foot against the log and worked the axe free.

Firal pursed her lips and caught hold of his jaw, grumbling about his mask beneath her breath. She touched his energies with her own and jerked in surprise when they pushed back with unexpected force. "That's impossible. It should have taken weeks for you to regain that kind of strength."

He batted her hands away and lifted his axe. "Turns out I'm a fast healer."

She frowned, but stepped back to watch him work. He got in several strikes before she noticed the damp, dark discoloration on the haft of the axe. "Not fast enough, I'd say." She caught his arm and pried his hand from the tool to inspect his palm. A number of scales had been torn loose, leaving raw, bleeding patches in the palm of his hand.

He pulled away. "I've had worse."

"Perhaps, but if you're going to be out here in the dirt, you're not going to leave that exposed. Whether or not you're feeling better, I'd rather not risk infection so soon after healing you." She picked up her skirts and started back toward the well, though she paused after a few steps to glance over her shoulder. "Coming?"

Daemon rolled his eyes, but he leaned his axe against the half-cut log and followed her.

She gestured for him to take a place on one of the makeshift seats as she dug around in her satchel. "Did you bring any gloves? If you're going to keep working, it'd be best for you to cover the bandages. That way they won't tear."

He snorted. "If I'd brought gloves, I would've put them on before starting work."

Firal uncorked a bottle and poured a bit of medication onto a cloth as she knelt beside his feet. Before he got comfortable, she caught hold of one of his hands and dabbed the cloth against his palm. He jumped and hissed when the tincture touched his raw flesh. She struggled to restrain a smirk. "Well, that will teach you to come prepared, I suppose. Does it sting a bit? Good, that means it's working."

"How much of your healing involves not hurting afterward?" He twitched and growled under his breath as she worked the salve across the bloody patches of missing scales.

"I save those treatments for people who haven't angered me." She held tight to his fingers as she retrieved her gauze and set to wrapping his hand. His blisters were in normal enough places. He did not have as many fingers as she supposed he ought, but the tendons and fleshy pads seemed to be similar enough to those in a normal man's hand. When she had more time, she would have to study the anatomy of his hands and feet more closely. With the gauze twisted between each of his fingers and wrapped around his palm, she knotted the bandage and tucked in the ends before gesturing for him to present his other hand. He obliged.

"So are we speaking again?" he asked, voice low.

She shrugged. "You were the one who decided to hide."

"I was going to tell you." He flinched again at the medicine's sting. "I wasn't planning on keeping it a secret forever. I just... I wanted it to be the right time. I wanted to be sure, instead of just relying on hope."

Her heart made an uncomfortable lump in her throat. She kept her eyes on her work. "Hope for what?"

"That you'd be willing to accept me like this."

She paused, then forced herself to keep working. He no longer reacted to the medicine on his abrasions. When she said nothing, he went on.

"You have to understand, I've spent my whole life hiding this. Afraid of being found out, afraid of being treated like I'm different—"

"You are different," she interrupted.

"I'm not," he protested. "What makes me different? My body? A shell? That shouldn't define me. I'm tired of being perceived as a monster because of something I can't help. I didn't choose to be this way. All I ever wanted was just to be a man. Normal. Like everyone else."

"If that's what you want, why do you keep hiding?" She twisted bandages around his hand. "All you're doing is distancing yourself, making it easier for people to see you as being unlike them. Just stop hiding. Things will change." She pulled the knot in the gauze tight and cut off the excess with the small knife Minna had packed for her. It was a wonder how the woman thought of things that never crossed her mind.

He rubbed at the bandaging on one hand and then the other. "It's not that easy."

"Nothing is easy. Speaking to you like this isn't easy." Firal stuffed her things back into her satchel with one hand. "At first, I didn't believe I had the strength to speak to you at all."

"I don't expect you to forgive me. I don't deserve it."

"None of us do." Firal reached up to touch him. Her fingertips slid against the cold steel of his mask. "Which is why the best thing we can do is extend grace to those who haven't earned it."

His eyes flickered behind the featureless steel. The shifting colors showed hints of anxiety, fear. "I hurt you."

"Yes," she agreed. "And nothing will undo that. But holding a grudge won't change things, either."

"I just regret that I—"

"Shh," she interrupted, cradling his jaw with a gentle hand and smiling when he relaxed into her touch. "I think you worry too much."

His eyes slid closed. She let her hand linger a moment more before she snatched the mask from his face.

Daemon spat a curse and lunged after it. She scrambled to her feet and danced backwards, holding it at arm's length.

"Give it back!" he snarled.

"I will not!" Her amber eyes flashed. "Stop using it as a crutch! You think this makes any difference in what people think of you?" She shook the mask at him, flung it it to the ground, and planted a foot atop it.

The work site around them grew deathly still. Daemon didn't come any closer, but her skin rose in gooseflesh and hair prickled on the back of her neck as she felt dozens of eyes fall upon them.

His clawed fists clenched tight at his sides and his head turned, almost imperceptibly, to let his snake-slitted eyes rove the faces around them.

"No one here cares what you look like." Firal kept her chin up, willing herself to look at nothing but him. "Most of them wouldn't recognize you, anyway. This isn't the capital, or the temple, where you've built a name and reputation for yourself."

Slowly, his eyes drifted back to her. For once they held no expression, no glimmer of emotion to betray what he might be thinking. He said nothing. She almost wished he had. Swallowing against the fluttering knot of fear in her throat, she drew her foot away from his mask and took a slow step back.

He moved forward and knelt to take it, his eyes never leaving her face.

"These people have always viewed you as a man, Daemon." Her voice softened and she leaned down to cradle his face in her hands. His skin was soft and surprisingly smooth beneath her thumbs as they traced over his features, eliciting memories of when she'd touched him the same way during their travels. "You're the only one who sees anything else."

He pulled away, head down as he fitted the dusty mask back over his face. "We'll speak tonight," he said gruffly, pushing himself up from the ground. The ruin-folk hurried back to their work, the clatter of tools and din of voices resuming as if nothing had happened.

Firal frowned at his back as he walked away, rubbing her arms as if that could keep her from shaking. "All right," she breathed, though no one was close enough to hear.

Bonfires in the street cast a flickering, ruddy light onto the new buildings, their incomplete walls and wooden skeletons throwing strange shadows out behind them. Had Daemon not said they would speak, Firal would have returned to her home in Core. Instead, she paced the dusty main street, watching workmen and their families pitch their tents for the night. Few of them paid her any mind, and those who did spared little more than a glance and friendly nod. She didn't mind; it was better to avoid attention after the brief spectacle she'd caused that afternoon.

The largest bonfire stood near the well. Numerous tents ringed the space around it and Firal wondered at where they'd come from. She already knew the soldiers camped frequently in the ruins, but she hadn't imagined how ready the ruin-folk were to return to the surface.

An iron cookpot beside the fire filled the air with the pleasant scent of sweet potato stew. Her stomach growled in response and Firal headed that direction. There were no proper chairs, but people sat on blocks of stone and logs. Daemon sat among them, his face bare. He met her eyes briefly before his attention returned to the bowl of stew he cradled in one clawed hand.

"So you're not ignoring what I said." She twitched her skirts out of the way as she sat next to him.

"It does make it easier to eat." He shoveled a spoonful into his mouth.

Nearby, some of the ruin-folk exchanged nudges and murmurs and slipped away with their food. More than one of the married women gave her long, meaningful glances, and she caught one sullen frown from a girl closer to her own age. Firal raised a brow in response. She wasn't sure if she appreciated the privacy or if their hasty retreat bothered her. Putting it out of her head, she leaned forward to take an empty wooden bowl from beside the fire and scooped a helping of stew from the pot.

Daemon stared into the fire as she returned to his side.

"They've been laughing over what you did this afternoon." His tone was level, without a hint of the agitation she'd expected.

She bit her lip, uncertain if she should reply, unsure if he would continue. When a moment passed and he did not speak again, she changed the subject between bites of food. "How are your hands?"

"Well enough, though they'll be a bit raw until I shed."

Her nose crinkled. "You shed?"

"Twice a year or so. Peel like a snake." He gave her an amused look. "Does that surprise you?"

"A little," she admitted. "Though I guess it shouldn't."

A silence fell between them and she didn't try to break it. Daemon seemed more interested in his food than conversation, so they ate in peace, listening to the cheerful voices in the rest of the camp. He set his bowl on the ground when it was empty, but didn't leave. It didn't take long before she'd had her fill and put down her bowl, as well.

He did not speak.

Worrying her lip, she excused herself to retrieve her satchel from where she'd left it beside the well. She returned to Daemon's side as she fished inside it.

He raised a brow at her.

She drew several vials from her bag before she found the right one. "I promised you a salve for your scales. I made an oil that should help. It's been ready for a while." She hesitated before adding, "I just didn't know if I could talk to you yet."

He grimaced. "I'm sorry."

"I can see now why you didn't want to tell me. Especially after the way everyone looked at us this afternoon. I don't agree with the decision, but I understand." She tugged at his sleeve a moment before he rolled it up for her. She uncorked the vial and drizzled thick oil across her fingertips. It was uncomfortably cool, despite the warm herbal fragrance. She rubbed her fingers together to warm it before she slathered it on his arm where the glossy green scales emerged from red and irritated flesh in rough, uneven patches.

"Are you still angry?" He rolled up his other sleeve, watching as she rubbed the oil into his skin.

"I wasn't angry to begin with." Her brow furrowed and the corners of her lips pulled down, but she gave her head a shake. "I was surprised. And deeply hurt. And very confused. All this time, all the ideas I'd formed about you... After I learned about your father, I thought that was why you'd always been so distant, always absent at peculiar times, always secretive about your life. I never would have imagined it was something like this."

"I don't think anyone would." He grew quiet for a time, just long enough for her to begin to feel uncomfortable before he spoke again. "There were times I thought I might tell you. More frequently, at the end. Especially when we were in the ruins together. But I've grown so used to never having anything I want."

"But you were raised as royalty," she said, dripping oil on her fingers again. She waited for it to warm before she applied it to his other arm. "You had everything."

"I never had you."

An icy chill rolled down her spine at the stark honesty of his words, even as her heart tried to climb into her throat. Memories flashed through her mind unbidden, accompanied by a tumult of emotions. The jokes and pranks, the way she'd blush and stammer when caught by one, the way she'd stifle her feelings each time her best friend pined for him. Kytenia had expressed her interest first. Kytenia had always been prettier. Always the better option. "I'm not Kyt."

He took her hand and rubbed the oil from her fingers. "I know."

"She's my best friend," she objected weakly.

"I know that, too." He spoke slowly, as if testing the words.

"I haven't missed the way she looks at me. Or, at who she thinks I am. But she doesn't know me."

"Do I?" Bitterness seeped into her voice.

Leaning closer, he drew her hand to his lips and pressed a kiss to her knuckles. "I don't know if I can answer that."

She struggled to find words, a flush rising into her cheeks.

Daemon traced shapes on the back of her hand with his claws, watching the trails of oil they made. "I never said anything, though I wanted to. It's not like the world we live in would ever let you be with someone—something—like me." He paused, flashing her a rueful smile. "I thought it would be easier if I made you hate me."

Firal shrugged. "I don't know that I care much for the world we live in, anymore. I'm not sure I intend to go back. I..." She trailed off, gazing at the fire. "I like it here. I'm happy here."

He laced his fingers with hers and gave her hand a gentle squeeze. "Stay with me."

"I wasn't planning on going anywhere. I think I belong in Core."

"That's not what I mean," he said. "Stay with me. Marry me."

Out of everything she'd expected, every possibility of where the conversation could have gone, that direction had never crossed her mind. For a moment, she wasn't even certain she'd heard him right. "What?" she managed, unable to tear her eyes away. His expression was gentle, sincere.

"Marry me," he repeated, holding her hand fast. His claws barely brushed her skin, despite the strength of his grip. "I can't offer you a lot, not here. I can't live the life my father expects, I can't give you riches or a place in his palace, fine clothes or jewels. I can't guarantee you a comfortable home, probably can't even give you children, but—"

Her head spun. She held a finger to his lips. "You're not making this a very good proposal," she said, trying to inject mirth into her tone. "What *can* you give me?"

"Love." Uncertainty burned in his eyes and in the way his

brow knit together. "I've tried so hard not to love you. I've tried since the very beginning, the very first time I saw you in the temple. I've never failed so miserably at anything in my life."

Firal tried to speak, but a growing lump in her throat stifled her voice. It took every ounce of her strength to keep the tears that stung her eyes from brimming over. She tried to blink them away. Despite her best efforts, she still choked on tears when she tried to speak. "I've never been loved." The confession stirred an ache in her heart. It had hurt throughout her entire life, knowing she was unwanted from the moment she'd been abandoned at the temple for training.

Cradling her face in clawed hands, he hushed her and turned her head, forced her to look at him. "You have been loved for years. Just because you didn't know it doesn't mean it's not true."

She blinked faster, hot tears spilling over her dark eyelashes. "What of Lumia, then?"

"Lumia," he murmured, shaking his head. "Lumia was the first to accept me as I am. She gave me hope. I owe her that, but nothing more."

"And what of me?" she asked.

Daemon brushed a strand of hair from her face. "I already told you. I'll take you for my wife, if you'll have me."

She studied him for a long time; studied how his eyes glowed, even in the firelight. How the faintest shadow of a beard lined his jaw and his dark hair fell in tangled strands about his face. "Ran—" She stopped short and swallowed hard at the myriad of emotions that stole her words.

"Is that what you would call me?" His claws rasped gently against her skin, the gauze wrapped around his knuckles soft beside the slick texture of his scales. She took his hand in both of hers. Her fingertips traced the scar on the back of his hand, just visible beneath the edge of the bandages.

"Rune," she whispered.

"Rune?"

Stroking the outline of the scar, she nodded. "A new name. A new you. No more hiding behind two faces. No more Daemon. No more Ran."

"Firal, I—"

She silenced him with fingertips pressed to his lips and laid her head against his shoulder. His arms crushed her to his chest before she realized he'd moved. One scaled finger tilted her chin upward, his mouth seeking hers with a hungry need. She clutched his shirt to keep her hands from trembling, though it did nothing to lessen the roar of her pulse in her ears. His chest beneath her fists was more real, more solid than anything had ever been. His claws tangled in her hair and his kisses begged her lips to part. She complied, sighing softly beneath the warmth of his mouth, the softness of his tongue. The sensations made her knees weak. Tracing his jawline with a fingertip when he pulled back, she smiled up at him through the darkness. "Yes," she whispered, daring to lean in and steal a kiss. "You asked me to marry you. I say yes."

He all but hauled her to her feet. "Find a rope. I'll gather everyone."

Firal gaped. "What, here? Right now?"

"I don't want to wake another morning without you beside me."

"What about Minna? Oh, we don't even have flowers, or seeds to exchange!" She held tight to his hand when he tried to walk away.

Daemon snorted. "Minna will forgive you."

"But I haven't a dress! And your father! What of him? And—"

"My father would be thrilled. Will be, when he hears. I promise." He gave her hand a squeeze before he let go.

Before she knew it, they stood beside the fire, ringed by ruin-folk as one of Daemon's officers wrapped their wrists with a rope in place of the traditional chain of flowers.

"Repeat together, after me," the officer prompted, leading

them through the vows Minna had taught her in a lesson on culture that now seemed long ago. Firal blushed, though she never looked away, a strange wash of comfort pouring over her as she heard the words echoed simultaneously in her voice and Daemon's.

"By the blessing of Brant, I give you my all. To love and to honor, through all things that are. By embrace of the Lifetree, take my heart and body. As all seeds grow strong, let us two be one. Until earth reclaims what was borrowed, and our lives shall be done."

NEW FOUNDATIONS

A SINGLE BEAM OF WARM SUNLIGHT STREAMED IN THROUGH THE small opening at the tent's peak, casting a pleasant patch of light across the blankets. Firal stared at the blue sky on the other side of the opening for some time before she shifted, stretching amid the comfortable collection of pelts that served as bedding on the ground.

Daemon glanced in her direction and offered a smile she dared say was almost timid. Then he looked away, his snake-slitted eyes returning to the unadorned mask he held in his hands.

Rune, not Daemon. Not Ran. She reminded herself silently of the new name she'd assigned him, the name she'd taken to calling him in private. "You don't need that anymore." She lifted a hand to touch his shoulder. The slim band of gold that decorated her finger still looked odd and felt odder, even after wearing it for days. The exchange of rings as a wedding gift was a practice she'd heard of, common on the mainland, less so on Elenhiise. But it was popular among nobles, so it wasn't strange that he'd insisted. Firal had been content enough with the traditional exchange of seeds.

They'd spent their first afternoon as a wedded pair in Core's marketplace, choosing just the right gifts to exchange. It hadn't taken long for them to agree on rings; a plain gold band for Rune, and one with a polished purple gem for Firal. It was a curious stone, with a star of light that flashed in its middle whenever the sun struck it.

"They call them serpent's tears," Rune had told her, while the goldsmith looked on in approval. "There's a myth that says they fell from the eyes of a beast when it wept." Then he'd laughed as he slid the ring onto her finger. "I don't know about that, but Brant knows I've been teased enough with the idea of crying gemstones."

Rings had been easy, but choosing the seeds to present to one another had taken hours. Firal finally settled on a pouch full of furry aspen catkins for Rune, a treasure imported from the cooler northern continent. He had presented her with a single lotus seed, a choice which Minna had approved of profoundly when they'd gone to tell her of their bond.

"It's strange," Rune said at last, laying the mask in the furs and shifting to gather her into his arms. "I've spent so much time hiding, I almost don't know how to be myself anymore."

"You'll do fine." Firal wrapped her arms around his neck and met his lips for a kiss that promised a most enjoyable morning.

When they finally emerged from their tent, she hefted her satchel of dwindling supplies on her shoulder and walked the construction site while Rune and the other men broke camp. As buildings began to take shape, fewer tents went up each night. Even without the roofs completed, many families were eager to move into their new homes.

Those who needed Firal's attention found her as she walked. Their split days between Core and the new village made her work difficult, but no one had complained about her dividing her attention between the two locations. By the time she finished distributing herbs and checking bandages, Rune had packed away their things and slung their bags against his back.

"Ready?" he asked as he intercepted her at the village's edge.

She smiled coyly and led the way.

When they reached the ruins, he caught her hand and twined his fingers with hers. Such displays invited teasing from the ruin-folk, which they didn't mind, save that it sometimes grew old. There was a measure of truth in their ribbing, Firal supposed. They were newlyweds and behaved the part.

"We won't have to walk between the outpost and Core forever," Rune said as he led her through the twists and turns. The corridors in this side of the labyrinth had grown familiar, but not enough to give her any real confidence. "I intend to use the Gate-stone to build us a permanent Gate between the outpost and Core's market soon. I just want to be sure about where I'm putting it, first."

"Wouldn't it make more sense to wait?" She slid a thumb under the strap of her satchel to adjust it. "I'd think we'd want the Gate to reach as far south as possible."

He shrugged. "It's a straight shot up from the coast, so the main purpose of the Gate is just to get through the ruins faster. If I have my way, Core will be most important. The city still has a lot to offer, which is why I'm not worried about how many want to remain there."

Firal made a soft, thoughtful sound in reply. The vast majority of the ruin-folk did remain in the underground city, which was the primary reason they traveled back and forth between the underground and the new outpost, as Rune called it. Core could not be left without its healer for long.

When they reached the underground city, a line of patients had already formed outside her infirmary's door.

"I'll be with you shortly," Firal said as she let go of Rune's hand and braced herself for the work ahead.

The squeeze he gave her shoulder was a mild comfort.

"I'll need more supplies soon," she murmured as they slipped inside. "I'll take tomorrow to work in the gardens."

Rune glanced at the clusters of herbs that lined the walls. Most of the time, multiple cuttings hung there to dry, but several pegs were empty. "I don't think I can help. Even if I were a competent healer, I'm to meet the army for drills. We need to establish new squads and determine their roles in the new settlement."

"Fine, but at the very least, you'd better carry a list to Minna. She keeps her own stash of herbs now that she's my assistant. She may have some of what I need." She crossed to the table where she kept her quills and inks.

"I can do that much," he agreed.

Firal pressed the finished note into his scaly palm and stole a kiss before she waved him away. Instead of heeding her gesture, he caught her hand and pulled her into a long embrace.

"I'll be late," he murmured into her hair.

"Then you'd best go before all your dilly-dallying makes you even later." She nudged his side and kissed his chin. Then she pulled away. "Send in the first to be healed on your way out, if you would, please."

"How do I decide who goes first?"

Clean water waited in a kettle by the fire. Firal hefted it into place over the logs and summoned a flame with a wave of her hand. "You ask them. If you can't tell what's urgent and what isn't after hearing their complaints, then you really are hopeless as a healer."

Rune flashed her a grin. "I think we already knew that."

She shook her head and chuckled to herself as she scrubbed her hands and arms with soap.

Beyond the initial healing of the gravely ill when she'd first arrived, none of the day's complaints had been unusual—though knowing people had to wait to have injuries or illnesses seen to while she traveled between the new village and Core left her with a brooding discomfort. They had been fortunate thus far, but sooner or later, an emergency would arise and she wouldn't be there to see to it. The permanent Gate Rune wanted to establish would help, but only to an extent. She couldn't be everywhere at once, which led her to the uncomfortable knowledge she would have to petition her new husband to press for more alliances.

They needed mages. And that meant negotiating with the establishment that had shunned her—and ruined him.

The thought alone made her stomach flutter with nerves. Dealing with the temple mages seemed frightful enough to her, and she'd only been expelled. Regardless of what it would do for their people, how could she expect him to work with those who had scarred him so badly?

For that matter, how could he negotiate? They'd spoken little more about his identity and his role in the palace after his injury —not because questions hadn't burned at the tip of her tongue, but because they simply hadn't had time. The subject arose now and then, but what time they did have was spent pushing forward, growing comfortable with one another, creating a bond.

His role in the temple, however, had never crossed her mind.

Regardless of where his skill lacked and what his role in Kifel's household was, Rune was a Master mage, subject to the Archmage's rules and whims. Firal didn't know how he'd escaped her clutches this long, but returning to ask that mages be conceded to their effort could only be a mistake.

Their effort. Firal wondered at how easily she'd slipped into that way of thinking. It wasn't wrong; the moment she'd agreed to marriage, she had adopted Rune's cause as her own. She did not agree with or understand all his methods, but whatever the means, there was a sincerity in everything he did. That, in its own way, was noble.

Still, the turn her thoughts had taken troubled her, and it made for a dark cloud over her day's work.

Nightfall came as the last of her patients departed. Fond as she was of her work, Firal still breathed a sigh of relief in the first moments of peace that followed. She filled a pot over the fire with vegetables and sat to mix and measure herbs for new tinctures while the meal cooked. She dined alone.

Her food stores, too, ran low. When they returned to the

village outpost, she would have to take time to forage. With the lush forest that split around the clearing, there was bound to be food nearby. With time, there would be gardens, and Core would finally thrive.

Long after Firal banked the fire and curled under the blankets, the door creaked open and stirred her from slumber. The familiar soft click of claws against the floor soothed her and she nestled deeper into the blankets as she listened to the comforting sound of his presence.

Rune paced around the tables and chairs that cluttered the room, his step slow and deliberate. No matter how stealthy he tried to be on the nights where his duties kept him away, his claws always betrayed him. Firal watched as he retrieved food from the pot left over the dying fire. He sat on the edge of the hearth and ate like a starved man, and perhaps he was—she doubted he took the time to eat when he was working. Such was the only thing she really wanted to change. He threw himself into his work with a near single-minded nature, to the detriment of himself and all else. Raw, bloody patches marred his hands where his scales were perpetually torn, yet he worked the axe and saws at the outpost with unmatched vigor every day they visited the budding village. She almost preferred those days; at least then, the nights were their own.

"You're supposed to be sleeping," Rune murmured.

She huddled her chin into the blankets. "How did you know I'm not?"

"I could feel your eyes." He cast her a glance that was both apologetic and amused. Then, the dish emptied, he put his bowl aside and stripped off his dusty clothes. No matter how tired he was, he maintained a certain level of manners she'd come to appreciate. He folded his clothing and put it on the shelf beneath the washbasin she kept beside the fire.

Firal did not know what she'd expected of him in the wake of learning his identity, but really, little had changed. He bore a remarkable self-sufficiency, given his upbringing. Yet with the roles he played among the ruin-folk, that was little surprise. They worked hard. He was no different. And despite his discomfort in his own skin, he moved and acted with such confidence that she wondered how he thought ill of himself at all. Her eyes traveled over his body as he washed. He was capable. Powerful. And handsome, despite the mark left by magic.

"I feel that, too."

"You're tense," she murmured in response. "You carry it in your shoulders."

"It was a difficult day." He ran clawed fingers through his hair and squinted at his hands. His hair, too, was full of dust. Instead of using the cloth, he caught the water in the ewer with his magic and drew it forth to wash his hair. When he finished, he twisted the water into a strand in midair and drew his other hand through it to separate it from the dirt. The latter fell to the floor in dry clumps.

Firal made a soft sound of approval. "You've gained a lot of dexterity lately. We haven't even had time for lessons."

The water rippled and slid back into the ewer. This time, when he ran his fingers through his hair, he seemed satisfied. "I learn a lot just being around you."

"I'll take that as a compliment. Come here." She beckoned him with a finger and smiled to herself when he hesitated, his eyes on the shelf. "I'll clean your clothes in the morning. You've come a long way, but I don't think you're skilled enough to use magic for laundry just yet."

"Laundry is one skill I haven't mastered, magic or otherwise." Rune crept to the bed and climbed in when she peeled back the blankets. She caught him by the shoulder, maneuvered him face-down into the pillow and ignored his grunt of protest. He turned his head so he could breathe. Her thumbs dug into his shoulders, yielding another grunt.

"Relax." It was an order, not a request, and she was pleased when he sank deeper into the pillow. A long, slow exhale escaped him, his whole body seeming to deflate. Knots in his muscles began to give way.

After a time, his breath grew slow and even, and Firal curled close against his side beneath the covers.

Morning, it seemed, always came too soon.

She woke to an empty bed, an occurrence that had grown familiar in the underground. Despite what she'd said, his dusty clothing was gone. Sooner or later, the man would work himself to death.

Few patients needed care in the morning and Minna's assistance meant they were seen to soon enough. Minna departed with the last of them, leaving Firal free to roam Core as she would.

The city received her differently now. They'd always been welcoming and respectful, but her bond with Rune had affected that, too. Some had grown warmer, greeting her as they would a long-time friend, while others had cooled and regarded her with stiff formality. Suspicion hung thick in some glances. Firal wasn't sure she could blame them.

If Lumia intended to seat Rune upon a surface throne, now Firal, as queen, would be beside him. Firal couldn't pretend to understand the woman's motives, but she understood why the abrupt change in plans could concern those who still sought to see Rune and Lumia united as rulers. No matter how warm a welcome they'd given her or what she'd done to benefit them, Firal couldn't change that she was an outsider. And when an outsider interfered with long-laid plans to help the ruin-folk return to the surface, she understood distrust.

Her intentions, however, remained pure. She scaled the inverted tower to the garden above. It had expanded under her instruction and she shuddered to think of Core's people leaving it behind. Perhaps the permanent Gate would alleviate those concerns, but she couldn't imagine the garden's location would ever be convenient for those outside of Core.

When her basket brimmed with fresh cuttings in the late

afternoon, Firal returned home. Already, her mind raced ahead to their return to the outpost, to the garden she'd have to plant. It would take years for it to compare to the garden in Core, but if nothing else, the village would have basic necessities. She put a handful of cuttings into bottles of water to try to coax them to root, then bundled the rest and hung them to dry.

Something thumped against the door. It creaked open a moment later to reveal Rune, his arms full of rolled papers and small boxes balanced in a precarious stack.

"What in the world is all this?" Firal met him at the door to relieve some of his burden.

He passed the boxes to her with relief. "Work." A roll slipped from his arms and thumped against the floor. He snagged it with the claws on his toes and tried to pull it closer. It turned sideways instead. Rolling his eyes, he left it where it was. "Can you clear a table?"

The corner table she used for writing hosted only a handful of bottles with herb cuttings. She left the boxes, gathered the bottles, and moved them to the hearth. "I thought you were doing drills today."

"That was yesterday. Today we established new patrol units, and now I need to establish where they're supposed to patrol."

Firal scooped the lost roll from the floor and laid it across the emptied table. "Well, I might have known that if you'd said anything before you left this morning."

The gentle goading seemed to have its intended effect, as he bowed his head and rubbed his brow with a knuckle. "Sorry. I never want to disturb you."

"If I didn't want to be disturbed, I wouldn't have agreed to marry you."

"I'd think being married to me is disturbing enough for most days." He unfurled one of the rolls across the table. A map of the island peeked out for a moment before the edges rolled back on themselves. He spread it again with both hands, the quiet rasp of his claws and scales against the coarse paper strangely pleasant.

"Most days," she agreed. The little boxes he'd brought sat at the back edge of the table. She retrieved them and sat one on each corner of the map. In the map's center, the tiny circle that represented Core seemed insignificant. Around it, a dotted line marked the borders of the ruins, a vast, empty space with no roads or landmarks.

"All that land," she sighed. "Yet here we are, forced underground because our ancestors couldn't agree on magic."

"We?" Rune chuckled. "You really are one of us now, aren't you?"

Sobered, she looked away. "Perhaps. Not everyone is happy about my place in Core."

"They never will be. Someone will find fault with you no matter what you do. The best you can do is keep on." He caught her hand and pressed a kiss to her knuckles as he sat. "Here, let me show you something." He retrieved a piece of colored wax from one of the small boxes and struck a jagged green line across the map. Now and then he paused to measure off small distances with his claws, then marked the map again. The line meandered from a point just east of the ruins to the southern coast, then back to the ruins to form a narrow strip. Above it, he traced the edge of the ruins.

Curious, Firal leaned against his back and peered over his shoulder. "Is all that your territory?"

"Ours," he corrected. "And yes. My father hasn't relinquished control of the ruins, but he may as well have. He doesn't monitor or use the space. With the temple empty, he doesn't watch it at all."

The thought of the empty temple gave her a chill. She rubbed her arms as if she could ward it off. "How do you mean to seize it?"

Rune grinned. "That's the easy part. I'm going to ask."

She blinked. "Just like that?"

"Just like that." His hand hovered over the map a moment before he marked the location of the new village on the surface, this time with a piece of charcoal. "We have our differences, but he's still my father. We're all on the same side, he and Relythes just can't seem to see that. That's half of why I need this."

The borders he'd drawn glowed a sickly shade in the weak firelight. Unsettled, she retrieved a stone from the small pile she kept on the corner of a shelf. It warmed beneath her fingers, a soft glow forming as she funneled her magic into a mage-light. "You think he's simply going to surrender land and not think you've betrayed him?"

"He's not surrendering anything. And I haven't betrayed him." Bright flickers in the glow of his eyes hinted at agitation. "I will admit some of the things I've had to do to get this far are... questionable. But everything I've done has been toward unification, not division. I'm not asking him to make a sacrifice. I'm asking him to trust me enough to let me reach places he can't."

Shadows splayed across the map as she rolled the mage-light between her fingers and set it aloft. It hung in midair when she drew back her hand. "I'm sorry." She drew her fingers across his shoulders, gentle and placating. "I didn't mean to upset you."

"You didn't." A shade too much heat lingered in his voice for it to be true, but the light in his eyes softened. He wiped his face with a hand. "I just... I need this to be perfect. This is the chance I've always wanted. An opportunity to prove I can do these things. I can make this island a better place, but he's never given me the chance. It's about time I made my own."

Warmth swelled in her chest, the mingled pride and sympathy as strange as it was familiar. His dedication no longer surprised her, but it remained novel. She threaded her fingers through his hair, tilting his head back to press a kiss to his forehead. "You're always working so hard."

He smiled haltingly and reached for the box of wax. "I have to."

"Just be careful not to overwork yourself. I'd like to have my husband sometimes, too."

"You'll have me tomorrow," he said. "I promise."

Tomorrow, she supposed, would have to be good enough. She returned to preparing herbs and tinctures while he worked. Now and then, she stole glances at the maps and charts as he drew existing borders and plans for expansion, proposed roadways, ideal sites for cities, convenient trade routes, and possible placements for Gates. He ate without seeing or tasting what she offered, but his murmured thank-you made her smile.

When her eyelids grew heavy, she crawled underneath the blankets and lay looking at him for a time. "Will you come to bed?"

He shot her an apologetic glance. "Soon."

For a time, she slept, but the unnatural glow of the mage-light she'd made for him pressed uncomfortably on her eyelids. Though bright enough to wake her, the light had grown dim, indicating several hours had passed.

"Rune?" Her voice was small, softened by sleep.

His hand paused over a sheet of paper finer than anything she'd made for herself, one of her quills caught between the sides of his fingers so it wouldn't be damaged by his claws. His eyes were faded, dull, but stubbornness still gleamed in their depths. Even so, he put down the pen and crept to the bedside to kiss her brow and draw the blankets closer to her chin.

"I have to get this right," he whispered.

She slipped an arm from under the blankets so she could cradle his face in one hand. "It can wait."

Rune caught her hand and kissed her fingertips. "No. I'm to travel to Ilmenhith to speak with him in three days. We're going back to the outpost tomorrow. It has to be now."

Unhappy, she tried to voice her disapproval. Instead, only a tiny squeak of a sigh escaped her throat.

"Soon," he promised, and returned to his desk.

When she woke again, the mage-light had all but extinguished, its feeble light just tracing the outline of his features where he lay sleeping against the desk, quill pen still in hand.

She slid from the blankets and padded across the room to brush her fingers across his back. He jerked awake and stifled a groan.

"Come," she ordered, pulling his arm. "Sleep."

This time, he did not argue. He followed her to the bed and collapsed into it, asleep before she drew the covers. Firal curled close against his back. For a fleeting moment, she took the sense of being his protector, and the uneasiness it formed in the pit of her stomach robbed her of all further sleep.

THE PRICE OF POISON

T{.sc HE LAST TIME} K{.sc IFEL SET FOOT IN THE RUINS, HE'D BEEN A YOUNG} man. Like any Eldani, he didn't show his years, but he felt them —more, as of late. He tried not to let the weight of time drag him down. Things would have been different, were he not alone. If only he'd been able to keep Envesi happy, kept her in the palace. Perhaps then he might have known his child.

Not for the first time since leaving Wethertree, he berated himself. Not only for his failures, but for that line of thought. Nondar was right; he'd always known Lomithrandel was not truly his son. Nondar himself had confided as much when the boy was first brought to Ilmenhith, daring to pit his word against that of the Archmage. But Kifel had always worried and wondered if he'd made a mistake in believing the old Master.

Despite all their wisdom, the mages didn't know what magic might do to an unborn child. It was not unreasonable to think a mage's child might be tainted. For years, Kifel had been torn between the hope that perhaps Ran secretly *was* his child, warped by his mother's magic, and the gut-clenching fear that came with knowing that if Ran was not his blood, then chances were his blood child was dead.

In spite of the now-certain knowledge that Ran was not his,

Kifel couldn't stop thinking of him that way. As his son, his child, the one he'd thought could be his heir. A daughter who was related by blood complicated the matter. His throat tightened. A blood child who was perfect, whole. Part of him felt relieved the offspring he'd begged Envesi to keep had not been twisted the way she'd claimed. Then guilt arose anew. Ran's condition did not dictate his worth. Yet, Kifel could not keep the thoughts at bay.

He followed the winding hallways of the ruins, pausing now and then to inspect the walls for sigils that were all but worn away. Their final argument still echoed in his mind, so many years later. It was the last time he'd seen her cry, the morning his wife, her dark hair yet unbleached by magic, had learned of the child growing within her womb.

She had suspected, but mages were unable to sense the presence of their own unborn offspring, their magic overshadowing the delicate strands of energy that constituted another being. Energy she had threatened to have drawn until the child was unmade. The idea still gave him chills.

Envesi blamed him for all of it, of course. For their arranged marriage, for her lost chance of attaining the rank of Archmage on the mainland. For any other woman, being the future queen would have been enough. It had taken all of his determination—and every ounce of his influence as crown prince—to strike the bargain that kept his child alive.

Only days after his father's death and Kifel's coronation as king, he'd let his queen leave. With her, she'd taken a portion of his wealth and his finest court mages, striking out to establish Kirban Temple on the southern edge of the ruins. All he'd held was the promise she would spare his child. Months later, Nondar delivered Lomithrandel to his door.

It would have been a lie to say he'd felt no repulsion at first sight of the infant. Kifel's first impulse had been to kill the miserable creature, to spare him a life that surely would have been nothing but pain. But pity—and the realization he would have no other chance at the family he so desperately wanted—won out. The loss of his bride had taken great effort to bury, and the idea of remarrying did not sit well with him as long as his wife still lived. Though she was estranged and the royal court had declared their marriage invalid, he was no widower. Truthfully, he'd always clung to some feeble hope that, once the temple was well-established, she might return to him.

That hope had been foolish.

The corridor ended abruptly, forcing Kifel to turn around. Without the aid of a Gate, the trip had already taken too long. The mages in Wethertree had tried to open a Gate to the temple, so he could continue on foot from there, but every attempt to create one ended with the portal going askew and falling apart. Only Nondar's expert hand kept the fierce energies from escaping the mages' control. The destination had changed too much from their memories of it, Nondar said, leaving Kifel with no choice but to travel from Wethertree by horseback. But he couldn't blame them. From the warped glimpses of the temple he'd caught through the unsteady Gate, he hardly recognized the place, himself. Not that the ruins were any better. The guide sigils had decayed to the point they forced him to make more blind guesses than purposeful turns.

How long had it been since he'd walked these hallways? Since before Ran was born, at least. It was strange and fitting that the boy had always found solace wandering the ruins, the same as Kifel had in his youth. But then, Ran was not so unlike him. They'd been close once. With effort, he kept himself from dwelling on how that had changed.

The winding paths spun him ever closer to the entrance to the underground he sought. He'd taken little with him. Half the waterskin on his shoulder remained, but the evening meal was nothing more than bread and a bit of jerky. Sleep did not come easy beneath the stars, not when he knew what waited for him below. Breakfast the next morning saw the end of his provisions, but noontime put his feet on the stairs into the underground.

Kifel had been to the tunnels often, but had rarely ventured into their depths. In his childhood, the ruins had been monitored closely. His father had sought to eliminate the last of the Underling forces, driven underground by a king now generations past. Kifel had thought it silly to expend time and effort hunting the remnant of a broken people, a notion he'd carried with him into adulthood. But the threat of enemies lurking underground made the ruins dangerous—and all the more appealing to a bored boy whose father dragged him about on the crown's business. Whenever they traveled to a guard post at the edge of the ruins, it had never taken Kifel long to find his way into the winding hallways.

Sighing, Kifel touched the sigils that marked the wall. They pulsed with a faint light whenever his fingers brushed over them, illuminating just enough for him to read what they said. He barely remembered how to work them; he pressed a hand flat against the wall to keep the sigils lit as he knelt to search for the line of marks carved where the wall met the floor. It took a moment to find them, but when he touched the age-worn grooves, they flared to life. Bright blue light shot down the hallway as the flowing script became visible. More knowledge lost to the ages, he supposed, forgotten along with whoever had been responsible for carving the tunnels in the first place. He'd discovered the lights by accident, tripping in the dark and catching himself on the wall. Those lights had often helped his father find where he hid.

The tunnels sloped downward at a steady rate. On occasion, the branching paths gave Kifel pause. Despite the sigils, he couldn't tell how far he had gone, nor was he certain where he was going. But as long as he moved downward, it was progress, and as he delved farther into the cool deep of the underground, he began to hear whispers and the scuffling of feet as denizens of the underground hurried to avoid notice.

Perhaps his father had been right in his desire to kill the last of the Underlings. Once Kifel took the crown, he'd called back the men stationed at the ruins. He'd watched his father search for years without finding anything. Kifel had believed there was no one there. It wasn't until Lumia was exiled and vanished into the ruins that he began to reconsider.

Kifel paused to glance over his shoulder. The sigils had dimmed behind him, leaving the path at his back hidden in shadow once again. Unsettled, he touched the hilt of his sword and carried on. Signs of life appeared in the form of lights, their cool illumination washing out the soft, comforting glow of the sigils that lined the floor. The twisted sconces resembled tangled vines, he thought, thorny shapes that struggled to choke out the lights they held. He trained his eyes on the dim passage ahead. When he reached the open doorway at the end of the hall, he found himself still once more, breath stolen by the sight before him.

The size of the great hall rivaled his throne room in the palace of Ilmenhith. Columns stretched far overhead and roaring fires in the iron braziers between them gave the room a pleasant warmth, though a haze of smoke obscured the lines and angles of the vaulted ceiling. Sweet-smelling wood chips and herbs mixed with the tinder drove away the mustiness of the underground. And at the very end of the room, perched upon a throne, was the woman who—had he his choice—should have been his greatest ally.

"You've come to me." Lumia's head tilted as she spoke, her words full of wonder. She was everything he remembered, dressed in ivory silk, with golden hair that glowed like the sun in the red light of the fires. Her hips still swung with a fluid grace when she walked toward him, her eyes still glittering like gems. She had always been magnificent, but her appearance was just one of the vanities that had been her downfall. "After all this time, you've come."

Kifel squared his shoulders. "I've not come for you."

Her expression melted into neutrality and her tone grew cool. "He will never be you." She stopped just within arm's reach and let her hand trail over his chest. "You've given him your strength. Your passion. But he will never be you."

He stared down at her impassively. "Have you really become so desperate, Lumia?"

"If only a king were so easy to replace." She snatched her hand away and glared. "At least your son fights for what he wants."

"You knew it was unavoidable. My marriage was arranged, I had no part in it."

"Because they wanted an Eldani mage for a queen." Her lip curled with a sneer and her eyes darkened. "I thought we were allies. I thought we wanted the same thing. Yet you surrendered everything. We had a chance to end this war. To end the power tearing our home apart. And yet you wed her."

"You never loved the idea of peace," he snapped. "You were in love with power. You envied my title. My palace, my crown. You pined for them from the moment you joined my father's court."

"Curse your father!" Lumia drew back and spat at the carpet underfoot. "Curse your mother and curse your queen! If magic sows discord, then we can only find peace through its decay."

"It's in our blood, yours stronger than mine. We cannot control that. There must be another way."

"And the answer was to found the temple?" She raised a brow. "To empower what should have been destroyed?"

Tamping down his anger, Kifel sucked in a breath. She would never understand the choices he'd made. In her eyes, her cause was everything. But no cause could replace the family he'd craved. The family he'd sacrificed everything for.

"Where is my daughter?" Kifel demanded.

Lumia's eyes narrowed, a cold smile twisting her mouth. "So you abandon your son so easily? The moment you learn the truth about the brat you sired, all those years together are forgotten?" She leaned close. "He's taken her, you know. I'm sure he's bedded her by now. How terrible it would be for either of them to know the truth—that the moment you learn of her, you care for your poor little foundling no more. Or that he received all your love, which should have been hers, even after what I made him."

The inflection in her words made his stomach knot. "What you *made* him?"

She chuckled and glided past him to circle one of the great iron braziers. "Perhaps he might have had a normal life, if I'd let him be. It's all your fault, you know. You supported the Archmage in that venture, gave her free rein over the future of magic. If not for that, perhaps I would not have carried on alone. Perhaps I would not have felt the need to corrupt the power as she brought the poor thing to life." Her voice lilted with amusement and she stared into the fire, a gleam in her eyes. The licking flames sent shadows roiling across her smile. "Oh, just remembering gives me chills. The way she screamed when I twisted the flows. The way it made his flesh blister and warp. I didn't know what to expect, really. I'm not sure why the magic gave him that form. Perhaps because I'd been watching that lizard as it scaled the wall."

Kifel's breath caught in his throat, his heart hammering in his chest as her confession sank in. "You ruined him," he choked. "You destroyed his life!"

"I saved his life!" Her eyes flashed, cold blue against the reflection of the flames. "I saved yours. What might your beloved queen have done if she thought herself capable of creating more like him? Mages that know no limit? With the strength of all creation at their fingertips? Please. She sought to overthrow you. If he'd turned out as your Archmage intended, he would have unmade himself by now and taken half your kingdom with him. Had she not considered the project a failure, you would be dead."

"How could you?" His stare carried every bit as much disbelief as his words. "He was a child!"

"He was an abomination!" she snapped back. "Even before I

touched him. A child born of magic alone can never be anything but a monster."

Kifel unsheathed his sword before he knew what he was doing. Anger clouded his vision, fury at the pain she'd caused his son bringing everything inside him to a white-hot boil. He surged forward and she squealed when the blue-silver metal of his blade shaved skin from her neck. He barely stopped himself from pushing it farther, his grip on the hilt of his sword tightening until his knuckles turned white. "Where are they?"

"It's too late for you to take them back. My tether is all that holds his might at bay," Lumia sneered. "Already they carve out land for their own kingdom at the edge of my ruins. Between me, your queen, and Daemon, you've already lost. You abandoned our cause and everything I thought we stood for, but you are no longer needed. I will have the support of your throne, the moment he takes your place."

His face softened into a strange serenity as rage washed over him. "You will have nothing." The rage swept away every emotion, leaving only a cool, calm hate as his blade slipped into her throat.

TREN STROKED HIS BEARD, STARING ABSENTLY AT THE POOL OF crimson on the floor. He hadn't moved her. Instead, he studied the way her vacant eyes stared at the ceiling, the way she sprawled with blood cooling in her pale hair.

She'd not been dead long when a maidservant's screams drew him to the throne room. Truth be told, he'd always assumed that if something happened to Lumia, he would feel it. He'd never been able to figure out the blood-bond or how it worked, just that it sometimes gave him a strange awareness of her, a peculiar sensation or an impression she was reaching for him.

But nothing had come from their link when she died. Not

anger, not hate, not fear. Idly, he wondered if she'd felt any of those things when it happened.

Whoever did it had been quick. It had been fast and clean, with not a trace left behind. A page mentioned seeing a man in the hallways not long before Lumia had been found. An Eldani in fine clothing, the boy had said. Tren could only recall one of their lot who had seen an entrance to the underground recently enough to know how to return. What had his name been? Venn? Von? Either way, it wasn't as if the young soldier had reason to do such a thing. As far as Tren knew, Lumia hadn't even been aware of the boy's presence.

Weary, he rubbed his eyes and leaned forward on the throne until he could rest his elbows on his knees. He had little time to decide what to do, and unless he could clear his mind, he wouldn't be able to do anything. He didn't even know what to feel, still numb from the shock of what lay before him. He ought to move her. Clean her up. He ought to wash the blood from her beautiful hair, wrap something around the ugly wound in her neck. He ought to do something.

And yet he felt paralyzed. A band of tightness constricted his chest, a thick, almost sore feeling in his throat making it hard to breathe and swallow. Perhaps she'd known that he found her beautiful. That despite all his plans to seize power from her hands, he never would have allowed anything to bring her harm. Perhaps that was what numbed him; the weight of failure that settled over his shoulders.

He became aware of someone behind him. Tren frowned, but did not turn to face the page. "We must avenge our queen." Very little emotion colored his words. If only he'd taken the time to tell her how beautiful she was. "The Eldani have done this. Send word. Gather the soldiers. We must react before the blood shed by their wickedness grows cold."

"My lord," the boy started, unable to keep the quaver from his voice. "The general is—"

"I am your general now!" Tren roared, surging to his feet,

wheeling on the boy with his sword drawn. The child yelped, scrambling backwards as Tren pointed the blade at him. "I am your leader. Do as I say! Daemon led the mages to Core and now Lumia is dead. The Eldani will pay for their crime and Daemon will, too!"

Much to his satisfaction, the page bolted without another word. Tren turned his eyes to the body of his queen one last time. He felt something now, anger filling him so completely that he thought he might burst. Anger, and the satisfying sense of power.

He stood tall before the throne as officers filtered in and assembled in front of him. "Arm the men and prepare them for battle," he barked. His gaze skimmed past them and lingered on the group of men that gathered around their fallen matron. However Lumia planned to take the Eldani king's throne, nothing would come of it now. He had no mind or patience for her twisted schemes, no desire to play the games that came from her petty grudges. Drawing himself up, Tren wondered briefly which jewels should adorn his crown.

"Tonight, our war begins!"

23

DUEL

"You could just Gate us there, you know." Firal swung her feet farther than necessary with each step, kicking up the hem of her plain brown skirt. It had grown loose in the waistband again, though it had only been a few weeks since Minna helped her adjust it. She had never been slender and probably never would be, but Core had changed her in many ways.

"I could," Rune agreed, "but no one expects me to, and it would take away from the time I get to spend with my wife." He lifted their joined hands to kiss her fingers.

She allowed herself a small laugh. "I suppose I shouldn't encourage you to be reckless with your Gift, besides. It's hardly responsible of me."

"Marrying me wasn't particularly responsible of you, either, but here we are." A mischievous grin flashed across his face before he caught it and tamed it into a more reasonable smirk.

"Depends on how you look at it," she said. "One could argue I'm shouldering a great responsibility, volunteering to keep you in line."

"Great and grave. A vital service to all living people." Again, he kissed her fingers.

They rarely hurried through the ruins. They hadn't hurried

out of bed that morning, either, and the sun rode high in the sky. Firal had been glad to see him rest. Though he hid it well, she recognized exhaustion in the tension of his muscles and in the shadows underneath his eyes that grew darker through the passing days.

"Well, I must admit not all of my motives were so selfless." She leaned her head against his shoulder for a moment. His step faltered and she grinned. No matter how composed and charismatic he seemed, there was a hint of awkward uncertainty just below the surface of his persona. Prodding it was both amusing and endearing.

Rune cleared his throat. "I suppose I'd have to disagree. After everything I've done, you'd have to be selfless to forgive me." He paused to pluck a wildflower from the weeds beside one of the ruin walls. He twirled its stem between his claws and tucked it into her hair.

The simple gesture put warmth in her cheeks. She ducked her head and hid her face against his arm. "Just because I've forgiven you for keeping secrets doesn't mean I've forgotten."

"Then I'll have to do my best to replace those memories with sweeter ones." He spun her into his arms and kissed her soundly.

Laughing, she pushed him away. "You're a bit of a romantic, aren't you? I never would have guessed."

"Well, I never thought my life would be like this, so I suppose anything is possible."

She tilted her head. "Like what?"

"Happy." His violet eyes shone bright, the unnatural light of his power granting them an ethereal glow even in the sun. "I never thought I would be."

Firal blushed again and hurried ahead. "Come. I'm sure someone at the village needs me by now."

More frames for peaked roofs greeted them. The clearing had grown a shade wider while they were gone, letting in more sun. The midday intensity of the light had driven most of the

SERPENT'S TEARS

outpost's occupants to the edges of the budding city, where lines of laundry spread between the trees in bright splashes of ivory and cream beneath the forest shade.

"So much progress," she murmured.

"Distributing the work evenly makes things faster. Everyone agreed to build the village, so everyone contributes." Rune motioned toward the far end of the clearing. "There. I want to show you something."

Curious, she trailed at his heels as he led the way to one of the newer structures. The skeletal frame was taller than the other buildings, with beams for a second floor overhead and an unfinished chimney rising from a stone hearth. He stepped through a gap in the frame that she supposed would become a doorway. His claws clicked on the plank floor as he turned to face her, pacing backwards. "Over here."

On the far side of the house, a small plot of fresh-turned dirt hosted a number of small plants, their wilted leaves indicating they were recent transplants. There was no fence yet, but posts stood in the ground to mark where one would be.

Firal squeezed between the bare studs. The ground was a good foot below, the earth soft beneath her boot when she landed. "What is this?"

"Yours. I asked that some of the herbs you use most be transplanted out here as soon as possible. I thought it would make things easier."

Her mouth fell open and she turned to look up at the framed building. "And this—?"

"Ours," he said, smiling. "The first floor is designed to function as an infirmary. There will be space for waiting chairs and private rooms for patients who need to stay overnight. The upstairs will be for us."

Tears pricked her eyes and she raised a hand to cover her mouth.

Rune's smile faltered. "I know you're fond of Core—"

"It's perfect," she interrupted, climbing back into the naked framework of the house. She all but threw herself into his arms and wrapped him in a tight embrace. "It's everything I could have hoped for."

His shoulders sank with relief and he hugged her close.

They barely had time for a kiss before a soldier Firal didn't recognize stepped through the would-be door.

"Sir," the man started in a rush, giving Firal an apologetic look as he drew to a halt before Rune, "all soldiers have been summoned to the palace in Core. It's an emergency. You must come."

"What's happened?" Firal stepped forward, but Rune gently pushed her back.

"You stay here." He brushed a strand of her unruly dark hair away from her face. "You'll need to tend injuries. And your new garden. I'll send word as soon as I know what's happening. I'm sure it won't take long."

She was loath to let him go, but he was right. If no one had called for the healer, she was more useful where she was. "Fine. Just be careful."

Rune flashed her a troublesome grin. "When am I not?" He pressed a kiss to her forehead and dropped their bags by the hearth, though he kept his sword.

She watched with a sigh as he joined the soldiers streaming away from the encampment in a long, narrow line. Women and children gathered in the street to watch them leave. Wedding him hadn't changed his role in the ruin-folks' army, Firal reminded herself, righting the satchel of medicines on her shoulder.

When a man sporting a broken hand appeared at the door of her incomplete infirmary moments later, she was glad she'd come prepared.

In the late afternoon, when she finished tying a bandage and looked up at the sound of shouting, the banners on the horizon made her wish Rune had stayed.

PEOPLE CROWDED THE CORRIDOR AND DOORWAY INTO THE GREAT hall. Rune shouldered his way past them with a growl. Grim faces followed him, some bearing looks so dark he might have been startled, if not for his irritation. Faces he recognized turned away. Some looked shaken, others sorrowful, but not a word was spoken. He pushed harder and the crowds parted to let him through. Then he saw what had silenced them.

A bier draped with red and white silk stood before the dark metal throne. Upon it, Lumia's body lay with her hands folded against her chest. Rune stared, frozen in place for what felt an eternity before he could move his feet. Slowly, he paced forward through the empty space between the soldiers and the body of their queen.

The blood had been washed from her throat, though nothing had been done to hide the deep, ugly slice that split it. He reached out, one green-scaled hand hovering over her cold form for a moment before he dropped it to his side. The last he'd seen her, he'd left her screaming on the floor without a shred of magic left. He'd never expected that to be his final memory of her. He stared at her face in disbelief, his chest tightening with a tumult of confusing emotions. What was he supposed to feel?

"What happened?" he asked, startled by the quaver that shook his voice. He turned to the crowd behind him and reeled backwards when a fist connected with his face.

"I've always wanted to do that," Tren sneered, shaking his hand and flexing his fingers as he stepped back. "That blasted mask was always in the way."

Rune touched the side of a claw to his busted lip with a grimace, glancing at his hand when it came away bloody. He licked the black ichor from his lip and spat at the floor. "Now isn't the time for this."

"You did this!" Tren thrust a finger toward the bier, his angry words reverberating throughout the great hall. "You're the reason our enemies knew where to find her! You're the one who brought one of their soldiers here!"

"That soldier saved my life," Rune growled.

"We'd be better off if he hadn't." Tren paced in front of him like a restless animal, his hand on the knife sheathed at his belt. "If you were dead, he wouldn't have come here. If you were dead, Lumia would still be alive!"

Rune's violet eyes narrowed. Surely the man wasn't serious. Rune had laughed back when Vahn told him he wanted to join the army. Vahn, who'd once cried over a stray dog injured by a cart's wheel. Vahn, who couldn't hurt a fly. "Dishonesty is unbecoming, Tren."

Tren charged without warning. His back crowded to the bier, Rune didn't have room to draw his sword. Spitting a curse, he ducked. Tren's knife caught the hood of his cloak and tore it to the edge. Rune staggered back, unable to regain his footing before his opponent came at him again.

"Only one of us can rule!" Tren snarled, feinting with his knife, darting just close enough to catch hold of Rune's sword before throwing him off balance with a kick to his middle. The soldiers crowded around them in a ring, jeering and shouting.

Rune caught himself at the edge of the crowd, sanguine shades flooding his luminescent eyes. "Just between you and me," he began, evading easily when Tren swung at him with his own sword, "you'd make a terrible king." The scabbard at his side now a useless hindrance, Rune unbuckled his belt and cast it to the floor.

Baring his teeth, Tren lunged at him with both blades. Rune skirted the sword and caught Tren's knife arm by the wrist, twisting hard. His talons dug deep, severing flesh and tendon. The knife clattered to the floor and Tren bellowed in anger and pain. He lashed out with his sword arm and struck hard with the hilt. Stars exploded into Rune's vision, pain blossoming in the side of his head. He stumbled and fell to his knees, hands out to keep him from prostrating on the floor.

"Move!" Davan's shout from the edge of the ring was all that kept Rune from falling senseless. He rolled to the side as Tren brought his sword down. Sparks flashed when it struck the stone, searing his eyes. Rune shook his head and blinked hard, struggling to find his feet through the spinning of his head. Black blood flowed from his temple, matting his hair. His limbs refused to cooperate. His hand brushed something and he curled his fingers around it.

He didn't have time to rise before the sword came down again. It wasn't until metal sparked against metal that Rune realized he'd gotten hold of the knife and used it to deflect the blade. Seizing the opportunity, he sprang forward, plowing his shoulder into Tren's gut, bowling the man to the floor. Tren was stronger than he anticipated. They rolled, and he pinned Rune to the ground.

"I expected a better fight from you!" Tren shouted. Rune barely caught the sword in his hands as Tren leveled it with his throat and bore down on it with all his weight.

Grimacing, Rune pushed back, struggling to ignore the way the sword bit into his scaly palms, the way the blood coursed down his arms. Frantic, desperate, he reached for the flows of energy around him. His eyes locked with Tren's and he lashed out with the full force of everything he could grasp.

Howling wind kicked up around them, overturning braziers and spilling ashes across the floor. Embers spun through the air as the fires went out. Icy gusts tore through the great hall and the ground beneath them shuddered. The wind drowned the voices of the men around them, roaring louder, battering their bodies until Rune felt nothing else.

Then, all at once, it was gone.

Rune fell back against the floor, gasping for breath, closing his eyes against the spinning of the room and the pain throbbing in his head. It was only when he felt the warmth and weak glow of torchlight against his skin that he opened his eyes again.

"Basilisk," someone said in a stunned whisper. The word

swept through the crowd with an awestruck, frightened murmur.

Above him, Tren's vicious snarl was frozen, the man's flesh turned to stone.

"WILL YOU BE LEADING US, THEN?"

Rune grimaced, half at Davan's question, half at the sting of the medicine Minna slathered on his palms. He could tell she tried not to look at him as she wrapped his hands with strips of clean linen bandage. It was no surprise the woman had become Firal's medical assistant. She'd grown adept with herbs and treatments, but he still wished it were his wife that tended his wounds. "I don't have a choice." He tried to move his fingers. The cuts were deep, but aside from the bulk of the bandages, it didn't seem like his movement was impaired.

Davan frowned, scratching his unshaven chin. "You make it sound like you don't want to. I always thought you intended to be our king."

"I just never thought it would—Ow." Rune flinched away from the poultice Minna dabbed at the split in his lip. "I just never thought it would happen like this. With Lumia gone, and Tren..." he trailed off, the vision of the man's face, etched in stone, sending a shudder through his frame. "I knew I was next in line, but I never wanted it to be like this."

"Some of the men will follow you," Davan said, nodding in understanding. "But some followed General Achos even when he wasn't general anymore. I don't know if you'll win them back."

"Maybe I'm better off without them." Rune leaned forward to cradle his head in his hands. Minna assured him he wasn't concussed, but his head still ached and probably would for a while, considering the bruise at his temple.

Davan hesitated, shifting uneasily.

Rune frowned. "What?"

"Begging your pardon, sir, but you'd best aim to have them under your control as soon as possible." The captain shook his head with a scowl. "Tren sent out his army before you and the men from the village arrived. The loyal officers and I tried to stop them, but all it did was stir up fights before they went."

A minor complication. Rune squeezed his eyes shut. "How many?"

"Five thousand strong, sir. Two to assault the villages on the eastern border, near the outpost, and three to attack western lands."

"What?" Rune shot to his feet and regretted it instantly. Minna grabbed his arm and clucked at him to sit down. He hoped Davan thought he was just humoring her when he sank back to his seat.

"He gave them the Gate-stone. I don't know how he got it. I'm sorry, sir, but there's no way of knowing where they are now." Davan's tone was truly apologetic, but it didn't do much to comfort him. Rune groaned and cradled his head again.

Even if he knew where they had gone, he was in no condition to open a Gate of his own. And if their army had split, that only made it harder. Which did he go after? The army that could put his new bride at risk? The larger army that threatened his father and the capital city? He felt torn in two directions. Five thousand! How had Tren kept hold of such a number?

"Prepare horses," Rune said at last, getting to his feet with a murmured thank-you for Minna. "I need you to send word to the village. Call everyone there back to Core on my order. I have to find the army that went into Kifel's lands. If he sees me with them, we might get out of this alive."

"Yes, sir." Davan started for the hallway, pausing in the doorframe to add, "Sire."

All Rune could do was stare. The full weight of his new position settled on his shoulders so swiftly, he was not sure how he would stand.

Firal wiped her hands on her apron and strode toward the edge of the village with her head held high. Most of the women and workers hid in the half-built houses, for lack of better place to seek shelter from the army moving toward them. The men left to guard the outpost, a scant two handfuls, followed close at her heels.

Several had tried to dissuade her from meeting the approaching soldiers, but she insisted. It was not a large band, perhaps fifty men on horseback, but they were well-armored and carrying good steel. If they failed to recognize her as a mage and ally, her magic would be more useful against them than any sword.

Most of the men at her back fingered their weapons, though she'd tried to convince them combat wouldn't be necessary. No one had taken her word, and they fanned out to either side of her as they waited for the horsemen to arrive.

They were knights, marked by the bands of silver on the edges of their capes. Two carried banners depicting the seven-pointed star of Ilmenhith on a field of blue. A cluster of horsemen moved to the front and she took a step forward to meet them.

"The lands ruled by King Kifelethelas lay at least five miles to the west," she called, resting her hands on her hips as they drew their horses to a halt. "What brings His Majesty's knights this far from his territory?"

"I am well aware of where the border is," the horseman in the middle replied as he removed his helm.

Firal blinked and swept into a bow that was only hesitantly mimicked by the men at her sides. "Forgive me, Majesty. I did not recognize you in your armor."

Kifel eased himself down from his horse. "I wouldn't expect you to, you've never seen me in it." He'd obviously been prepared for the worst, riding into what he believed were lands still held by Relythes. The scant number of armored ruin-folk that stood in front of his band clearly surprised him.

Firal licked her lips in nervous uncertainty. The king was the last person she'd expected to see. All the things she'd planned to say scattered from her head. "I apologize, the village is not prepared to welcome such prestigious guests. I would offer you wine or tea, but I'm afraid we have neither here."

"I'm not here for tea," Kifel replied. "I've come seeking someone."

"Rune—Ran isn't here." She gestured toward the well in the plaza some short distance behind her. "Shall I have water drawn for your horses?"

He shook his head. "No, thank you. And I'm not here for Lomithrandel."

Her brow furrowed. "I beg your pardon, Majesty?"

"Pardoned," he said with a nod as he passed off the reins to his horse. "While I would love to speak to my son, I've come to see you. I would speak to you in private, if we may."

The soldiers around her tensed. Firal lifted a hand as if to soothe them. "Of course, sire. One of my men shall accompany us for propriety's sake. Your men are welcome to rest by the well in the meantime."

"Very well." Kifel gestured for her to lead.

She hesitated a moment before she started for the nearest house. One of the soldiers who had flanked her peeled away from the group to join them. He remained close to her side, his hand poised to draw his sword at any moment. Dedicated, determined, despite that she didn't know his name.

There were no furnishings in the building yet, but like her infirmary, a hearth stood finished in the center of the far wall. She stopped beside it, unsure whether she should sit on its edge or remain standing. Even having met him before, she still did not know how to behave around Kifel. That she was now married to his fostered son only made things more confusing. Was she to tell him of their bond, or was it best to leave that for Rune? Did that make Kifel her father-in-law? Or would that only have counted if Rune was his blood child? Lifetree's mercy, she was entertaining the *king*. Why was he even there?

"What is this about?" Firal asked, clasping her hands together for lack of something else to do with them.

The king looked at her for a long time before he spoke. "It's come to my attention that the Masters of Kirban never told you of... of your parentage." He fumbled over the words. That was odd enough on its own, but his choice of subject struck her as stranger.

"They have not," she said calmly. "Surely you haven't come all the way from Ilmenhith to discuss this."

"It's very important that you know," he insisted. He rotated his helmet, worrying its edge with both hands. "Had they told me, I would have come to you much sooner. I realize that the timing is poor, what with the conflict, but you must know. The Archmage Envesi—she is your mother."

Firal's heart fell to her knees. Memories of the Archmage flashed through her head—her frigid expression and the cold venom in her voice as she declared Firal expelled. Her *mother*. Only steps away throughout her entire life, never having spoken a word to her before the moment Firal had been discarded by the temple. Her mother had cast her out without a second thought, without so much as batting an eye.

Firal blinked against tears and swallowed hard. "If... if you believe that means I would stand against you because of her secession, you are mistaken." She struggled to keep the tremble from her voice.

Kifel's mouth fell open in surprise and stepped forward with a hand outstretched. "No, please! That isn't what I mean. You must understand, the... the Archmage is—was—my wife."

She didn't realize she'd sat on the edge of the hearth until she put her hands out to steady herself. His wife. Her mother was his *wife*. She struggled to wrap her mind around the picture, to make herself understand what he was saying. All of a sudden, the royal crest she'd been given as a child—the one that had belonged to her mother—made sense. The Archmage had broken her ties with Ilmenhith's court to found the temple. Broken her ties with the *king*.

Kifel was her father. That was what he'd ridden from Ilmenhith to tell her. The king was her father. The man who had adopted her husband. The man who had raised him as his own.

"Does Ran know?" she choked out.

"No." Kifel knelt before her. It took some effort, his armor cumbersome. "He doesn't. Even I didn't, until Nondar told me. It has been no more than a week."

"Nondar," Firal repeated as a wave of bitterness washed over her. The Master who had all but raised her, been all but a father to her. He'd known, all this time, and never told her.

Kifel's gauntleted hand brushed her face and she blinked at him through a haze of tears.

"I'm sorry," he said softly, searching her eyes. "I've spent days thinking of how I would tell you once I got here. I couldn't think of any gentle ways."

"My lady!" A voice cried from the doorway.

She shot a fiery glare at the soldier as he leaned inside. "Do you not know what privacy means?" she snapped, shoving Kifel's hand away and scrubbing tears from her face.

The soldier bowed with a hand over his heart. "I apologize, my lady, but it is urgent. You must return to Core."

"For what reason?" Firal stood. Beside her, Kifel did the same.

"Word from the captain just arrived. By the general's order, we are all to return to Core immediately. Lord Daemon rides to join the army that moves against Ilmenhith."

"What?" Kifel's emerald eyes widened and then turned hard.

"Brant's roots, man!" the soldier who had escorted Firal roared from the corner, making her jump. She'd all but forgotten he was there. "Do you not see the King of Ilmenhith standing right before you?"

305

The man in the doorway grew pale and his jaw went slack.

Firal scowled. "I will not return to Core. If Daemon rides to Ilmenhith, then I will see him there."

Kifel shook his head. "We have no extra horses. Even if we did, we'd not be able to beat them to the capital."

"There is more than one way to reach a destination, Majesty." Her words were cold and formal, the title tacked on as she shoved the new knowledge of her lineage to the back of her mind. She didn't know which mages might be in Ilmenhith or who she could ask for help, save one.

She pushed past the soldier in the doorway and marched into the open street. The budding village already boiled with frenzy as ruin-folk scrambled to gather their things and escape. Firal didn't doubt they now thought the presence of Kifel's men meant the village was under siege. The knights kept tight rein of their horses, the animals stamping and whinnying in displeasure as people filled the street.

Firal pushed past villagers and soldiers alike, her bodyguard lost in the crowd, though Kifel managed to stay at her heels. She sucked in a deep breath as she marched past the edge of the village and into the empty space beneath the trees, the madness of evacuation behind her. She locked the old Master's face in her mind and gathered energy to the center of her being.

With one powerful thrust, she sent the pulse of the Calling. A strange, pins-and-needles sensation echoed back. She sent another pulse, laced with emotion, pleading, and the impression of herself and a Gate.

A long moment passed, Firal's uncertainty growing by the moment. Kifel's men gathered around them, quieting the horses. Uncertainty became desperation, desperation melting to disappointment.

And then the air before her sizzled, and Nondar and a half-circle of Masters emerged from the invisible Gate before them.

"Child," Nondar laughed, a look of relief on his face. "Who

ever taught you such a thing? Opening a Gate to a person instead of a place. Who would have imagined such an idea?"

"It was all I could think to try," Firal said as she wrapped the Master in an embrace.

Nondar started to speak, but stopped in surprise when his eyes fell on Kifel. He grew solemn, dipping his head in reverence.

Firal released the old Master and stepped back, swiping her eyes with a thumb.

Behind the mages, crackles of energy broke the sky into shards that fell away to reveal the courtyard of the palace on the other side.

"Prepare my armies at once," Kifel ordered as his men poured into the courtyard with their horses. "We must ride immediately. Nondar, summon Medreal. Tell her—" He paused, and his eyes fell on Firal. "Tell her my daughter is coming home."

24

WAR

"WAR HAS CHANGED." KIFEL MOVED COLORED FIGURINES ACROSS the map laid on his desk. "My forefathers fought to establish nations, uphold principles. They never faced battles like this."

Medreal set down the tea tray, mindful of the markers the king placed. "War never changes, my liege." She filled several cups; he assumed it meant they would have guests soon. She added honey to his tea before she pushed it across his desk. "Since the dawn of time, blood has been spilled in the name of everything. Revenge is no exception. History repeats itself, sire, writing more bloody chapters for scholars to read."

He frowned, taking the thin silver teacup in both hands. That she'd taken to serving him in silver instead of fine porcelain hadn't escaped his notice. Perhaps she feared he'd ruin another tea set. He let the cup's warmth seep into his fingers as he tore his eyes from the figurines that represented the army moving into his territory.

Estimates put the number of men at less than he expected, but still a large enough army to cause considerable damage. Kifel had expected retaliation, but he hadn't expected his son to lead it. Surely they didn't think they would stand a chance against the armies of Ilmenhith. Ran knew what they were up against. Why lead his men to slaughter?

"Where is Firal?" he asked. With everything on his plate, he needed at least one piece of good news.

"Avoiding you." Medreal took a teacup for herself and blew steam from its top. One for him, one for her, and two others on the tray. At least one Master mage would be joining them, he wagered. "Almost as soon as the lot of you arrived, she said she wanted to visit the mages in the chapter house. I suppose after the fracture, she wishes to know where she stands among them."

"She has friends there, no doubt." A good thing, Kifel suspected. Something to help anchor her to Ilmenhith. He didn't intend to let her slip away. If only recovering his son would be as easy. "Has she seen her quarters?"

"She has been told of them. I'm sure she remembers from her last visit. I took the liberty of placing her in the same room as before, to lend whatever comfort I can." The old woman sighed, shifting on her feet and staring into her tea. "I'm afraid I don't know when she will return. I imagine your meeting this afternoon gave her quite a shock. She will need time to settle. Rushing will only make it worse."

Kifel grimaced. The stewardess knew him too well, knew he was anxious to announce Firal's presence and place a crown on her head. He'd always intended to declare Ran heir to the throne, blood or not. But now his son led a rebellion, and Kifel could not risk entering a war without an heir.

"You could have crowned Lomithrandel long ago," Medreal said, as if hearing his thoughts. Perhaps she could. She'd been a mage of the old ways, long before the temple was founded. He didn't really know what she could do.

"I wanted to. I would have. But how could I? For all that he wanted it, if only as a chance to impress me, how could I? He would have been trapped, forced to spend the rest of his life hiding, keeping secrets. He could never walk in his own skin around the council, around a wife. He'd never have heirs. Even if he is able to father them, what if the taint that ruined him passed on to his children? Would he risk that, just for sake of passing down the throne?" He shook his head and let his shoulders slump. "I couldn't do that, Medreal. I couldn't condemn him to that. And now I'm afraid he'll never understand that I never named him because I wanted better for him."

"It's never too late to say these things, my liege." Medreal drained the last of her tea and placed her cup upside-down on the tray before she made for the door. She reached it just as someone knocked. If she couldn't hear thoughts, Kifel had no idea what trick was up her sleeve. The stewardess drew the door open, and two white-robed Masters swept in.

"Majesty," Anaide greeted him with a stiff but formal bow as she positioned herself beside the desk and surveyed what lay before her. Edagan was only a few steps behind, but the stern-faced Master of Earth said nothing.

"Good of you to join me." Kifel gestured for the women to sit as Medreal moved chairs closer. "I trust you have something to contribute to the situation?"

Edagan sniffed as she took a seat. "Of course. As we understand, there is a powerful mage present in the approaching army?"

"Lomithrandel will be with them, yes. You don't need to pretend you don't know what's going on." He tried not to sound as irritated as he felt. Perhaps the Masters thought they were being polite by failing to mention Ran's name, but they weren't fooling anyone. Short of the Archmage herself, Ran was the only mage they feared.

"Of course." Anaide settled and laced her fingers together in her lap. "I'm sure you understand what a challenge his presence will present. As a result, we feel it best that your men be accompanied by mages who can provide shields and healing on the battlefield."

Kifel frowned. "Do you have enough seasoned mages to spare for such a thing?"

Edagan nodded. The two of them intended to tag-team him, it seemed. "Even the youngest of our magelings are capable of shielding, and we have several who are quite skilled with healing. Not all of our mages wear white, but I assure you they will perform most admirably."

"Very well," he ceded with a sigh. "Medreal will collect your mages and add them to the ranks."

Anaide rose as quickly as she'd sat. "Good!" she exclaimed. The look on her face was startled yet pleased, indicating she'd expected a fight. "We will see to it immediately. You will not regret this decision, my king."

Kifel waved them away with a hint of agitation.

"I will see to it that all choices are appropriate, my liege," Medreal said, dipping in a bow as graceful as her words before turning to escort the mages from his office. Kifel gave her a grateful nod. If Firal was with the mages, Kifel did not want her to be swept out to the battlefield alongside them. He was relieved to see Medreal didn't need any prompting.

But then again, she could likely read minds. Would that she had known his thoughts before he'd charged into the ruins, fueled by anger that had simmered within him for decades.

He'd made a mistake in killing Lumia. She'd been an ally once. Perhaps they could have been allies again.

"One more thing," Kifel said before Medreal could depart.

The stewardess faced him expectantly.

He returned his near-forgotten teacup to its tray. "Summon my generals and their messengers."

"All of them, my liege?" Medreal asked.

"All of them," Kifel confirmed. "War is at our door."

THE WAY FIRAL WAS GREETED WITH HUGS AND HAPPY TEARS WAS ALL too familiar. Had they been in the palace, instead of a dormitory room in the chapter house the mages now called headquarters, she might have found it eerie.

"I can't believe you're here!" Kytenia repeated, squeezing her until she couldn't breathe.

Firal tried to pry her off, to no avail. Rikka came to her rescue and wrenched Kytenia's arms loose, and Firal sucked in a gasp of a breath. To her relief, the hug Marreli gave her was gentle. "I already told you," she said when the younger girl let go, "I'm not staying. I'm only here until this whole mess blows over. Is Shymin here?"

"She's a messenger today. The Masters are all in an uproar with these men marching on us." Rikka grabbed at Firal's hand when she caught the glint of the star-gem in her ring. "What's that?"

Firal jerked her hand away and hid it in her skirt. "Is it true the Masters plan to send mages with the army? I overheard the blue magelings discussing it on my way in."

"Yes, it's true." Marreli tugged at her braids, though whether that expressed fright or excitement, Firal couldn't tell.

"All of us are going," Kytenia said. Her bright hazel eyes darkened with concern. "Vahn will be furious when he hears."

Firal blinked. "Vahn?"

"Vahn and Kytenia have been courting," Rikka giggled. "I think he means to write Kytenia's father to ask for her hand. He fusses and frets over her as if they were already married."

Kytenia flushed and averted her eyes. "He doesn't fuss like that," she murmured, though the protest was weak.

"That boy and your friends will be fine, but you will certainly not be joining them." Medreal stopped beside the girls with hands on her hips. Firal grimaced.

Rikka raised a brow and shimmied closer. Her fists settled on her hips in mimicry of Medreal's stance as she sized up the old woman. "Who is this?"

"Medreal, adviser and steward to King Kifelethelas." Medreal lifted her chin. "I've been sent to collect the mages that are to accompany the army. And you, child, will be returning to the palace. The king wants you as far from that madness as possible."

"I will go where I please," Firal snapped. "I know their general. He wouldn't just move an army against the king like this. There must be some sort of misunderstanding."

Medreal's mouth took a sour twist. "There's no misunderstanding, child. We know perfectly well why they rise against us. It was just yesterday the Underling queen was slain."

Firal's heart dropped like a stone. "Lumia is dead?"

The stewardess gave an almost imperceptible shrug, spreading her hands in a gesture of helplessness. "It's foolish to move an army against a stronger foe for vengeance, but men do very foolish things in the name of women."

An odd tightness rose into Firal's throat and she swallowed hard. Rune had left her alone in the border village and ridden off to war without saying goodbye? Hardly more than a day before, he'd sat up half the night working on the proposal he meant to give his father. With that in mind, she'd thought he might have changed his plans and departed early, believed his army a well-intentioned but stubborn group of men who refused to stay behind. But this? A war of vengeance started in the name of another woman?

He was the leader of the military force. If Lumia was gone, he was leader of everything. The people would want vengeance for their queen, but he should have quelled it. Why didn't he quell it?

She bit her lower lip and forced herself to straighten, breathing deeply to stifle the anger that chilled her inside and out. Cold and formal, she turned to give Kytenia a gentle hug. "Please be careful, all of you. I'll be waiting for you when you return."

"There'll be thousands of men out there to protect us. I'm sure we'll be fine," Rikka laughed, though her mirth sounded forced. She embraced Firal in turn and offered a bright smile as she stepped back to let Marreli take her place.

"Don't worry, Firal," Marreli said, grinning up at her. "They'll never reach the city walls."

Firal feigned a smile. Pretending to be happy was difficult. The ruin-folk had become her people in the same way the mages were still her people. No matter what, if blood was spilled, she was on the losing side. "Good luck. Try not to have too much fun without me."

"Shall I escort you back to the palace?" Medreal asked.

"No, you attend to your work here. I can find my way. Thank you, Medreal." Firal inclined her head to the older woman and left before her friends could stop her.

She retraced the path she'd taken through the meandering halls of the chapter house and paused when she heard her name. The hall behind was empty, as was the hall ahead, but one of the office doors stood ajar. She turned toward it to answer the summons, then stopped. It wasn't a summons; it was conversation.

"We can't forget they've sheltered her. She may not be as firm as we need, moving forward," a woman said. Master Edagan.

Firal inched forward to peer through the gap. Beyond the door, Edagan and Anaide stood together, their backs turned to the door as they conversed with someone on the other side of a desk.

"You know that was the least of his intentions," Anaide muttered. "Don't forget he was made Master just before the secession. Before the temple burned. His name was on the logbook of those requesting records be pulled. What other reason would he have to grant her shelter within the ruins?"

"You cannot be sure he meant ill," Nondar's deep voice rumbled from behind the desk.

Edagan grunted. "You give him too much credit. He's never wanted anything more than to take the throne. What better way to solidify his claim than to claim the heir for himself?"

A chill tore down Firal's spine. She'd heard that before—the suggestion Rune meant to use her. The thought summoned Tren to mind and she shuddered. The Master mages were right; if they were wed and she was Kifel's blood, it gave Rune a link to the throne in Ilmenhith that couldn't be denied.

"He is cunning, I'll give him that," Anaide said. "He's always excelled at manipulation. We were foolish to let the Archmage give him more power. She wanted a distraction to detract from her unethical practices. Well, she certainly got it."

"And now we'll clean up after it," Edagan sighed. "You saw them in Alwhen. How deeply is she snared?"

"That's not for me to say," Nondar replied. "However, I don't think it coincidence he chose to travel with her. I believe there is some level of intimacy in their relationship."

Anaide rubbed her brow in frustration. "Just what we need. The rightful heir to the throne trapped with the enemy's illegitimate child."

"Peace," Nondar said. "We don't know that for certain. We could not keep the pieces from being laid, but it's still possible for her to be freed from his grasp."

"And how are we to do that?" Edagan asked. "We couldn't even keep him from persuading the Archmage to cast her out. The girl has suffered enough without being told she's become a tool toward her father's downfall."

Firal's heart plunged and she took a half step backwards. She'd blamed the Archmage for that decision, for shattering the remnants of the life she'd had left after the temple burned. It had been *him*? Mind reeling, she tore herself away and hurried on. She slipped out of the chapter house and into the bustle of the street without noticing men and horses that flocked toward the castle's courtyards.

The Masters were right. She made an ideal tool in a game for power, and one Rune hadn't been afraid to use. Firal kept her head up and her face placid, moving through the crowds with a gliding grace. It was not until she reached her quarters that she

316

let her facade fall, the first sob racking her body as she collapsed into the pillows on her bed.

———

THE SUN RODE LOW ON THE HORIZON WHEN THE ARMY MOVED FROM Ilmenhith in a long line of glistening silver armor framed by flags of blue and silver. Mages in every color rode single-file down the center of the column, most too nervous to show any pride at their position of honor in the middle of the army.

"In other times, battles were fought with honor and prestige in mind. The wars continued throughout the day and ceased when both sides had had enough. There was no fighting at night. They'd retreat to their camps in peace, then resume the fight the next day." Vahn didn't look at them as he spoke, but Kytenia knew how concerned he was without seeing his face. He'd positioned himself near her on purpose. Shymin and Marreli rode some ways behind her, Rikka a few horses ahead. All three were as solemn-faced as she.

"If we're moving as far as the Masters seem to expect, we may not see any fighting until tomorrow morning, anyway." Kytenia shifted on her horse. Riding was not difficult when such a group surrounded them. Soldiers on foot surrounded the mages and the few cavalry riders who led the column, and the horses moved of their own accord. A small relief, and one less thing to worry about. She suspected the beast wouldn't stop even if she fell asleep in the saddle.

Vahn shook his head. "I doubt they're all that far off. More Masters arrived at the palace today from the borders, and soldiers with them. They say Relythes has men on the move now, too. If his men had time to travel from Alwhen to the border after hearing things were unsettled, I'm sure this fight will be right at our doorstep."

Kytenia gripped the saddle horn a little tighter. Though tensions between the eastern and western halves of the island always simmered, things had been calm for most of her life. But the mages had been on Kifel's side then, and Kifel had no interest in expanding his territory, content to maintain the borders his father had established. With mages answering to Relythes now, it was no surprise the balance had shifted and he was ready to strike. She toyed with the reins as they moved steadily farther from the city. "Are you nervous?" she asked at last, glancing at Vahn from the corner of her eye.

"Nervous?" He almost laughed. "I'm terrified. Wars are awful. Especially when you ride into them with someone you care about."

Kytenia flushed and bowed her head. She hadn't thought things between them would grow serious as quickly as they had. She'd fancied him when they'd danced during the solstice ball, certainly, but things had changed the moment she read his first letter. It had been tender and unexpected, and she'd penned a reply as soon as things settled in the temple. She hadn't known whether or not he would receive it, with his battalion on the move, but he'd sent more. The letters that followed only grew more sweet.

In the same window of time, Marreli had asked about Ran, and each question had stirred an odd pang of emotion within her. Kytenia didn't fancy him like she once had, and they'd not seen him since the temple fractured. King's son or not, he was still a Master, and she could only assume his absence meant he'd ended up on the other side of the divide. Perhaps it was better that way. It was bad enough for Vahn to face riding into battle alongside the woman he was courting. Riding alongside his childhood best friend as well might have been too much to bear.

"What are you thinking about?"

The question jerked her back to the present and she gave Vahn a sheepish smile. "Just the way everything has changed. I'm not even a high-ranked mageling, never mind a Master. I never imagined we'd be in a situation like this."

Vahn nodded, staring toward the horizon. "Well, you don't have to worry. I'll protect you out there."

Kytenia raised a brow. "And who will protect you?"

He laughed as the last rays of the sun winked out behind them. "I suppose we'll have to protect each other."

The army traveled until sunrise and rested until midday while scouts continued ahead. From noon they traveled until sundown, when the officers at the front of the line stopped them and ordered them to take positions. The wagons that traveled at the rear of the company were drawn into a circle and campfires dotted the hillside. No one removed their armor and no one put down their swords, but everyone settled for the evening meal and laughed as though they weren't riding to war.

"The army has grown soft over the years," Vahn told Kytenia in hushed tones, staring at his bowl of stew more than eating it. "Elenhiise is so secluded, and there's been no real need for battle since Kifel took the throne. They say we're riding against several thousand men. Our numbers may be greater than that, but if they're good soldiers, this may be a harder battle than the officers expect."

The moon had just passed its peak when the sentries raised a panicked call. The camp burst into activity. Kytenia scrambled to her feet and scanned the slope of their encampment for the rest of her assigned group. Unable to ride and wield magic at the same time, the mages left the horses to the soldiers and clustered together on foot. Around each group, men sorted themselves into ranks.

Somewhere, someone roared an order to begin the march. Kytenia still hadn't seen anything. It wasn't until her company crested the hill that their opponent came into view, and her heart sank.

Marching into the plain between swells were men in dark armor, their numbers hard to distinguish, though moonlight glinted off their weapons. At least a thousand that she could see, and the flow of men over the opposing hilltop showed no signs of stopping.

"Mages!"

Kytenia gave a start and joined the other three mages she'd been grouped with as they seized energy. They worked in unison, tying the flows together, spinning them into a shield over their company. It was all but invisible, a faint ripple in the air all that gave it away. It took two tries for her to set her share of the energy into a cycle. She tuned out the sounds of the officers as they issued orders to the men around her, focused instead on her own deep breaths.

Her sister stood with another group close by and appeared no more at ease. Kytenia gulped and tried not to look at her again. Instead, she watched the men ahead of them. The king rode among the officers, his horse gleaming white in the darkness. It made his presence a clear, reassuring beacon in the night. Her eyes drifted farther and she paused when her gaze fell on Vahn, not far off. He gave her a reassuring smile and she had just enough time to return it.

A bugle sounded.

The long, clear note spurred the men onward with their weapons drawn and shields ready. Kytenia and the other mages had no choice but to move along with them, shifting the flows of the mage-shield overhead to make it follow. The whistle of an arrow drew her eyes overhead and she flinched in spite of herself when its flame-shrouded tip bounced off the transparent barrier. One arrow became hundreds, and her gasp was lost amid the war-cries as the energy shield above them shattered.

Wounded men fell in the crowd as others rushed to meet the enemy with steel. Gouts of flame burst forth from the hands of several mages as they pushed to the front lines. Others cast massive mage-lights into the air, where they hung as if on invisible strings to light the battlefield below.

Kytenia darted from one wounded soldier to another to tend what injuries she could, her feet carrying her ever farther into the chaos. Her heart skipped a beat when she found herself beside a man in dark armor, her hands on him before she realized he was one of the enemy. Her pulse raced. She was a healer, bound to help those in need. If she refused to aid the enemy, she was a traitor to her own beliefs. Yet if she answered her own calling, she'd be a traitor to the crown.

"Look out, mage!"

Kytenia wheeled and shrieked as she flung her hands out in defense. A burst of energy deflected the sword meant for her head and sent her attacker reeling.

She scrambled to her feet, picked up her robes, and ran. She'd gotten too close to the front lines. Men clashed in combat around her, no matter which direction she tried to go. Frantic, she moved from cluster to cluster, desperate to find someone she knew.

"Kytenia!" Marreli's voice rang high and reedy over the sounds of battle. Kytenia migrated toward it like a moth to a flame. The smaller girl held out her hand, beckoning her into the circle of Eldani soldiers she moved with.

"How many are there?" Kytenia gasped as she gathered her thoughts enough to spin another mage-shield over the cluster.

"The captain said three thousand!" Marreli ducked under a soldier's elbow and wove her way toward the next group of men. "Have you seen the others?"

Kytenia ran to keep up. "I haven't seen anyone!" Someone grabbed the sleeve of her robe and she screeched before she realized it was one of their own.

"Best keep your wits about you, girl," the soldier growled, turning his head to show the bloody gash in the side of his scalp.

Kytenia swallowed against the lurch of her stomach as she pressed her hands to his cheeks and let magic flow through him. In the span of the heartbeat the healing took, she looked around again.

Bodies littered the ground, not all of them whole, and more

than one in colored robes. The soldier she tended tapped her arm to dismiss her and she let him go.

The sound of her name made her look up. Vahn jerked his blade from the enemy he'd felled and almost tripped over his feet in his haste to get to her. A clean slice decorated his cheek, blood on his dented armor indicating it wasn't the only cut he'd received. "You have to move back!" He caught hold of her arm and shoved her toward the thinning rear of the army.

"You need me!" She twisted to lay both hands on his face. He gasped as her magic coursed through him, electrifying and energizing as it mended his wounds.

"You're no use to anybody if you're not in one piece," he said as he urged her onward. She stumbled, but didn't protest again. Vahn hovered close behind her, herding her toward safety.

Kytenia glanced over her shoulder. Marreli was somewhere close. She thought she'd seen Rikka as well. "What about the others?"

"They're fine, I've seen them. Duck!" Vahn all but threw her to the ground. He spun and raised his sword, just in time to catch the weapon of a soldier in black. He stepped over Kytenia as he pushed the enemy back, their blades shedding sparks in the half-illuminated night.

"Vahn, behind you!" she shrieked, too slow to find her feet.

Too slow to spin a mage-shield to deflect the spear that drove into his back.

Flame exploded within the armor of the spearman behind him, leaving Kytenia blinking against the glare. Sizzles rose above the man's screams, silenced only as he crumbled to ash. The sight of Marreli on the other side, hands outstretched and dark braids half undone, was the last thing she expected.

Vahn fell to his knees, wheezing as he groped for the shaft of the spear. The swordsman before him raised his blade to deal the killing blow. Marreli rounded on him and a shockwave of energy threw the man back.

Kytenia scrambled forward on hands and knees. "Vahn!" she gasped, grabbing for his hand.

"I'm okay!" He grimaced and moved her hands to spear's haft. "Pull it out! It just grazed my side, I'm okay."

Kytenia gritted her teeth and jerked it out of his armor. Vahn stifled a shout, clapping a hand over his ribs and collapsing with a laugh of relief. She didn't have time to laugh with him. Above them, Marreli's face was ashen, her brow beaded with sweat. She struggled to hold a mage-shield around the three of them, repelling oncoming soldiers with blasts of power thrust from either hand.

The blood drained from Kytenia's face. "Stop!" she cried, scrambling to her feet. "Marreli, stop!"

"It's okay," Marreli said, voice soft. She turned from ashen to white, a serene smile wreathing itself on her face.

Kytenia screamed her name, reaching out just as her friend spent the last of her energy reserves. The mage-shield fell and Kytenia's hands closed on empty air. She fell to her knees, breath freezing in her chest, eyes burning with tears.

Glimmering motes danced all around them, riding currents of air, the last shining remnant to show that Marreli had ever been.

25

VENGEANCE

CLICKING TO HIS HORSE TO PICK UP THE PACE, RUNE SILENTLY cursed the animal's flagging strength. He'd ridden hard, but he couldn't stop now.

Heading straight for Ilmenhith had been a blind guess, but once he'd found traces of the army, there was no question where they'd gone. Attacking the city directly was beyond foolish, but Tren had no way of knowing what Kifel's armies were like, and it was even less likely he would know what the city's defenses were. Rune didn't think the man had ever gone far from Core. Now he never would.

Shaking the thought of Tren's demise out of his head, Rune nudged the horse's side with the claw on his heel. He'd changed horses several times, paying fistfuls of unminted gold for animals at stables across the country, riding with all the speed he could gather.

With any fortune, the army Tren had sent against Relythes moved slower. If Relythes had caught wind of Tren's men marching for Alwhen, retaliation would have already begun, and the outpost the ruin-folk had only just begun to build would be a lost cause. Rune had left Davan in charge of moving everyone back to Core. He only prayed Firal would be safe there.

Rune reined his horse to a trot as he crested a swell in the landscape and an encampment came into view, bathed in moonlight. Men he recognized sat with the supply wagons at the rear, looking as surprised as he felt. Several climbed to their feet and came to greet him.

"The battle's already started, General," one said, reaching for the reins of his horse.

Rune pulled back, drawing the animal just out of reach. "Where?" He was too late to stop combat, then. The thought put a knot in his stomach.

"They marched several miles to the west, told us to wait here. Said it would be safer if we were away from the mages."

Spitting a curse, Rune turned his horse westward.

"Wait, General," another voice called from the circle of wagons. Had it not been a crowkeeper, Rune wouldn't have paused. Impatient, he locked eyes with the man.

"There's word from one of the captains in Core, arrived not half an hour past," the crowkeeper said. "We didn't know you were coming until the message arrived for you."

Resisting the urge to move his horse onward, Rune lingered. "What does it say?"

"The new village on the border, sir. It's been burned. Siege by an army. They struck just as you ordered the outpost evacuated. Some say they carried blue banners, some say red. Some made it safely back to Core, but..." The crowkeeper trailed off.

"Some?"

The crowkeeper hesitated.

Rune's hands tightened on the reins. "Where is Firal? The mage, where is she?"

"General, I..."

"Where is she?" he demanded.

The man swallowed. "Captain Davan sends... regrets. The bodies were burned, sir. By all accounts, the healer mage did not return to Core."

Rune found no words. The cool night breeze blew through him, leaving him chilled to the bone.

The village had burned nearly two full days past, if Davan sent word right away. And Rune was on the other side of the island, moving farther away by the moment.

At last, he drew a breath. "Are they certain?" His voice cracked.

"I mean all respect, General," the crowkeeper said softly. "I don't think the captain would say it unless it was true."

Whether the banners were silver-rimmed blue or rich vermillion didn't matter. If Firal hadn't made it back to Core... Rune closed his eyes but couldn't banish the thought of her in the burning village, too determined, too bullheaded to leave anyone with injuries behind while she still stood.

"Do you wish me to send a reply, General?" the man asked.

Rune flexed his left hand, too aware of the ring he hadn't yet grown used to wearing, of the tight pulling of the scar Lumia had given him. If not for Lumia's death, he'd have been in the village with Firal. Where he could protect her. Where he should have been.

He looked to the east, toward the village he'd left behind, face solemn. Flames filled his head; flames and her face. "No," he said, spurring his horse into motion once more.

The gentle swells and slopes of the plains south of Ilmenhith fell away beneath his mount's hooves.

The sounds of battle loomed closer. Mage-lights hung in the night sky ahead, the iron scent of blood sharp in the air. Lathered from the last miles of the journey, the horse faltered as it crested the final hill. Rune slid from the saddle and left the animal behind as he strode into the valley where combat raged.

His face was stone as he flowed past the warring men. His slitted eyes burned crimson, the sword he didn't remember drawing weightless in his hand, the muscles in his arm and shoulder wound tight with anger so strong it made him shake.

Mages stilled to look at him. Soldiers moved from his path as he found his target in the crowd. He unfastened his cloak and let it fall behind him as he walked with a singular intent. Raising his blade, he advanced as his opponent turned. He brought his sword down with all the strength of his fury.

Kifel's pauldron shattered where the sword struck and the king collapsed beneath the weight of the blow.

"You did this!" Rune spat, drawing his sword back for another strike. "The only one who knew the way into the underground was you. She's gone because of you!"

The king barely made it to his knees to deflect the second swing. "Get hold of yourself!" He climbed to his feet as Rune recovered. "Look at what you're doing. You've started a war! Do you have any idea how many will die because of this?"

"I started it?" Rune's clawed fingers splayed against his chest. "I did nothing! I had everything planned. For the first time, I was happy. You've taken everything from me!" He adjusted his grip on his sword and took a fighting stance.

All around them, combat ceased. The magnitude of the challenge etched itself on the king's face. Accepting the challenge meant an end to the battle, though his opponent had nothing to wager. If Rune was struck down, an end to the battle was all Kifel could receive. But for the king, both life and the right to the throne lay on the line.

"Think carefully before you do this," Kifel urged. "Please, Ran."

Grief and fury spurred him on. Rune swept in to meet his opponent in a clash of steel. Kifel deflected each strike almost without effort, the two of them spinning in a dance of blades they'd practiced countless times before. Master and student no more, they collided as equals for the first time, no longer practicing, no longer playing.

Kifel forced Rune back with a flurry of strikes, each glancing blow threatening to upset his balance. Rune reevaluated his position and shifted accordingly. His sword's edge, already riddled with chips where it had met with his father's unusual blade, put him at a disadvantage. Kifel was a king; a king's magic-enhanced blade never broke. He moved slowly, considering, drawing a line in the earth with the tip of his sword as he circled. Then he leaped forward and his blade flashed upward in a rapid slash.

Kifel spun aside and turned the momentum into a stab that only just grazed Rune's side as the two came together, face to face with only inches between. Grimacing, Rune shoved him away. He adjusted his grip on his sword and again took a moment to consider his attack.

He stalked the king like a hunting beast, the centers of his eyes narrowed to paper-thin slits. From the way Kifel looked at him, and not for the first time, he felt more animal than man. But he didn't let the king's unsettled stare lull him, and when Kifel moved, he expected it. Rune twisted away from the jab of Kifel's sword but missed the intent. The strike of the king's gauntlet against the side of his head sent him to the ground.

He all but howled, clutching at the side of his face. The bruise at his temple from the blow Tren dealt him days before was still visible; striking it was a dirty trick. It took a moment to find his feet again, a moment Kifel used to strip away the hanging pieces of broken armor that hindered his shoulder and settle into a ready stance again.

His head throbbing, Rune flexed his clawed toes against the ground to gauge the traction. He waited until Kifel met his eyes before he moved again.

Dashing forward, Rune feinted one direction before striking in another, shaving sparks from the king's armor more than once. He gritted his teeth and threw himself to a gamble. He moved, granting an opening.

The king took it.

Rune lashed forward with a hard sideways strike aimed directly for Kifel's sword. Rune's blade shattered; Kifel's sword spun from his grasp. The king's gaze followed his weapon, and Rune's hand surged forward to catch him by the throat.

Kifel choked and clutched at Rune's wrist as the grasp on his throat threatened to lift him from his feet. "Will you take my crown, then?" he asked, breath ragged.

"I never wanted your crown," Rune growled, luminescent eyes flickering in the feeble light of pre-dawn. "All I ever wanted was your recognition."

Kifel's face crumpled, sorrow shading his eyes. "You've always had it. From the moment you first came to me. You've always been my son, Ran." He struggled to breathe. "You'll never know how proud I've been to call you that. But this has to end. No more bloodshed... it has to end."

Searing pain blossomed in Rune's side as the king's dagger pierced his leather armor and sank deep into the flesh underneath. He roared in agony, his hand clenching as his knees gave way. Too late he remembered where his hand lay and, as the talons on his fingers tore through artery and flesh, the cry that escaped him was of regret as much as pain.

Kifel touched his fingers to his throat, confusion and then understanding dawning on his face. Side by side, they fell to the ground, and the voices of soldiers and mages alike echoed in screams around them.

Rune struggled to turn over. He gasped, reaching for Kifel, reaching for the energy flows all around him as his father's name refused to form on his lips. Desperate, he tried to catch the flows he'd always sensed Firal using when she worked her healing magic. He brushed them, and they slipped just beyond his grasp.

Someone grabbed his shoulder and rolled him over. He stifled a shout, his claws digging at the wound in his side. Vahn stood above him, Kytenia at his back.

"Help him!" Rune pleaded, reaching for the mageling girl. Kytenia shook her head. She didn't look at him, tears rolling down her face.

"We can't," Vahn said, face somber. "It's too late. I'm sorry. It's already too late."

Someone pulled Vahn away. Eldani soldiers Rune didn't

recognize crowded above him and pulled him up. He bit down on his tongue and strained against the urge to scream. Voices around him were arguing, people shouting, shoving.

"You can't make him travel like this!" Vahn yelled as he tried to force his way back to Rune's side. A knight in battered silver armor pushed him away.

"He's a murderer," the knight snapped. "He'll hang in Ilmenhith for what he's done!"

Murderer. The single word echoed in Rune's head, panic gripping his heart. "Wait! I didn't mean—I wasn't—" A backhanded blow across his face silenced him, all but knocked him from his feet.

"He will hang," the knight repeated as the sack thrust over Rune's head blotted out the first rays of the morning sun.

———

FROM THE TIME SHE'D FIRST TAKEN THE MANTLE OF NURSEMAID AND cradled him in her arms, Medreal knew this day would come. Her magic was different from that the temple mages bore. Theirs could prolong their lives for centuries, but hers did something different. Outliving everyone around her was painful, but inevitable. She'd known this day would come, but had not expected it yet.

Breathing deeply, she willed herself not to let the tears well up again as she turned back to the table of arguing mages that occupied the council hall. They hadn't ceased their argument since the pigeon arrived with the message. Medreal took small comfort in that the army had taken pigeons with them instead of corvids; the message had been enough without being delivered by a black-winged, cawing harbinger of gloom.

"No council will be able to stand up against contestants for the throne, regardless of who is a member of it!" Anaide slammed her palms on the table as if to punctuate the sentence. "The Eldani are used to following a monarchy. They cannot

BETH ALVAREZ

adapt so quickly. Even if they could, how long can we refute claimants touting the idea their blood is somehow connected to the royal family?"

Medreal held her tongue with her teeth until she returned to the table. "If I may, Masters, I served as adviser and confidant to the king throughout his entire life and rule." She laced her fingers together and studied the faces of the councilors. "I realize I have no formal position on this council, but I do ask why none of the councilors consider the blood heir present in the palace."

Edagan gave her a look to chill bones. "What are you on about?"

"A most curious thing happened while the rest of you were planning retaliation against the Archmage and preparing for this battle," Nondar said. It was the first time Medreal had heard him speak. He looked almost amused. "The king was made aware of his daughter, as the Masters desired. Did I neglect to mention his excursion to collect her? I would have thought you'd seen her in the chapter house the day before yesterday."

Anaide blanched. "The girl is here?"

"You asked how we were to free her," Nondar said. "I believe the king saw to that nicely."

Medreal gave a wan smile. "She is quite comfortable in her quarters, though I fear she is in mourning. She was already in tears, I assume over the battle, when I took her word of her father's death."

Edagan leaned back in her chair, stroking her chin. "So, then. We have a queen."

"The Archmage will likely argue we already had one." Nondar replied. "Without previous public knowledge of Firal's existence, it will be difficult to contest whatever claim the Archmage may make. Kifel was the last of his line. Many would sooner see the Archmage lead us than an unknown relative. We will have to see to Firal's coronation immediately. A queen seated is harder to dethrone."

332

"And will she be easy to guide?" Anaide looked between Nondar and Medreal, her words far too blunt to be insinuation.

"I doubt you will be able to control her." Nondar apparently saw no need to mince words, even if the other mages cringed. "It will take time for her to learn and she will rely on us at first. But she will grow into the role. And she will accept guidance from those she trusts once she has settled into it."

With a sniff, Anaide slapped the table's edge. "Good! Best to fetch her immediately. The situation will not wait."

Medreal bristled. "Have you no heart? She just learned of her father the other day, and today she hears he's been slain!"

"Yes, and she will be responsible for sentencing the treasonous wretch who has slain him," Edagan said with a wave of her hand. "Hurry along. Tell the girl we wish to speak to her. Better to have the crown on her head this morning so we can have the murderer's head tonight."

Medreal opened her mouth to protest but found herself silenced by a sharp glance from Nondar. She had no love for the three mages who had nestled themselves in Kifel's council so soon after their arrival in Ilmenhith, but at least he seemed somewhat concerned for Firal's wellbeing. Regardless of whether or not she had been there for the girl's childhood, Medreal had always served as chief attendant to the royal family. She did not plan to change roles now. "Very well," she agreed, though her reluctance was clear in her tone.

She did not wait to be dismissed before she left the council hall to wind her way through the palace. Servants bowed and smiled at her as she passed. The staff carried on about their work without any idea of what had transpired in the hours before dawn. It made little difference to them who ruled, she supposed, as long as they were paid. But Kifel had been loved by his people for his simple way of speaking and his modest way of life. He'd been lenient in taxes and generous in trade, fostering good relations with the mainland countries that used the island as a waypoint in their travels. With any luck, Firal would share her father's keen mind for business and economy.

Of course, with any luck, Kifel would not have died.

Medreal sighed and smoothed her skirts and silvered hair before she knocked on the door. When no answer came, she tested the handle. The door was unlocked and swung open soundlessly on well-oiled hinges.

Firal sat in a chair beside the window, staring down at the courtyard and walls below. With the city streets visible beyond the walls, Medreal considered it fortunate that the army had not yet arrived. It would at least give the girl a little time to prepare herself.

"Child, are you well enough to speak?" She tried to sound pleasant, though she felt anything but. Her heel nudged the door closed behind her to keep out unwanted eyes and ears.

Firal shrugged. She turned something small and golden between her fingers. It was that she was staring at, Medreal realized, not the city beyond the windows. From the distant look on her face, it seemed she didn't see anything else.

Medreal hesitated by the door. Her instructions were to direct the girl to the mages, but only the Lifetree knew how gentle they would be with her. She stood still for a long time before she finally joined Firal by the window. "Your father was a good man," she said, staring into the gardens below. "I am sorry you will not have time to know him. You will never know the joy it brought him to find you were alive and well."

"He told me once that he wanted grandchildren." Firal closed her eyes and slipped the thin gold band onto her finger, twisting it as though she considered removing it again as soon as it was in place. "I always thought he hoped I would marry Ran."

Medreal frowned. "I don't know how good of a match you might have been. Ran has his... peculiarities."

"I know."

The simple words caught her off guard and Medreal blinked at the girl. "Do you, now? What sort of secrets has he told you?"

Firal grimaced and said nothing more.

Medreal waited in awkward silence until her eyes glazed over with thought, and she no longer saw the gardens through the window. "Ran was never crowned, you know. Until you arrived in Ilmenhith, Kifelethelas had no recognized heir."

Firal's amber eyes widened and darted to Medreal's face. "Heir?"

"You will be crowned before the day is out." Getting the words out was struggle enough without trying to make them sound positive. "I'm afraid you'll have a very challenging first few days as our ruler."

"I can't rule!" Firal cried. She lifted a hand to her mouth and pressed the other to her stomach as her face blanched. "Oh, I feel ill. Please tell me you don't mean that!"

"My apologies, dear girl." Medreal dipped in a bow and drew back. The poor child. She couldn't blame her in the least. One shock after another, with no time to think on any of it. Being thrust from the position of a temple exile to that of queen was jarring enough to unsettle anyone's stomach. "I'll step down to the kitchens and have them make a kettle of peppermint tea. I suspect you'll need it for your nerves in the coming hours. In the meantime, the three Masters from the chapter house would like to speak with you. About your coronation, I am sure. Best not to keep them waiting. I'll have your tea delivered there."

Partly for the girl's benefit and partly for her own, Medreal made her retreat from Firal's quarters hasty. Still, as she pulled the door closed, she was unsure of whether the sound Firal made behind her was a sob, or the girl retching.

EVEN WITHOUT THE USE OF HIS EYES, THE FAMILIAR SOUNDS AND smells of the city would have been enough for Rune to know they had reached Ilmenhith.

The wagon driver clicked at his horses and snapped his

whip, loose boards rattling in the bed where Rune lay. Though the mages had mended the wound in his side just enough to ensure he'd live to reach the city, no one thought him capable of riding. He might have been grateful, if not for the way they'd tied his hands behind his back and bound his feet with his ankles crossed before they'd thrown him in the back of a wagon with the supplies.

The mages hadn't been gentle, either. He'd earned a new respect for Firal's healing when the magelings had twined their energies together to tend to him. Firal's healing hadn't been comfortable, but what these mages unleashed on him had been agony. Better to still have the dagger in his side, better to have it slowly rotating in the wound than to feel that again.

Once more, Rune decided to try his bonds. He'd almost succeeded the first time, cutting the binding that wrapped his ankles with the claws on his hands. They'd seen him moving and stopped the procession, wrapping his hands with cloth so he couldn't do it again. But there was still hope for escape, a chance to right things after retrieving his amulet from Core. Before they'd covered his head, he'd seen none of the soldiers who might recognize him without his amulet—except for Vahn, and had Vahn told the others that the creature they'd bagged and bound was the king's son, they'd have laughed in his face. Not that they should have taken him prisoner at all. Kifel had consented to the duel and Rune had won. Kifel's army should have withdrawn.

Breathing deep, Rune shifted from his side to his stomach and willed himself to relax, despite the jarring of the wagon and the ache in his side that made it impossible to concentrate. He rolled his shoulders back, folded his knees, arched his back to bring his hands and feet together. Just a little more. A little more, and he could catch the rope that held his wrists with the claw on his heel. The half-healed wound in his side pulled. He gritted his teeth and stretched a little farther before it started to open and a lance of pain shot up his side and through his middle.

Gasping, he abandoned the attempt and tried not to focus on the pain.

The things that came to mind were no more pleasant. His father's face, still fresh in memory, the moment he realized he was going to die. The look of worry Firal had tried to hide when he'd left, unknowingly abandoning her to die, as well. His eyes stung and he squeezed them shut behind the cover of the sack. He hadn't cried since childhood. He fought it with everything in him now, though he knew it was a battle he'd likely lose.

Without warning, the wagon jolted to a halt. Thoughts jarred from his head, Rune tensed and waited for someone to come for him. The dull roar of a crowd obscured the sound of individual voices. There was music, too, somewhere nearby. Not the dirge one would expect from a city that had just lost its ruler, but something happier, upbeat. Celebrating his capture and impending death, perhaps.

"You're a lucky one, aren't you? The queen's all ready to receive you in the palace." Hands dragged him out of the wagon bed. Cold steel against his ankle cut his feet free as they forced him to stand. He rolled the words over in his head and everything in him turned to ice.

The queen. A vision of Envesi filled his mind. Of course she'd rush to seize Kifel's throne, eager to claim more power. That was why she'd ingrained herself with Relythes, after all. That was why she'd made him. A tool, a weapon, something with which to sow discord. The icy feeling in the pit of his stomach shifted to roiling hate. Hate for the Archmage, hate for what she'd made him. Hate for the things that had happened at his hands. Hate for himself for doing them.

The wound in his side had made it hard to focus. Now, acting on pure instinct, Rune reached for the energy flows that moved all around him. He rose to his full height, ignoring the throb of pain, and let the soldiers maneuver him around the wagon and through the courtyard.

"Well that certainly put a spring in his step," someone behind him laughed; a harsh, unpleasant sound. He put them out of his mind and focused on the energy flows, winding them close, holding them tight, struggling not to let his wound distract him. He'd only have one chance, one opportunity to strike the Archmage with all the strength she'd given him.

The sound of people faded behind him as the soldiers entered the palace and guided him through the expanse he could have navigated without them, eyesight or not. The doors to the throne room groaned as they opened.

"May we present to the queen," someone said as they crossed to the throne's dais, "the criminal responsible for the death of King Kifelethelas."

Hands on Rune's shoulders forced him to his knees and held him there. His breath quickened as he gathered the flows close and braced to let them free. Someone tore the hood from his head, and when his blazing eyes landed on the queen, all his anger fell away.

She was glorious, dressed in green silk and wearing gems in her ebony hair. She stiffened on the throne and raised her chin, though she caught herself before shock could show on her face.

Magic slipped from his grasp. "Firal," he breathed, hardly believing, unable to look away. He tried to rise, but the soldiers to either side forced him back down.

"You?" she asked. He saw the hurt in her amber eyes and the way she tried to tamp it down.

"The village burned, I thought... They told me..." His voice was husky from disuse, unsteady with emotion. He stared up at her, his brow furrowed. How had she gotten here? Why did she wear that silver circlet on her brow and perch upon his father's throne? He dragged his tongue over his dry lips and managed to swallow before he spoke again. "What's happened? What's going on?"

"You killed the king." It wasn't quite a statement and not quite a question, either. "He was my father. His kingdom is now mine."

Rune opened his mouth, but Firal rose from the throne before he could say a word.

"I cannot speak to this man," she declared, turning to the white-robed mages he hadn't noticed beside her.

"My lady, you must!" Anaide insisted, wringing her hands. Anger sparked in him again when he recognized the Master.

"I cannot!" Firal shouted, ignoring the gasps and murmurs of the soldiers and high-born gathered in the throne room around them. "I sit on a throne that's been cold for less than a day, and already you ask me to act against a man I cannot bear to look at. He is a liar and a traitor, a wicked and manipulative monster. How dare you lay this before me before my eyes have dried! If it means so much that he be cast into the dungeons today, then the council may speak without me. As I'm sure you intend to, anyway."

"Child, please," another Master—Nondar—said as he moved toward her. The old mage looked more aged and frail than ever. He clutched his cane in near desperation as Firal lifted her skirts and started for the stairs that led to the private quarters above.

"Wait," Rune called after her, struggling to rise. "Firal!" Again the soldiers at his sides held him in place, forcing him to remain kneeling before the throne. He craned his neck and strained to see her as she disappeared.

Exchanging worried looks, the mages remained silent for some time before Anaide moved to stand before the throne. "Very well," the Master said, lifting her voice and staring down at him with a sneer. "As the queen wishes, her council will act in her place, as she is still too stricken with emotion over the loss of her father. As a high member of the sitting council, I hereby charge you murderer, guilty of treason and the slaughter of our king."

Rune's eyes flicked down to the Masters and a look of warning flashed across his face. "You know who I am, Anaide," he said, voice stronger, determined. "You know I wouldn't have killed him on—"

"Be silent!" Anaide snapped, and the room seemed to tremor with her words. Nondar turned away; a hint of a smile played on Edagan's lips. Rune tried to speak again and found himself unable, muted by some trick of the Master's power.

Anaide drew herself up and stared at him with a gleam in her eyes. She did know him. He saw the recognition in her eyes. "As penance for your guilt, admitted just now by your own words," she continued, a grim look of justice on her face, "I sentence you to hang by the neck until dead."

26

WORTH FIGHTING FOR

"THERE IS WORD FROM THE BORDER, CHILD." NONDAR GRIMACED and corrected himself. "My queen, that is. I apologize. It will take some time for me to grow used to that."

Firal squeezed her eyes closed and rested her forehead against the windowpane. She no longer saw the gardens below, but she stood there, nonetheless. It would be strange when she moved to the royal family's quarters. She still thought of this room as her own and would for some time. Of course, being in a part of the palace appropriate to her new position might come with benefits. Perhaps people would even knock before entering her room.

"I don't think this is a good time, Master Nondar." Kytenia patted Firal's shoulder. She hovered close to her friend's side, as she had all morning. Her eyes were red, but she did a good job of disguising that she'd been crying moments before.

Nondar sighed, remaining in the open doorway. "I wish it could wait for a better time, but it must be tended now. I understand there was a village being erected near the edge of the ruins. Relythes sent men to destroy it. Now those men move westward and have begun to threaten outposts under your control."

More bloodshed. Firal shook her head and drew a shuddering breath. "Forgive me, Kytenia. I must speak with Nondar. If you'd like to go find Rikka and Shymin, I'll join the three of you as soon as I am able." It was strange not to include Marreli in the group, strange to realize she'd never see the girl's dreamy eyes or dark braids again. Marreli had always been quiet, shy, but she was a precious friend from a time where Firal had few. She'd have even fewer now that she was to rule.

"Are you certain?" Kytenia asked, frowning when Firal gave her a nod. She looked as if she wanted to protest, but no objection came. Instead, she embraced her friend and then strode past Nondar to leave the two alone.

The old master watched Firal by the window for a time before he stepped inside and shut the door. "I realize you have much to mourn, child. I know handling this matter now cannot be easy."

Firal turned to give him a shadowed look. "Everything is falling apart around me, Nondar. I only just learned who my father was. Now he is dead. Marreli is dead and there aren't even ashes to send to her family. Now I receive word that a land I don't know how to rule is threatened, and there is to be an execution before the week's end!"

He held out a hand in gesture of peace. "I understand your distress, child, but Anaide is certain that the best course of action is for the captive to be—"

"He was my husband!" Firal shouted. Nondar's eyes widened with shock. Tears pricked at her again and she blinked hard to keep them at bay as she reined in her emotions. "Regardless of whether or not he sought to use me. I know who he is and I know you do, too. The only thing he was ever truthful about was his love for his father. He has committed any number of crimes against the crown, but I don't believe for a moment murder was one of them. I expected better from the mages. To hang him with a falsehood is to spit on your king's grave."

Visibly shaken, it took some time for Nondar to find words.

"Your Majesty, what Anaide passed as sentence is appropriate for his crime, regardless of who he is. I realize you lived among those Giftless people for some time, but their ways and customs are not recognized here. You cannot let such things cloud your vision of justice."

"Those Giftless people are my people." She pressed a hand to her heart. "They live within the ruins, which stand on my lands. Their ways are a part of our ways and we will protect them as a part of our people."

"If that is the case," Nondar said slowly, "I suggest you decide how we shall handle the issue of the men Relythes has sent against us. If you claim the people in the ruins as your own, then there are more of your people at risk than I realized."

Firal hesitated, biting her lip in thought. "What of the Underling soldiers that marched against Ilmenhith? Where have they gone?" She didn't like adopting their old name; she'd grown accustomed to calling them ruin-folk, but it was a name those in Ilmenhith were unlikely to know or use.

Nondar shrugged. "The army retreated when they saw their leader captured and bound. Shaken by the breach of tradition, I would assume. Our own soldiers pursued them, but the officers claim when they crested the hill, the Underling forces were simply gone."

Firal twisted her ring. To be in one place and gone so quickly meant a Gate, of course. She doubted anyone else knew of the Gate-stone that had passed into possession of the Underlings, but she was willing to wager the army had used it. If they had, the soldiers would be back in Core now, which meant they could defend themselves if necessary. "No need to concern ourselves with Core, in that case," she mused, thinking aloud. "I will approach the Underlings when all this is settled and I am able to do so. We shall have to defend the border against Relythes, but how to quell the fighting?"

"If I may suggest," Nondar said as he moved toward the windows, "I believe that as a new ruler, it would be best for you to meet with Relythes to reestablish your borders. And if I may be bold, I believe you may be able to negotiate between the mage factions, as well."

"I trust you have ideas on how to do that?" Firal gestured to the chair beside the tall windows. She'd been too restless to sit.

He accepted the invitation a grateful nod, easing himself down and folding his hands atop his cane. "Of course. We shall start with how to extend an invitation for the meeting." The old Master settled into the placid tone he'd used so often when giving lectures. Firal leaned against the window as he spoke, her eyes unfocused as she stared out across the city that was now hers. She didn't like all of his suggestions, but she could see the wisdom behind them. It was good fortune that Nondar had ended up on her side. For things to end well, she'd need all the good fortune she could get.

Though the council hall held mostly court mages and Masters from the chapter house, a handful of magelings in colored robes dotted the room as well. The Masters rarely left the chapter house without them, insisting they required magelings for assistance. Assistance, of course, meant they were little more than servants while in the palace, but it was an understandable necessity. With the preparations for Firal's formal coronation ceremony and subsequent feasts underway, the palace could spare no staff to assist them.

Most of the mages sat in their places at the long council table, though a few seats remained notably empty. Firal's place at the head was flanked by places for the three Masters that now led the mages in Ilmenhith. Each of the four seats lacked an occupant. The magelings did not dare borrow those chairs for rest, sitting on the floor or milling about the room instead, refilling wine goblets and otherwise making themselves useful.

No one noticed the door had opened until Master Nondar

spoke. "Our young queen has written a letter to be delivered to King Relythes at once." He waved the scroll and glanced over the faces gathered.

"I will deliver it." Shymin stood, earning surprised looks from Rikka, Kytenia, and Vahn. They'd been sitting in the corner for some time, saying little and doing less.

Nondar beckoned her with a finger. She offered her sister and friends a smile before she joined the white-robed old man. A small cluster of Masters formed around them, stretching and mumbling as they prepared to open the Gate. He held out the message and clasped a hand over Shymin's fingers when she took hold of it.

"You are to deliver it to Relythes alone," he told her, expression hard. "No one else."

She eyed the parchment and nodded. "Are we going to war with the eastern lands, Master?"

Nondar shook his head. "That is not for me to say, child. Deliver the message. We will open the Gate for your return in an hour's time."

"Yes, Master." Shymin bowed her head and stepped back to wait as the Masters opened a crackling Gate against the wall. The light was blinding; she squeezed her eyes closed against the brilliance. When she reopened them, she blinked at an image of the palace in Alwhen. She'd expected the building the mages had been given, not a direct Gate to the king's location. Sparing a look over her shoulder for her friends, she tried to reassure them with another smile before stepping through.

The tingling energies of the Gate were hardly pleasant, but she'd grown used to them. Shymin smoothed her robes as the Gate's power winked out behind her to leave shimmering sparks in the air. With fortune, she'd be able to deliver the message and have time to speak to the Archmage before the Gate to take her home opened.

Sentries at the palace door gave her nods of greeting as she slipped inside. The air within was thick with smoke and she

345

restrained a cough. She couldn't imagine why Relythes hadn't replaced torches with mage-lights after the mages arrived in Alwhen.

Shymin hurried to the throne room, but slowed when the people seated nearest the king came into view. Fortune smiled upon her, it seemed. The Archmage and her Masters sat beside King Relythes.

"Another one of your magelings for a meal," Relythes grunted, giving Shymin a thoughtful look. "Do you lack proper accommodations for feeding your people, mage?" The tilt of his gaze indicated he spoke to Envesi. Shymin expected an outburst at the disrespectful tone he used, but to her surprise, the white-haired woman smiled as if it were in jest.

"Majesty," Shymin said, spreading the skirt of her robes as she dipped in a bow. "I come bearing a message from Queen Firal of Ilmenhith."

The Archmage's smile cooled and a startled look flitted over her features, if only for a heartbeat. Then she caught herself and settled into a look of frosty neutrality. Shymin tried not to cringe. She'd not had time to deliver information regarding Firal's claim to the throne to the Archmage. Naturally, Envesi would be displeased by the surprise.

"Queen!" Relythes scoffed. He rested his elbows on the table and held out his hand. "Give that here, girl."

Shymin crossed the room without looking at the Archmage again. The roll of fine paper was light in her fingers—too light for the burden it must bear—as she deposited it in the king's hand. Then she stepped back, clasped hands before her and waited with her head bowed. She felt Envesi's eyes boring into her like daggers of jagged ice.

A long silence dragged past as he read. Shymin glanced at Melora and Alira, the other Masters at the table, and studied their faces. They were close enough to read the message, but neither of them tried. Both white-robed women wore pinched expressions that still managed to show no more feeling than what the Archmage displayed. She almost wished one of them would read over his shoulder, just so she could catch some sort of emotion that would reveal some hint as to what she'd just delivered.

Relythes snorted and let the letter roll itself closed. "She's invited you, as well," he said, with a sidewise glance toward Envesi.

"Invited me to what, my king?" the Archmage asked with a smile too tight to be genuine.

"The coronation and festivities afterward. It seems their good King Kifelethelas has gotten himself killed, fighting the same filth that tried to rise against me. Bah!" He flung the roll to the floor and cast Shymin a look that made her stiffen. "You, mageling."

"Yes, Majesty?" She fidgeted with the skirt of her robes.

"Tell your *queen*," he sneered as the word left his tongue, "that I have no interest in this little party of hers."

Shymin flinched at his tone and opened her mouth to speak.

"But," he said, holding up one thick forefinger to forestall her. "I will gladly attend the execution of Kifel's foundling prince."

Shymin was not the only one who gasped.

Melora almost leaped from her chair. "They cannot be serious!"

"Lomithrandel should have been next in line for the throne! What madness has taken the capital?" Alira demanded.

"Hush, both of you." The Archmage did not raise her voice, her words enough to silence the Masters.

Shymin swallowed. Her head swam. She found herself staring at the king before she realized he was watching her, waiting for a response. "I shall tell her, Majesty. Thank you." She bowed and turned to excuse herself. Silence ruled the throne room and her footsteps echoed loudly on her way to the door. The moment she passed out of sight, a fierce argument erupted behind her.

BETH ALVAREZ

Foundling? Lomithrandel? Execution? The Underling general's face flashed through her mind. The sight of him bloodied and snarling like some sort of beast as he battled the king was still fresh in memory, but to recall it now was jarring. She hadn't known him, with his darker hair, snake's eyes, and the scales that marked him some sort of monster. But it *was* him.

Her knees trembled and she stumbled to the benches in the courtyard to sit. She turned the thought over in her head a thousand times before the air shifted with the power of an opening Gate. A handful of Masters appeared in front of her and offered no greeting before another Gate slid open for her return to Ilmenhith. On the other side, Nondar and the rest of the Masters waited.

It took all her strength to get to her feet and cross through the portal. Her sister hurried to meet her as she stepped into the council hall.

"Shymin, what's wrong?" Kytenia reached for her arm. Grateful for the contact, Shymin gripped her sister's hands for support.

"They were not very happy," she said, shaken. "Relythes said he would come for the execution."

Nondar's face grew grim, but he nodded. "Very well," he murmured. The mages released the Gate and he turned to leave. "I shall inform the queen. Sit, child. You've done well."

Shymin sank to the floor where she stood. Kytenia sank with her and watched the tired Masters as they scattered. Shymin waited until they'd vanished, waited until Rikka and Vahn joined them on the floor to speak.

"Oh, Kytenia," she started, blinking against tears. "I think there's been a terrible mistake."

———

FIRAL RAN A THUMB OVER HER CARVED SEVEN-POINTED STAR pendant, its surface worn from years of such caresses. There had been a time she'd been happy to have her pendant back in her hands, when she'd lost it in the ruins and feared it gone forever. But that was before she'd known who her mother was, and that for all the years she'd thought herself abandoned, her mother was only on the other side of a closed door. Now, the pendant seemed a harsh reminder of everything she'd wanted and lost.

Still, it was her father's crest. Her crest. Throwing it away seemed wrong, though she'd gone without it long enough that the chain felt odd around her neck. Perhaps she would put it away, stow it in some jewelry box where it would be buried with the other riches she'd have lavished on her.

It was difficult to imagine that only days ago, she'd owned three dresses. Now she had half an island, and not everyone on it seemed pleased at the sudden appearance of their new queen. She'd overheard Edagan and Anaide speaking of riots and letters from angry lords declaring their right to the throne. No such letters had reached her, though she was not surprised.

"They think me unfit to rule," Firal said, staring down at the pendant she wore. The door had made no sound when it opened, but she'd already grown used to the odd feeling of Medreal's Gift. It had the same note of wildness she felt in Rune. Her chest tightened at the thought of him. "The only reason the mages wish for me to have the throne is because they think me a puppet that will dance when they pull my strings."

Medreal quickly shut the the door behind her. "All rulers begin with no idea how to rule." She offered a smile as she held up the tea tray. "Even if they think they know what they will do when they take power, doing it is another thing entirely."

"And what of those who don't know what they will do at all?" Firal tried not to sound hopeless.

Shrugging, Medreal set the tray on the floor, of all places, and gestured for Firal to join her as she sat. "They're usually best served by taking time to think of what they want, first."

Firal crept closer. She did not sit, but hovered above the old woman as she poured the tea. Medreal always seemed to know when one's nerves needed soothing, and when a cup of chamomile could help. When the stewardess raised a cup in offering, Firal sank to the floor beside her. "I've haven't even been queen for a week and I've already made the worst mistake. I wasn't strong enough to face him, not then. I thought they'd simply stave off his sentence. I don't want Rune... Ran," she corrected herself. Everyone seemed to know him by a different name; she wasn't always certain which one to call him. "I don't want him to die, but I don't know how to undo the judgment Anaide passed. Nondar said I can't. He says Ilmenhith is ready to rise against me as it is, and I cannot afford to offend the city's people by not putting him to death."

"Nondar is correct." Medreal sipped her tea, her eyes distant. "Kifel was a quiet ruler, but he was loved. You are already in a precarious position, taking his place when you are all but unknown."

"But I didn't want his place!" Firal protested.

Medreal arched a brow. "Would you prefer your mother take it?" When Firal clamped her teeth shut on any further protests, the stewardess chuckled. "Not all is lost yet, dear girl. He is a stubborn boy and will not go without a fight."

Firal sighed. A fight was what had gotten him into this mess to begin with. Again, resentment bubbled up in her as she thought of his betrayal. The idea of being used to access the throne made her ears burn with anger and her stomach roil. And the records. She would have to ask Nondar for the logbook she'd overheard them speaking about. She and Rune had traveled to Ilmenhith together—long before she'd known who he was—for the sole purpose of seeking the identity of her parents. He had already been a Master then. If he'd known the answer before they departed, then their venture had only served to help him into her graces. She could think of no other reason he would play along.

Then again, if gaining her favor had been his intent, some pieces of the story did not make sense. The burning of the temple had driven her away, and despite everything, his claim he hadn't been involved still seemed sincere. She rubbed her ring with her thumb and stared absently into her cup.

"He gave that to you, didn't he?" Medreal nodded in understanding even when Firal did not reply. "I knew from the moment he brought you into my palace that he'd find a way to have you. Stubborn, spoiled child would tear down the stars before giving up on something he wanted."

"He didn't start any wars for me," Firal said bitterly. She tugged the ring free of her finger and left it on the tea tray with her cup.

"Perhaps not. But he gave you a war to quell, and that is certainly a good way to start your rule. When the people hear of the bloodshed you were able to avoid, they will come to respect you." Medreal swallowed the last of her tea and put her own cup back on the tray.

Quelling a war. Nondar and the other two Masters kept saying the same thing. Firal fought her exasperation. "Everyone expects me to stop the war, but no one will tell me how they think I should do it. Nondar said I would know what to do by the time Relythes arrived, but he'll be here at sunrise and I haven't any idea."

"I would have thought it obvious, child." Medreal's eyebrows lifted in mild surprise. "You'll have to marry him."

Firal's jaw dropped. "You can't be serious!"

"Well, what could be better?" The old woman frowned at her. "You'd unify the island under one rule. He's Giftless, so you'll outlive him easily. Even if you bear him children, they'll have to wait for you to die before they can take your place as ruler."

"I cannot!" Firal cried.

"You can, and if you know what's best for your kingdom, you will. When Relythes arrives tomorrow, you will make the suggestion when you break your fast with him. You are young and quite lovely. He will not turn you down. Now, if you will excuse me, my queen, I must return this to the kitchen." Medreal bowed and excused herself as quietly as she'd come.

Again, Firal found herself feeling ill.

"WE ARE NOT SO DIFFERENT, YOU AND I."

Rune struggled to open his eyes. His muscles burned with exhaustion; fire lit in his neck and shoulders just from the effort of lifting his head. Fitted with manacles and chained in place, he dangled uncomfortably from chains not long enough to let his knees reach the floor. He was trapped, unable to rest. It had been deliberate, of course. If they kept him tired enough, there was no chance he could summon the magic he needed to break free.

He cast one baleful look at the old woman crouched on the other side of the iron bars before he let his head fall. "How are you anything like me?"

Medreal grasped the bars and leaned against them. She studied him, pity in her eyes. "The jailer has not been kind to you."

Rune snorted a laugh. If he was fortunate, the jailer would dump another bucket of cold water over him, wash away some of the grime and blood and sweat before their next session. The man seemed rather fond of his scourge; dozens of thumb-wide welts and wounds promised to leave ugly scars across Rune's back. "The threat of execution wasn't punishment enough, it seems."

"Perhaps I am at fault. Had I been braver, perhaps I could have taught you. Perhaps if I had, you would not be caged." Her smile didn't touch her eyes. "Perhaps if you'd learned your magic from a proper source, you'd never have needed to return to that dreadful temple of theirs."

Ignoring the pain it caused him, he lifted his head to look at her again.

"I've done you no favors by not speaking of my own Gift,"

Medreal said, sitting on the floor and smoothing her skirts around her. "There are none left here that practice the old ways, save you and I."

He studied her face for a time, uncertain. He'd never heard of any other forms of magic, though the fact his was special had been drilled into his head since before he could remember. He'd always known Medreal was a mage, but had assumed she was like any other. Looking at her now, he wasn't so sure. It was impossible to say how old she was, but she hadn't bleached the way other mages did. Her hair was white, but it was the yellowed white of age, not the stark white that came from the surging energy of magic, and her eyes were still so dark they looked black.

She nodded. "Yes, you see it now, don't you? My power is not like theirs. My power is like yours. Unrestricted. Unrefined. All the power of this world flows through me, I do not need to bend it to my will. I ask, it answers. You ask, it answers. We are the same."

"Why are you telling me this?" Rune twisted his wrists against the biting iron cuffs that held them.

"Because you have a choice, child." Medreal reached for a pocket hidden in her skirt. "You may die tomorrow, or you may fight. And if you choose to fight, you should know what lies ahead for you."

"And that is?" He met her gaze when she lifted her eyes. The sight of them startled him, chilled him. Their color was unchanged, but her eyes glowed with a soft, otherworldly light, reflecting all the power she'd mastered and now embraced.

"Eternity, Ran. Our kind live forever, unless we are killed. It is a long path, a lonely one. But it is yours to choose." She searched his face and smiled at his surprise. "Thought you were special, did you? Thought you were the only one whose eyes could shine with the strength of all there is?" She chuckled. "With time, you will learn to shut the power out. It won't always feel like it's trying to consume you."

He shook his head and let it drop. "I don't see why I should fight, if an eternity of being alone is all I have to look forward to."

"Because, child," Medreal said as she leaned forward and placed something on the floor of his cell. "Some things are simply worth fighting for." Then she rose to leave, and he waited until the echo of her footsteps died before he opened his dimly glowing eyes again.

There, on the floor, lay a simple ring of gold crowned with a serpent's tear.

27

ESCAPES AND EXILES

AS THE SUN'S FIRST LIGHT PAINTED THE CLOUDLESS SKY IN MUTED pinks and yellows, Firal still lay awake. Weariness sat heavy in her bones, weighing her down in the bed she couldn't bring herself to leave. She'd spent the whole night struggling to think of something, anything, that could solve the problems that would rise with the sun. But the moon set, the stars faded, and when sunrise began to peek over the trees on the horizon, she had come up with nothing. Nothing sound, in any case. There was always the possibility of running away and letting the Archmage take Ilmenhith while she disappeared into the underground. But they'd hunt her, she was sure, eager to eliminate any threat she could present as direct heir to Kifel's domain.

And there was the thought of pulling Rune from the dungeons. Letting him masquerade as the former king's fostered child again. She wasn't eager to let him walk free, but she didn't want him to die, either. Her life would be easier if she could just sweep him under the rug, maybe send him off with the mages so she wouldn't have to look at him again. He had been a Master, after all; it wouldn't be unreasonable for him to resume living beneath that guise. But that was unfair, forcing him to spend the rest of his life hiding, and there was the matter of finding some criminal in the dungeons to disguise as Kifel's murderer and hang to pacify the crowds—deceit that didn't sit well with her.

Dealing with Lomithrandel's disappearance was another matter. If she was to marry Relythes and mend the rift between the factions of mages, she couldn't pretend he'd fled to the eastern lands. Groaning at the thought of the Giftless king, she turned to bury her face in her pillow.

Her head ached, and not just from lack of sleep. She'd cried herself dry more than once during the night and her eyes still felt swollen. She'd not bothered to rise and check the mirror. Rising would mean beginning a day she didn't want to face. Rising meant receiving the eastern king and the mages that would accompany him, and seeing the hastily-built gallows in the wide avenue just outside the palace gates.

"Still abed, are we? Well, you'd best get up. I've brought a gown and a drink to wake you." Medreal's quiet entrance was no surprise; Firal had felt the woman's energies from a good distance down the hall. She carried a tray, as she always did, but the drink it held was not tea. It had a rich aroma, pleasant and eye-opening. Firal lifted her head from the pillows.

"Shall I brush your hair for you this morning?" Medreal put the tray on the small table in the corner. She turned toward the bed as she lifted the gown from her arm and shook it out for Firal to see. It was the same inky blue as the night sky, and tiny crystals and white pearls nestled among silver and pale blue embroidery gave the impression of stars.

"Is that what I'm to wear for my coronation?" Firal threw back the covers and pushed herself upright with a sigh.

Medreal blinked at the dress. "Why, do you not like it? I thought it nice, considering it has the kingdom's colors in it. Shall I fetch something else?"

"No, no." Firal waved a hand and smoothed her thin nightgown. "It will do fine, I just thought I might wear something else for breakfast. Imagine me getting jam on the front, then standing before the whole city to formally receive my crown."

The stewardess chuckled and shook her head. "I'm certain I could find you another dress before your coronation, were that to happen. But there are other events due to happen first."

Firal tried to push those other events out of her head. She got to her feet and made her way to the table to pour herself a cup of the dark, steaming liquid before Medreal could beat her to it. It certainly smelled good, though the first taste was exceedingly bitter. Grimacing, Firal put down the cup and reached for the sugar and cream.

"It is a bit strong, isn't it?" The old woman laughed. She drew Firal's unruly black hair back over her shoulders and set to working out the tangles with a brush retrieved from the top of the dresser. "Coffee, they call it. It's quite popular on the mainland, I understand. Your father liked it for difficult mornings."

"I can see why. It would be hard to think of anything more bitter than the taste of that." Firal scraped her tongue against her teeth and stirred a liberal dose of sugar into her drink.

"That could be why he drank it straight, yes," Medreal agreed.

The rest of the morning's preparations passed in silence. Medreal worked gems and pearls into Firal's hair and buttoned her into the dark blue dress without the need for her to suck in her stomach. Tailored dresses instead of ill-fitting hand-me-downs were another thing she'd have to grow used to.

Anaide waited for her in the hallway, nattering about how Firal was to behave from the moment she opened the door. Firal did her best to nod and say little, tucking away all the instructions in the back of her mind. She understood what she was expected to do, understood why they expected her to do it, but nothing said she had to enjoy it.

A small group of maidservants had collected at her heels by the time she stood at the palace doors to await the entourage from Alwhen. She gazed into the courtyard and tried not to look at the gallows on the far side of the gate. Already people gathered around it, impossible to ignore even if she didn't look at them. The noise they created was thunderous, though whether it was anger or eagerness that stirred their voices, Firal couldn't tell.

"Are you even listening to me, girl?" Anaide asked, lip curled back in a snarl.

"I hear you, yes," Firal replied. Edagan and Nondar were somewhere behind them, but where, she couldn't care less. She wished Anaide would join them and leave her be. When the crackling light of a Gate came into view, she found herself relieved, if only because the sheer power of its spiderwebbing energies silenced the Master. The air split, allowing a view of the courtyard on the other end of the portal.

"How many mages does it take to create a Gate that can be seen and used from both sides?" Firal asked absently.

"Many," Nondar murmured at her back. "A great many."

Two by two, mages in Master white with bands of vermillion on their sleeves moved through the Gate. Their ranks parted to allow Relythes into view, the Archmage close at his heels. Firal offered a warm smile as the Gate flickered out behind them, its shimmering energy remnants dancing on the wind.

"Fair morning to you, Relythes of Alwhen." She gave her head the slightest incline, acknowledgment of an equal and nothing more.

"And to you, Firal of Ilmenhith," Relythes replied, though his tone was as guarded as his expression.

"I am honored to receive you on such short notice, though I regret we are not meeting under better circumstances. Please, come. Break your fast with me." Firal turned and gestured into the palace with the sweeping grace Medreal had spent part of the morning drilling into her. She did not look to see if he followed, the footsteps of his dozen-plus mages close behind her serving as indication enough.

The breakfast laid out in the formal dining hall was decadent, to say the least. She waited to sit until Relythes reached his chair. The Masters had chosen his place carefully, putting him across from Firal at the center of the table. He motioned the Archmage to his side. Then queen, king, and the whole gathering of white-clad mages sank to their seats in unison.

Relythes took a long draw from his goblet before he turned toward her. "You are familiar to me. Have we met before?"

"We have." Firal did not look at him as she spread butter over a slice of bread with a careful hand. "I served as mage to Daemon of the Underlings then. I hoped to act as his mentor during my time with his people, but it seems he and I ultimately did not share the same ideals."

"And so you've gone from court mage to queen, fancy that." His eyes narrowed.

She did not rise to the bait. "It is quite common in our culture for the children of nobles to study magecraft. Better that we understand their practices, so that we may understand their importance and move them about the island appropriately. My parents, of course, thought it best that my name not be widely known during my studies." Her eyes flickered to the Archmage's face. Envesi's expression was as cold as ever.

"And is it common, too, for nobles to use their magecraft to aid enemies?" Relythes challenged.

Firal hesitated. This was something the Masters had not prepared her for, but aside from Nondar, she didn't think the Masters knew she had been to Alwhen. She should have assumed Relythes would recognize her. "On the contrary," she started, choosing her words carefully, knowing the heated stares she received from the Masters would be the least of her concerns if she phrased herself poorly. "Though they sought to claim independence from my father's rule, the Underlings have always called the ruins their home, and the ruins fell under my father's jurisdiction. They are my people, whether they like it or not. They struck out against both of us, but it seems that matter has already been dealt with." She raised an eyebrow at him, as if to ask if he knew she'd been aware of what his army had done.

The king grimaced and leaned back in his chair. "Ah, yes. I apologize for the matter of crossing your borders. My men merely thought to stamp out the stragglers after we flattened the lot that attacked us."

"No need for that." Firal smiled, though his lie made her want to scream. She was sure the expression looked as fake as it felt, but if anyone recognized it as forced, they didn't show it. "Though I must admit the state of the borders is something I hoped to discuss with you."

Now Relythes shifted forward, uncomfortable. "How so?"

She maintained her false front of sweetness as she raised her cup to her lips. "I'd like to eliminate them."

The visiting mages stiffened at her words. The Archmage's eyes widened, if only for an instant, and her mouth puckered as if she'd tasted something sour. Stepped on someone's toes, had she? For a moment, Firal's smile was a bit more genuine.

The Giftless king eyed her as if he hadn't heard correctly. "And how would you propose something like that?"

Firal's brows rose. "I understand you are unmarried, is that correct?"

Understanding lit his face, but Relythes said nothing, considering in silence.

She licked her lips before going on. "I believe the merging of our two kingdoms would be of great benefit to the island. The land itself is better suited to unification. Even our coastlines complement one another, and I dream of what our ports could do if we were able to expand and work together. We'd waste no resources on battles between us. Trade could flourish between our cities."

"It could," Relythes conceded, eyeing her thoughtfully. Perhaps more than thoughtfully. The way his eyes raked over her form reminded her of a hungry animal.

"I trust you will consider it?" she asked.

"Consider, yes. But I'm not here for you, girl."

Consideration was better than nothing, perhaps even the best she could hope for. The Masters had made it clear this was the best option, but Firal hoped he would decline. She thumbed her finger beneath the table, startled by her ring's absence. She couldn't remember where she'd left it. "I understand, and I realize you are eager to see justice dealt. I can imagine it stung to allow a group of people to remove land from your holdings, only for them to strike out at you before the ink on your treaty could dry."

"A group of people you claim responsibility for," the Archmage added. Firal eyed her. It was strange that Envesi had kept quiet until now. She couldn't tell if the woman thought to play her like the other mages tried, or if she was feigning ignorance.

"I take responsibility for their wellbeing," Firal said as she returned her silver goblet to her lips. The spiced cider inside smelled good, but she didn't drink. Her stomach gave an unpleasant flutter. "But if we're speaking of their behavior, we both know you're the one responsible for that, Archmage."

Envesi's ice-blue eyes widened as if she'd been struck. Relythes turned his head slowly. Somewhere farther down the table, Firal heard Nondar cough.

"Is this so?" Relythes asked. The Archmage drew herself up and opened her mouth, but Firal spoke before she could.

"I'll not insult your intelligence by pretending we don't all know the name Daemon was raised under. It was because of his identity you decided to chance giving the Underlings land, was it not? Hoping he would use it to rise against my father?" Her amber eyes narrowed as she addressed the king, though she gave him no chance to respond. "No, I don't blame you. It was safe to assume he would, given the bitterness he held over having no chance to inherit the throne. You had no way of knowing he harbored just as much anger toward the Archmage for making him what he is."

Envesi leaped from her chair and slammed her hands flat against the table. "How dare you? I am the Archmage of Elenhiise, not one to sit here and suffer these baseless accusations!"

Anaide snapped to her feet and glared up the table at the Archmage. "The queen has been under the counsel of mages who know firsthand of your treachery. If not for your manipulations, the boy might have had a chance to be normal!"

"Normal!" Edagan barked a laugh. "He is an affront to all Lifetree's creation! Only Brant is meant to give life. Who was she to twist the flows into such an abomination?"

"Enough!" Relythes roared, bringing the room to silence. Only Firal remained cool and calm, sipping her cider and managing to look unruffled. She did not even flinch when the king turned toward her with a glare.

"Explain this!" the king demanded.

Firal bowed her head. "As was mentioned before, Relythes, I am a mage." She stood her goblet beside her plate and turned it by its base. "I learned the laws governing proper use of magic at a very young age, so you can imagine my dismay at learning what vile things the Archmage has done with her power. You see, the three Masters that sit on my council were present at Daemon's creation."

He looked to the white-robed mages for verification. Anaide and Edagan avoided meeting his eyes.

Nondar cleared his throat. "All we were told was that she needed assistance," he said. "A circle of mages to lend strength and control to some astounding discovery she'd made. We knew not what she attempted until it was too late. A child with no parents, birthed of magic, of the very energy of the world around us. Power given physical form, created in mimicry of the mages of old. Those who were not bound by affinity or element. What the queen says is true. By attempting to imitate the life-giving strength of the Lifetree, the Archmage violated ancient law."

"If Brant did not mean us to do it, he would not have made us capable!" Envesi snarled.

Relythes shook his head in disgust. "We're capable of countless things we know better than to do. You shame yourself with such feeble excuses." He turned to Firal with a grim glint in his eye. "My lady, I have no desire to be entangled in such wickedness. Had I known, I never would have granted the Archmage refuge when she fled your lands."

"There is no need for apology," Firal said, though her expression grew hard and cold when her eyes fell to Envesi. "But if we are to speak of justice today, I would see the Archmage punished accordingly."

"You would hang her?" Edagan questioned, aghast. Even the Archmage seemed taken aback, recoiling from the table with a look of horror on her face.

"I'll see no mage hanged." Relythes scowled. "Let us not forget our own culture. Exile her. Cast her out from our island and retrieve your mages from my city. I want nothing more to do with Eldani or magefolk." He brushed his hands together as if dusting away his involvement, his breakfast abandoned on the table.

Firal dared not wet her lips, though they felt dry. "And what of my proposal?"

"You keep your borders, girl, I'll keep mine. Once I'm back in Alwhen and you've taken the rest of your kind from my keeping, we shall speak no more."

Relief washed over her like a wave, soothing the raw nerves she only concealed because she must. "Very well," she agreed, turning her eyes to the Masters on her council. "Seize the Archmage. She will be dealt with as soon as King Relythes is returned to his own kingdom."

"You have no power to do this!" Envesi shrieked. She stumbled backwards even as Firal felt the other mages wrest energy flows from her hold. The Archmage clawed after them, clearly certain she was strong enough to overcome them.

Individually, perhaps she was, but Nondar, Edagan, and Anaide worked in unison, their magic entwining to paralyze the white-haired woman before she could flee.

Firal rose from her place at the head of the table and dabbed a napkin to her lips. "If you would follow me," she said to Relythes with a gesture toward the door, "I will escort you back to the courtyard and have you returned to Alwhen at once."

"Of course," Relythes agreed, obviously unsettled but unwilling to appear weak.

As Firal led the king from the dining hall, she felt a strange tingle of satisfaction at the Archmage's furious screams.

———

JINGLING KEYS ECHOED DOWN THE HALL WITH THE FINALITY OF A death knell. Rune had expected the sound for hours; the jailer had told him the executioner would come for him at sunrise. There'd be some show and some fuss, and then he'd be walked to the gallows. He didn't see why they bothered to tell him—sunrise was an abstract concept in the dungeons buried beneath the palace—unless it brought them pleasure to see a doomed man's face. He'd taken care to show nothing.

Voices quieted when those keys jingled. No doubt the petty thieves and criminals locked away with him believed the jailer was coming for them. He wondered how many others had been told of the gallows, or told it was for them.

"Ran!" a voice whispered on the other side of the bars.

Rune's head jerked. Exhaustion blurred his vision and he squinted against the feeble light, unsure if he could believe his eyes. The keys rattled against the cell door and the lock clanked. A small grumble of frustration reached his ears. Finally, the hinges groaned as the door swung open.

Two figures rushed into his cell, little more than shadowed outlines in the dark. One reached for the manacles that trapped his wrists and kept him half-suspended. Cold iron brushed his arm and the manacles snapped open, one after the other. Rune fell hard, and the unforgiving stone of the floor knocked the air from his lungs.

"They've done a number on him, haven't they?" a woman murmured at his side. Soft as it was, her voice was familiar. Rune struggled to push himself up, but gentle hands on his arm stopped him. "Shh, not yet."

"Kytenia?" His voice cracked with the question. When his eyes finally focused, the dim light from the lantern at the guard's station was just enough for him to see her grin.

"Take it easy, you oaf. I can't heal you now or they'll know we're down here. There are several hundred mages upstairs, fresh back from Alwhen, who would sense me doing it." She held him still until the irons on his ankles were undone.

More carefully this time, he pushed himself to his hands and knees. His eyes scanned the floor twice before he saw the narrow band of gold Medreal had left behind. He caught it with a claw and clutched it in the palm of his hand. "Where is Firal?"

"Out in the courtyard," said the other familiar voice from his other side, "seeing the mages brought in. They're about to exile the Archmage."

Rune turned his head. Vahn's extended hand hovered beside his face. He clasped it and groaned as his friend hauled him to his feet. The moment his legs were under him, his knees tried to buckle.

"Come on, now. Stay standing." Vahn draped Rune's arm over his shoulders and hefted him up with a grunt. Though they were close in height, Vahn was slimmer and lighter. They wouldn't be able to move fast.

Kytenia hurried to the narrow hallway between cells and peered out before she motioned them forward. Rune stumbled more than he walked and Vahn all but dragged him out. Kytenia took up his other side, her small, warm hands wrapped tight around his scaly wrist to hold his arm steady over her shoulders. "Rikka and Shymin are distracting the guards. They won't be able to give us much time. We have to hurry."

Angry cries and helpless pleas rose from other prisoners as they moved past. Hands grasped at their clothing and caught Kytenia's skirts more than once, but they pushed on.

"The guards won't hear us down here," Vahn said. "Shymin put a ward around her and Rikka before we came down here, made it look like they were gossiping. No one will know she spun it out over the guards, too."

Rune nodded. The idea was clever; it was only too bad she hadn't found a way to make a mask for their magic as well. Perhaps then Kytenia could have done something for the wounds the whip had left on his back, or his exhaustion, at least. His whole body ached. He tried to focus on the ring in his hand, the match for the one they had not removed from his finger.

When they reached the stairs, Kytenia returned the keys to the jailer's empty desk. They struggled up toward daylight together, pausing twice to catch their breath. When they reached the courtyard, Vahn motioned for them to stay back as he slipped Rune's arm off his shoulders and crept ahead to peer into the courtyard.

"Nothing," he whispered. "I don't know what Rikka and Shymin did, but they did a good job." He returned to Rune's side and together, the three of them emerged into the courtyard and cut toward the wide gardens that stretched to the palace walls. Hundreds of voices echoed from the city beyond. "The city is so crowded that no one will notice you, as long as you're careful," Vahn said as they inched across the cobblestones. "Everyone's distracted with the Archmage being cast out. No one will know you're gone until it's too late."

Rune grimaced. "And when they know?"

"I'm pretty sure we can peg your disappearance on the Archmage, too. I'll take care of it, don't worry." Vahn led them toward the back of the gardens, where the flowering trees grew.

A figure rose in the shade beneath the trees and, startled, Rune dug in his claws to stop.

The hooded woman turned toward them, her arms full of cloth, and when a sad smile wreathed itself on the old stewardess's face, he allowed himself to relax.

Medreal closed the distance between them with short, quick strides. "Best get steady on your feet, boy. You've quite a trek to make before people begin to look for you." She passed the bundle to Kytenia and pressed a hand to Rune's cheek. He shuddered and gasped, the transfer of energy unlike any exchange he'd ever felt. Instead of the cold, ice-water sensation that came from other mages touching him with power, Medreal's magic zinged through him like a shock. His feet grew more solid beneath him and he shrugged away from Vahn and Kytenia's help. The old woman patted his cheek affectionately, her dark eyes troubled despite her reassuring smile. "I'd do more for you, but I fear we'd be noticed. As it is, that may be enough to draw them."

Kytenia separated the pile of cloth into several garments and pulled a tunic over Rune's head so fast, he barely had time to shove his arms through the sleeves before she threw a cloak around his shoulders. Vahn helped fasten it at his throat while Kytenia thrust strips of linen into his pockets. "For you to bind your hands and feet later," she said. "Better if they think you a leper than a... well, easier if they avoid you than try to kill you."

Then Medreal stepped close, balancing a burlap-wrapped bundle in one arm as she held out a small leather purse. Rune gave her a questioning look.

"Coin for the trip," the old woman said. "I would Gate you myself, but I know nowhere to send you, so we cannot do it without involving Masters. They'd never let you leave."

His stomach dropped. "Where am I going?"

"You can't stay on Elenhiise, Ran," Kytenia murmured. "Relythes means to close his borders. The Masters want Firal to flush the Underlings out of the ruins and settle them in a proper city, and you certainly aren't safe in our territory."

Medreal closed his fingers around the purse. Coins clinked inside. He tried to push it back into her grasp. "I'm not leaving Firal here alone," he protested.

"You don't have a choice!" Vahn hissed in a whisper. "They'll kill you, do you understand? Firal can't protect you. She can't save you. They'd be as likely to hang her for trying."

"At least this way we have a chance for things to settle," Kytenia said. "A chance for her to rule in peace."

Medreal crept toward the wall, drawing Rune along with her. "Your best bet is to make your way north, to the harbors. Find a ship destined for the mainland and buy passage." She pulled up the hood of his cloak with her free hand. "There's enough money there to pay for food and the trip, but not much else. I'm afraid that's all we can offer you. There was no time for anything else. That, and this." She thrust the bundle in her arms into his hands.

Rune folded the burlap back just enough to see the gleaming black hilt of his father's sword. He tried to return it. "I can't take this. The sword of the king belongs to Firal by right."

"I'm certain he would want you to have it," Medreal said, stepping back. "Now, go."

Swallowing, he looked from Medreal to Kytenia, from Kytenia to Vahn.

"Go," Kytenia whispered.

Vahn nodded. "Go, Ran. While you still can."

Everything in him objected, fought against what he knew made the most sense. Rune turned to the wall. Everything he wanted lay behind him, but his only chance at survival lay ahead. His grip on his father's sword tightened. "Vahn, Firal—"

"I'll look after her," Vahn reassured him.

Rune closed his eyes. "Promise me."

"I swear," Vahn said, clasping his friend on the shoulder. "Anything I can do to protect her, anything to keep her safe, I'll do. I promise."

Nodding, Rune forced himself to move. Medreal had tied the sword's coverings with loops of rope. He slid his arm through one and dug his claws into a gap between stones in the wall. He reminded himself to breathe as he pushed himself upward. His energy was back, but the pain lingered. It took every ounce of strength in his body to scale the wall, reach the top and drag himself over its edge. But looking back—at the solemn faces of his friends below, at the palace he'd grown up in, now belonging to the woman he loved—looking back and then leaving took everything he had.

Setting his jaw, he turned and slid down the far side of the wall before they could see the tears in his eyes.

2 8

NEW LIFE

A SMALL TAPPING AT THE OFFICE WINDOW MADE FIRAL PAUSE AND lift her pen. The reestablishment of the temple and its chapter houses was more work than she'd expected, but writing formal letters to the Eldani nobles was a simple task. Time-consuming, more than anything, but time was something she had.

"Another messenger pigeon. They must have closed the coop again." Medreal sighed and pushed herself from her chair. The white-feathered bird strutted on the window ledge, pecking at the sill with a single-minded intent. "Well, at least it's not another ugly crow. I'll see that it's let in. Shall I bring you anything when I return, my queen?"

"Some mint tea, perhaps," Firal said, flicking the feathered end of her quill against her chin. "All this stress has me feeling ill again. I've not the fortitude for politics, not of mind or stomach."

Medreal eyed her strangely, but nodded before she made her way out.

The office had already been rearranged to suit Firal's liking, though she had only taken it a few days before. She preferred simple furniture in warm tones, but had allowed some of the lavish blue-cushioned couches and chairs to stay beside the windows. Medreal spent a great deal of time in Firal's office, helping with what she could, even if it was just providing a fresh cup of tea. Firal appreciated the older woman's company; Medreal's presence was calming.

Ilmenhith still bustled with activity, though with the coronation postponed, it now prepared soldiers to gather mages from Alwhen and return to the temple. The same soldiers would scour the land for the king's killer, turned loose by the Archmage during the fit of rage that preceded her exile.

Firal didn't buy that story for a moment, though she and her loyal Masters were content to let the rumor spread. She'd known it was a lie from the moment Vahn told it, only minutes after they pushed Envesi through the Gate that carried her back to the mainland. Her court Masters had never left the Archmage's side. Their hold on her power had never faltered. Firal herself had barely let the woman out of her sight once Relythes had returned to Alwhen. But if Rune was gone, she had a suspicion she wouldn't see him again. As for how she felt about that, she was not sure.

"Come in," she called absentmindedly as she dipped her quill. The knocks came so frequently that she almost didn't hear them anymore. It took a moment, sometimes, for her to distinguish it from the sound of the clock that ticked above the mantel.

Nondar shrugged the door open and cleared his throat as he stepped inside. Cane in one hand and a piece of paper in the other, he wore a puzzled frown. "I received this note from your desk first thing this morning. I've read it a dozen times, but I'm not entirely certain I grasp what it's saying." He made his way to her desk and nodded his thanks when she gestured for him to sit. He dropped into a chair with a sigh. "I realize that as our queen, you have every right to name the next Archmage, but I cannot help but question this decision."

Firal penned the rest of the sentence she'd started before she put her quill aside. "As your queen, I'm not sure you have the right to question my decisions." Her words were softened by a smile. She folded her hands together at the edge of her desk. "I can't think of anyone better suited for the role, Nondar. You may not be as strong in your Gift as the others that head Houses of affinity, but you are undoubtedly the right choice."

He inclined his head in respect, though his expression was troubled. "I am honored, my queen, no doubt, but I fear this will cause quite a stir among the mages we've drawn back into our fold."

"I couldn't care less what they think." She expected there would be some fuss, since Nondar had been the Master in charge of her training. The cries of favoritism would be rampant, but her fondness for the old man had nothing to do with why she'd chosen him. "With Melora and Alira removed from headship over their affinities, I need someone I can trust to raise Masters to their places. I don't feel that's something I can ask of Edagan or Anaide. Anaide is far too self-serving. Edagan might make a fair choice, but I think her friendship with Anaide makes it easy for her opinion to be swayed. On the other hand, your loyalty to my father never wavered."

Nondar shook his head. "The right course of action should be its own reward, my queen. I have no desire to earn rank or privilege for doing what any subject of the king should have."

"That isn't the only reason," Firal said. "Since the temple's founding, Envesi has been its only Archmage. Our kind are very long-lived, Nondar. One should not lead for an eternity."

His thick brows knit together. "You mean for me to take power because I will soon die?"

Though she grimaced at the way he made it sound, she nodded. "Yes, to put things simply."

"And after I die?" he asked, stroking his long beard with one knobby hand.

"There are other half-blood mages who can be trained to take your place. I trust you're capable of seeing they receive a proper education. You still have quite a few years left in you. We'll have to make the most of them, breaking down any reservations the others might have. If the other Masters really do want me to remove the Underlings from the ruins, that means integrating them into my country. Intermarriage will happen. Half-blood mages will become more common with time."

Nondar pondered her words with a distant look in his mage-blue eyes. At last he nodded, though he gave her a rueful smile. "I suppose it's best for me to accept, then. As my queen bids me, I obey."

Warmth lit her face and she leaned across the desk to touch his hand atop his cane. "Thank you, Nondar. I can't say how much it means to me to have you on my side."

Another knock interrupted the conversation and Firal sighed. "Come in!" she called, settling back in her chair as the door opened. She wasn't surprised to see Vahn with a message tube. No doubt Medreal had waylaid him in the hallway and told him to deliver whatever news the carrier pigeon had borne.

"Sorry to bother you." Vahn glanced between her and the Master mage. "I have a letter. Should I just leave it?"

"No, no." Firal waved him in. "You might as well wait. So much correspondence comes and goes now that I'll likely need you to carry a response back to the coops." She drew a fresh sheet of paper from the stack at the side of her desk. It was a wonder no one had ever found a way to use magic for communication, other than the demanding sensation of the Calling the mages reserved for emergencies.

Vahn handed over the tube and shuffled back, letting his eyes roam the office. He was uncomfortable in her presence now, the easy banter they'd shared at the temple long gone. She imagined it was difficult to decide how he should behave around her now that she'd gone from the best friend of his intended to being his queen.

Firal popped the seal from the end of the tube and fished out the rolled parchment with a fingertip. It wasn't very big, as expected by nature of its delivery. She skimmed it, and when she read it more closely a second time, her brow furrowed.

"What is it?" Nondar asked.

"It's from Minna. Well, from her husband, but I recognize her handwriting. She's one of my friends in the ruins. It says they received the message I sent. I asked to meet to discuss moving them from Core and recognizing the Underlings as a part of my country, but it says they have something to do before we can." Her lips felt suddenly dry. She licked them before she went on. "They ask if Daemon... Ran, that is... was successful in his attempt to stop the army before there was battle."

Neither Nondar nor Vahn said anything, their faces as grim as her own. Her heart sank to the pit of her stomach. His attempt to stop them? She'd thought he'd sent the army, thought he moved in retaliation for Lumia's death and in attempt to seize the throne. He'd tried to *stop* the retaliation? Blinking rapidly, she read those words again. She tried to find something she'd misread, something she'd misunderstood. But the words were simple and straightforward. She laid the note on her desk and stared down at it.

Nondar's brow creased. "Your Majesty?"

"A misunderstanding," Firal said. "The battle, Kifel's death, Ran's sentence, it was all a misunderstanding." Her fingertips searched her left hand for the ring that wasn't there. She cursed herself for taking it off. It was gone, now. Gone like Kifel. Gone like the man she'd loved.

"Will you send a reply?" Vahn asked, interrupting her thoughts.

Firal drew a breath and steeled herself, putting painful emotion aside. There would be time for tears later. Still, the idea that she could have done something nagged at her from the back of her head. She'd come to Ilmenhith to stop him and her own folly had kept her from even trying. If she hadn't misunderstood his intentions, she could have done something. Helped things end differently. If she'd not doubted him, doubted when he'd told her there was nothing between him and the Underling queen, doubted when he said he didn't want the throne. She knew better than that, but still let it get the best of her.

"Yes," she said at last. Her fingers trembled when she took her quill and she stared at the paper in front of her for a long time before she penned a simple note. Perhaps the anger she'd directed toward Lumia was misplaced. If not for the destruction of the temple, nothing ever would have changed. She'd still be Firal, mageling of Kirban Temple. Not Firal, queen of Ilmenhith and half of Elenhiise isle. "We'll arrange to have the remaining officers of their military brought here to discuss things. I'll have to convince them to select a new leader. Perhaps Davan. He's level-headed enough, and worked closely with Daemon when he served as general." Then she lifted her head and glanced toward the door.

Since her arrival in Ilmenhith, Firal found herself more aware of the presence of other mages. She'd heard that Masters could always feel the presence of others with the Gift, that one knew they had neared their full potential when they stopped focusing so much on their own strength and began to be aware of the strength of those around them. She attributed her growth to the training sessions she'd held with Rune. Toward the end, some lessons had tested her skill as effectively as his.

Of course, if she had already reached a plateau in her abilities, she had to admit disappointment. She'd always expected she'd be stronger, that she'd graduate to mageling blue and refine her abilities in pursuit of the white. That she was the Archmage's daughter reinforced that belief, though she had to remind herself that Kifel's bloodline played an equal part—a bloodline he'd once admitted was mixed with Giftless lineage. Firal smoothed her hair as the thoughts played through her head. The door opened, and she straightened.

Kytenia stepped halfway into the office before she caught herself. Blushing, she retreated into the hallway to knock.

"Come in, you goose." Firal couldn't help but smile. "I called you up here so we could visit before you all go home, why wouldn't I let you in?"

Sheepish, Kytenia pushed the door open again and held it for the other two mageling girls at her heels. "Well, you're an important person now. And you have company. I didn't want to interrupt." Her eyes darted between Nondar and Vahn. Her gaze lingered on the latter with a hint of a smile.

Rikka held no such restraint, almost prancing to the old Master's side. "Nondar, the other Masters said you've been asked to be Archmage of Kirban! Is that true?"

Nondar grunted, displeased. "Now how would the other Masters know that?"

Shymin stayed by the door and fidgeted with the skirt of her robe. "Edagan was snooping at your desk this morning while you were at breakfast. I planned to tell you, but you left the chapter house before I could."

The old Master's eyes narrowed until Shymin squirmed. Firal couldn't fault him. No one liked a tattle-tale, but worse was one who could have tattled before gossip spread.

"Well," Nondar grumbled, giving her a dour look, "she'd best break herself of that habit. I've decided to accept the title. Spying on her superiors is unacceptable behavior."

For some reason, Shymin reddened and averted her eyes.

Kytenia cleared her throat. "In any case, Firal, I passed Medreal in the hall. She said that she'd bring you something to eat with your tea. Are your nerves still bothering you?"

"A bit. That or I've started to come down with something. It would figure, me catching ill just before my coronation and the festivities." Firal tore the note from the top of the paper and held it out to Vahn. He plucked it from her fingertips and collected the message tube from her desk.

"I'm sure that's not it, but I can check if you'd like." Kytenia pushed up her sleeves as she crossed the room, positioning herself behind Firal's chair before she had permission. "I know you're nervous, but you'll do all right. You'll have Nondar to look after the temple for you and Medreal to advise you here."

Firal sat straighter as Kytenia laid her hands on her shoulders. "But I don't know the first thing about being a queen!" The feeling of her friend's magic coursing through her, probing for illness, made her shiver.

"You'll learn," Kytenia laughed. "Now, let's see. You'd probably feel better if you slept, for one. Your energies are pulling at mine like you haven't had a minute to rest all week. I think that—oh," she interrupted herself and stopped short.

"What?" Firal craned her neck to look over her shoulder.

Kytenia bit her lower lip. "Master Nondar, would you?"

Nondar raised a brow but pushed himself up from his chair and took Kytenia's place. He'd barely touched Firal with his energies before he jerked back his hands. "Oh, heavens, child."

"What?" Firal cried, looking between the two of them in panic. The eyes of the others in the room weighed heavy on her skin.

Kytenia's mouth worked a moment before she could speak. "When you went off into the ruins with... with Ran, did you, ah... Were the two of you..."

"Of course they did," Nondar snorted. "Don't be daft. They were married!"

Firal's eyes widened, the uneasiness in her stomach suddenly a lead weight. "No," she managed, the single word thick with disbelief.

Nondar rubbed his brow. "It's been a handful of weeks. If the timing was just right, it would mean you'd begun symptoms early, but that's not unheard of."

Rikka clapped hands to her mouth. "Firal and Ran were married?" Her bewilderment was mirrored in Shymin's face. Only Vahn didn't look surprised, though he shifted uncomfortably on his feet.

Firal's stomach churned harder than before and she laid a

hand against it. "But I didn't think—He said he didn't know if—"

"Not knowing doesn't mean it's not possible, dear girl." Nondar patted her shoulder.

"But it can't be!" She raked fingers through her hair, unable to fight the tears that brimmed in her eyes. "I'm to be the queen, Nondar! There's not even been a formal coronation yet, I can't be unmarried and have a child! What would they call me? What would come of it? They'd hang me if they knew where it came from!" Never mind what they would do if it was born looking like its father. Would it? The idea made her heart skip. Could the magic that twisted his form be passed on to his children?

Kytenia planted her hands on her hips. "You'll get married," she said, pausing before she corrected herself. "Or remarried, that is. If you marry now, no one will know. If anything, people will just think the child was born early."

"I don't think it's so easy as that," Shymin said.

"Well we can't just say she was married before, that would raise too many questions," Rikka added, rubbing the back of her neck. "But where is she supposed to find someone to marry without causing a fuss?"

"Simple." Kytenia's face fell. "Vahn will marry her."

"What?" Vahn cried. The message tube dropped from his fingers.

"You must," Kytenia pleaded. "Think what would happen if you don't! To Firal, to the kingdom, to all of us. You're the perfect choice to play the part. Your father is the newly-retired Captain of the Guard, descended from nobles. High born enough that no one would cry foul, low enough in rank that no one's been watching you."

Nondar eyed the young man. "It's possible." He tugged at his beard and smoothed a hand over his thinning hair. "I believe we could make it work. A coronation and a wedding at the same time, that should settle things in the city."

"But Kytenia, I can't! I won't come between the two of you," Firal protested.

"I don't believe you're in a position to object, child." Nondar's stern frown silenced her.

"Besides," Kytenia said, struggling to smile. "You made a promise, Vahn, remember?"

He flinched at the reminder, but nodded. Firal blinked, uncertain what she'd missed.

"I did," he agreed, though his shoulders slumped. "And it would be an honor to serve my queen and country, no matter what is asked of me."

As if to punctuate the statement, Nondar thunked his cane against the floor. "So it's decided, then. As Archmage, I will inform the council and the mages and see that preparations begin. Shymin, run and fetch Anaide and Edagan. Tell them I would speak with them at once."

"Yes, Archmage." Shymin dipped in a bow and hurried out the door. Nondar followed not far behind, though he paused to hold the door for Medreal to enter with her tea tray before he continued on his way.

Medreal stopped just inside the door and searched the troubled, forlorn faces still in Firal's office. "Oh!" she exclaimed. "I've not brought enough teacups."

A NAME

"Is everything all right?" Vahn struggled to keep his voice calm, though calm was far from how he felt. He'd grown tired of watching the city through the high windows in the hallway. Now he tried to ignore the people in the courtyard below. The entire palace was aflutter with excitement. He felt rather aflutter, himself, though it was more anxiety than excitement.

"Of course." Medreal pushed the door halfway closed behind her. "A healthy child. A daughter. Are congratulations in order, king-regent?" She offered him a smile despite the sorrow that still glazed her eyes. The months had been long and difficult for all of them; it seemed there wasn't a soul left in the palace or temple that had not lost someone dear.

He hesitated to reply. "Yes," he said at last, leaning to look past her into the now-quiet bedchamber. "They are in order, thank you."

Medreal opened the door again and gestured for him to go ahead. Vahn lingered just inside as his eyes adjusted to the muted light. Maidservants were cleaning the room, and a Master he recognized as a healer stood alongside the midwife. In the center of everything, Firal reclined in a mass of pillows on the bed. Her bedraggled dark hair framed a weary face, her eyes trained on the tiny, linen-wrapped bundle she held at her breast.

"And it may take a few days before you've the milk to feed her properly," the midwife was saying, hands on her hips. "In the meantime, I can call for a wet-nurse if you think there is a need."

"Thank you, I will keep that in mind." Firal caught sight of Vahn from the corner of her eye and turned her head to offer a feeble smile. His throat constricted oddly and he did his best to smile in return. Through the months that followed their wedding, he had come to love her in a way, though it lacked the fire and passion he always hoped to find. Still, she was lovely, and she was queen. No man in his right mind would be displeased with that.

"A girl, is it?" The king-regent clasped his hands behind his back as he moved across the room. He settled on the edge of the bed and smoothed her hair back from her face.

"I'm afraid she doesn't look like you at all," Firal laughed, though a shadow of sadness veiled her eyes.

Vahn chuckled at the jest. She was always so mindful of the way she worded things, so careful to conceal the awkward truth of their relationship, lest it engulf them in scandal. He pulled back the linen and smiled at the sight of the infant's dark hair and delicately pointed ears.

"She's a good-sized child for as early as she's come. Strong and healthy, nothing to worry about." The midwife nodded in approval and folded her arms over her chest. "We'll leave the three of you for a bit of peace. Please call for any of us if you need assistance."

Firal nodded. "We will, thank you."

Vahn watched as the maidservants and attendants filtered out of the room. When the door closed behind them, he allowed himself to breathe. "I suppose everything is... normal, then?"

"Ten fingers, ten toes." Firal shrugged. "She is blessed to take after me."

"What would we have done if she hadn't?" It was an honest question, one he meant kindly, though he couldn't quite keep the relief from his voice. "A life in hiding is no life for a child. Especially not a royal."

She swallowed. "I don't know. I tried not to think about it. I tried not to think about much of anything."

He watched the child sink away from her mother's breast, her eyes rolling open and settling closed again. He gave a start at the color; a vivid, otherworldly violet.

"Just like her father," Firal said with a bitter smile. "But they aren't snake's eyes."

"Fortune takes kindly to her," he agreed. A long silence passed before he found the will to speak again. "What will we call her? We never discussed any names."

"Something familiar. Something to represent unity," she murmured as she shifted the babe in her arms. "Something to draw the island's people together. I..."

Vahn raised a brow and waited for her to go on.

Firal nodded as if she'd made up her mind. "I thought we might call her Lumia."

GLOSSARY

Affinity – One's natural inclination in magic. There are five major affinities: Earth, water, fire, wind, and life. These provide the primary source of power a mage can draw from and manipulate. While there are smaller subcategories affinities may fall into, granting specific talents in narrow fields, they are generally related to one of the five and, as result, only the five major affinities are recognized.

Alira – (*uh-LEER-ah*) – Master of the House of Fire.

Alwhen – (*OWL-when*) – The capital of the eastern half of Elenhiise island, a region known as the Giftless Lands.

Anaide – (*uh-NAYD*) – Master of the House of Water.

Archmage – The leader of Kirban Temple, generally recognized as the leader of all mages.

Core – An underground city beneath the ruins, home of the Underlings.

Daemon ~ (*DAY-mun*) – An Underling soldier. His tainted magic has twisted his body into a monstrous form.

Davan - An officer among the Underlings.

Edagan – (*ED-ah-gan*) – Master of the House of Earth.

Eldani – (*ell-DAN-ee*) – The only inhabitants of Ithilear who are known to be Gifted. Eldani are long-lived, due to their magic, and differ from humans only in their pointed ears. Diluted bloodlines are recognized by the reduced point of an Eldani's ear, which directly corresponds with their prowess as a mage.

Elenhiise – (*ELL-en-heese*) – A small island in the middle of the Lantaaran sea, generally used as a waypoint in trade between the region's northern and southern continents. The island is ruled by two factions, the Gifted Eldani and Giftless men.

Envesi – (*in-VESS-see*) – The Archmage of Kirban Temple.

Firal – (*fur-ALL*) – A green-rank mageling at Kirban temple.

Flows – The natural ebb and flow of magic, which mages are able to seize and manipulate.

Gift – The ability to use magic.

House – A subsection of mages, ruled by a particular affinity. Mages within the House of Healing, Fire, etc. may take classes together, but their education is overseen by the Master of their House.

Ileara – (*ill-ee-ARE-ah*) – The second moon. The smaller of the two, Ileara is known as The Mother and is stationary in the sky. As it is only visible in the far western regions of the known world, such as the Westkings and the Chains of Raeldan, some residents of Elenhiise and the other eastern regions do not believe Ileara exists.

Ilmenhith – (*ill-men-HITH*) – The capital of the western half of Elenhiise island, which is under Eldani control.

Ithi – (*ith-EE*) – The first moon. The larger of the two, Ithi is known as The Soldier and circles Ithilear once per day. The thirteen months of the year are framed around Ithi's phases; its cycle is 28 days.

Ithilear – (*ith-ILL-ee-arr*) – The world. The name is derived from the two moons, Ithi and Ileara. In folklore, the moons are lovers. Ithi ventures forth to patrol and protect their child, Ithilear, while Ileara remains in one place to provide a stable home.

Kifel – (*kiff-EL*) – Full name Kifelethelas Penedhionn. The Eldani king and ruler of the western half of Elenhiise island.

Kirban Temple – (*KER-ban*) – Founded by Archmage Envesi, Kirban Temple is the only school of magecraft on Elenhiise Island. A prestigious college sponsored by the Eldani crown and located near the southern edge of the ruins.

Kytenia – (*kit-teen-yah*) – A yellow-rank mageling at Kirban Temple and Firal's best friend.

Lumia – (*loo-MEE-ah*) – Queen of the Underlings.

Mageling – A mage in training. Magelings are divided into five ranks before they graduate to Master and wear robes in corresponding colors. The five ranks are gray, lavender, yellow, green, and blue.

Marreli – (*mah-RELL-ee*) – A gray-rank mageling at Kirban Temple. One of Firal's friends.

Master – A mage recognized as skilled enough to wield magic without supervision. Masters outside the temple act as healers and scholars, and are in charge of scouting Gifted children to send for training. Masters who remain within the temple are generally teachers. Master mages are the only mages allowed to wear white. Court Masters and Masters of an affinity mark their eyes with black ink to distinguish their rank.

Medreal – (*mee-dree-al*) – King Kifel's stewardess.

Melora – (*mel-LOR-ah*) – Master of the House of Wind.

Minna - An Underling woman who befriends Firal.

Nondar – (*non-DAR*) – Master of the House of Healing, also known as the House of Life. Nondar is one of few recognized half-Eldani Masters and is unparalleled as a medic.

Ran – Full name Lomithrandel. A blue-rank mageling at Kirban temple and the only part-time student allowed. He considers Firal a friend, while she considers him a nuisance.

Relythes – (*rell-uh-THEEZ*) – The Giftless King, ruler of Alwhen and the eastern half of Elenhiise island.

Rikka – (*RIK-kuh*) – A yellow-rank mageling at Kirban Temple. One of Firal's friends.

Ruins – A sprawling labyrinth in the center of the island. The ruins fall entirely on Eldani lands.

Rune - A new name given to Daemon.

Shymin – (*SHY-min*) – A green-rank mageling at Kirban Temple. One of Firal's friends and Kytenia's elder sister.

Tren – Full name Tren Achos. Lumia's general.

Underlings – Giftless people driven into the ruins by war, rumored to be monsters and believed to be legend.

Vahn – Full name Vahnil Tanrys. A low-ranking soldier in Ilmenhith's military.

Made in the USA
Monee, IL
05 February 2022

90706474R00236